Ken Eulo

Million-Copy Best-selling Author of *The Brownstone*, *The Bloodstone*, and *The Deathstone* . . . Creates His Most Terrifying Thriller Yet, a Spellbinding, Nightmare Novel of Death in the Still of the Night

NOCTURNAL

Praise for *The Bloodstone* . . .

"A particularly powerful and well-written horror novel . . . ALMOST HALLUCINATORY IN EFFECT."

—*Publishers Weekly*

"CHILLING . . . THE WORD *SCARY* DOESN'T DO IT JUSTICE."

—*Chicago Tribune*

And *The Deathstone* . . .

"Harrowing supernatural ordeals . . . Eulo builds up the tension expertly, insidiously . . . A SUPERIOR THRILLER."

—*Publishers Weekly*

"The Deathstone crackles with the kind of intensity that makes an outstanding horror novel. Mr. Eulo weaves a strange and terrifying tale; and the ending is deeply chilling. AN ALTOGETHER UNFORGETTABLE PERFORMANCE!"

—Whitley Strieber,
author of *The Hunger*

Books by Ken Eulo

The Brownstone
The Bloodstone
The Deathstone
Nocturnal

Published by POCKET BOOKS

Most Pocket Books are available at special quantity discounts for bulk purchases for sales promotions, premiums or fund raising. Special books or book excerpts can also be created to fit specific needs.

For details write the office of the Vice President of Special Markets, Pocket Books, 1230 Avenue of the Americas, New York, New York 10020.

NOCTURNAL

KEN EULO

PUBLISHED BY POCKET BOOKS NEW YORK

The quotation from "Avatars of the Tortoise" by Jorge L. Borges, from the collection *Labyrinths, Selected Stories & Other Writings*, is reprinted with the permission of New Directions Publishing Corporation. © 1964 by New Directions Corp., translated by James E. Irby.

Another *Original* publication of POCKET BOOKS

POCKET BOOKS, a division of Simon & Schuster, Inc.
1230 Avenue of the Americas, New York, N.Y. 10020

Copyright © 1983 by Ken Eulo

ISBN: 0-671-43065-3

First Pocket Books printing December, 1983

10 9 8 7 6 5 4 3 2 1

POCKET and colophon are registered trademarks of Simon & Schuster, Inc.

Printed in the U.S.A.

For my brothers, Joe and Don.
And my good friend, Bob Stark.

NOCTURNAL

PROLOGUE

THE ROOM WAS QUIET NOW, EXCEPT FOR THE SUDDEN LOW hum of the elevator in the hallway. The man in beige turned at the sound. His heart raced, but he steadied himself at once.

He sat very still for an instant, listening, then moved to the small mirror over the dresser. Here the light fell in tinted, dusty beams through stained-glass panes and draped itself over the bottom part of the dresser and around the legs of the bed. When he stepped into the splay of light, his brown, plain shoes turned as red as blood, and he gave a little start and looked into his own mirrored eyes.

He remained that way for a long time, studying his image, memorizing the subtle changes that had taken place over the years. With each flash of light from the hotel sign beyond his window, he could see his face clearly, then darkness, but still his image lingered.

Ah, yes, he thought, and slowly, dreamily, not making a sound, touched his fingertips to the mirror.

Now his fingers traced the outline of his face, moved exquisitely over the landscape of features set in glass.

Time passed; how much he neither knew nor cared.

He whispered: "You have a short time to reach your true self." He repeated the phrase over again, and then again, each phrase blending into the next, nonstop. . . . "You have a short time to reach your true self you have a short time to reach your true self you have . . ."

Tiny sparks of chill flickered across his skin, the little proofs that his exhaustion was contracted into an intense cluster. The neon sign flashed again, brushing his face with a fresh patch of light.

Hesitantly, almost timidly, he turned and moved to the black overnight bag on the dressing stand. Carefully, he removed an art magazine and laid it open at the foot of the bed. He had bought the magazine two years ago and had continued to look at it every day since. He smiled and nodded. He knew the page well. He went right to it and there she was.

The photographer had placed her nude, lying on her stomach on a deserted stretch of sand. Her legs were spread wide, her back a graceful arch that allowed her head to tilt slightly and her hair to flow in a seemingly soft current of air that carried her away into her own private world . . . his private world. She wore no jewelry, no flowers in her hair, nothing to spoil the perfection that was hers. His fingers grew moist as they glided over the glossy surface of the picture.

Then he closed his eyes, content to be alone with her in his mind. It was within his mind he knew her best. Where vivid pictures of the past lingered like buried jewels. The loveliness of her youth. The softness of her innocence. She had been such a lovely child. Then more images as she had grown older, her face and body changing to that of a young lady. And then two years ago he'd seen her picture in a magazine. The woman he'd imagined she had grown to be.

But he had to be sure. Absolutely sure he wasn't mistaken. So he had purchased other magazines to see if there weren't other women who more aptly fit his vision. But they were always repulsive to him—vulgar and cheap. Just looking at the others had caused violent disturbances within him. He didn't like looking at the others. No, he wanted only to look at her. To be with her. Forever.

"Only you," he breathed, and was not aware of the relaxing or the letting go. He was just, suddenly, in the middle of a warm shapeless seascape with her. And something else. Something that pulled him forward, a compulsion, an obsession, until he stood naked, held by the splendor of a white sandy beach that twisted and turned to infinity, while the ocean sparkled with luminous ripples that danced at the discretion of currents and wind-huffs.

The excitement inside of him grew stronger, stronger and still stronger, as if her closeness was expanding to become all of him . . . He did not exist except for her, except for this shuddering sensation . . . and now . . . now he was experiencing the explosive climax of an orgasm.

Gradually the feeling subsided, the seascape retreated, and he found himself alone, feeling—

—enchantment.

—Until the neon sign flashed again, vanished beyond the drapes, blurring the corners of his mind. He opened his eyes a hairline crack. The blackness of the room, unflawed by light, began to thicken around him. He turned, confused. Pure ecstasy. She was . . . but no . . . no, no . . . something was wrong . . . unpleasant . . . the terrible tension in his shoulders again . . . that same screaming tension that had gripped him this morning . . . crawling up his neck now.

Now a procession of images, girls smiling, lips smeared with lipstick, cheeks coated with rouge, bodies stuffed into flimsy clothing, moving, gyrating . . . buzzing . . . that dreadful buzzing in his head.

He had known it would come; he had felt it coming for days, the quiet rumbling, the blinding white light. But it was bad; it was worse than he had imagined it would be.

The second wave of dizziness came quickly, threatening to overwhelm him. The pain began to scale the walls of his skull, whirl in the complexities of his mind, and, rattling louder, more thunderous, mount into a rush of blood that raced through his arteries and veins, heading dead center for his brain.

He had to relieve the pressure. Obliterate the sensation. In an instant he had drawn a knife from his overnight bag. It was a switchblade knife with an ebony handle. It would not be painful. He had done it before. The bloodletting. Just a small slicing of the vein and his circulation would return to normal.

He brought the tip of the knife against his forearm . . . just the tip. He pressed the blade in so that his skin gave way in a little slit, a tiny eruption, and then suddenly there was a spurt of blood. Then another. The blood was very bright, very red. It flowed steadily into the basin.

After a few minutes the bleeding stopped.

Slowly his body began to reshape itself; his shoulders—a little large for so thin a frame—straightened, and he rose, if not steadily, yet with such solid footing that his temporary weakness was erased in his stance.

"Those who are not with me are against me," he muttered, the weak and scratchy sound of his voice mixing with the sudden buzzing of the elevator. His eyes turned inward. The elevator ground to a stop. Viciously he gripped the knife. His eyes moved over its deadly blade, then rolled back into his head until they saw only white. The sides of his mouth pulled back, baring his teeth, gums, tongue. A smile flickered across his lips, like a tic, and he knew, absolutely knew that the time had come.

Quickly he slipped the knife into his jacket pocket.

The next time the neon sign flashed—the small hotel room on Twenty-fourth Street was empty.

PART ONE

CHAPTER 1

SHE WAS USED TO NEW YORK CITY BY THIS TIME. IT DIDN'T brutalize her any longer, but rather it brutalized around her. Somehow she had learned how to step aside and not get involved. Just yesterday, she had seen an old man enraged. Standing in the middle of a crosswalk, he had taken his cane and viciously beaten the hood of a cab. Then, as though his actions had been normal, he nonchalantly crossed the street and disappeared into the crowd.

Thinking of it now made her giggle a little.

Or maybe her light-headedness came from the amber-colored wine in her glass. For over an hour, Rose had been sipping wine and hanging onto Rachetti's best outdoor table where the last rays of mid-October sun pressed under the awning and touched her upturned face. Today there was none of the usual autumn zip to the air; rather, a deceptive indolence claimed Manhattan, taking away anticipation and leaving in its place a hazy calm.

She sat alone for the moment, waiting for her friend Lottie to get off the outdoor pay phone. From time to time, she caught sight of Lottie's kinky black hair bobbing up and down on the other side of the glass partition. That excited nod could mean that the sale had come through on Rose's new painting (rather obscurely entitled *Goldilocks*). Or then again, it could be Lottie refusing to hear how *Goldilocks* just wasn't that good a painting. Lottie, of course, would find such talk unacceptable. She was a dedicated positive thinker, always reaching out for life.

Perhaps that was why most artists in the area eventually gravitated to Lottie's Greenwich Village gallery. The Soho crowd, the loft dwellers, the New Jersey dropouts, all gathered around Lottie to partake of her faith and to listen to her talk about art and about painters.

Rose felt singularly grateful to have become a special friend, more than merely one of the flock, and many a night they would sit together after the gallery had closed, talking and drinking wine from cut-glass carafes, Lottie's German-Jewish face beaming with excitement.

No, sir. Lottie would not accept the fact that any of her artists—especially Rose—were capable of producing bad work. Controversial work, maybe. But not bad.

Rose nodded to herself now, reassured that it was most likely a sale, and leaned back in her chair. Almost at once a tall figure of a young man came to stand beside her.

"Excuse me," said the long-haired youth, somehow appealing through the eyes and chin, "but you have a wonderful look about you. Are you an actress?"

"No," Rose said placidly, not adding that she was a painter. That fact would be sure to guarantee the lad's seizing a chair. Then what?

"Something in the arts," he persisted.

"No. Sorry." It was a gentle turndown. She had perfected the knack of it. If I were available, she seemed to say, but I'm not. And if she were being perfectly honest, she would add: I really couldn't get interested in a face under thirty. It takes thirty or more to get me involved.

The boy hesitated, then modestly moved on, while Rose sat idly by considering their brief encounter. For once, the mere act of a male come-on hadn't sent her reeling into one of her guilt trips over Lance. It was a definite step forward. Only four months and twenty days since Lance had disappeared off the edge of her earth (transferred to Atlanta wasn't it?), and she felt pretty decent and ready to go on with her life.

The divorce had been a quickie (half of her had simply been amputated without anesthetic), and she sat there four and a half months later well enough for a rather charming young man to say she had a wonderful look She resisted wondering if Lance would still think she had a wonderful look.

Instead, she peered into her wine glass and met her own swimming eyes. She had a startlingly clear flashback: herself as a solitary little girl so emotionally fragile that she could be stricken by a glance. A normal little girl and yet very different.

Then she saw an older self, in college, where people tried to understand her, tried to get into that place that would make her no longer solitary Rose.

That didn't happen until after college. She had gone to a dinner party and sat next to a sensitive-looking young man with a wicked laugh and a way of looking at her that melted down the barriers. That was Lance. On an impulse she had flung herself into a heated courtship which had ended in marriage.

The very thought brought Rose up to a rigid seated position in her chair. After her marriage, like dry cake under the icing, had come the divorce. The result had caused a struggle inside her between two forces—a feeling of defeat that said that she might as well give up, and a driving determination not to quit but to battle back. She had resisted defeat, but she could see how some people might not. And she wondered how many breakdowns had resulted from divorce. How many lives were permanently shattered.

The thought suddenly made Rose realize that she still hadn't quite recovered. Even as she sat in her own tiny spotlight of sun, she could feel a sudden ache and the locomotive of pain beginning to take off, coming toward her for a head-on collision.

Across its brooding course blundered Lottie, her black velvet cape flopping around her large lavender-bloused shoulders. Her feet seemed immense in old-fashioned Minnie Mouse type pumps. Her skirt was black and flowing and so much longer in the back than the front that it seemed to be a train. Like a cross between Mae West and the queen of some mythical and swinging isle, Lottie came striding. Past this broad spectacle no locomotive of pain could pass, and Rose reflected fondly that with help from Lottie she had once again shaken off the past.

"About *Goldilocks*," Lottie hissed, dropping in the chair opposite Rose's. "I sold it for two hundred and fifty dollars. Which is only a fifty-dollar reduction. Which is worth it when I tell you who bought it."

Rose waited expectantly. "Who bought it?"

"Not so fast. I want to tell you how it happened. I was at Milton Gold's party last night. I know you don't like him, but you don't own a gallery. It's the Milton Golds who keep my doors open."

"Anyhow," Rose said, "you like him. You like everyone."

"Well, not everybody." Lottie frowned, trying in vain to come up with someone she didn't care for. "I'm not overly fond of bad waiters when I'm hungry," she said after a moment. "But after I've eaten, I usually forgive and forget. Now stop getting me off the subject. Milton's party was a smash last night. The people were coming out of the woodwork. Rachel and Mark were there, of course. Oh, and Baby Jane Simon—"

"Oh, God," Rose groaned, "Baby Jane Simon."

"He likes *you*," Lottie said severely. "Well, anyway, it seemed everyone, including Milton, was talking about your latest paintings. Impressive, no? It may mean the big time if you continue growing the way you are." Lottie smiled. "Does the thought of success make you nervous?"

"No, not very." Rose hesitated. "Well, maybe. I'm not sure."

"Not sure? Well, you better get your nerve up. You're heading in that direction. Well . . . anyhow, after all the talk last night, I just floated out the door like a blimp on a string. My toes were a foot off the pavement. All of a sudden, I looked down from my heights and noticed a most impressive male animal who seemed to be asking for my card. Before I could get my sexual allure together, he was off in another direction. It was Rose Carpenter he was interested in. He collects promising young painters and, by God, he thought maybe he'd like to collect you. So today he came by and we exchanged compliments and such things and just now when I called the gallery, I found out he came up with the bucks. It's official. You're collected by A. Adam."

Rose gazed at her fixedly.

"Well?"

"I never heard of him," Rose said after a moment. "Did you?"

"Well, not actually, but . . ."

"And he asked for a fifty-dollar discount?"

"Honey, you've worked at my place often enough to know that makes him legit. They all do it."

"A. Adam." Rose hesitated. "What does he look like?"

"Umm, umm, good, like the soup." Lottie glanced at her watch. "I've got less than an hour to get to the gallery before closing. I've got another new girl." She scooped up her hat and gloves. "Don't you have to go to that dive you work at?"

"The Cottontail Club," Rose said with dignity, "pays my bills."

"But it's so bleak," Lottie protested. "A girl who looks like you should own the world."

"Maybe so," Rose said, "but in ten weeks, Nick Nuzzo was the only man to offer me a job. Jobs are scarce these days, or haven't you heard?"

"I guess." Lottie shrugged. "But as a cocktail waitress?"

"Yes, well . . . Lance didn't give me enough notice to sharpen up my secretarial skills. And I didn't want to take a dollar from Lance, beyond the two thousand that seemed fair."

"Forty thousand, plus alimony, sounds fair to me," stated Lottie. "But then I'm not you. If I were you, I wouldn't be at the Cottontail Club. I'd have lied like hell about my experience and be at a classy place uptown." Lottie smiled patiently. "Well, forget it. Think about A. Adam."

"I'm thinking," Rose said solemnly.

"What's the matter, honey? You've got an odd look on your face . . ."

"I wish I'd heard of that man," Rose hastened to say. "I was hoping he was a famous collector." She had captured the waiter's attention, and stood somewhat precariously and slipped on her lightweight coat. "The wine's on me today."

"Nope. My treat."

"Today, it's my treat." Rose paid the waiter before Lottie could make further objection. The wine was making everything spin just a little. Not an unpleasant sensation, actually. A bit of giddiness never hurt anyone. "Let's get out of here before I change my mind and sit down again," she said grinning, then glanced at the sky. "Lottie, I'm going with you in the cab, okay?"

"The subway will be quicker."

"Well . . ." Rose continued to take in the subtly darkened sky. "I think I'll take the cab anyway."

Inside the cab they were quiet and very much alone as the driver had closed the plastic partition in front of them. Lottie then began philosophizing about art and continued to do so until they had reached Greenwich Village. Abruptly, she brought up the seascape, that particular painting of Rose's she liked the best.

"You'd have thought Mr. Adam would have chosen that one, wouldn't you?" she began. "I was sure he'd choose it. But he went straight to that awful distorted face of that little girl. Whatever made you paint such a thing?"

Rose drew a thoughtful breath. "It came from something that happened to me once when I was a little girl."

"Oh, dear," Lottie said, stricken. "Surely it wasn't something that bad. And here I thought your childhood was all like that beautiful seascape."

Rose smiled. "Need I remind you he didn't buy the seascape. He bought reality. The way life really is. Not that the seascape isn't reality, but—"

The cab suddenly came to an abrupt halt.

"Gotta run," Lottie cut in, and distractedly flopped from cab to curb, then turned back. "By the way, have you heard from your parents?"

"I just got a postcard. They're in Denmark."

"Denmark? They really do intend to take in all of Europe, don't they?"

"Another two months' worth."

"Good for them. Now don't forget Saturday."

"Five o'clock. Guggenheim, right?"

"Right. Drinks afterwards?"

"Can't. I have to work."

"How perverse of you." Lottie leaned forward to close the door, and in the same action pressed taxi fare into Rose's hand. She was gone before a protest could be uttered, and Rose sank back in her seat, letting her head loll about on the soft upholstered backrest. Not until that moment had she been able to really slow down and think what was urging itself to be thought.

It was extraordinary, but she'd had a dream last night. In it, she was pursued by a tall man, someone whose face she could not see clearly. Now did it or did it not happen that in the dream she had turned and said to the man: "Who are you? Why are you following me?" And the man had answered: "My name is A. Adam. And you are mine, Rose. All mine."

CHAPTER 2

THE COTTONTAIL CLUB HAD BEEN A LAZY, SLOW-MOVING neighborhood bar in the Village when Nick Nuzzo bought it for a song. In less than a month, he liked to brag, he had redecorated the place, installed a stage to the right of the cash register, hired a few topless dancers, and tripled his business. Which only went to prove that one could go broke on respectability, whereas cheesecake paid the bills. But tonight, business was slow.

Rose stood aside and watched Nick swallow the last of his scotch. He bore an abject look of disgust. Above his head, a bored heavy-eyed damsel seductively rolled her hips to the music, but she just didn't have it. She was supposed to make the men restless and drink more. Instead, the few men who were there merely nursed their drinks and talked among themselves. About the room candle lamps flickered; all but two tables were empty. One of the men at the closest table motioned to Rose for another round.

Rose called for the drinks and waited, the room appearing even more bizarre than usual in one of those brief flashes of clarity where reality seems twice as real—in this case, disturbingly so. Lottie was right. She really didn't belong working in a place like this. She felt rather silly, standing there dressed in tight black slacks with a bunny tail sewn on, a black velvet cap with ears, and white ruffled blouse with bow tie. Thank God, Nick hadn't gone for the scantier type of cocktail outfit. "No," Nick had said, "what we're selling is right up there on that stage."

The dancer moved faster now, trying to generate some excitement.

Rose lowered her eyes. She was still unable to accept the variance between her dreams and what her life actually was. Oh, for the savage matter-of-factness employed by most of the other girls who worked at the club. Whereas she hadn't even been able to write her parents about the divorce yet. Her alibi: she hadn't wanted to interrupt their lifelong dream of taking in Europe. She knew how worried they would be, afraid that she wouldn't be able to cope alone. They had been so relieved when she married.

Damn.

Rose looked up as a little nudge of anxiety jabbed her rib cage. Beneath the crystal globe the dancing had stopped and the Cottontail Club had shrunk into a muted silence.

Nick shook his head. "Hey, Rose—how'd you like to go home early?" That's what made Nuzzo a good businessman. He knew when to cut his losses.

"Sure," Rose said. She wasn't feeling too hot anyway. She deposited the drinks on the table and thanked the man for the dollar tip—would it have been two dollars if topless, one for each breast? She quickly glanced into the man's eyes to see if he had read her mind. Apparently, he hadn't. There was hope in the world yet.

She moved back to the bar where she paid the bartender her bank, retrieved her purse, then moved toward the back room for her coat. She stopped suddenly when she realized she still hadn't opened the letter that had arrived in the morning mail. She removed the envelope from her bag and stood squinting at a scribbled return address she couldn't decipher.

"Who's it from?" Nick asked. "A fan?"

"I don't know. I haven't opened it yet. I've been carrying it around all afternoon."

"Well, open it!" Nick was apparently more curious than she was.

Rose tore open the envelope and extracted the single piece of white bond typing paper. She held it up to the small circle of light at the service area, glancing first at the signature line. Cheryl Arthur. It was a short letter with some of the words fractured by a cheap portable typewriter. Perhaps, Rose reflected, a letter from the past should always be typed this way, the type as fragmented as one's memory of things almost forgotten. Cheryl and she used to be classmates at Florida Tech. Wasn't that a hundred years ago?

Anyway, it wasn't easy to read in the dim light, but it went something like this: "I will be arriving in New York on Thursday, the sixteenth of October. I haven't much money. I was hoping you could put me up for a few days. I'll call you as soon as I get in. If you are unable to accommodate, I'll understand. And thanks. Cheryl Arthur."

Strange, Rose thought, and reread the letter. Something was so formal about the wording. Almost self-conscious. "I will be arriving . . ." "If you are unable to accommodate . . ." Then the abrupt cutoff. Maybe it *was* a hundred years since she had last seen Cheryl, who had possessed a certain frothiness of personality. It was Nick who finally snapped her out of it.

"What's the matter, kid? You just get drafted?"

"Sort of," Rose said. "An old classmate of mine is coming into New York on Thursday and wants to know if I can put her up for a few days."

"Is she stacked? Because I can use another dancer—"

"She's a nun," Rose said, feigning sincerity. It was the quickest way to end the conversation.

Nick blinked. "You're kidding. A nun? A real nun?"

"Would I kid about a thing like that?"

"A nun," Nick repeated, and with exaggerated gravity dropped onto the nearest barstool.

Smiling to herself, Rose ducked into the back room, changed out of her bunny outfit, then had her coat on and was heading for the front door. Fourteen dollars in tips—a very low night. Still she had actually sold a painting today. She was heading for the big time. But then, it seemed as if she had been heading for the big time forever. No wonder her feet hurt. She glanced at the clock behind the bar. 12:15 A.M. She'd be getting home early. Thank God.

"By the way," Nick said, "this stinks."

Rose turned and almost bumped into a customer who was lost in concentration staring at the sketch pad Nick now held in his hand. "Why? What's wrong with it?" she asked.

"There's no lips, for Chrissakes—and the ears . . ."

Rose moved closer and tried to see the sketch through Nick's eyes. "I think it looks exactly like you."

"Bull!" he snorted, sliding from the stool. The customer giggled, a silly sound.

Rose smiled. "Nick, there are many ways of seeing reality."

"And this is how you see me?"

"Sometimes."

Saying the word, she watched the subtle change in Nick, a little shrinking created by a word, the glance at the sketch pad in his hand and back again to her.

"It doesn't even look like me." His nose wrinkled in dissatisfaction. "I asked you to do a portrait, but this—"

Nick's hair was more gray than white, and greased down, it clung to his skull like a bathing cap. Even his eyebrows seemed greased. His eyes roamed around beneath his brows like a pair of dull marbles. Rose took the pad and stuffed it into her shoulder bag.

"See you tomorrow, Nick," she said.

"You better give it up, kid. An artist you ain't."

"Right," she said, and hit the street. The city had once again grown cold and there was no moon. The sky was clouded, without stars. It was the kind of night when no one should be on the streets alone.

The IRT lurched to a stop. Rose had just folded her magazine back, crossed her legs and was prepared to read, when she saw him. She would only see half of his face, but she was sure that it was Lance. He looked like a young god standing there on the opposite platform, his shoulder resting against the blue column, a newspaper held properly folded in his right hand. His face was tanned, with blond hair tossed casually back, setting off his honey-colored eyes.

The magazine fell to the floor as Rose scrambled from her seat and moved for the open doorway, but she had been too late. The passenger doors had slammed shut. In a sudden jerk-like motion, the train lurched forward and she could feel the wheels grind on the tracks, could feel the swaying motion, and whirled to the furthest part of the door, still trying to get a last glimpse of the platform where Lance stood. She could feel her body slacken.

The young man was not Lance. The face was too thin, the mouth too wide, the forehead too broad.

"Sixty-sixth Street—next stop." The conductor's raspy voice

came over the loudspeaker and once again Rose knew that Lance was no longer part of her life.

Silly, she thought. What would Lance be doing in a subway station? For that matter, what would he be doing walking a dog in Central Park or waiting for a bus at Eighty-first and Columbus? He was in Atlanta. Atlanta, she reminded herself.

Shivering slightly, she returned to her seat, her long slim legs tensing against the pitch and sway of the train. Dropping into her seat, she let her shoulder bag fall free of her arm. Absently, she pushed the long black bangs from her forehead and closed her eyes.

Frustration, apprehension—you bastard, she thought, and the last, fast-fading image of Lance shattered into a thousand pieces.

Her clean flow of anger freed her for the moment, and she opened her eyes to find herself back in the present and being observed. A little black boy who lay cradled in his mother's arms had zeroed in on her in such a hostile and totally unexpected way that Rose instinctively groped for her sketch pad. She was amazed at how she was beginning to see things. An image within an image. She rapidly transformed the boy's tiny face into the features of a man. The small beads of belligerence became the eyes of someone much more mature, much more intelligent in his hatred.

She frowned. The black skin . . . no, that didn't seem at all right. The man she was suddenly seeing seemed to have white skin, the dead white of someone who rarely sees the light of day.

A night person.

She glanced at the picture again.

A night person would not be heading home, not until dawn. The night was his element, not by choice, by birthright. A night person was not made, he was born. A night person forced to function in daylight was a bit self-conscious. Awkward.

Good. The picture was starting to work on her.

"Rose," someone said.

She glanced up inquiringly. Someone had called her name and disappeared. The sliding door at the front of her car had opened and closed. It probably hadn't been Rose he was saying at all. Or maybe it was a couple and the girl's name was Rose.

She found herself staring idly at the door's dirt-encrusted

window. Now really, this was ridiculous. Someone, a friend most likely, was playing a joke. She was gazing at a distorted face. Nose, mouth, all features squashed against the glass in a caricature of longing.

All right, she thought, come back into the train. It's dangerous traveling out there.

The blurred face strained forward.

Rose now felt herself tensing, a warning reflex which started in the pit of her stomach and made its way up the base of her spine. This wasn't a joke. She realized that now. It was the kind of instinct she had developed night after night at the Cottontail Club.

Get up, she told herself, and felt a helpless anger. Anger at her inability to act. The train pushed its way into the lighted station. Sixty-sixth Street signs began to fly by. Another and another.

Rose turned to stare out the window, hoping to see a policeman standing on the platform.

Suddenly she heard the door between the cars slide open; before she could turn back, someone came flying forward like a bullet shot from a gun.

Stunned, Rose realized that the train had stopped, that the outside doors of the subway had opened and he had shot through them, closing himself on the outside as the train began to move again.

She tried to relax. She was more shaken up than usual over such an occurrence, probably because she had made the mistake of thinking him a friend. She was used to the creepers of the city, but she was not usually fooled into making a semblance of contact with them.

Rose . . .

Strange. He had known her name. How was that possible?

When she had reached Seventy-ninth Street and come up into the cool night air, her anxiety had not left her. The night seemed filled with his presence: by the distorted features of his face pressed against glass.

She glanced down Broadway toward Seventy-second Street. The feeling she had was strong. That he was coming toward her. Closer.

Shifting her pocketbook to her opposite shoulder, she swiftly made her way up Seventy-ninth Street, glancing back to the corner, picturing him running up Broadway, trying to reach her.

She quickly crossed Amsterdam Avenue.

Still she could feel the man getting closer. She kept telling herself not to be ridiculous. He had gotten off at Sixty-sixth Street. The train had only taken another minute to reach Seventy-ninth Street. How could he be anywhere near? How could he know that she was getting off at Seventy-ninth Street?

She was walking swiftly now with all her New York paranoia intact. And in her mind was one continuing image. That damn picture.

A night person.

Standing outside her apartment door, Rose realized she had done it again. She had pushed in the lock on her doorknob before leaving the apartment, but neglected to slam the door hard enough. The top lock she had simply not bothered with at all. The door stood half-open, mute testimony of her transgression.

Cautiously, she stepped over the threshold and looked around. There was that moment of dread before she relaxed, having observed in the light of the always-burning lamp that her furniture and TV were still in place. Stupid damned lazy burglars, she thought, throwing her bag on the dining room chair. Here she was just asking to be robbed, begging for it, and they had screwed up their chances once again.

She was still shaking a little, but in a moment she had shrugged it off. Now as she hung the coat in the hall closet, she could feel her heartbeat slow to normal, the fear replaced by a more familiar loneliness. Resolutely she turned to face the first ghost of Lance.

Yes, there he was; she could see him stretched out on the couch, legs dangling, pillows crushed under his head, shoes kicked off and lying on the floor next to a cold cup of coffee, fast asleep. Anyone else would see an empty couch, its two large floral pillows untouched, but to her it was eternally occupied. She ought to sell the damned thing, ghost and all. She sighed, wishing that she hadn't been such a stickler for a tidy apartment. Was that part of it, their breaking away so suddenly as they had? Perhaps, but the whole issue was more complex than that. Lance was more complex than that. Had she ever really known Lance at all?

Rose turned tiredly back to the door, checked to see that it was firmly closed this time and locked, top and bottom. Coming home to an empty apartment was so predictable. Rose could never get used to the lack of possibilities of an empty room.

She wandered into the kitchen and switched on the light, thinking of hot tea. She always had it after work—that was predictable too, despite the fact she had never especially cared for tea. Drinking tea was just a vaguely comforting thing to do, and she was quite sure that somewhere out there were thousands of people who didn't especially care for tea, drinking it. Gallons of it. Well, not tonight.

Rose turned from the cupboard and came face to face with her reflection in the smooth back side of the copper frying pan. She tried to smile. She had lost a good deal of weight over the summer, which pushed her naturally high cheekbones even higher, giving her face a sucked-in look. Her green eyes, somewhat large and generously irised, appeared even larger. There was a haunted look in them now that hadn't been there before. It was this look that drove her to the refrigerator. She opened it.

There was an unpleasant odor. Nothing definable, stale air likely. She very rarely ate at home. She wasn't in the mood to start now. Slightly hungry, she left the kitchen, heading for the bedroom.

The bed was unmade; the quilt lay in a heap on the floor. In some obscure way—too late to please Lance—she had changed. The orderliness of the apartment no longer mattered.

On her dresser were two large sketch pads and a dozen charcoal pencils. Beyond them were various pieces of driftwood from her summer outings; stones and seashells now faded; and a paperweight holding down scores of little notes, scraps of paper with which to remind herself of the week's activities. Art classes Tuesday and Thursday. The Museum of Modern Art on Friday.

A loose scrap of paper had drifted away from the others and she picked it up. In the way one rarely needs to make a note of the major messes one commits oneself to, she didn't especially need to be reminded of this one. Friday night she was scheduled to take off work and spend the evening at the Institute of Parapsychology. The twenty-five-dollar testing fee would hardly compensate her for a lost night's work, but it had seemed like a fascinating idea at the time. Do artists have innate ESP ability? She was inclined to think not, but Dr. Cindrella had been so convincing. During his initial phone call and then through two preliminary interviews, he had somehow known how to pluck the right chords to get her interested. He was quite a magnetic person. And ESP was a compelling subject. Especially for an artist. Anyhow, that was Friday night. Saturday it was the lecture at the Guggenheim with Lottie. Quite a busy schedule. Just your typical datebook of a mad divorcée.

She shoved Cheryl's letter into the stack, removed her clothes and, slipping into her nightgown, went to the bedroom window. A few lights glowed, but most were out. New York had gone to bed.

Suddenly, staring out over the ugliness of concrete and run-down brick buildings, she had an overwhelming intuition that she had been mistaken ever to come to New York in the first place. Back in Connecticut, the images would be cleaner, her focus more on nature. It was all a matter of what message you wanted to send the world. Love of nature and hope, or despair and a collection of pinched faces and warped outlooks. Despair was easier to get recognition for. It was called profound. But perhaps the world was already top-heavy in despair. Perhaps it needed a lighter brushstroke.

In a way, she could remember Connecticut better than she could see New York this very moment. She saw the house she was raised in, a simple house, set back in the Connecticut woods, the unpaved road in front of the house, the winters buried beneath snow, the summers on the beach, her childhood friends still back there, still vibrant. She had so many fond memories of those quiet summer nights she would sit on the front porch with her bare feet propped against the flower box, listening to the creaking of the porch swing as her mother and father would rock back and forth, talking, laughing or just sitting still listening to a choir of crickets.

Of course, there had been that one time of awkwardness where she had known something had happened. She had tried not to listen, but occasionally she would hear them talking at night, Rose's mother crying, and the "she" they had talked about was the reason for it all. The other woman. When it was over, it was over so abruptly, it was merely like a dark cloud had passed. The pain, even the awkwardness, had evaporated, and after that, Rose had wondered if all couples didn't have to go through something like that, that it was so ordered somewhere on the marriage license in invisible ink.

She was sure that the image of *Goldilocks* had come from that dark period of time. That time when her mind had become so confused.

A. Adam, Rose mused.

A. Adam . . .

The building was totally quiet now or else she wouldn't have heard it—the windows in the living room rattling. The wind, she thought. The super had promised to weatherproof them. She'd have to remind him again tomorrow to get the job done. If not, they'd rattle all winter long.

She moved back into the room, set the alarm for 9:00 A.M. She'd have to work the next few days getting things ready for Cheryl's arrival. She adjusted the quilt, got into bed and put out the light. She had just drifted off when the window in the living room rattled again.

Slowly, very slowly, she felt herself nudged awake. She sighed and rolled over. Again she stirred. She felt tired, deadly tired, but something in her mind was forcing her into an alertness when all she wanted to do was sleep.

"Rose? Wake up, Rose."

The voice drifted up from beneath her, so close that it might have been within her own body. But the voice, a whisper actually, sounded artificial. She knew that it did not arise through any volition of her own consciousness. It was being forced into her, mechanically, from an outside source. She kept her eyes shut and struggled to make the voice go away—but gradually the strength of her very willing exhausted her, sapping her of all resistance. She found herself hating the voice.

"Wake up, Rose."

And then she felt it, sensed it—his presence again, the man on the subway, coming at her from a faraway place. The basement. He was just rounding the first-floor landing leading up from the basement. He stopped just long enough to remove a knife from his coat pocket. Rose could see the blade sparkling in the light and his eyes as he caressed the blade—made love to it. After kissing the blade several times, he started slowly up the stairs toward Rose's apartment.

"Oh, God—no," she moaned.

He had reached the seventh floor now. So close—he was so close. She could feel his body pressing in on top of her, suffocating her. And the sheets, her body—all covered over with sweat and . . . blood. The lower portion of her body was covered with blood.

"No!" she screamed.

Her body shot straight up. Was she dreaming? She had seen him clearly, coming up the fire exit stairs. She glanced at the luminous digits of the clock: 3:05 A.M.

She had been dreaming. But the feeling that he was drawing near was still with her. She sat up in bed, listening to the ticking of the antique clock in the living room.

The ticking grew louder. She turned, startled. He was close to her. Closer than ever before. She suddenly felt that he was standing in her living room. She tried to rise but couldn't.

What was wrong with her?

She'd been having, she knew, strange sensations for days now: fantasies of an indistinct voice, smells, an occasional sense of someone near her, observing her, but never this strongly. She had supposed it was just a side effect of too busy a schedule and not enough time to relax. But what she was experiencing now was different. It was as if she were being hurled away from herself, being drawn deeper into someone else's reality.

Abruptly, to free herself from her own disturbing thoughts, she rose from the bed. Her mind was suddenly determined to put a stop to the nonsense. She quickly moved into the living room, which was totally dark.

She turned on the sofa lamp. The room was empty. She moved to the front door, unlocked both locks and opened it. She leaned forward and glanced down the corridor. Empty. She slammed the door shut and locked it. Then she moved to the clock, opened its back, and stopped the pendulum from swinging back and forth, stopped it from reminding her that seconds, minutes, hours were ticking away. Stopped it from reminding her that she was alone.

After that, she crawled into bed where minutes later she drifted into an extraordinarily peaceful sleep. No dreams.

CHAPTER 3

Wednesday, October 15
6:00 P.M.

DR. REESE CINDRELLA HAD NOT EXPECTED TO SEE SO MUCH blood. He was not prepared for that. Neither was he prepared for the casual attitude Mana displayed as the blood dripped from his arm, each drop helping to form a large red floral design on the laboratory floor.

Reese's first knowledge of Alex Mana had come through a pamphlet mailed to him by the National Parapsychology Society. The article it contained had riveted his attention. Mana's reported demonstrations of paranormal phenomena were so spectacular that they defied credibility. Reese had known almost at once that he wanted to test the man further. If the reports proved to be true, he had finally found the man he had been looking for.

Correspondence with Mana eventually resulted in a date set for a special session in which Mana would demonstrate some mind-body coordinations as a research subject. He had stipulated, however, that it was to be a closed session. No observers were to be allowed, and Dr. Cindrella was not to record the session. Terms agreed upon, Alex Mana said he would fly to New York on Monday, the twelfth of October, but that he would not be able to meet with Cindrella until the fifteenth.

Today's session had started simply enough. Nothing spectacular.

The sailmaker's needle Reese had used to puncture Mana's bicep had remained buried about three-quarters of an inch deep. Mana had made no particular sign of pain. His heart and breathing rate remained normal. He just sat there, relaxed, his silky black hair hanging limp over his forehead. His quick, intelligent blue eyes barely moved, yet Reese had the feeling he was taking in the entire room. Over six feet tall, muscular, he was obviously a man who kept his body in perfect physical condition.

Reese stared at him distrustfully. He could be a nonbleeder, a nonpainer. Reese had taken precautions against fraud, still he was unable to believe wholeheartedly in Mana's reported abilities.

Yet the report on Alex Mana had been most specific. By holding a Geiger counter in his hand and concentrating intensely, he had been able to make it jump from 0.7 counts per second to over two hundred times the normal rate. Nothing had influenced the Geiger counter except Mana's mental concentration.

In further tests, all under controlled laboratory conditions, metals were bent by the slightest touch of Mana's hand; he had shattered crystal tightly sealed in a plastic container, moved compass needles forty to fifty degrees, and caused major changes with a magnetometer simply by concentration. All tests had been conducted in the Kansas City State Prison where Mana had just finished serving six years for brutally molesting and beating a girl of sixteen. The two young doctors who had performed the tests on Mana were both well known in their field.

Still Reese knew that he could perform this experiment a thousand times and it wouldn't prove that Mana had control of bleeding unless he knew that bleeding was natural to him. There had been known cases where people rarely bled unless they were severely cut. If this were the case, the needle in Mana's arm would prove very little.

"Alex, I have a question," Reese said quietly. "Is it going to bleed when I take the needle out?"

Mana glanced at him with surprise. "No. Not unless I want it to. Or unless you want it to."

Reese knew Mana had him pegged and squirmed uneasily.

"Tell you what," Mana said. "I'll give it to you both ways. I'll let it bleed just to satisfy your curiosity—then I'll stop the bleeding, okay?"

Reese was worried now. Perhaps he had projected the possibility of fraud too strongly, thereby interfering with Mana's coordination between conscious and unconscious processes. It wouldn't have been the first time a subject had picked up his thoughts, perhaps even his subconscious ones.

"Don't worry—go ahead, pull it out," Mana said.

Reese hesitated, then pulled the needle from his arm. That's when the blood began to flow. Immediately and from both punctures.

Mana laughed. "Hey, how's that for a bleeder! You want more or should I put a cap on it?"

Reese was too busy mopping up the blood and never realized Mana had asked him a question. He found that he was trembling, his muscles jerking as if out of control under his skin. His mind raced on. Man consists of two separate entities. What does it mean to be part of universal forces?

He paused to breathe deeply, a breath that seemed to fill his nostrils with blood, his mouth with the bitter taste of the past.

Reese Cindrella had come up the hard way during the late 1950s: sensitivity training, encounter-group therapy, and a wide variety of personal "inner-development" programs. Textbook stuff. Discussions, constant arguments.

To experiment is better than to argue. That was the thought which had freed Reese Cindrella. Little by little, he began to experiment on his own. His primary interest—dream telepathy, the apparent communication from one mind to another other than through channels of senses. Thought transference—was it possible?

With the advent of new techniques for monitoring dreams, Reese thought it had become feasible to explore dream telepathy. In 1961 he began his planning: he would need an electroencephalograph, a sleep laboratory, a staff, and people who would be his willing subjects. In December of 1962, Reese formed the Institute of Parapsychology, N.Y.C., threw up a shingle and started to wander aimlessly through people's minds.

From the very beginning, Reese had problems: family problems, financial problems, and finally not being able to handle it all, suffered severe illness. It was a bleak, snow-covered day in the winter of 1965 when he delivered the news. His hands shook and his lips trembled as he informed the staff the Institute was closing.

But the Institute hadn't closed. No, he wouldn't let it. It was not in him to let it. The first problem to solve was financial. He would lecture: Psychic Powers, Telepathy, ESP, Hypnosis, Clairvoyance, Christ, Satan, Sex, Drugs—he didn't care; whatever people wanted to hear, he would lecture on it.

And he must have been a good lecturer in those days because she was taking notes, writing faster than he was talking. Amazing! Her face was lovely, composed; it was obvious she had a great interest in Reese's work, at least it appeared that way from where he stood, on a tiny stage in N.Y.U.'s student hall. It was also obvious that she had loads of money. Gobs of it. Reese eyed her for a moment, her head inclined slightly to one side, her thick red hair arranged in coils, layers; Reese found himself staring at her and thinking . . . money.

The fact that she was young, very young, made no difference to him. That dreamlike face would become his dream. He would use her and think nothing of it. The fact that he instantly hated her was of equal indifference; the hatred was involuntary, sprang out of him against his will. He would not let it stop him. The lab mustn't close.

It took only three weeks: two drinks at the St. Moritz, a ride in a hansom cab, lunch at The Four Seasons, and several lavish dinners at the 21 Club. Three weeks to the day. They had gone to bed only once during that time. It wasn't an earth-shaking occasion for either of them. She was used to those eighteen-year-old N.Y.U. stallions and Reese hadn't the competitive spirit that day. But it was enough to clinch the deal.

The next week Reese was notified that the Institute had received a very generous three-year grant from the Nathan J. Morris Foundation. This marked the first time the foundation had supported a project investigating dream telepathy, or anything, for that matter, less conservative than the more classical forms of the arts.

Nathan J. Morris was the girl's father, and resented the hell out of Reese Cindrella. Reese, on the other hand, cherished Morris's hatred. Thrived on it. Morris believed in the material world. Let him die by it. A lush, rich, fragrant world—it made a good grave. And Morris and his daughter were always digging theirs. They were born to be taken, and Reese Cindrella took plenty. In 1968 the Nathan J. Morris Foundation granted Cindrella another grant, this time for five years.

For the first time Morris and Reese had had a solitary drink together, the night before the papers were signed. There was a silent rider to the contract, Morris had explained. His daughter was hereafter off limits. Reese smiled. "I'll drink to that," he said in all candor, and was amused at the sudden gleam of respect in Morris's eye for not having played the game.

But what would Reese do when the grant ran out? He had immediately reassured himself there would be others. And there had been others. Many of them. And each one he hated more than the last, but then—they had helped him support his habit—dream telepathy.

"It stopped." Mana now looked at his arm in a detached way.

Reese spun around like a man lost in a sudden blindness. "What?"

"It's stopped. Here—take a look."

Reese dropped the bloody towels into the wicker basket and examined Mana's arm. To his amazement, the two punctures in Mana's skin had drawn shut; the bleeding had stopped. Reese couldn't help but be impressed. Mana had done exactly as he had predicted—he had bled and then had stopped the bleeding. But could he prevent bleeding entirely? Reese made this an audible question.

"Why not?" Mana said, and allowed Reese to reinsert the needle in the opposite arm. This time the needle was pushed through a small vein as it broke through the skin.

Reese waited.

No bleeding. Reese waited longer, still the blood did not flow. Instead, the wounds closed up around the needle. Finally, after two or three minutes, Reese withdrew the needle. Immediately, the skin drew shut completely, leaving two small bluish-red spots, barely perceptible. But no blood.

A smile slipped over Alex Mana's lips. "Charlatan or miracle worker? Which am I?"

Reese looked at him reflectively. "I'm not sure."

Mana pressed his upper lip with his forefinger and thumb, molded it. "You think on it. In the meantime, I believe we set the price at two hundred dollars a session. I'd say you were getting a bargain." Again Mana smiled, crossed his legs and ran his fingers through his hair slowly, crimping it in the same motion.

"Why don't you tell me something about yourself?" Reese suggested. "Whatever you think I should know."

Mana began at once to talk, settling back in his chair and wandering into a long rambling monologue that concluded with a gloomy discourse about death.

He's afraid of dying, Reese thought. Death—it frightened people; the ignorant, the intelligent, rich, poor, healthy, sick— all had the same question on their minds. What is it like to die?

"For the living know that they shall die: but the dead know not anything," Mana said softly.

Reese barely moved, aware that Mana had just picked up his thoughts, almost before he was able to have them. It was absolutely uncanny. Could Mana actually know what people were thinking? No. Reese didn't think so. Probably just has his mind running on all the time and then a wild guess. Still, there would have to be other tests.

"When?" Mana asked.

Looking into Mana's smiling face, Reese shuddered. Impossible, he thought, staring, the image before him pale and still.

"Tomorrow at three," Reese said hesitantly.

"Can't. Let's make it Monday."

"I thought you were only staying in town a few days?"

"Changed my mind."

Reese hesitated. "All right. Monday—at three."

"Fine."

Like parapsychologists who had gone before him, Reese believed telepathy to be the original archaic method by which people communicated, and which had been pushed into the background in the course of evolution, and might still manifest itself under certain conditions. But what conditions? Could Reese convince Mana to sleep over Monday night at the laboratory? Mana had an incredible power and the best way to monitor this power was while he slept. "I'd like you to sleep here Monday night, if that's all right with you." Reese's words came out too fast, his anxiety hanging apparent in the air.

Mana smiled. "Sure, why not."

"Good." Reese relaxed. "Here, I'll write you a check for this session."

"No checks. Cash."

"I don't have—"

"Next time, okay? Monday—three P.M. I'll be here, bag in hand. You don't mind that, do you? I'll need my bag."

"Of course not. And if you don't mind, I'd like to call in an observer on Monday. I'd also like to videotape the session."

"Let me think about it. I'll call you at home tomorrow night."

"I'll write my number down."

"555-3313."

Again Mana had picked his brain. Reese Cindrella's number was a private, unlisted number. There wasn't any possible way Mana could have known. "How did you know my number?"

Mana avoided Reese's gaze, appearing awkward and self-conscious, as if he had been caught stealing something that didn't belong to him.

"Think of a number?" he said.

Reese laughed and was startled at the harsh sound of his own laughter. "What?"

"A number. Think of a number."

Reese pivoted slowly on his heels and thought: *Good Christ! What is he up to now?* "All right," he said. He had thought of the number one.

"Now think of another number."

"I've got it," Reese said, having thought of the number nine.

"Now the last number," Mana said.

Reese tried to focus mentally, but the number nine repeated as a double image in his mind. He tried to erase the image and begin again.

Mana said suddenly, "No, that's fine. Pick up the pad on the table behind you. I wrote the number down before while you were on the phone."

Reese glanced at the yellow pad which lay face down on the table. He turned it over. It read, "1999."

When Reese next looked up, Mana was gone. All that remained was the sound of footsteps, curiously hollow, as they padded their way down the long hallway.

Moments later, Reese made his way down that same hallway. Outside, the wind had picked up, throwing rain in hard bursts against the window pane. There was little light left in the low sky. He entered his office and closed the door behind him. It was already seven o'clock . . . where had the day gone? Irritably, he ran his fingers through his hair. His hair was too long. Must get it cut soon . . . soon. He suddenly caught a glimpse of himself in the glass bookcase.

Throughout the day he was always catching glimpses of himself like that. Sometimes in one of the many small mirrors scattered throughout the Institute, sometimes in the shiny surface of an instrument. He was fascinated at the way his appearance changed from day to day. Today he looked especially tired, yet his steel-gray eyes had remained clear, penetrating, even through the amber tint of his tortoise-framed glasses. His lips seemed thinner today, his jaw more pronounced. If not for the gray hair, he would have thought himself a much younger man.

All at once his mind clicked onto a small private picture of his mother. Yes, good. He would find her home when he got there. And his brother Michael was coming home tomorrow evening. Yes, good.

He moved to the desk, picked up his chart and studied the profiles of his other two dream session volunteers. The experiment would begin on Friday, October seventeenth, and run for seven unconsecutive nights. Thus far, his timing had been perfect.

He let his gaze run down the chart.

SUBJECT: Rose Carpenter. Age 25

    Occupation: Cocktail waitress/Artist.
    Marital status: Divorced.
    Education: High school. Four years of college.
    Parents: Living.
    Tested: Subject was open to ESP experience. Interesting, motivated, capable of establishing rapport with others quickly. Expressive.

                    Medical History: Age nine, suf-
                              fered an eight-
                              month regression.
                              Schizophrenia. In-
                              stitutionalized Wil-
                              lowbrook, N.Y. No
                              other medical prob-
                              lems.

AGENT: Jack Squadron. Age 33

                    Occupation: Composer.
                    Marital Status: Married.
                    Education: High School. Four
                              years of college.
                    Parents: Living? Whereabouts
                              unknown. Of spe-
                              cial interest: Jack
                              had been placed in
                              an orphanage at age
                              six.
                    Tested: Open, confident, capable
                              of becoming emo-
                              tionally involved in
                              the target. Expres-
                              sive. Very inter-
                              ested in others.
                    Medical History: None applica-
                              ble.

   Reese stood perfectly still for a moment. A pulse beat strongly
in his temple. Exhausted, he put the chart aside and turned out
the light. Seated alone in the dark, he let his mind wander. An

image of Rose Carpenter flashed before his eyes. He knew a good deal about her background; in fact a good deal more than Rose herself was aware. Now her image rolled over in his mind, became unreal, as if it had been cut from a magazine. Tensing, he tried to envision what Jack Squadron looked like. An image formed. Then froze.

CHAPTER 4

Wednesday, October 15
7:00 P.M.

JACK SQUADRON STILL WASN'T CONVINCED HE BELONGED IN a psychiatrist's office talking about his wife who knew nothing of the visit, and who was now convalescing in Roosevelt Hospital. The fact that Frank Austin was a longtime friend as well as a psychiatrist didn't lessen Jack's anxiety. Neither he nor his wife had ever used Frank professionally, but Frank had thought it might do Jack some good. So there he was.

At first there had been a lightening of atmosphere, a young secretary talking around them, a phone call downstairs for take-out food, a drink poured from Frank's private stock and then a settling back.

It had all been, of course, the prelude to a more serious matter. Jack had barely put down his drink when Frank told his secretary to hold all calls. Perhaps it was the phrase itself: Hold all calls. Or perhaps it was the tone in Frank's voice. Whatever the case, Jack knew the dreaded moment had finally arrived.

"And now let's talk about you. Off the record," Frank said, and smiled.

The conspiratorial smile made Jack uneasy. "You mean let's talk about Cara."

"No, you." Another smile, a crooked one this time, with a chuckle to follow. "Relax, Jack. Let's just BS like we do at the club."

"We're not at the club."

"Don't let the shingle outside the door scare you," he said good-humoredly. Then he asked, almost in the same breath, "Is it true that you hate young women, Jack?" As he asked the question, he leaned back and seemed to disappear in his deep and comfortable black leather chair.

"What the hell kind of question is that to ask?"

"Cara says you do. That every time you and she go out, you always wind up arguing with young, pretty women. Is that true?"

"It's not only not true," Jack said angrily, "it's absurd."

"All right," Frank said. "Let me put it another way. Perhaps you really don't hate young women. Perhaps you just want to show Cara that you're not interested in them. Is that possible?"

Jack frowned, took a cigarette out of the brown leather case on the desk and lit it. Through the pale screen of smoke, he watched Frank's thin face, watched his blue eyes, peering intently. Good education. Upper five percent of his class. So sure of himself, Jack thought enviously, and realized if there was one thing he had never been, that was it—sure of himself. He caught Frank's reproving eye and straightened obediently in his chair like a schoolboy caught in the act of daydreaming.

"The mind is unbelievably complex," Frank went on. "In this case we're dealing with two minds. Yours as well as Cara's. I'll need to understand both of you if I'm to help Cara."

Jack met his gaze evenly. "It's been ten years. Do you realize that? When I married Cara I had just turned twenty-three."

"Well, time flies so quickly . . ."

"No, Frank—it's not time that has flown, it's our marriage. Cara and I have become different people. We need different things."

"When you say you need different things," Frank said gently, "are you saying you don't need Cara any longer?"

"Cara is not an object. She's a woman. She is the most remarkable woman—"

"Sounds like too much protest, Jack . . ."

"You are not going to bend me into saying other than what I feel. Cara has been everything to me. How can I say I don't need her? You know better than anyone else that I worshiped Cara from the minute I set eyes on her."

"Yes, but Cara doesn't look exactly the same now, does she? Still quite a woman, of course, but not exactly the same."

Jack was silent, feeling the undercurrent of some running tide of truth difficult to deny any longer.

"Funny," he said, and put his cigarette into the ashtray. "I really thought we were going to get past all this. I thought Cara would go back to work, make contact again with the outside world. I thought it would help take her mind off me for a while. We both need time alone, but somehow I can't seem to make a move without her being there." He shrugged. "She refuses to leave the apartment. When I suggest we have friends over for dinner, she says let's just be alone. We never go out anymore. We just always seem to be on top of each other. It's gotten so bad that I've thought about leaving her. I don't want to, but I don't know how much more of it I can take. Look at me. What am I? A broke-on-my-ass songwriter. Why? Why do I keep on trying?" he went on, disdaining reply. "For some, the words, the music come easy. For others, it's a long, bitter agony. I don't mind that. I really don't. But it takes time. Time alone. Something that Cara just isn't able to give me at this point."

"Does she know all this? How you feel?"

Jack shook his head. "I didn't have the heart to tell her she's suffocating me."

"I see," he said, almost meditatively, then leaned forward in his chair. "Jack, Cara's condition seems to be primarily an ego sickness. What happened this morning, her deliberately burning her hand like that, was an eruption of unconscious life into the field of consciousness, an encroachment possible only in the face of ego breakdown . . ."

There was no escaping it. Frank was now fully embarked upon a clinical lecture as to the direct cause of Cara's problem. Jack turned away to face the window, letting his mind drift beyond the orchid-colored drapes. Letting his mind drift back to the beginning.

Cara Lucille Gassner. What a woman, what a name! Jack loved her, right there on the spot, the first time they had met. She was having breakfast on the terrace of the Evergreen Club, a private tennis retreat in the Hamptons. She had come highly recommended. "She's a great tennis pro, Jack. You'll learn a hellofa lot. She's expensive, but what the hell—you'll have the best backhand in show business."

Perhaps it was because Jack was so impressionable that he found Cara's beauty overwhelming. For the first few weeks he could think of nothing else, whereas her mind was definitely on tennis. She would go to great lengths to teach him. He, on the other hand, would go to great lengths to be awkward, barely responding to her instructions, drawing her attention even harder to him. She wasn't used to failing, Jack knew that. The more he fumbled around the court, the more she felt it necessary to spend time with him. "Let's try again tomorrow, all right? The lesson will be on me." Jack hadn't heard her; he was too busy staring.

Thirty-nine years old, he thought. Impossible. She had the vitality of a younger woman, much younger. Her face was a deep tan, her teeth white and even; she looked the picture of health. Beneath her tennis outfit, Jack could see the movement of her strong, athletic body, and he felt the excitement growing inside him. "Can I buy you lunch?" he asked, and she said, "Sure, why not."

He took her to the Fisherman's Inn. It was immediately apparent they enjoyed each other's company, and that their relationship could become more than teacher to student. "You mean you can play tennis better than you've been playing it?" she asked.

Jack smiled. "What can I tell you?"

They had breakfast the next morning at her apartment, then lunch the following day and dinner the night after that. Cara began neglecting her other students. Instead, she and Jack would take trips into New York. They would go to Broadway shows, Madison Square Garden, and sit afterwards in the Top of the Six's for hours, talking. For Cara, it was pleasant. For Jack, one of the great crushes of the Western world. A crush that came to a climax three weeks before the summer was to end.

Jack had just finished playing several sets of tennis with Frank and, covered with a light sweat, dropped onto the couch in the living room. Frank had gone back to the guest cottage to change.

"Jack, is that you?"

"Yes," he said, and watched Cara pause at the top of the stairs wearing a blue satin gown with bare midriff, the light from the bedroom behind her—tall, sleek-headed; hand on her hip. A goddess, he thought. Right out of a Greek legend. She paused briefly to toss back her hair, then descended the stairs in erect grace.

"We don't have all that much time, you know," she said, leaning over and kissing him. "You had better hurry and get dressed."

Jack watched her tall, graceful form move to the mirror; watched her peer into it; pure profile lighted on his side. Gorgeous.

He stood, stretched. "Sorry, the match took longer than I figured."

"Did you win?"

"Are you kidding? Austin's got the best backhand around. Even if I did win, he'd start analyzing my victory until I realized that it was my hidden aggression that won, and not me."

She's putting on lipstick, he said to himself, watching her. So unnecessary—there's nothing she can do to make herself more beautiful than she already is. . . . Doesn't she know that?

In a hesitant voice, he said, "I love you, Cara. I want to marry you."

Cara turned as if suddenly jolted by an unseen force. She glanced at Jack's face for a moment. "Jack, please don't." She straightened, pressed her fingers to her earlobe, adjusting her earring. "I really don't want this to turn into something sticky." She forced a smile. "Now hurry up and get dressed. The Talbotts will be here any minute."

". . . I wish they weren't coming."

"Why?"

"Last night—today. The whole damn week. It all seemed so perfect."

"We agreed, Jack. Nothing serious. A week here, a few weeks there. Tomorrow I go back to my job, and you . . ." She came to him and placed her fingers to his lips. "And you . . . will now march up those stairs and get dressed."

Jack turned sharply away.

"Jack, don't act like this." She moved toward him. "Where are you going?"

"I am now going to take a good long swim," he said calmly. "And you can talk it all over with yourself and decide whether or not you love me, want me, want to be Mrs. Jack Squadron."

He tossed the racket onto the couch and started out the patio doors leading to the beach. "Oh, yes, there's one more thing I almost forgot: I get a feeling of great elation every time I swim in the nude—a really tremendous joy watching myself navigate the waves bare-assed; although I must admit I never do feel sexually drawn to do it unless I'm pissed, and I'm never pissed unless I'm in love. I am in love with you, Cara! I am also pissed! I am now going to swim bare-assed! Please keep the Talbotts indoors; I wouldn't want to embarrass you."

He turned back toward the doors, ripped off his shirt, dropped his drawers and dashed onto the beach, his legs taking long strides until his body disappeared into the white foam and splash of the ocean.

Cara ran her hand through her red, slightly wavy hair and said: "Oh, do you really think so?" In less than a minute, she had removed her dress and walked off naked down the beach to where Jack was floating like a walrus, atop the water. Before going into the water, she caught sight of her neighbor seated beneath the beach umbrella, the expression on her face seeming to say, "You can expect that woman to do anything."

Cara smiled. "Hello, Sally."

"Hello!" Sally pressed the bridge of her nose, adjusting her sunglasses.

Cara turned back to Jack, winked and plunged in. They were married in a simple ceremony, on the beach, in the presence of a few friends including Frank Austin, two weeks later.

"Jack, for Chrissakes! You're not even listening to me." Frank was standing now, his tall, rangy figure impeccably tailored in blue slacks and a dark gray sports coat. Thick gray hair curled over his ears and over his blue shirt collar, leading one to expect the wild inner workings of a poet.

"Sorry, Frank. You caught me in the act of admiring a very beautiful lady."

"Do you still love her?"

"I don't know. Christ, Frank—I don't know what I know anymore. I've been out of touch with everything for so long."

Frank crossed his arms on his chest. "Jack, listen. I'm going to ask Dr. Grayson to keep Cara in the hospital for at least another week. Her hand is pretty badly burnt. I'll use that as a pretext. In the meantime, she'll be in a neutral territory where she might relax. I'll drop in as a friend—maybe we can get her problems worked out. In the meantime, you have to get out. Start circulating."

"And do what?" Jack asked, fumbling for another cigarette.

"Come on, Jack. Don't make the going any rougher. Go to a bar—drink. You still drink, don't you?"

"Yeah."

"Well, there you are. You play chess, don't you? Go to a chess parlor. Play chess!"

"I'll lose. I don't like to lose." He smiled and drew in on his cigarette.

"It'll do you good."

"That's what you say every time you beat me in tennis. It never does me any good, believe me." Jack let out a huge cloud of smoke. "Anyway, I'm going out Friday night."

"Oh?"

"The Institute of Parapsychology. Have you ever heard of it?"

"Not really."

"Interesting place. It's run by a Dr. Cindrella. He's experimenting with dream telepathy. You know, when people communicate to each other through their dreams. Actually, I'm sorry I agreed to it."

"Why's that?"

"Dreams really don't interest me much. I used to have them all the time as a kid. But now, well . . ." Jack broke off.

"Are you going to see Cara tonight?"

"Yes."

"Good."

"Frank, what made her do such a thing?"

He shrugged. "She's forty-nine, you're thirty-three. Did you think it was going to be easy for her?"

"But to do a thing like that. To place her hand over the burner . . ."

"Does it make you angry?"

"Angry?" Jack forced a laugh. "How can you be angry with someone who deliberately tries to destroy herself?"

"For making it harder for you to leave her?" he suggested.

"I told you—I never mentioned it. We had a few bad times, but nothing to make her think I wanted to leave her."

"The fact is, something helped to shatter her ego. What do you suppose it was?"

"I don't know!" He scowled. What the hell was he getting so hot about? What was the sense of that? He suddenly caught sight of himself in the polished silver back of a picture frame on Frank's desk. That the frame was a strategically placed trap was a certainty, and yet it gave him an odd sort of comfort staring at himself. He marveled that the image in the frame had retained its clean-cut good looks, that the mouth retained its sensitivity, the eyes something of their youthful curiosity. Still boyish at thirty-three, but rugged, with a full head of sandy-colored hair and broad forehead.

"Did you say something, Jack?" Frank asked.

"Not out loud, I didn't." He paused. "Okay, so maybe she is taking her age badly. It's not my fault."

"All right, Jack—let's take a look at where we stand."

"Good. I mean, that's the only reason I agreed to come here. No offense. It's just—"

"I understand." Frank unbuttoned his jacket, sat in the chair opposite Jack, and let his hands glide gently one into the other. So fatherly, Jack thought. It was hard to believe that there were only four years separating them.

"Cara seems to be all right now. But then, she's on fairly strong medication. But with this type of disorder, we can't be sure that it won't reoccur. That depends on a multitude of influences. Why she did what she did in the first place. What caused her to do it. And . . ."

"Me."

"Yes, you." He paused, then added: "Cara mentioned an apartment cluttered with magazines."

"Come on, Frank. So I like reading *Playboy*—an occasional *Penthouse*. Why should that suddenly bother her?"

"Forty-nine is a tough age for a woman. Real tough." He shrugged. "It's a tough age for anyone."

"So what do I do, read them in the closet like a schoolboy?"

Frank eyed him skeptically. "Was it your idea that she go back to work?"

The abruptness of the question was disconcerting. "Frank, for Chrissakes—I had two flops in a row. Broadway isn't exactly banging my doors down these days. We needed the money. Cara suggested she work."

"But she prefers to be home with you. Isn't that right? Did you try to find other financial solutions before suggesting she go back to work?"

Jack looked at him in surprise. He hadn't. For weeks now

he had walked around the apartment like a bear. Moody, sullen, thinking himself trapped. He told Cara it was his inability to write music; good music, bad music, it made no difference, he just couldn't hack it. But the truth, the absolute truth was . . .

"Jack, listen to me. If you don't love her anymore, well— we have to find the right way to approach this. In the meantime, you have to— I hate to say this. You have to fake it. At least for the time being. She needs you."

"Yeah," Jack said, half defensive, half apologetic, letting his arm slide from the arm of the chair, knowing exactly what Frank was going to say and yet obligated to sit there and listen to it. So he sat, back straight in a pose of deep concentration, a pretense, while the nerve above his left eye started to twitch. Frank spoke soft reassuring words, Frank's own language, psychiatrist's talk—impressive. But Jack was becoming impatient. "I gotta go, Frank."

Jack's last impression of Frank standing at the office door amused him. Ironic in a way. He pictured Frank carrying a green canvas case that unmistakably held within it a tennis racket. Obviously in a hurry, Frank appeared full-blown as a cartoon character ready to enter the great green arena reserved for weekend warriors, ready to attack the first tennis ball hit in his direction. Isn't that funny, Frank? Me picturing you like that? What was it that Frank was saying? Oh, yes—something about how Cara would be in a receptive mood.

"See you around, Frank." As Jack made his way to the elevator, he heard the door close behind him. It was somehow a very ominous sound.

CHAPTER 5

Thursday, October 16
3:00 P.M.

GETTING READY FOR CHERYL'S ARRIVAL HAD ACTUALLY BEEN very pleasant, one of those simple acts of charity that make a person feel useful. Rose had rearranged the furniture so the sofa bed would easily fold out in the evening, bought new sheets and towels, and stocked the refrigerator. Even the wooden floors had been buffed and the windows cleaned.

Rose felt an odd anticipation about seeing Cheryl again. They had been good friends at school. At least Cheryl had been in and out of her daily life, much like a bobbing cork. Not much of a serious thinker there. Not much to talk about, come to think of it. Rose wondered if the visit wasn't going to be a disaster. But when Rose opened her door an hour later and Cheryl was suddenly there, bag in hand, in one of those blank beige business suits, Rose was taken aback.

Drab, drab, drab, she thought. But in that split second people take before committing themselves to contact, she already knew the image was wrong. Not really drab. Deliberately drab. She could hardly tell how she knew this. Perhaps it was the way Cheryl wore the suit . . . like a costume she was unaccustomed to wearing. The low flat shoes were dreadful and brand new. And the naked look of Cheryl's face. Would the Cheryl she had known go around without makeup? With her hair barely curled and hanging? Was this the same Cheryl who had put on a new face three times a day and washed her hair every morning?

Cheryl smiled and extended her hand, but she would not meet Rose's eyes. "Sorry about this," she said.

"Hey, don't be silly." Rose gave her a brief hug, feeling

Cheryl withdraw slightly. "Come in. Come in . . ." Rose was remembering what she told Nick. A nun. That was exactly what Cheryl reminded her of. A nun in street clothes.

The door closed behind them with a dull thud.

Two vodka tonics with a twist of lime later, Cheryl still hadn't relaxed. She walked up and down, back and forth, and then sat. She was not the same person Rose remembered her to be. There was something missing from her, and not just her attitude or physical appearance, although they certainly had changed. But it was the emotional difference that was most obvious.

In college, Cheryl had had a great sense of humor and a strength or whatever it was that allowed people to survive the worst kind of disasters, then rise above them. Cheryl had been able to do that very well. Rose had a dim memory of Cheryl making light of a tense situation involving bad grades and possible expulsion from the university. But this resiliency seemed lost to her now, and whatever it was that was bothering her, she was keeping it to herself.

Rose smiled, clinking the ice in her glass. "You must be tired from your trip."

"Not really."

Rose looked at her with concern. "Are you sure you're all right?"

"I feel fine." She unfastened the front of her jacket. "You still look very pretty." __

Rose flinched. "Lord, Cheryl—it hasn't been that long."

"Four years."

Rose burst out laughing. Cheryl laughed too. Who was it that said laughter was good for the soul? "I hadn't thought it was that funny," Cheryl said. "But when you think about it—"

At that point Delgoto appeared—that was his name, Delgoto. An excellent pizza had arrived. One of the best pizzas. One of the really great ones. Delgoto was carrying it like a gourmet chef, wearing his tennis shoes and jacket. He was obviously in a hurry. "I think it's a fine one," he said to Rose, who tipped him a dollar. "It has the cheese spread just right. And the sauce . . ." A few more remarks and off he went, down the hall and into the elevator.

Both girls dug in.

"You'd think we were ancient," Rose said, popping an anchovy into her mouth.

"Twenty-six and I still don't know what to do with my life." Cheryl forced a smile. "You?"

"What?" Rose had drifted. "Oh, twenty-five."

"No. I mean what you're going to do with your life."

Rose shrugged. "I have to start all over again, I guess. Lance and I divorced four months ago. Oh, but then you didn't even . . . I got married right after college. A sort of graduation present."

"Oh," Cheryl mumbled. "Have you heard from him since you broke up?"

"He called once to see if I was still alive. Long distance no less. I told him I was and his conscience went back to sleep. I haven't heard from him since."

Cheryl gazed at her with stricken eyes. "It still bothers you, doesn't it?"

Rose started to tense. "In the beginning, it was terrible. I couldn't stop hoping he'd call and say it was some kind of horrible mistake. I don't know, I felt alone, even in a crowd. People stopped inviting me to dinners because they didn't know what to do with me." She shrugged. "That left me a lot of time by the phone. Still, there are times I—" Rose broke off and reached for her glass. It was empty. Dragging her fingers through her hair, she waited for Cheryl to ask the usual questions. How long were you married? Answer: three years, two months and one day. She had even figured it down to the hours and minutes, but lost interest after the second week. Question: Did you love him? Answer: Yes. Question: Was it another woman? Answer:——

What was the question? Oh, yes. Was there another woman? Answer: Yes, I think toward the end there was.

But Cheryl didn't ask Rose any of these questions. Instead she continued to stare at her with pale sympathetic eyes, as though she could almost imagine for herself how hard it must have been. Perhaps, Rose reflected, Cheryl had been through something similar. That would explain the tightness around her mouth, the clinching of her hands around the arms of her chair. Something had turned Cheryl into this stranger.

The afternoon ran into late afternoon in a blue-gray rush, and time passed, along with all the memories of college days.

Rose made a few more attempts at humor. But Cheryl wasn't really paying attention and Rose found herself feeling uneasy.

"Another drink?" she asked.

"No. No, thanks."

And then Rose heard it. Softly at first. Then louder, stronger. Children singing. She looked around, trying to pinpoint where the sound was coming from. Crazy. Yet there were children singing. Could Cheryl hear the children? There was a frantic sound of music now. Suddenly gone. Replaced by a quiet, almost serene quality to the atmosphere. People speaking in muted voices. Ssssh.

Rose watched as Cheryl's face became strangely distorted, then saw her body explode into a thousand pieces as if someone had shoved a stick of dynamite into her mouth. Kaboom!

"Rose?"

Blood suddenly splattered over the walls and then began to drip. Everywhere, pieces of human flesh—hair; Cheryl's severed head lay smiling at Rose's feet.

"Rose!"

The room had all at once become enormous, disproportionate, the walls and ceiling metallic-red and glowing, the glare bathing everything in a crimson brightness. Rose blinked, trying to adjust to the glare. When she looked up, Cheryl was standing beside her.

"Hey, are you all right? What happened?"

Rose shook her head. "I don't know. Something must be caught between my contacts. I'll be right back." She moved through the room with one eye closed for effect, and part of her brain—the part that wasn't clouded—said, "Damn, look at how cool you're making it through this. Heads rolling, blood gushing, so real you could throw up. And here you are walking with one eye closed so Cheryl thinks it's contact lens trouble."

She went into the bathroom, locked the door, and with eyes of a great gray owl, she peered at herself in the mirror. Then she really did get sick. With her head bent over the sink, she tried to gag as quietly as possible, letting the water run to cover the sound.

What is happening to me?

Again she glimpsed her image in the mirror and saw tears rolling down her face. She had no idea what was causing this flood of anguish. Just that all of a sudden, as she stood there, staring at the first faint glow of moonlight coming in at the window, life had become very perplexing and difficult. She dabbed her face with water, but the solemn set expression remained. If anything, her mood darkened like a fist tightening.

When she reentered the living room, she found Cheryl standing by the window. The moon sat low in the sky and a light mist drifted over rooftops, diaphanous puffs of vapor that swirled suddenly, driven by the wind that moved over the city like a pair of nervous hands.

And then it happened. As if a curtain had been suddenly drawn away from the window, allowing in the light. There was no warning. It was a simple understanding of the whole situation. She just opened her mouth and said:

"You can't stay here. I want you to leave—now."

Cheryl turned and seemed to know exactly why Rose had said what she'd said. "I'd expected as much. You know, don't you?"

"That you've been having an affair with Lance? Yes." Rose didn't know where the thought came from, how she had come by this sudden awareness, but she knew it to be true.

"We met in Florida. Lance was on a business trip."

"I don't need the details."

"I was shocked when I discovered you were married to him."

"Do tell," Rose said coldly.

"Please, Rose—"

"Out of curiosity, is this the way you dress for Lance? Sophisticated sackcloth? Or is that a guilt trip for my benefit? A sort of smearing on of the ashes . . ." But Rose wasn't capable of listening to Cheryl's answer. The hallucination had suddenly repeated itself. Cheryl's head went exploding over the walls; the children were singing in the background.

When was it? What other time had she heard those same children singing that same song? She had been ten—no, nine years old. She remembered the day very well. She had awakened that morning with a sense of fear. She had parted the curtains and gazed out. The day had the appearance of extreme cold. People milled about, heavily bundled.

She had shrugged, as if the shrugging would shake off the ominous feeling, and had begun to dress. The feeling dogged her.

Still uneasy, she had kissed her mother goodbye and started

to walk toward the schoolyard. She had not been able to shake her gloom. Shivering, she had pulled her coat tighter around her neck to shut in the warmth of her body.

When she had reached the school, everything was quiet. So quiet that the thumping of her heart echoed with insistence within her brain. All at once she had heard children singing. She stopped to listen, and at that instant panic washed over her. She was late. Everyone had already entered the school. Class had begun without her. The thought had sent a disturbing sense of unreality coursing through her body. She turned suddenly and no longer recognized the street. The school, a building of three stories, made of dark-streaked brick, swirled elusively before her gaze as the singing grew louder into a mocking chant. *You don't belong here. You don't belong here.*

Instantly a dazzling light had blinded her eyes, and with horrid anxiety that caused her to break out sobbing, she ran home.

She had never thought of an explanation for what had happened. Except that it had happened around the time when she had discovered her father was seeing the other woman.

In the month that followed, Rose had lost all touch with reality. She had been hospitalized for a very short time. At nine, long ago—she had been hospitalized.

As the memories drifted away, Cheryl's face came into sharp focus. Rose hesitated, blinking massively.

"I've got to go to work," she said. "When I get back, I don't want you here." She moved to the hall closet.

"Rose, please—we must talk."

"There's an extra set of keys in the vase on the table. Lock the door when you go. Leave the keys in the mailbox." She slipped easily into her suede jacket.

"Rose, please. I didn't come here about Lance."

"Oh, then why did you come?"

Cheryl hesitated. "It's not easy to explain. I mean, it's going to sound crazy. But ever since I found out Lance was your husband— No, that's not it at all. Every time I think about you, I . . ."

"Please, Cheryl—say what it is you've come here to say."

"Damn it, it's not that easy. I think of you and I feel things. Dream things. I have these odd sensations come over me."

Rose looked at her sternly. "Guilt can do strange things to people."

"It's not that at all. This is different. I feel as if someone is watching me. Then the images come, one picture flashing to another quite different from the one before, but I see them. Rose, something isn't right. I know it. I feel it. It's so real that it's almost driving me crazy. Please, Rose, we must talk."

Rose stared evenly in her direction. Her sense of herself, which had been lost for a moment, driven back, as far back as childhood, had returned to her. With a curt nod, she turned and passed through the door, slamming it behind her.

"Rose!" Cheryl cried.

The voice was as distant as the past. Faded and muffeld. As faded and muffled as the closing of the fire exit door. Rose turned. The door was just swinging shut.

She stared at the door for a long time. Whoever had closed the door was now in a hurry, clamoring down the stairs.

CHAPTER 6

THIS SAME THURSDAY, AT A QUARTER PAST TEN IN THE EVE-
ning, Reese Cindrella sat slumped in the darkened living room
of his home in Manhattan Beach, an exclusive suburb of New
York City. He was watching a Chaplin movie. One of those
rare vintage types, fast-moving and silent. From time to time
he took sips of coffee from his cup. Otherwise he sat perfectly
still.

It had grown quite cold again this evening but Reese had
devoutly ignored that environmental fact. Instead he sat close
to the projector and stared idly at the screen, the faint flickers
of light bleaching him and hollowing his cheeks.

Presently an abrupt movement diverted his attention. He
glanced into the darkness. One could barely discern the seated
figure at the opposite end of the room. She sat quite still for
a time. Then, shifting her weight in her chair, his mother sighed
heavily.

Usually they would sit together for an hour or so each
evening watching old movies. Comfortable. Silent. Allowing
the other's separate flights of fantasy to go undisturbed. But
tonight Reese's mind was unable to take wing and settled instead on the last few days.

Alex Mana had done remarkable things at the Institute yesterday. Reese was anxious to conduct further tests. Monday,
three o'clock. It seemed a thousand days away.

Hesitantly, he smoothed back his hair, removed his glasses,
and pressed his fingers into the corners of his eyes.

Almost at once his mind took a quick step backward.

Christ, twenty-one years (had it really been twenty-one

years?) since he'd started the Institute of Parapsychology? He remembered the strength and vitality with which he had performed his work then. The enthusiasm, the vigor. He was on fire in those days, a shooting star—and a handsome son-of-a-bitch to boot. That had always made him feel good, having both sexes constantly attracted to his good looks. People had trusted him back then, trusted his looks. They had opened up their minds to him so easily. Yes, it had all been so easy then. Uncomplicated.

But then again, he had just turned twenty-seven years old at the time. At twenty-seven, everything seemed easy. Mana was twenty-six. Was youth power? Reese wasn't sure, but knew he had to find the answer to his question soon. Power meant control. And control was what he desired the most. To control his destiny. To see that his long-awaited dream finally came true.

Reese now settled back and allowed his mind to wander. Thoughts came and went, until finally he straightened, the last of his thoughts being of his mother, and his heart twisted.

Now sound and light and shape wafted back through the latticework of his senses. He placed his hand on the back of his neck and stroked it. It was sore; all of him sore, he realized; his palms were sweating and his hands were trembling slightly. He had lost control. That was the biggest difference between then and now. Control.

Dimly at first, then sharper, eyes, nose, mouth emerged from the shadows.

"I'm tired, Reese," his mother said, shifting her position in her chair to lend emphasis to what she was saying. "Reese, did you hear, I'm tired. Michael isn't coming. He won't be here now, it's too late. I'm going to bed."

"He'll be here."

"No, I'm going upstairs now."

Chaplin continued to struggle, his comedic posture contradicting his inner turmoil. Hat cocked over one eye, he leaned forward on his cane, which immediately slipped away, sending him sprawling to the ground. Still, Reese's mother did not stir from her chair.

"I had another dream today," she said. "Did I tell you? A man—hanging. Suspended in midair with his neck broken. It was most exhausting. Not for the man, naturally, he was dead.

But rather for me trying to determine the nature of his crime—if indeed he had committed a crime. Innocent perhaps—a victim. I awoke smiling. Isn't that odd—smiling. What do you suppose it meant?"

Reese remained silent.

"I'll have to ask Mildred the next time I see her." She took a deep breath and released it as a sigh.

In a sudden flapping of celluloid, the film was over. Reese stirred from his chair and switched on the overhead light. He moved to the projector and began removing the reel.

"It's going to be nice having Michael with us again, isn't it? I hope he comes alone." She pressed her lips into an unsteady smile.

"What would you like to see now?"

"You need a haircut."

"I haven't had time."

"It will be long enough to braid soon."

"I will, Mother, I will."

"You look terrible. You need a haircut." She watched Reese put the film carefully into the canister. "My hair is a mess too, isn't it? I should have gone to the beauty parlor today." She sat stiffly with the long narrow fingers of each hand locked one in the other. Resting in her lap, a dark cloak covered the lower portion of her body, protecting her against the reawakened October chill.

Reese stared at her. Her face was pasty white, so that her makeup looked as though it were painted on. She wore too much makeup for a woman her age. Much too much. There were dark circles under her eyes. Her silver-gray hair was tucked crudely under, attempting a pageboy style of sorts. Her face remained expressionless.

"Your hair looks fine," he said, placing the canister on the shelf. His lips formed a tight smile.

She tried to return the smile, but she couldn't seem to manage one. "Don't lie, Reese. It's frightfully sloppy. I should have gone to the beauty parlor."

"Then why didn't you?"

"What will Michael think when he sees me looking like this?"

"Michael won't notice," he said almost to himself.

"Speak up, Reese."

"I said, Michael won't notice."

"Oh, yes. Yes, he will. Your brother notices everything. He is very aware."

"You haven't answered me."

"What is it?"

"What would you like to see next?"

"No more Chaplin movies. The man is a communist." She watched Reese open a new canister. "Something unusual, but without communists." Reese hesitated. "What are you putting on?"

"World War Two." Reese had spent the better part of two years conducting dream therapy with survivors of the holocaust. He had obtained a rare print of the atrocities committed during that period and had studied the film with morbid curiosity. Still he had been unable to come to grips with the cause, the effect on the victims, himself—the world at large.

Each dream that had been told to him seemed to contradict the next. Each individual had viewed his or her life during confinement so totally differently, with emotions, thoughts, dreams so mixed that finally he had given up the project, unable to put all the pieces together. He had always felt that it was his greatest failure in dream therapy.

"You know I don't like that movie," she said with a certain amount of urgency. "It's disgustingly horrid. Perhaps explaining my recent nightmare. I can still see that man hanging. No rope—nothing supporting him, just hanging. It frightened me."

"Dreams."

"What?"

"You have dreams, Mother. Not nightmares."

"How would you know? Were you there?"

"'I awoke smiling,' you said. A dream. Tears would indicate a nightmare."

"I tell you, I was frightened."

"If you say so, Mother."

"Don't humor me, Reese, I don't like it. And I don't want to see that movie ever again. Do you understand? Not ever again." Their eyes met, coldness against coldness.

"As you wish." He closed the canister.

"I cried at Michael's wedding. Was that a nightmare?"

Reese felt his body stiffen.

No matter what, he loved his mother, closing his mind

against her repetitive complaints and the fact that she had always preferred Michael's company to his. He loved her, murmuring the strange word "love" to himself while she continued to abuse him.

"Reese, why do you suppose Michael married Inga? Oh, not that I've got anything against her. Michael's son is healthy enough—intelligent. And the child does look like him. Michael is going to place him in a private school, did you know that? An architect or a lawyer, perhaps." She closed her eyes momentarily, and spoke in a soft dreamy tone, her words coming away from her mouth in a seductive chant. "No. No, somehow I pictured Michael's wife looking different—different, somehow, than she does. I saw her once, the girl I hoped he'd marry. Oddly enough, she looked like me. Like I looked when I married your father. It was at a celebration—an anniversary, I believe. I argued—"

"She's strong," Reese interrupted.

"What?"

"I said, Inga is strong."

"So?"

"That's why she married Michael . . . and Michael married her. Because she's strong."

"Would you like children of your own someday, Reese? You will never get married if you let it be known that you don't want to have children."

Reese sat there, his face expressionless, waiting for his mother to change the subject.

"Reese, I found those filthy books again. The books with women in them. You left them right out in the open this time. Is that what you do when you go to your room? That's not right, Reese, you . . ."

Reese sprang to his feet. He stood there shaking. "I've told you never to go into my room. What's there is mine. It belongs to me. What are you searching for? All that I am is right here in front of you. There is no more. Don't you understand that— there is no more!" Reese looked sternly in her direction, then moved suddenly toward the kitchen.

"Where are you going?"

"To warm your milk before bed."

"But Michael will be here any minute."

"No. You're right; I don't think he's coming."

From the kitchen, Reese watched his mother rise, her thin, seventy-year-old frame draped in a green polka-dot dress. She clung to her necklace given to her by Michael. Carrying a box of candy in the other hand, she padded her way to the mirror and stared at herself for a moment. "What day is it, Reese?"

"Thursday, the sixteenth of October," he said, pouring the milk into the saucepan.

"Thursday? Is it Thursday? I thought it was Sunday. Isn't that strange?"

"Michael always spends Sundays at home. You know that."

"Yes." Carefully, she removed a rose from the vase. "I'm all alone."

"What?"

"I said, I'm all alone."

"The milk will be ready in a minute."

"You know, Reese, you really should have children. At least one. A house always seems empty without them. Oh, I know, they would probably drive me mad in no time, but it would still be a comfort. I need someone here—especially during the day. I asked Michael if he wouldn't consider moving back here with us. For a while, not more than that." Reese appeared at the kitchen door with a glass of warm milk.

"I don't like Inga very much, did you know that?" She tore a petal from the rose, letting it drop to the floor.

"No, I didn't know that."

She continued to pick apart the rose. "Because I've kept it well hidden. Michael wouldn't like me saying that, would he? That I disapprove of his wife? No, he wouldn't like that at all."

"You're tearing the petals from the rose again, Mother."

She shook her head, pretending confusion.

"Here, drink your milk."

After a moment, she said, "Why do you suppose he married her?"

Reese looked at her face and saw that she was daydreaming. He wondered if Michael really knew how much she loved him. They stood in silence for a moment, and then he said, "Why, to give you a grandchild. Why else?"

"Yes. I'm sure you're right. I'm sure that was it." She drew a deep breath. "I'm going to my room now. To read." She moved toward the stairs.

"Mother?"

"Yes?"

"You've forgotten your milk."

"Why, yes, so I have."

Reese moved across the room and handed her the glass.

"Reese," she said softly. "I wish you wouldn't waste your money on candy. You really can't afford it and, well . . . I don't like candy." She finally smiled, and then she was walking slowly up the stairs, her slippered feet dragging audibly up one step at a time.

Reese stood motionless, eyes locked, until his mother was gone. His face tightened. He tried to unclench his hands, to force them to open.

Without conscious thought, he moved to the hall closet.

The gloves were black leather with a fur lining and elastic cuffs that held in the heat of his hands. His hands were sweating. He forced the gloves on even tighter, put up his coat collar and left the house, heading for the subway. His hatred had centered dead on before his eyes—a dot. That was all he could see. Just a dot.

CHAPTER 7

THIS SAME THURSDAY, AT ELEVEN-TWENTY IN THE EVENING, Jack Squadron opened his eyes. He sat perched on a barstool, his body aching, the dull red light from the stained-glass window filtering onto his face and across his hands that lay folded on the bar in front of him. He could hear the steady sound of song.

"Just turn and walk my way . . ."

A tall good-looking blues singer dressed in red sequins whispered the words into the microphone held professionally in her right hand. Her ruby lips seemed to caress the head of the microphone, as if making love to it.

Absurdly, given the setting, Jack imagined his world shrunk to the size of a tennis ball. He had thought about that all day, turning it over in his mind. The feeling grew stronger when Cara had refused to see him at the hospital tonight. He had had a vicious fight with the head nurse who finally told him to fuck off. Not in those exact words, but close. Very close.

"Walk closer and closer and closer . . ."

Jack sat there trying to reassure himself that his world wasn't the size of a tennis ball, trying to build himself up, placate himself, and convince himself that he belonged. In short, he found himself talking bullshit. Was the feeling he felt self-pity? If so, did he have the right to wallow in it? Cara was sick, not he. Yet knowing this, knowing that Cara's condition was precarious, only made him feel all the sorrier for himself.

"Until I'm in your arms forever . . ."

Jack's mind suddenly went blank, like a slate that someone

had wiped clean. He seemed afflicted with a few other infirmities as well. His eyes burned like hell, and he felt sick to his stomach.

He leaned forward on the bar and waited for his condition to improve. He realized he might have a long wait. What the hell was wrong with him lately? Sitting there in a bar—where was it anyway? A slum area—Thirteenth Street and Eleventh Avenue. A real gem of a spot, all right. Half the room was pimpled with white folks, the other half black. It was a salt-and-pepper club. Most of the people formed couples and resembled a patchwork of dominoes.

The Domino Theory. Knock one down, they'd all fall over. That's the way he felt; Cara fell, knocking him down, and he was about to knock the next person down. He was about to start a chain reaction. Who would be the last to fall; that was the question.

"Until the night fades away."

She really was a knockout. Jack stared at her large breasts. Firm, rounded—he could make out her nipples through her almost transparent sequin top. Her legs, the right one visible up to her thigh, were perfectly shaped, long and connected high to her firm young butt. A knockout. A one-in-a-million, lady-be-good-to-me knockout. Would she be the one he'd knock over?

Not likely.

She turned her burning eyes toward him and smiled. Was she eyeing him, Jack wondered. Christ. Amazement wasn't the right emotion to describe how he felt. Confused perhaps. Even scared. An hour ago he was ready to take on all comers; he was Mr. Cordiality in person. Now he suddenly felt deceitful and stupid, wanting only to crawl into some deep, dark hole where no one could find him.

His gaze slid away until it landed on his glass. Slowly he lifted his bourbon and soda, reflecting vaguely that his life thus far had been rather worthless. A couple of frivolous songs, a few flop shows on Broadway, and a ten-year marriage that was about to go kaboom. The thought overwhelmed him, filling him with a sudden rush of frustration.

"Then you and I will be together . . ."

Jack placed his drink against the bridge of his nose, and now, as he peered through it, his mind was filled with a full-blown image of the blues singer, young, big-busted and delicious. There she was, stretched out across his bed, naked. So he really had come here to score. He really had become, after all was said and done, just another horny guy set loose on the city, prowling, probing, looking for a target to bang all his frustration into, bang away until he went limp, until he had nothing left in him, nothing at all to disturb his peace and quiet, and then maybe, just maybe, things would be all right again. Maybe.

He sighed heavily and turned to face the bar, to face his own solitude. He knew exactly when it had all started to go wrong. About a year ago, someone had mistaken Cara for his mother. Since then, nothing had been the same. Not for Cara. Not for him. It was always there between them now. Jack knew Cara was self-conscious of being seen with him. But it wasn't just her. He felt it too. He was always waiting for the casual wrong word that could kill them worse than they were already killed. The worst thing—Jack did find himself looking at younger women. As though the all-knowing observer was expecting it from him—waiting for him to fall into the trap. If Jack did hate younger women for being there, well, he hated himself worse. "Much worse," he muttered aloud, as though the bartender were both judge and jury, and those two words spoken aloud might soften the verdict.

He shook his head. He really needed to get some sleep. Dammit, he was sorry as hell now that he had agreed to play guinea pig tomorrow night. Most likely he'd be asked to do the impossible. He'd be asked to dream. *Tell me, Dr. Cindrella, how can I dream if I can't sleep?*

Suddenly he was distracted by a pair of eyes. Big green eyes under heavy dark lashes belonging to a brunette sitting two stools away. She wore dark-colored slacks, with a white blouse that clung to her braless breasts, their fullness accented by a large silver pendant that snuggled between mountainous cleavage. Her mouth was small and coated with pinkish lipstick; her hair black, cut short—almost butch.

She glanced away and ordered a bloody mary. Drink in hand, she took a sip, her green eyes gleaming in their sockets like Christmas tree ornaments. The liquor moistened her lips, which the pink tip of her tongue immediately licked dry. First the top lip, then the bottom. She stuck a cigarette into her mouth and lit it with a small gold lighter. The flame bounced off her high cheekbones, accenting how pretty she really was.

She turned to face him.

Jack attempted a smile. Ignoring him, she drew in deep on her cigarette. Conditioned reflex was instantaneous. Like Pavlov's dogs, Jack panted. Slowly, he removed a cigarette from his pack. He pretended to look for a match. He was doing it, he thought. He was actually playing the game. He fumbled through his pockets just long enough to catch her eye, then turned and said, "Got a light?"

She smiled. "Sure." She pushed her lighter across the bar in his direction. He lit his cigarette, then glanced at his drink, as if undecided whether it should travel with him or not. It did. He slid one stool closer and handed her the lighter.

"Thanks," he said casually.

"Sure." She eyed Jack like a dealer examining a piece of used furniture.

"Can I buy you a drink?" he asked.

"I just bought one."

Jack grinned. "I know."

Her lips licked the tip of her cigarette. "Well, then . . ." she said pleasantly, "why bother to ask?" She moved her face close to Jack's, smiled, and then whispered, "Take a walk, creep."

"You don't have to act like that," Jack said, his body stiffening.

"You're out for kicks, right? What's the matter—wife ain't givin' you none?" She dragged her long fingernails across the bar, digging them into the hard wooden surface, deliberately trying to agitate him.

For a moment Jack saw nothing, thought nothing, and in the next instant he had grabbed her by the arm and started to squeeze hard. He felt himself turning livid.

"Hey, what the hell are you doing—let me go." She wrenched her arm away, trying to free herself.

But Jack was oblivious to her resistance. He rose, shaking with anger, still squeezing her arm. "You had better watch who you fuck with. Or someone's just liable to cut out your goddamn tongue."

For a split second she gaped up at him in utter fear. The top part of her blouse had fallen partially open, exposing a large portion of her breasts. Frenzied, she jumped to her feet.

Jack whispered, "Braless bitch."

The bartender quickly ducked under the bar door and emerged on the other side. But Jack's eyes stayed pinned on the girl.

"Fucking creep!" she screamed, ripping her arm free.

"What's going on?" the bartender asked, moving between Jack and the girl.

"Nothing," Jack said hoarsely, still blinded with rage. Christ, this wasn't really happening—was it? Not really, not to him. But there he was, hands trembling, voice stuck in his throat, looking to bust this broad's ass. Looking to . . . Calm down, for God's sake. He stared at her, never looking directly at the bartender.

"You a smart ass or what?" asked the bartender.

Jack watched a second bartender slip from behind the bar and move up behind him. He was carrying a small blackjack. "No," Jack said, his anger still full in his throat. "She's a damn tease, that's all."

"Fuck you, weirdo," she hollered, more defiantly now that the bartender stood between Jack and her.

"Don't let me catch you alone," Jack warned. "I'll—"

"You'll do what?" The bartender turned him slowly around, pressing his body full against Jack. "Look, just finish your drink quietly. You know, nice and calmlike, okay? And then I suggest you leave."

The first bartender stepped around so that both bartenders were facing him directly. "Or better still, why not just . . . leave."

Jack stared at the two bartenders for a moment, then turned and glared at the girl. He moved his hand slowly to the bar, tossed off his drink, and left the bar to the accompaniment of, "And don't come back."

Jack was about fifty yards down the street when he ducked into the doorway. He stared at the bar for a moment and decided to wait. It didn't matter how long it took. He would wait.

CHAPTER 8

AT THE END OF HER LONG NIGHT OF TEARS AND FRUSTRATION, Rose Carpenter had a dream. The dream came upon her swiftly, leaving her no chance for escape. She was swept forth by a sudden power and passed like a spirit through a veil of thin mist that stretched out before her. Light flashed and she turned and began running through the reddish glow of darkness, balancing a load of paintings in the upturned palms of her hands. The paintings were stacked one on top of the other and reached so high that she was unable to see over the tops of them, and with each step she took they shifted and wobbled and their weight pressed her down until finally she couldn't run any further.

Rose! Rose!

Her arms stiffened and she was terrified but held firmly to the towering stack of paintings to steady them, shifting her body to correct the balance, moving her arms wildly because the paintings mustn't come down.

Rose, run! Run!

I can't! she cried. I can't!

All at once the dream changed and Rose found herself an observer rather than a participant. Through a strange light she saw someone running. A girl. The half-demolished walls of an abandoned building. A pinkish glow. Overhead a streetlight flickered, and through a windowless frame, Rose watched the girl running for her life.

Images flickered—a girl, a man, a girl, a room. Another room . . . larger—blacker. Rose tried to open her eyes, to wake herself before it happened. But it did happen. Vividly, behind fluttering eyelids, as if she were the girl whose life was in danger instead of lying asleep in her own bed.

Rose turned, and as she turned the girl lost her balance and plunged to the ground. Behind her a metal door slammed open. The dim, long walls of the room wavered and Rose saw her . . . no, heard her first. "Please, don't hurt me . . . don't . . ." She was moaning more than speaking. Then Rose saw her, her clothing torn, the tears streaming down her face. It was Cheryl.

Rose's body stiffened.

Cheryl. Dear God, it was Cheryl.

Stumbling to her feet, Cheryl moaned louder. She darted across the room, past the jagged clutter of twisted metal and splintered boards, trying to reach the opposite door.

She didn't make it. Arms grew out of the darkness to grab hold of her. Instantly she was thrown to the ground. Laughter now as the man stood over her. Rose couldn't see who the man was, but could see him reach down and forcibly part Cheryl's legs. She screamed.

A hand was smashed across her mouth.

This time Rose felt the hand. Felt the fingers covering her face, making it almost impossible to breathe. The light flickered and Rose saw his face. Thought she saw his face. It was all happening so fast. He laughed. Cheryl screamed.

No, it was Rose screaming.

Cheryl was dying.

She would be dead soon.

The knife's blade glinted in the darkness, flashed, then punctured her white flesh. The blood trickled at first, then gushed. Cheryl screamed louder, stopped to suck in air, screamed again.

Amidst rows of greasy oil drums, broken glass and stacks of old newspaper, he entered her. At the moment of penetration he groaned with pleasure. Cheryl kicked for her life, using her arms and legs and hands as clubs, trying to topple him. The sound of thrashing and heavy thuds shattered Rose's mind, dashed her thoughts to rubble, and then a long painful grunt—and then silence.

Slowly he rose. Cheryl's lifeless body lay at his feet. Methodically, he wiped the knife's blade across his pants. His back remained toward Rose. His shoulders jerked suddenly and then his body went limp.

Quickly now, he dragged Cheryl's body to the corner of the room, lifted it, dumped it into a metal drum. Light flickered. He heaped old newspapers, rags and pieces of wood into the drum to cover the body. He stared at the drum for a moment, inflating his lungs with air.

After moving to the far door, glancing back every few steps, he bolted—clattered down the wooden staircase, dashed through the bottom room, banging into piles of wood and broken brick until he had reached the street. Light flickered. Flickered again.

Rose awoke in the space of a blink.

For a moment she heard the sound of an airplane passing overhead, and then there were no sounds at all. It was as though someone had made the city vanish, had whisked it away: the streets, the buildings, the people—all gone. All bundled up and carted away. The dead weight of a Valium-induced sleep clung to her, the weight enormous, and she wondered if she were not still in the dream.

Her eyelids fluttered but refused to open. Her thoughts swirled lightly. A hazy, unexplainable lull caressed her body and started to rock her back to sleep. The night was taking her to a place she had never been. It was a peaceful place, where nothing seemed to matter. Rose always believed death would feel like that. Peaceful, calm.

Moonlight and death, death and moonlight. The shimmering of night: shadows, now blue, now black, now purple; the faint sound of wind chimes; the clouds moving across the faceless moon; the night as pure as the Lord's pain—the very thought was of such piercing intensity that Rose awoke completely.

The dream. She had seen it so clearly.

. . . I saw . . . Her eyelids fluttered, then opened. She felt tired and satiated. She shook her head fiercely to dislodge persisting dream fragments, then turned on the bedside lamp.

She was awake. She was in her own bedroom. A place of quiet away from the city hustle. It was a dream. Only a dream. But even as she heard the first drops of rain fall outside her window, she wasn't convinced that it had been.

Caught in a half-world between the dream and her narcosis, she gradually became aware of her growing fear. She had told

Cheryl to leave the apartment. Not to be there when she returned. She had asked Cheryl to put the keys to her apartment in the mailbox. But when she'd returned home, she hadn't checked to see if the keys were there.

Slowly Rose left the bed and blinked into the darkness of the living room. Everything was quiet, and with the quiet came a message: Beware. Don't go in there. But it was a false message, she told herself.

She started forward, stopped, started again. At the living room door she reached out and turned on the light. The radiator in the corner hissed, letting go of short puffs of steam. Everything in the room was the same. Untouched.

She moved to the front door. It was locked. Both locks, yes—were locked. She stood there, listening, thinking about those damn keys. She told herself to forget the keys, to go back to bed. But after looking at the front door for a moment, she knew she'd have to retrieve them.

She had just stepped away from the door when the phone rang. She turned with a start. It rang twice more before she picked it up. "Hello?"

There was a remote, dead quality of sound on the other end of the line.

"Hello?"

She heard a click and then a dial tone. She stood there with the phone in her hand, shivering. The rain was coming down harder now, pelting the windows, sending huge drops of water running across the glass in strange patterns. She watched her own image in the glass become distorted, mixing with the raindrops that zigzagged down the steamy windowpane.

Suddenly she slammed the receiver down, moved into the bedroom and tossed on her sweater and jeans. She glanced at the clock: 1:20 A.M.

Locking the front door to her apartment, she started down the hallway. The single overhead light sent her shadow ahead of her. Reaching the elevator, she pressed the button. The fire exit door to her left stood ajar. She stared at it, remembering her dream vision on Monday. The man coming up the stairs, those exact stairs, with a knife in his hand.

She hit the button again. The door slid open. She stepped into the elevator and pressed "1." Her head felt as though it were about to topple from her neck. She closed her eyes for a moment. When she opened them again, she was staring into the lobby.

Quickly she moved to her mailbox, inserted the key and opened the small brass door. The spare set of keys to her apartment wasn't there. She jammed her hand into the box, groped. Nothing. Not a damn thing.

She was shaking her head now, trying to free the strange notion that twisted and knotted her thoughts. And then she heard it. A scraping noise. It was coming from the fire exit stairwell. Like someone was dragging a heavy object up from the basement. At one-thirty in the morning?

The sound abruptly stopped.

She turned and there he was, his body silhouetted by the light directly behind him, just standing there staring at her. Exactly as he had appeared in her dream Monday night. The exit door was closed, but she could see him as plainly as if the door were open.

Rose blinked and stared again, so powerfully did the image affect her. The same light that had shown his image so clearly now began to fade. Rose backed up slowly, inch by inch, then turned and made a dash for the elevator. Pressing the button, the elevator door opened. She moved inside and waited for the door to close. She was unable to see the exit door from where she stood. But when the exit door opened, she heard it. And she knew it was him.

She pressed the button again.

Close, damn you. Close!

Slowly, mechanically, the elevator door slid shut. She collapsed against the wall as the elevator began its climb. She dared not move. Anxiously, she tried to reassure herself that it was all a bad dream. Just a bad dream that would vanish once she was safe again in her apartment.

But when she stepped from the elevator and glanced at the indicator panel and saw that the number 1 was lit, she realized it wasn't a dream at all; someone had actually pressed the button on the first floor.

"Goddamn it," she muttered, and moved to her apartment. The two keys slipped easily into their locks.

Once inside, she quickly bolted the door. Her heart was pounding. Almost at once she heard the elevator door open. She waited, disbelievingly—surely she had imagined it. But when she heard the elevator door close, she knew that she hadn't imagined it at all. Someone had just gotten off on the tenth floor. A neighbor? Yes, that was it. The architect and his wife living at the far end of the hall. They were always getting home late. She waited to hear the familiar sound of keys being placed into their locks.

The sound never came.

Rose stared fixedly at the light filtering in beneath the doorsill. If someone did come to her door, he would block out part of the light. Eyes glued to the tiny slit, she waited.

Outside the rain had begun to slow.

For a moment she had no sense of his presence anywhere near. But she hadn't heard the elevator. He could have left by the stairwell, or maybe he'd never been there at all. Maybe Cheryl had just forgotten to leave the keys.

Damn.

Damn you, Rose Carpenter, she thought. Get hold of yourself. Her mind skipped back to when she first had entered the apartment. Cheryl had left a note. Where had she put it? Not in the usual pile of mail. Not on the table beside the bed. A small piece of lavender stationery with harsh hurried scrawl. Not a woman's handwriting at all. Where— Rose had it. She had thrown the note into the garbage can in the kitchen.

Carefully now she smoothed the note flat on the kitchen counter. Her eyes moved over the words once. Then she read it again, slower this time, trying to find new meaning.

Rose: As soon as I find a hotel room, I will try to make contact with you. If not at the club tonight, on the telephone. I'm sure once you give me a chance to explain, you will see things differently. Please, we must talk.
Cheryl.

Rose shook her head. There was no mention of keys. She read the note several more times. Had Cheryl gone to the Cottontail Club tonight after she had left? Was she at the club now?

Rose glanced at the front door and then at the telephone. Propping herself on the kitchen stool, she dialed. She listened to the sound of the phone ringing . . . and ringing . . .

"Hello—Cottontail Club." Rose could hear the crowd in the background and music.

She inched forward. "Nick, is that you?"

"Yeah, this is Nick. Who's this? Wait a minute, hold on." His voice became distant. "Cut the crap, will you." Loud laughter came next. "Okay. Go ahead."

"Nick, it's Rose."

"Rose, for Chrissakes. You told me you were sick. So why aren't you in bed?"

"I am, Nick. That's where I'm calling from."

"So why aren't you asleep? Guilty conscience?"

"Nick, I'm sorry for leaving the club early tonight. But I really did feel sick."

"Forget it. Take a pill and get some sleep. You're my little girl, you know that. I was just telling . . ."

Rose bit the inside of her cheek. "Nick," she interrupted, "I was just wondering if anyone came in tonight asking for me."

"Yeah. Paul Newman!"

"Please, Nick. It's important. Was there a girl in there tonight asking for me?"

"No, not that I know of."

"Are you sure?"

"Sure I'm sure. Why?"

"Just curious."

"Hey, what's going on? You're supposed to be sick. So get to bed."

"All right, Nick."

"And listen, about tomorrow night. That damn dream clinic. They're not going to keep you up all night, are they?"

"No, I don't think so."

"Good, because I'll need you on your toes Saturday night. You hear me?"

"Right, Nick. Listen, I have to go. See you Saturday, okay?"

"You got it, kid, and—"

"Good night, Nick." She broke the connection.

She had just moved to turn off the kitchen light when the telephone rang. She heard the ringing as if muffled, from a great distance away and not in her apartment at all. But the phone was ringing. Her phone.

Hesitantly, she lifted the receiver. "Hello?"

The breathing was light and airy and had a quality all its own. It was barely perceivable but it was there nonetheless.

"Cheryl? Is that you?"

A voice whispered, ". . . I see you."

"What?"

"I . . . feel . . . you . . ."

"Who is this?"

And then a click and the phone went dead. The silence was replaced by a dial tone. It was him. She had never heard him speak, but she was sure the voice belonged to him.

She had barely put the receiver into its cradle when the phone rang again. Only part of her mind heard the ringing, just the echo of it, hardly a sound at all. And then another ring, fuller, louder. She did not move; she pressed the sound from her mind. But the ringing persisted.

"Oh, Jesus," she groaned, and realized she was panicking. Get hold of yourself. What can he do to you? Deal with him. Show him you're not afraid. Make him understand he's wasting his time. She laughed to stop herself from crying. Choked on it. The phone continued to ring.

"Leave me alone!" she screamed.

The phone rang again.

"Please, please—leave me alone."

Her body began to tremble like the subtle shaking of an earthquake and she tried not to remember the breathing, not to feel the jerks of her lungs and muscles, as the tears sprang from her eyes, rolled down her cheeks until the naturalness of her makeup became unnatural and her eyelids closed, sending her into the pitch blackness of night.

Suddenly the ringing stopped.

CHAPTER 9

Friday, October 17
9:00 P.M.

SOMETHING WAS WRONG. REESE COULD SENSE IT BUT WASN'T sure what it was. His memory had lapsed. Suddenly he could not remember what he had done after leaving the house last night. He hadn't returned home, he knew that. He had slept in a hotel. He wondered now how he'd come to be there. He remembered lights, a door slamming, the scuff and scrapes of a razor. But nothing else. He was sure he'd had a dream but wasn't able to recall a single aspect of it. Yet he had felt something happening. A shifting of some kind. Perhaps it had been just the dropping off to sleep. But if that were the case, why wasn't he able to remember?

He glanced at his watch. Nine, exactly. The traffic outside his office was unusually heavy for that hour of the evening. Drawing back the curtains, he stared out. People rushed along as if their clothes were on fire. An older couple dressed in soiled rags jerked and twitched under the hard yellow glare of street light, then disappeared into the shadows.

Reese drew his breath, staring after them.

A madhouse, he thought idly, letting the curtains fall back into place. Inexplicably, he felt a part of the madness.

What had he done from eleven o'clock last night until eight o'clock this morning?

He wasn't sure. He stood motionless, puzzled, then went to the filing cabinet where he took away the Rose Carpenter/ Jack Squadron file. He studied the file for the next hour, trembling with rage at his inability to think. Just before ten, the phone rang.

"I'm really sorry, Doc," Alex Mana's voice whined. "I

meant to call you last night. Really, I did. But, well—I sort
of got tied up." Then, in a tone loaded with self-reproach, "I
should have called you, I know. I'm sorry."

Reese smiled in spite of himself. He had forgotten Mana's
promise to call him last night. In itself, it signified nothing,
but within the framework of recent events, Reese's lapse transformed in his mind into a symbol of discord.

"Hey, Doc—you there?"

"Yes. Yes, I'm here. It's all right. I understand." His hand
tightened around the receiver.

"I wanted to talk to you about Monday. Our session."

Reese paled. "You're still coming, aren't you?"

"Oh, sure. I'll be there. But I've decided I don't want the
session taped. No observers either."

A dozen retorts sprang to Reese's lips, but he could not
bring himself to utter them. What good was the session if it
wasn't certified by a professional observer? If Mana was capable of paranormal phenomena, Reese needed documented
proof. "Alex, I'll need some certification on the session. Just
my saying such and such happened isn't good enough."

"It will have to be. If you're not interested—let's just forget
it."

"No, I didn't say that. But at least let me tape the session."

"Give me time, Doc. I mean, that's all they did while I was
in prison. Every move, every gesture recorded and examined.
I'm not a guinea pig!" he snorted vehemently.

"All right, Alex—take it easy," Reese said, clasping and
unclasping his fist, thinking that Alex was testing him. "We'll
do it your way."

"No hidden cameras or tape recorders. Because I'll know,
damn it. I'll know."

"Listen to me, Alex. There are rules of being a research
subject. One—it is not to be a game between us. We must be
brutally honest with each other." Now his voice rose shrilly,
and he began to shout, "If I tell you I will not record the session,
then I won't!"

Mana laughed. "So we both have a temper, right? Always
that fury lurking inside, if you know what I mean."

"No, I don't know what you mean."

"Like last night. You were furious."

Reese felt a touch of panic. "What are you talking about?"

"You remember last night, don't you?" Reese was unable to reply. "You think about it," Mana said. "It'll come back to you."

"Alex, what do you know about—"

"See you on Monday, Doc. And remember, it's strictly a closed session."

"Alex, wait. Alex?" Reese hit the disconnect button. When he lifted his finger, he heard the dial tone. Slowly he lowered the receiver and sank into his chair. All day he had seen the world through a blue haze induced by cigarette smoke and coffee. Now the haze moved inward, as a shadow recedes noiselessly into the darkness beneath a crag, and his thoughts turned on him with a ferocity he had never known. He tried to remember last night. There were flashes, little specks and images, but nothing that added up to a whole picture. He removed the last of his cigarettes from the pack and lighted it. Hands shaking slightly, he crushed the pack and flung it into the wastebasket.

Suddenly the sound of the doorbell penetrated the room. He looked up, the bell vibrating through his mind, the harsh sound unnerving. As he moved into the hallway the doorbell rang again. Jack Squadron stood slouched, peering through the small octagon of cut glass to the right of the door.

After letting him in, Reese latched the door and led the way through a small antechamber and then into his office where he offered Jack a cup of coffee. Jack declined the offer.

"It's going to be a long night," Reese said. "Are you sure you wouldn't like a cup?" He could smell the heavy aroma of liquor on Jack's breath.

"All right," Jack said. "I can use it, I guess."

Reese turned, and as he turned Jack surreptitiously took in the rest of the office. Sitting on the corner of the desk was a large antique frame whose gilded edges embraced an elderly woman whom Jack took to be Reese's mother. The picture was carefully placed and seemed to dominate a room which bespoke a scholarly presence. The walls were lined with bookshelves upon which, in precise order, sat numerous volumes richly bound in red and black leather. On the shelf close to the door Jack was surprised to see a small collection of *Penthouse*, *Playboy* and *After Dark*. Also, even more surprisingly, a few Spanish girly magazines and *True Detective*.

When Reese Cindrella looked up he saw Jack staring at the magazines.

"What you see," he said matter-of-factly, "is subject matter for dream therapy evaluation."

Jack nodded politely while trying to rid himself of the negative reaction he'd formed of Reese Cindrella. "So," he said, "when do we get started?"

"As soon as the girl gets here. Rose Carpenter; you wouldn't happen to—"

Jack shook his head.

"Sometimes it's a small world," Reese said, and Jack thought of a tennis ball and smiled.

"Did I say something amusing?"

"Just a private joke."

Dryly, he smiled at Jack, then sat and studied the folder on his desk. "I see here that you're a composer."

"Of sorts."

"And that you're married."

Jack sipped his coffee and wondered whatever had possessed him to sign up for this experiment. Cara and he had argued about it. She had insisted he cancel the appointment. Only after Jack had pouted around the apartment for a few days had she insisted that he go through with it. "Married. Yes," Jack mumbled.

Reese leaned back in his soft swivel chair. "I'm still not sure whether to use you as the agent tonight, or the subject."

"What's the difference between them?" Jack asked.

"Well, the subject is the person who sleeps. Who dreams. The agent is the person who remains awake and sends the subject images." He indicated a stack of large envelopes to his right. "The agent goes into a separate room, opens one of these envelopes and concentrates on the picture that is contained within. We call this picture the target. Each envelope has only one picture. Naturally, there is no way for the subject to know which picture is selected. I monitor the subject as he or she sleeps with an electroencephalograph."

"A what?"

"EEG for short. It's a kind of a polygraph or lie detector device that's attached to the scalp. The small electrodes transmit the natural rhythms of the brain by registering changes in the electrical discharges and pulses. Then the agent concentrates, the subject sleeps and I monitor. Soon the subject's eyes begin to make rapid movements as if watching something. And indeed they are. They are watching their own dream. This rapid eye movement is called REM obviously enough, and represents a time of vivid dreaming. Once this occurs, I wake the subject and record the dream. We do this four, perhaps five times during the night. After the subject goes back to sleep, I check to see if the dream had anything to do with the target picture. If they match, we have experienced telepathy. Mind-to-mind contact. A paranormal phenomenon."

Jack nodded. "I'll be the agent."

"Any particular reason?"

"I don't dream. You'd be wasting your time."

Reese smiled, a superior smile that Jack didn't particularly like. Reese saw his annoyance and quickly slid into speech. "All people dream. It's actually like becoming two people when we dream, one part of us creating the dramatic moment of the dream while another part remains a surprised spectator. We all dream; it's just that some of us are afraid to remember our dreams."

Jack stopped a frown from forming on his lips by asking, "Paranormal phenomenon. What does that mean?"

"When knowledge of events or facts is gained without recourse to the five senses—or when the knowledge is obtained in apparent disregard of the limitations of time and space. We call this extrasensory perception. If this occurs, we have paranormal phenomena."

"Well, I can tell you this. If I do dream, it's just your ordinary stuff. Normal."

"Normal. That's a nice word, but I'm afraid in the darkness of the bedroom, it really doesn't count for much. Could you be more specific?"

"I don't know. Food, I guess. Success."

"Sex?"

"What?"

"Do you have dreams involving sex?"

"Am I supposed to?"

"It depends. Millions of people dream every night; and in dreams the range of possibilities is infinite. So are the causes. One way or the other, dreams have a way of expressing the truth. That's why it's important to understand our dreams."

Reese moved forward again to examine Jack's chart. Without looking up, he added: "Dreaming is as necessary as breathing."

Jack forced himself to respond, reluctantly, more to keep up his end of the conversation than for any other reason. "You make it sound as though dreaming is a life-or-death situation."

"It is," Reese stated calmly.

Jack fumbled for a cigarette and lighted it. Through the thin vaporous smoke that hung over the desk, Jack studied the man with sloped head in front of him. With long gray hair wild upon his head, he made Jack feel frivolous for simply being alive. He wore his tortoise-framed glasses like visors and rarely looked Jack in the eye. But then, there was something in his attitude that said he didn't have to. That it was Jack's job to gape, and not his. He wore a loose-fitting woolen sweater, lusterless shirt and trousers; only his necktie seemed to betray an attempt at appearances. Still, he was an imposing figure.

The man behind the desk glanced up suddenly. "More coffee?"

"Just a little." Jack shifted uncomfortably in his chair.

Reese stirred and made his way across the room. "You see, dreaming is a safety valve. If we open it, we avoid buildup. It helps us to cope."

"With what?"

"Anxiety. With who we really are. I don't mean who we pretend we are, who we think we are, but who we *really* are."

Jack searched desperately for a way to break through the wall of hostility he was beginning to feel toward Cindrella. How strange, he reflected, that the man didn't seem to notice or care.

"You see," Reese went on, "each of us contains within ourselves another person whom we do not know. This person communicates to us in our dreams. Makes us aware of who we really are. If we refuse to listen, we remain, well"—Reese handed Jack his coffee—"divided."

"I don't know," Jack said. "It sounds risky to me."

"How so?"

"What if the other person within you is stronger than you are? He starts telling you lies about yourself in order to manipulate you."

"It's a risk we all must take." Reese turned to stare at the picture of his mother. "I remember going into a movie house one day," he went on. "I was sixteen years old, maybe seventeen . . . I'm not sure now. It was a dismal day. Rainy. The theater was dark. Very dark. I had a hard time finding my way. Finally, I was able to locate a seat, to the side, away from all the other people. The movie hadn't started yet, still the theater was very dark. Suddenly I had a terrible feeling . . ." Reese paused for a moment, smiling enigmatically. "My hands started to shake. At least I thought they were shaking. You see, I had fallen asleep and wasn't sure of anything really. I found myself locked in a small room, alone. I was huddled in the corner of that room, knees propped under my chin, arms wrapped around my body. Above me—and here is the strange thing—above me was a huge, bloated, human form. I knew immediately that whatever this thing was, it was there to hurt me. I tried to tell myself not to panic, to remain calm, but when the form moved, reshaped itself and moved closer to me, I panicked and tried desperately to rise, to get out of the room. But my body refused to move. I was paralyzed. This form, whatever it was—I really don't know how to describe it—started to descend on me, close in, until I was covered by its suffocating existence. I couldn't breathe, but somehow I did manage to scream. And scream I did. I yelled my head off. Suddenly my body shot straight up in my seat and I realized that everyone in the theater was staring at me. I wasted no time in running from the theater. As soon as I had gotten outside I felt better."

Jack stirred uncomfortably in his chair as Reese moved to the coffee table where he helped himself to a cup of coffee.

"For several weeks," he said, dropping a sugar cube into his cup, "I spoke to no one. Both my mother and brother thought that I had gone mad. Each night I'd experience the same dream. This horrible human form coming into my room, seeping in through the walls, the ceiling, and always enveloping me, trying to suffocate me. I finally told my mother. Very soon after beginning analysis, I understood that this form was nothing more than my own fear, my own guilt. I was creating this horrible creature. It really didn't exist, but because I believed that it did, I helped form the materialization of this creature so completely that there was no way for me to believe otherwise. For me, it did exist. It hounded me day and night until I was sure that I was near death. The point is this. Dream reality is as valid and real as waking reality and it affects our daily lives. During this period of time I was very depressed. Naturally. But the more I experienced this depression, the more this human form appeared in my dreams. It became a vicious circle. Only by identifying what this form represented was I able to free myself. The dream has never returned."

Jack suddenly felt a sharp chill run up his arms. He tried to counteract the feeling by half smiling. "Well, what's that old saying? 'Let sleeping dogs lie'? As for—"

"There's a difference," Reese interrupted. "We're not animals, Mr. Squadron. We have the power to reason, to think; we create—understand, feel. We must use our minds to move forward."

"To where?"

"Anywhere!" Reese said anxiously. "It's all possible. Anything. Everything. Once you find the key. Let your mind go. All of it—possible."

His voice had changed and his demeanor suddenly had transformed itself. No longer was he the under-control, self-appointed, self-styled man of wisdom. Now he spoke with passion, speaking before thinking; a crisp, broken language that somehow made Jack feel more comfortable in his presence.

"And someday, somehow—I'll prove that," Reese was saying. "You write music, don't you?"

"Yes."

"Have you ever woken up in the middle of the night and heard a song inside your head that you've never heard before?"

"Not really."

"But it is there. All the songs ever written, that will ever be written. They're all there."

"So why aren't they coming out?"

"Because you're blocking them."

"Or maybe the other guy in there is," Jack countered. "He could be jealous, destructive. So—"

"But that's just it. Get to know him. Trust him. If you don't, half of you will always be walking around distrusting the other half. Do you prefer it that way?"

Jack had trouble coming up with the answer. He was suddenly exhausted from a bad night's sleep. How long had he been standing in that doorway last night waiting for her to leave the bar? He had been another person standing there, not himself at all. He had wanted to hurt her, he remembered that. To inflict some kind of medieval revenge. He had waited, shivering in the darkness. And when the waiting was over, he had refused to acknowledge his actions. He remained unconnected to them, as if he hadn't been a participant at all, but merely an observer.

Images started to move in his mind now, spinning around, whirling; he visualized what he had imagined happened, but the pictures were different now, different than he had thought them to be. Something incredible was happening right before his eyes. Incredible.

CHAPTER 10

IT WAS A FEW MINUTES PAST TEN WHEN ROSE FOUND HERSELF hurrying down Central Park West heading for the Institute of Parapsychology. Beneath a marble black sky, the city hummed. Automobiles flashed by, and across the street a man stumbled from a doorway, performed a slow blundering dance around a fire hydrant and staggered down the street.

As Rose came to the corner, she pulled her raincoat tighter; the wind was more turbulent and colder than she had expected. Beneath her feet, she could feel and hear the subway grinding over the rails as it approached the Eighty-first Street station. For a moment she thought of him.

She stopped walking. She turned. Behind her the walkway was empty.

She started to move again, hearing the light clicks of her heels against the pavement, listening for other sounds.

It occurred to her that she had begun to walk with precautionary alertness. All at once she was imagining footsteps that weren't there. It was absurd. There was no threat hanging over her. No menace lurking in the darkness. She slowed, an involuntary smile creeping to her lips, and thought of the last few hours she had spent at the Museum of Modern Art. It had been good for her, like a health cure, almost. The art on display had seemed especially open and warm, and the people friendly.

It was Milton Avery's paintings that had captured her imagination the most. Nothing esoteric or theoretical, nothing mystifying, but rather images of surpassing courage; tranquillity in the face of anguish. That he knew life in its imperfection was all too apparent in the face of the old woman who stood staring out to sea; there was an acceptance in the calm lines of her mouth and eyes that was humbling. Avery had beckoned Rose, inviting her to share in a multitude of untroubled emotions. And the world, for the moment, had reshaped itself into something less frightening.

Only once during the day had she really felt uneasy and closed in—when the locksmith appeared at her door. The man had gone about his work swiftly, professionally. He had tried to sell her other locks, larger and more secure. "You know, miss, if someone wanted to get in here, these locks wouldn't stop them. You need bigger locks."

"And if someone really wanted to break in, would bigger locks stop them?"

"Well, you're right there. If people want something badly enough, they always seem to find a way to get it."

Still, she had felt a great relief once the locks had been changed. Cheryl hadn't called all day, and God only knew who had the keys to her front door. It was this that had kept her awake the whole night. She'd cuddled up on the sofa in front of the TV set. Only once had she dozed off. Moments later she had awakened in the throes of a bad dream, her eyes riveted to that damn door, thinking that someone had entered her apartment.

In many ways she wished that someone had broken in. That she had come face to face with another type of intruder. A young boy looking to rip off jewelry or cash. She could have survived this type of intruder and even forgotten him in time. But the stranger who had subtly taken hold of her imagination was much more elusive, moving at will between the recesses of her conscious and subconscious mind, that subtle gray area between reality and fantasy. But it wasn't fantasy, was it? She had actually come face to face with him on the subway, hadn't she? He was real. He was there.

Rose stopped suddenly, as if without calculation, and glanced behind her. Still she saw no one.

"Watch out!" someone hollered, and Rose jumped back as the car sped by, missing her by inches.

A small squat figure stood on the sidewalk, motioning Rose to move out of the street. Rose remained where she was for a second, swaying slightly, still stupefied. Then slowly she began walking toward the woman. "I thought you were a goner," the woman said. "You all right?"

"I never saw the car coming," Rose said.

"The crazy bastard didn't have his lights on, that's why," the woman said. "Jesus, my heart is pounding like a hammer. You going to be all right?"

"Yes. Thank you."

"You got to be careful at night. They'll just run you down and think nothing of it. You must be from out of town." Then in a louder, firmer voice, she asked, "Are you? Are you from out of town?"

Rose shook her head, staring at the woman who held two large shopping bags in each hand. The woman's nose seemed to dominate her face and to reduce her eyes and mouth to mere details. She was a bag lady, Rose thought. A person who had decided not to seek help, but preferred to live on the street, living out of her bags with no real home to speak of, nothing but herself and the bags she carried and the clothes on her back. Yet this frail woman, as thin and brittle as kindling wood, was a survivor.

A survivor, Rose thought, and reached into her pocketbook and took away a twenty-dollar bill. "Here," she said.

The woman hesitated. "I . . . I don't need that."

"Please. Take it." She pushed the money into one of the shopping bags. "And thanks."

"But—"

Rose moved away down the street until she stopped in front of the Institute of Parapsychology. She paused before pressing the bell.

Inside the Institute, Jack Squadron twisted nervously in his chair, his hand squeezing the coffee cup. Dr. Cindrella stood beside him. He appeared calm, sure of himself.

"Mr. Squadron, it's important for you to relax."

"What? Oh, yes." Jack quickly placed the cup on the desk. His hand shook visibly.

At that moment the front doorbell rang. Dr. Cindrella responded quickly. "She's here," he said, and left the room, leaving Jack sitting in his chair, a fine layer of cold perspiration covering his forehead.

Jack glanced into the darkened hallway, then stood and backed toward the service bar. Beneath him the ground shook. A subway was passing under the building, winding its way through the intestines of the city.

Jack hardly had time to think. Rose Carpenter was in the room now and they were being introduced. Dr. Cindrella was laughing about something, and then Rose and Jack sat in either chair in front of his desk. Dr. Cindrella paused to light Rose's cigarette, then sat comfortably in his leather chair.

For the briefest of moments, there was a silence.

Rose gratefully took in a lungful of smoke. She felt calmer now than when she had first entered the Institute. Jack Squadron had a pleasant face, she'd noticed. Not exactly handsome, or was that because he didn't seem interested in her? Rose always found it easier to be immediately attracted to people who were immediately attracted to her. Jack had remained aloof, barely looking at her as they shook hands.

Dr. Cindrella was speaking now in a very relaxed manner, overly casual. Rose took it as his way of putting them at ease. Still she sensed a vitality in his words. From the corner of her eye she watched Jack abruptly turn to look at her, his gaze hard, penetrating, so fierce that involuntarily she sat back in her chair and returned his gaze. Jack smiled, then looked away.

"The knowledge that individuals are somehow in communication with one another by extrasensory means is undoubtedly one of the most revolutionary discoveries ever made," Cindrella was saying.

Rose exhaled slowly, but her mind was moving at an incredibly fast pace. Very sharp. There had been something at once repellent and seductive about Jack's gaze. She imagined that he was a warm person, loving, to the right woman. She wondered if she could be the right woman. But the very wondering brought back a memory of the last time Lance and she had made love. Lance had barely entered her, when instantly she had begun to climax, her entire body gyrating with pleasure. It had gone on. And on . . .

"Am I that good?" Lance had asked.

She had reached for her robe, flipping the hair away from the back of her neck, which was covered with perspiration. What frightened her was that it hadn't been Lance at all who had supplied her with such sexual pleasure, but her own fantasy. The fact that she could not identify the fantasy made her feel violated and abused.

"The transference of thoughts, the ability of sensing the past or the future cannot be merely accidental . . ."

Rose often wondered what that sudden erotic flash had been that day. A fantasy, yes. But a fantasy without images. It had been made up of pure feelings, pure emotions. A flood of emotions that seemed to rush at her without explanation. That's what had frightened her. She had always led a very conservative life. Sex included. That she had gotten so carried away without really understanding why seemed to violate a code of decency she'd been taught to observe. As if without warning one part of herself had suddenly decided to work independent of the other. As if half of herself had wanted to taunt the other half. Was that possible?

While pondering this, Dr. Cindrella's phone rang; it was his mother. Rose put out her cigarette and reached for another.

"Yes. I'll be home. Yes?" Dr. Cindrella rose from his chair, stopping the phone to his chest. "I'm sorry, I'll be right with you." He moved away by the window, turning his back to the room, trying to make the conversation a bit more private.

Rose turned suddenly and asked Jack for a light without knowing why. She had matches and a lighter of her own. Jack lit her cigarette awkwardly, and this time Rose acknowledged that there was something interesting-looking about him. He looked at once very hard and very soft. As though he'd been a rough pudding mix whipped into a creamy finish.

"So," Jack said, shaking out the flame on the match, "this should be interesting."

Rose smiled.

"You nervous?" he asked.

"Yes. Something like that."

"Look on the bright side. At least you get to sleep." Rose looked worried. "Don't feel like it, huh?"

Rose was starting to dislike him. She sucked in hard on her cigarette, saying nothing.

"Sorry. I just thought since we're in this together . . ."

"Right." She flicked an ash from her cigarette into the ashtray. The oddest thing was that she was feeling sexy. But it wasn't him, was it?

"Good, I'll see you then," Doctor Cindrella was saying.

Rose turned to face Jack. "Look, I'm sorry."

"For what?"

"For acting like a real . . ." She half smiled, realizing what she was about to say.

"It's all right," Jack said, returning the smile.

Embarrassed, Rose turned away and watched Dr. Cindrella put the receiver into its cradle, saw an agitated finger tap the receiver as anxious eyes fluttered over the surface of his desk. "I'm sorry for the interruption," he said. The thin flicker of an apologetic smile rapidly fell from his lips, replaced by a thin tight line of concentration.

Seated again in his chair, he seemed stiffer than before, a prototype of a psychologist, as he explained the night's activities. Instructions given, he said, "The experiment tonight is not intended to be a psychotherapy session. I will not force you to talk or ask you to do anything you don't want to do. I'm only interested in whether telepathy is possible between two people who do not know each other. Two people who are involved with the arts."

"Why the arts?" Jack asked.

"Art is a thing of the mind," Reese said evenly. "To see properly, we must isolate and select. Nothing is arbitrary; everything follows a logic." He turned toward Rose now, speaking in firm, slow enunciation. "That is what makes an artist. The power to be selective. Rose, her painting. You, your music. The eyes and ears of reality."

"Logic from dreams?" Jack queried.

"If you stay with them long enough, yes. Nothing is more yours than your own dreams. To see your dreams clearly is poetry, prophecy, and religion—all in one. The true sense of life in all things."

Jack nodded. "I guess what I'm asking is, why us? Specifically why did you choose Rose and me?"

Dr. Cindrella leaned forward and placed the palms of his hands flat on the desk, as though the desk's surface was a Ouija board and would supply him with the proper answer.

"I selected twelve artists in each category," he said. "Only half agreed to be interviewed. Of the dozen I did interview, you two emerged as the most interesting. I had also been fortunate enough to see both of your work prior to the interview. Rose's work as it hung in La Galleria in Greenwich Village. And I saw your show on Broadway two years ago. A most interesting concept for a musical. I believe you both share an open-mindedness. A willingness to accept the free flow of ideas and images without question. In a way, this is a subtle form of ESP. To be able to see past the obvious. To be able to see what others are not able to see. In an odd sort of a way, you two are perfectly suited for each other."

Rose glanced at Jack. He shifted his position in the chair slightly, lifting his body with his arms. What was he thinking, she wondered.

Dr. Cindrella was talking again. After several more minutes of explanation, he removed his glasses and pressed his fingers into the corners of his eyes. "Are there any questions?"

Rose stirred uncomfortably. She hardly knew what she was being asked to do. Dr. Cindrella had explained it, but she wasn't sure she had gotten it right. All that was required of her was to go to the sleep subject room and sleep. She would be woken up each time the electroencephalograph indicated that she was in the process of dreaming. Jack was going into another room, away from her. He would concentrate on a picture. The object was to see if she could dream what Jack was concentrating on. In detail.

Jack broke the silence. "Will you and I be communicating with each other?" he asked Cindrella.

"Yes. I can leave the monitoring room, but I would prefer that you do not leave the agent's room. Each room is isolated and soundproofed. If you need anything, just pick up the phone. I'll be on the other end."

"Fine." Jack nodded his approval.

"By the way, Jack, you also have a bed in your room. If you want to lie down at any time, feel free to do so. But take the picture with you. If you find yourself dozing, call me."

Rose could sense that there was a change in the two men. They were both suddenly wide awake and deadly serious about the whole thing. Like two little boys about to play a game of sorts. Like it was going to be the Super Bowl of dreams. She just sat there watching them. Not talking.

"Does it feel funny to be doing this, Rose?" Cindrella asked.

"Funny? Strange, you mean?"

"Yes—strange."

She shrugged. "I'm tired."

Both men laughed.

"Then let's get started," Cindrella said.

He led Rose into a fairly small room with one glass wall, thick green carpeting, and only one bed and one chair.

Rose had a hard time listening to Dr. Cindrella explain the essence of dream therapy. She wanted only to lie down, to let herself sink into deep sleep. The doctor spoke in gentle tones, words that had an immediately lulling effect on her. She felt safe and hopeful that she would finally be able to get a good night's sleep.

She watched as he carefully attached the electroencephalograph electrodes to her temple and neck. Then he smiled faintly, reaching into his sweater pocket for a fresh pack of cigarettes. Almost at once he withdrew his hand with a sudden irritated jerk. "I keep telling myself one pack a day. But it's rough."

Staring down at Rose, he felt something behind his eyes tug, tug again. Who was this girl who had placed herself so willingly into his hands? In his mind, two images merged. One was that of an artist. The other that of a cocktail waitress. He looked at her differently now . . . as if he had never seen her before. He began to imagine her body beneath the sheets; she wore only a pair of pajamas. He was sure she wore no bra or panties. The thought caught him off guard. He had never experienced a lustful feeling for a female subject before.

"Is something wrong?" Rose asked.

He shifted uncertainly, barely smiling. "I just want to be sure that you're comfortable."

Rose nodded. "I'm fine."

"Good. Good." He pointed to the telephone on the wall. "Remember, if you need anything—call."

"All right." Her large eyes blinked back at him.

He shifted his weight again.

Rose had let herself relax completely. Oddly, there was something comfortable about Dr. Cindrella. He made her think of her father. As a little girl she had always waited for her father to come to her room. No matter how busy his day had been, how tired he was, he would never forget to kiss her good night. Sometimes he would sit for a moment or two and hold her hand. When she looked up, what she could mostly see was his large blue eyes. It was the only time she was ever alone with him, really alone with him. He belonged to her and she belonged to him. He would kiss her cheek and, at the same time, brush the loose curls away from her face, as if he had wanted her to look perfect. His touch was tender and Rose felt a sensation that she had labeled later as Holy. It was a complete feeling that sometimes made her feel as if she were going to cry. She never did. The feeling stayed locked away inside of her where she let it rest, cherishing the very existence of it. A tear of deep love that continued to bathe her innards.

"Well, now—you get some sleep." Reese stopped at the door to glance back at Rose, held there for a moment, then turned off the light.

CHAPTER 11

JACK SQUADRON SAT HUNCHED AT A TABLE IN A SMALL ROOM similar to the one Rose was in. Through the glass window he watched Reese enter the monitoring room where he began turning dials on the EEG machine.

The experiment had begun.

In front of Jack on the table lay a stack of large envelopes, a stack of plain white bond paper and several pencils. Jack selected an envelope, tore it open, and removed a picture print of Goya's painting *Saturn Devouring His Child* (ca. 1820).

Jack stared at it with loathing.

It essentially portrayed a raw destructive violence. The huge arms and legs of Saturn seemed to express his innermost hatred as he gripped the naked body by the neck, letting the body dangle between his legs like a rag doll.

Jack inched forward in his chair and looked closer at the body in Saturn's hands. Not a child's body at all, but that of a voluptuous woman. Buttocks and legs well shaped, well rounded; even the hair style was that of a sophisticated woman. Had the artist meant the body to represent a child?

Almost at once his mind shifted to an image of Cara when, stepping naked and wet from the shower, she would luxuriate in the gentle chafing of the towel. He would study the slow full curve of her hips, her large firm breasts and legs, which were taut and shapely. He had always felt naive in her presence, especially when she allowed her body to be viewed so openly. He also felt excited and tremulous.

Cara had always been so ready to accept Jack, so eager to please. She never complained when he playfully wanted to make love amidst blaring music, on the living room rug, in the kitchen—on the rooftop, under the George Washington Bridge. Anytime, anyplace, she was always willing. Jack smiled, imagining how she would have responded had he been a bit kinky. Listen, kiddo, I'm going to tie you bottom side up in that chair, spank you, and then . . . Jack's smile broadened. She probably would have comedically howled in terror and gotten the rope.

In a tight embrace with the past, Jack's smile faded. How painful it must have been for her to watch him retreat into his own private world. His melancholy must have been unbearable for her. When he had moped around the house like a witless child—what must she have felt?

Jack found himself focusing hard on the picture now, Saturn's hands strangling the life out of his victim. And that's what Cara was really, Jack's victim.

"So, how is everything going in here?" Cindrella stood in the doorway, rubbing his jaw.

"It's not going to be easy," Jack said.

"It takes a little getting used to." Cindrella moved into the room. "You're not used to concentrating on just one image. None of us are. So we drift, lose ourselves in the constant parade of images. Some coming faster than others, some slower. But they keep coming."

Jack chewed at his lower lip.

"That's what the paper is for. If you'll sketch the image you've selected, it may intensify the image sent to the subject. It will also give you something to do."

"How is she?" Jack asked, surprised that he found himself suddenly concerned for Rose's well-being.

"Fine. She looked tired. I believe she'll be asleep soon."

"Well, I'd better get started then." Jack picked up a pencil and slid a piece of paper in front of him.

"I'll leave you to yourself then, if that's all right?"

"See you later," Jack said without looking up. He heard the door to his room close, and then he did look up to see Cindrella disappear into the monitoring room. For a moment everything was still.

Jack stirred uneasily, lit a cigarette, and with his free hand started to sketch with harsh lines the image of Saturn. He was sweating heavily under his turtleneck sweater. He stopped momentarily to wipe the palms of his hands with a handkerchief. Palms dry, one last deep drag on his cigarette, he began again to sketch steadily, peering.

It was eleven o'clock when Rose finally drifted off to sleep. Just before going under, she felt an odd sensation in her neck, felt her head drop limp, as if it had been dislodged from her neck and just lay suspended on the pillow all by itself. Her body sank next, allowing the sleep mechanism to take over completely.

She floated deep in sleep, suspended in an airless, soundless vacuum, her body transparent and weightless. Yet, even in her deep sleep, she was aware that something was wrong. Her heart began to beat in rapid thuds; her breathing became shallow, harsh. Something was closing in on her. Something that meant her harm. She tried to open her eyes, her mouth—to scream out for help. She had to wake up, find a way out of the sleep she was trapped in. She was having a nightmare. No, more than a nightmare. The pressure around her body squeezed inward, crushing her. She was being crushed—pushed deeper into another world. His world. It was him—she knew it. Her night person. He was coming closer, calling to her, pulling her under; like a drowning person, she kicked with her legs, struck out with her arms, trying to stay afloat, trying to stay on top where she could breathe.

"Rose, wake up. Rose."

As she began to wake up, she tried to catch her breath, to get her bearings, to make sense out of what had just happened to her.

Dr. Cindrella was sitting beside her. "Rose?"

"Yes?"

"You were dreaming. Please tell me about it."

She sat up in bed with a sudden jerk of her body. The fear inside of her was now a running battle—she fighting to maintain her composure, while something inside of her closed in, pushed and probed and shifted her to a new place. A place she didn't want to go.

"Can you remember, Rose?"

She couldn't remember, but she tried.

"Tell me—was it a memory?"

"No, I don't think so."

"A thought?"

"A thought?" Rose tried to think. "Yes, a thought."

"Not a dream?"

"No, just a thought—a feeling . . ." Rose turned in confusion.

"Go on."

"That someone—"

"Yes—"

"I don't know—that someone wanted to destroy me. That I was being . . ." She struggled for the right word. "Strangled."

"What did the person look like?"

"Person?"

"Yes. You said that you felt like someone was strangling you. Did you see them?"

"No."

"Then there was no one there?"

"No. He was there, but I couldn't see him."

"Him?"

"Yes."

"Then he does exist?"

"Yes."

"Pardon me, I didn't hear you."

"Yes."

"Would you recognize him if you saw him?"

"I think so—yes."

"Then you can describe him. Try, Rose. Try to describe him."

She paused. "I think . . . he was big . . . very big. This is just an impression though . . . I didn't . . . there was no image or anything . . . just a feeling . . ."

"Go on."

"Powerful . . . huge hands and body . . . that's all."

"Can you remember anything else?"

"I'm not sure. I felt like I . . ." She hesitated. "That I was about to die. That's all. Just a feeling."

"That's fine, Rose. Just fine. You can go back to sleep now."

After informing Jack that he should select another target picture, Cindrella quickly returned to the monitoring room. He would wait for the EEG to signal him that Rose had once again begun a rapid eye movement period.

In the meantime, he would play back her last report, record

it on the transcript sheet. This entry would please him because her first dream had been a direct hit. She had received the target picture of *Saturn Devouring His Child* accurately. It was, thus far, a very successful evening.

Rose lay in her bed, feeling the tightness in her arms and legs. Small beads of sweat had begun forming on her chest. Last night's dream of Cheryl repeated itself in her mind, then vanished, leaving in its wake a sensation of chill and a fear that she could not lose.

Something had momentarily awakened her. It was Dr. Cindrella moving past the glass window toward the agent room with a cup of coffee in his hand. He had barely passed from view when she fell once again into a deep sleep.

Time passed and with it the subtle shifting of shadows. "A. Adam," she murmured, and fought the paralysis that clung to her limbs. The face that had been staring at her vanished. She woke suddenly and realized she had been dreaming. Or was she still dreaming? Jack stood by her bed smiling. She reached out to him.

"Jack, help me," she pleaded.

"I . . ." He lifted a hand toward her, then backed away.

"Please," she said, and watched him fade from her vision. She stared at the small orange light shining at the far end of the hall. She couldn't tell whether she was dreaming or not. She was caught in the middle ground between awareness and unconsciousness.

Something began to ache in her brain. She missed a breath, panicked because she could not draw it, waited, swaying inwardly like a reed caught in the wind. Then slowly, very slowly, she sighed. In the few seconds it took to exhale, her face relaxed and she once again drifted off to sleep.

Dr. Cindrella sat in the monitoring room watching her; then he stood and began to pace. Rose had not shown any sign of rapid eye movement in the last two hours. Yet all of her readings indicated that she was experiencing a peaceful sleep. Everything checked out normal. Under such ideal conditions she should be experiencing REM. Added to this unexpected complication, Jack had begun to tire. What had started out so promising was starting to fizzle.

Once again, he checked all of her vital signs on the monitor.

Normal. Absolutely normal. Perhaps Jack hadn't been the right choice for the agent after all. Perhaps he should have chosen someone younger, stronger. Someone who could reach out to Rose.

Cindrella was starting to feel anxious now. If Jack didn't work out, he would have to start all over again. He would lose precious time.

He sighed heavily and dropped into a chair. No, he reassured himself. He had gone over it all a thousand times. He had been involved with parapsychology too long to have made such a crucial mistake. All he had to do was sit tight. Be patient. Eventually, he was sure, Jack would fulfill his role.

Moments later, Jack dropped wearily onto the bed.

It had occurred to him that everything he touched disintegrated after a while. He was a great starter, a lousy finisher. Cara, his music, his tennis . . . all great, then kaput. Frank's word, the last time they had met on the tennis court: "Jack, your game has gone *kaput*." And now this. It had started like magic. Rose had actually received the picture he had been concentrating on. But now too much time had elapsed. The magic was starting to fade.

Jack tried looking through the window into Rose's room, but it was shrouded in darkness. His eyes traveled to the monitoring room. Dr. Cindrella sat in half shadows, his head bent forward, his eyes focused on the chart in front of him. Suddenly Jack felt his mind playing tricks with him: not only did Cindrella's head appear devoid of skin, but the dead and broken skull seemed to be suspended in midair.

Jack hung along the edge of this fantasy for a while; then his head cleared. Absently, he reached for the next picture. He had studied it before; now he tried to see it anew. He went over its detail very carefully because here was the tricky part: he was starting to fall asleep. Cindrella had given him his third cup of coffee, but it hadn't helped.

He closed his eyes and lay back on the bed, the picture resting across his chest. He thought about writing Cindrella a thank-you note and tiptoeing the hell out of there. Instead he just lay there thinking he hadn't meant to cause Cara so much trouble, hadn't wanted to hurt her, he was just a guy who suddenly found himself anxious about his future.

He hadn't meant to upset her, really. Yes, he wanted out,

sure he had lied to her, and yes—younger women were starting to turn his head. Did that make him a bastard? Probably. Would Cara ever forgive him? Probably not. Could they get the old magic back?

Jack didn't know what was possible and what was not, but on general principle, he decided anything was possible.

It was very quiet. Too quiet. And something inside him snapped.

·   And then Rose heard it. In the distance, coming into her mind very slowly. What was that sound? Padded steps, not human. Muffled, weird. Something started to rise above the horizon of her mind. And then she saw it. Barely at first, but it was there. The huge shadowy figure of a horse. It began to move toward her.

On the soft sand by the sea's edge the horse advanced leaving no footprints. From within the horse's eyes Rose could see herself lying on her stomach, legs spread wide, stretched out across the sand, totally naked. Gulls cried in the yellowish haze of sunlight as fish leapt from an azure ocean. Suddenly the horse raised itself into an enormous arch and then, whinnying, lowered its massive body.

On top of Rose now, he looked down at her with a strange stare. Then, with a gentle nudge of his head, he rolled her up onto his back. Breathing fire, he tossed his mane and started to move away into the sea. Slowly, very slowly, they disappeared into an onrush of blue-white waves.

"Rose, wake up," Cindrella said over the intercom system. He had decided not to enter Rose's room this time, fearing his presence the first time had upset the delicate balance of her sleep process. "Rose, are you awake?"

Rose sighed. "Yes . . ."

"You had another dream. Can you tell me what it was?"

The silence thickened around her.

"Rose?"

"Yes?"

"You were dreaming, weren't you?"

"Yes."

"Will you tell me about your dream, please."

"I was . . . It was a horse. Yes, a horse. And the ocean . . ."

"Could you repeat that, please."

"What?"

"You were dreaming of a horse, and . . ."

". . . the ocean." She could hardly think. Her mind was too busy trying to figure out where the voice was coming from.

"Was there anything else?"

She mumbled something that he couldn't understand.

"I can't hear you, Rose."

"I was . . ." Something stopped her from saying naked. A long pause followed. "I don't seem to remember anything else."

"Did the dream remind you of anything?"

"Religion. Very . . . Holy." Rose was hardly able to finish her sentence.

"Okay, Rose. You may go back to sleep now."

Dr. Cindrella was amazed. Another direct hit. Jack had been concentrating on a picture print of icon art depicting King George astride his horse, the horse being the predominant element of the picture. In the background the ocean blended with the sky, which was filled with an extraordinary burst of light as though God were about to appear at any moment.

Rose could hear Dr. Cindrella whispering to her. No, he was whispering to someone else. Not her.

Doctor Cindrella gently shook Jack's shoulder. "Are you all right?"

Jack was crying, his body twisted and convulsed and doubled up with sobs. The crying gave no warning. One minute he was lying there, dry-eyed, the next he was caught up in a gush of tears.

"I don't suppose you want to talk about it?" Cindrella asked, handing him a handkerchief.

"Not really." Jack reached for the handkerchief, wiped a few times, sniffed. He felt better.

"You want to stop?" Cindrella asked.

"No. I'm okay."

"She had another direct hit."

Jack shook his head. "You're kidding."

"No. It's amazing, really." He studied Jack's eyes. "Look, we can call it off for tonight . . ."

"No, we seem to be hitting, so why stop?"

Cindrella handed him a cigarette.

"Thanks." He paced the room a few times, inhaling deeply. "I feel awake now. I'll get started."

Jack quickly sat and tore open the next envelope. With his body jammed between the back of the chair and the table, he appeared a twisted mass of hard lines and awkward angles.

"Are you sure you're all right?" Dr. Cindrella inquired.

Jack nodded, a reluctant calm touching his rigid features. "Two direct hits," he said. "That's pretty impressive." Without further comment, he began sketching the picture he had selected.

Cindrella hesitated, then backed slowly from the room.

Somewhere around five o'clock Dr. Cindrella suddenly looked up. His body felt leaden and his head stuffed with rags: a state of dullness that was most disagreeable. He had been dozing. Dreaming. Through his semiconscious state he had heard a number of disturbing sounds. At one stage he'd heard sharp intakes of breath and tense stirring coming from the subject room.

Now the breaths, the stirrings were louder and he didn't like it. Something wasn't right. Rose had had two REM periods within the last hour. Both dream reports were scored as direct hits. But each time he had spoken to her, she seemed to be trembling, with her breath coming in quick, harsh bursts. And the way she had lain there, not moving. As if paralyzed, as if her voice hadn't really belonged to her, but to someone else. He had considered stopping the session, but her powers of telepathy were so remarkable that he had felt it necessary to go on, risking the consequences.

Hesitantly, he straightened behind his desk. His hand shook as he lighted his cigarette. The view of the subject room was not favorable from this position. He could only see a small portion of the room, and could barely see the subject.

He glanced at the monitor. Almost at once he began to panic. It was impossible yet it was happening. The EEG machine scanning Rose's brain was running wild with odd readings. First higher voltage brain waves. Too high. Much too high. Then a sudden drop to low voltage. Almost in seconds back to higher voltage. Low voltage. High voltage. And her heartbeat was running at a fantastic pace. A pace that no heart could withstand for any length of time without bursting.

He jumped to his feet. He couldn't believe his eyes as he looked into the subject room. Rose was gyrating in her bed as if some force had taken hold of her. She had torn away the covers, torn off her pajamas, her head lashing forward now, her hair flagellating her naked body.

From inside her room came an ear-shattering sound. Cindrella hit the intercom button. "Rose? Wake up. Wake up!"

He quickly hit the agent room button. "Jack. For God's sake—get out here quick." Then he raced into the hallway. Rose was pressed against the wall of the subject room, her eyes bulging, her hands slashing the air in front of her. He pulled on the subject room door. It wouldn't open. Rose had locked the door from the inside.

Jack appeared in the hallway. "What is it? What's the matter?"

"Rose? Rose!" Cindrella beat his fists on the window, trying to get Rose's attention.

"Jesus Christ," Jack gasped, his mind suddenly wrenched. He couldn't believe what he was watching. Because of the soundproofing, Jack couldn't hear Rose, but he could see she was laughing wildly, fondling herself, pinching the nipples of her breasts.

"For Chrissakes, do something!" Jack screamed.

"She's locked the door." Cindrella banged on the glass again. "Rose! Rose!"

She stopped to look at the two men who stared at her. Her expression tightened. She ran to the window and scowled. Then with a sudden sharp gesture, she stuffed her fingers into her mouth and bit down hard. Doubling over in pain, she dragged herself toward the bed. Fear was now plainly written on her face. Desperately, she reached out to Jack.

"Oh, God, God," Jack cried, and dashed to the door. "Rose, open the door. Rose, please!" He turned wildly to face Cindrella.

"How could you let this happen?" he screamed.

Rose was on the bed now, her body face up off the mattress, resting on her feet and elbows; she was pumping up and down with her pelvis area, pushing hard, her eyes rolling back into her head, her tongue licking the outside of her lips.

"Stop it! Stop it!" Jack screamed, at her, at Cindrella, at anyone who had the power to do something. With sudden fury he flung his body against the door. It refused to give way.

"Oh, Jesus," he whimpered, his mind barely able to comprehend what was happening.

"The key," Cindrella said. "Maybe I can find the key." He moved swiftly toward his office.

Jack turned to peer through the glass.

In the next instant Rose flipped over on her stomach, pinning her arms beneath her body. Something seemed to be pushing her down, forcing her face into the mattress; blood trickled from the corner of her mouth, her buttocks rose suddenly, as if someone had grabbed hold, had entered her from behind, and was now having violent intercourse with her.

A wild shriek erupted over the intercom, bounced off the monitoring room walls, then gushed into the hallway; a cry, half-human, half-animal—horrifying in its intensity.

Cindrella came rushing back toward the door with a ring of keys. He tried the first key but it would not fit. He stabbed at the lock with a second key; it was blocked. Another key. Another. None of the keys would fit into the lock! He turned to stare at Jack wide-eyed, body shaking, unable to function.

"Help me!" Rose's voice rang out over the intercom. "Help me-eeeeee!"

Her scream pierced Jack's stunned mind. He felt something grab hold of his stomach and chest. He glanced quickly at Rose, then back to Cindrella. The man stood grim-faced and defeated.

Clutching her throat, her eyes rolling back in her head, Rose opened her mouth. A long howl of pain came rumbling over the intercom, then exploded into the hallway. Jack became a part of the sound. He lunged, himself screaming, his body braced in a powerful arch. With one sharp plunge, he threw himself into the window. Everything seemed to freeze for a moment; then slowly, unhurriedly, his world seemed to shatter into a million specklike, crystallized splinters.

CHAPTER 12

ROSE SAT QUIETLY IN THE OFFICE AND SIPPED COFFEE. THE room was semidark, but at the curtain edges there were strong intimations of daylight. She felt tired yet relaxed, and the coffee tasted especially good. She waited for Dr. Cindrella to finish showing Jack the laboratory to the rear of the building.

"What do you mean, not tell her?" Jack was furious.

"She has undergone a great ordeal. I've never seen anyone in a trancelike state like that before. She was unconscious, unaware of anything for almost an hour."

"I realize that. That's why she must be told."

"And then what? We could trigger her all over again. Anxiety is obviously her problem. I won't risk exciting her again."

"But she'll have to see a doctor."

"For what reason? She's not physically sick. What would a doctor be able to do? She's not running a temperature; her pulse and heartbeat are both normal. Her eyes are perfectly clear. She's not suffering the depression which would be expected under the circumstances, and she seems in excellent health."

"Are you telling me what I watched was all in her mind? Triggered by her mind?"

"Exactly."

"Bullshit. I'm going in there and tell her." Jack moved to the door. "If she—"

"Please, wait a moment," Cindrella interrupted, perplexed. "She had five out of five direct hits. Even the last experience. I believe that she entered into the picture so completely—she became part of it. The picture does have sexual and horrifying aspects to it. Here, see for yourself."

Jack refused to look at the picture in Dr. Cindrella's hand.

"I don't believe this. You're telling me that what she did— what we saw came out of me sending her that image and her receiving it?"

"Precisely. If her actions hadn't been connected to the picture, then I would be just as skeptical as you are. But her actions were a vivid acting out of the picture. We must also remember she had hit each of the other targets. And look here." He flipped open the transcript. "With each target she got closer to the image. More intense about what she was experiencing. She had three REM periods in less than an hour. I believe her behavior was nothing more than a dream overdose. Similar to the taking of drugs. Once the drug wears off, the person is fine. You don't go to a doctor after every LSD trip."

Jack shook his head. "I think the first thing she should do is see a doctor. She was having spasms. I saw it. Spasms. She could have a nervous disorder or something."

"Then you're saying that it was just a coincidence. That after four direct hits—the fifth one just happened to be a direct hit as well, but that we should discount this."

"But she didn't act like that with the other four."

"Neither does a drug user on small dosage. But given large quantities, there is no telling what the mind and body will do. That's why she couldn't recall ever having the dream. Or her actions."

"What about the blood?"

"She bit her lip; you saw that." He moved closer to Jack. "Believe me, I'd be the first one to panic if I thought the girl was in any danger. You saw the way she reacted once we brought her out of the deep sleep she was in. She was perfectly relaxed. A little tired perhaps, but relaxed. When I asked her about her health, she said that she had just had a physical checkup. Her results were A-one. I'm sure . . ."

Jack was shaking his head, looking down at the tiled floor. "I don't know. I . . . I still think we should tell her. Then let her decide what she wants to do about it."

For a moment, Dr. Cindrella was silent. Then, "Well, go on. If you want to go in there and tell her, well—go on. I know what her reaction will be."

"Yeah? What?"

"The same as mine would be."

"Which is?"

"Embarrassed. Perhaps shocked. But I certainly wouldn't run screaming to a doctor. What would I tell the doctor? That I was in a dream telepathy session, had a few dreams, woke up perfectly relaxed, but then I was told a horror story of my strange behavior—not that I remember it—but here I am anyway."

"Ah, shit." Jack looked away in disgust.

"Jack, there are no symptoms here for a doctor to go on. He wouldn't know where to begin." Cindrella paused, then added, "You see what I mean, don't you?"

"Yeah, I guess," murmured Jack.

"I've given her a sedative. As soon as she catches up on her sleep, she'll be fine."

Jack paused, preoccupied, a fingertip pressed to the center of his forehead. "How about a psychiatrist?"

"For her anxiety? Perhaps. She has been recently divorced. That could be it. Those things are never very pleasant."

"Yeah." Jack knew only too well.

"But as you yourself say, a psychiatrist is her decision, not ours." He watched Jack nervously fidget with the bandage on his left hand. "You feeling any pain?"

"No," Jack snapped.

"You're lucky. The way you shattered that glass, it could have been a lot worse."

"Don't worry, I'll pay for it."

Cindrella shook his head and smiled. "Hey, relax. You're overreacting to this whole thing. Everything will be fine," he soothed. "Let's just wait and see, shall we? In the meantime, we'll complete our experiment long-distance."

"You want to continue with this?"

"She has remarkable powers. Or you do."

"Me?"

"Yes. I'm not quite sure whether she is a gifted receiver, or you are a gifted sender. We would need more tests. But not here at the Institute. Without a doubt, it was being in strange surroundings that interfered with the sleep process. At home in her own bed, she'll be relaxed. For this purpose"—he took a box from a lower cabinet—"we have what is called a dormiphone. It's a tape-recording device with a timer for long-distance dream telepathy. You place it by your bedside. She does the same. You both set your timers at the same time intervals. Four in all. At four separate intervals during the night the recorder is activated. There is a matching sound on either machine. You are both awakened at the same time to the same sound. Upon hearing the sound, you write down what you had been dreaming. At the end of the week we all get together and compare notes. Will you do it?"

Jack gave a helpless shrug. "Christ, I don't know. It's just hard, you know—after seeing her like that. What if something should happen?"

"Jack, try to understand what we are dealing with here. If Rose is anxious, if she is repressing something, then we must help her find out what that something is. We must help her deal with it. As I've already stated, we are each the sum total of two people, not one. Sooner or later Rose is going to have to deal with that other person. This experiment can help her do just that."

For a moment Jack Squadron looked at Cindrella blankly. There seemed to be a hell of a lot of people in the world, Jack had come to discover, who had problems. But why was it that he seemed to attract these people to him the way garbage does flies. The truth of the matter was that Jack had become almost obsessed with helping Rose . . . or meddling around in her life, depending on how you looked at it.

Jack hesitated a moment longer and then sighed. "Oh, Christ—all right."

CHAPTER 13

JACK AND ROSE LEFT THE INSTITUTE AT 7:20 A.M. SHE SAID SHE was hungry all of a sudden and he said he could eat something too and she said it was a nice morning and he said yeah but they both knew they were stalling.

He wondered if there was a restaurant open in walking distance and she said her apartment was close and he wondered if she was suggesting they go there for breakfast and she said for breakfast, yes, but they both knew something had passed between them during the night and that they didn't want to say goodbye just yet so they both stopped the bullshit and headed for her apartment.

"It feels strange, sitting here," Rose said. She hadn't sat at the dining table in days, no less with a man, eating breakfast. "You're lucky," she said. "I just stocked the refrigerator. It's the first time in weeks I've had food in the house."

Jack smiled.

"So," Rose said after a moment. "More coffee?"

"Please. But you sit there. I'll get it."

"No, I—"

Jack rose and indicated that he would prefer she let him get the coffee. "How about you?"

"Thanks."

Jack took both cups into the kitchen. "Nice place. Have you been here long?"

"Four years. Ever since . . ." She broke off. She had been about to say ever since she'd gotten married. Protocol: ex-husbands were not good dating conversation. Thinking of Lance made her think of Cheryl. Her eyes darted to the telephone on the kitchen counter. She suddenly wished that she knew if Cheryl were all right. And what had Cheryl meant when she said that she had seen things, that she had had dreams? Dreams, Rose thought impatiently. More dreams. As if dreams meant anything in the real world. Sometimes one needed more than dreams. Much more.

Rose blinked as Jack placed the coffee cup in front of her. "What are you thinking?" he asked in a soft tone, respecting her reverie.

"Nothing." She forced a smile.

"You were really something last night," Jack said, sitting again at the table.

"Oh?"

"Five direct hits. Not bad. Especially the last one."

"I couldn't remember the last one."

"Oh, I forgot."

Rose paused, looking at Jack's face closely. His eyes were soft and kind, and she knew that she wanted to sleep with him. But she never expected to say it. It just came out of her mouth full-blown, and it was a proposition and there was no way to take it back. "I want you to take me to bed," she said softly. "Make love to me." She paused. "Will you?"

Inside the bedroom they sat on the bed, naked, her back to his chest. He brushed her hair aside and kissed the nape of her neck. He began to gently press his body against hers, at the same time slipping his hand around her waist, pulling her closer to him.

Taking his hand, she kissed it and placed it to her breast. He moved forward, closer, and she felt his phallus pressing against the lower portion of her back.

Soon, they had turned to face each other. She pressed her parted lips against his chest, feeling the rough texture of his matted hair, taking small strands between her teeth in playful bites while she reached down to fondle him. With his hands gliding up and down her back, she felt him rise slightly, and knew what he wanted. He wanted her to kiss it, but she'd never done that with anyone before, not even Lance, and was afraid she'd appear foolish, incompetent. She continued to fondle him as he lay back on the pillow.

"Come up here," he said, pulling her up to kiss her. Gently, he rolled over on top of her, kissed her lips, her eyelids, her forehead; at the same time he entered her. He kept her face pressed between his hands as he moved inside her, and it felt so wonderful and loving, so gentle that she wanted to cry.

She was moving with him now, her entire body searing with pleasure. She held him tighter; then, kissing his mouth, she laid her head back and let him bury his face between her breasts. She moaned, wanting him to know how good she felt.

She moaned again as he gently bit the tips of her nipples. She could feel his breath, hear his rapid breathing.

He had hold of her buttocks now, lifting her; she willingly arched her back.

Just then she thought she would scream with pleasure. She groaned, digging her fingernails into his back. Instantly, mutually, they exploded and it all felt so incredibly good, so damn good, and the feeling lasted until they had stopped moving and then they clung to each other until their bodies melted into a peaceful loving embrace. And then sleep.

The music coming from the clock radio beside the bed had changed to hard rock, the disc jockey's voice as irritating as the music. Rose was shocked to discover that they had slept for almost nine hours.

Stepping from the shower, she wrapped a towel around herself and moved back into the bedroom. Jack was still asleep.

"Jack?" She pressed her fingers gently into his shoulder. "Jack," she said, "I have to go to work."

"What time is it?"

"Seven-thirty. We slept all day."

"Jesus."

She switched off the radio and got dressed. Jack just lay there, still wondering where he was.

"Sorry I have to run like this," she said, slipping on her skirt.

"It's okay." He took no notice of her, but stirred out of his lethargy, looking around the room. His face twitched slightly with the effort of memory. "Do you want me to leave?" he asked.

"When you're ready. Just close the front door. It locks automatically."

"That's convenient."

"Yeah." She shrugged. "I just had it fixed that way."

"Are you sure?" he asked.

"Of what?"

"That I can stay?"

She looked down and smiled at him. "Why, you going to rip me off?"

He smiled. "Not if I can help it."

She knew what he meant. "Thanks." She leaned over and kissed him.

"Are we going to see each other again?" he asked.

She didn't answer. Instead, she slipped on a white satin blouse, buttoned it and dabbed on perfume. She hadn't expected him to want to see her again. Her passion was stirring again just thinking about the possibilities. She had to force herself to say, "I'm not sure we should."

Jack didn't say anything. Pulling himself to a seated position, he reached for a cigarette. She looked him over curiously. She wondered what secrets lay behind those dark green, catlike eyes.

"That painting. I like it," he said, indicating the easel in the far corner of the room.

They held together in silence for a moment. Outside, the sky had turned an inky black and a few stars lay embedded in it. On the easel sat the painting of a huge winged insect trapped inside a glass bubble.

Rose shook her head. Another fantasy. Another nocturnal trip into the unknown. Just then the phone rang.

Jack continued to stare moodily at the painting as Rose moved across the room, the creaking of floorboards, the soft sound of footsteps mixing with the ringing of the telephone.

"Hello?"

There was silence on the other end. "Hello?" Rose listened as the phone went dead. Then a dial tone. She hung up. She stood there without looking at Jack.

"Is something wrong?" he asked.

"No—wrong number, I guess." She turned to look at him.

Jack felt kind of stupid, sitting in her bed naked. He wondered if she thought him stupid. If she considered him just another lay or what. He had no idea where he stood with her. Whether she was interested in him or not. He continued to gaze at her. In the bedroom's light, her hair appeared jet black. She had it swept up. It accented the planes of her face, and a dimple in her cheek called attention to itself. He hadn't noticed it before, having concentrated so hard on her eyes. Green eyes, like his, but lighter in color and more dazzling. He looked at her hands, delicate and pretty but very strong, hanging absently by her sides. The hands of an artist, he thought. He hesitated an instant before saying, "You're a very pretty girl."

"You're not so bad-looking either," she said softly.

He could see her blush.

"I really have to go," she said gently, and reached for her shoulder bag.

"I'll . . . I'll hook up the dormiphone for you before I leave," Jack said quickly, trying to hang on to her for a moment longer.

"We begin Monday night?"

"Yes. I'll set the timer for twelve, two, four and six o'clock. All right?"

"I don't get home until two."

"We'll make it three, five and seven then. Three times should be enough if we're dreaming the same thing." He smiled, liking the sound of what he had just said. Wouldn't it be something if they would, if they could, dream the same. His smile broadened. "Okay?"

Rose suddenly felt all mixed up. She didn't want to go to work. She wanted him to hold her. Yet, something held her away—telling her not to get involved. Not now. Not with a married man. She did not want to do to someone else what had been done to her. She did not want to be "the other woman."

She stared glumly out the window. The apartment lay in a strange vacuum of silence. There was an uneasy sense of crisis in the air, of an odd force that harbored an undefined threat to her, and Jack, unwillingly or not, was part of this force.

"Jack, about seeing you again, I . . ." She ground slowly to a halt. She could feel her heart thumping precariously like a bubble about to burst. She looked at Jack, a touch of anxiety clouding her face. "I'd like to see you again. I really would. But—"

"I understand," Jack interrupted.

There was a long pause.

"I'll be dreaming with you anyway." She forced a sad smile.

"On Monday then?"

Rose nodded uneasily. "On Monday then."

They looked at each other in silence, mildly disconcerted by their arrangement, and seeing, for the moment, nothing beyond it.

Rose walked nearer the subway, but before she had actually reached it, her body turned, propelled almost against her will. She ducked into a phone booth in the lobby of a hotel on Broadway. After dialing, she said in a shaky, hesitant voice, "Jack?"

"Yes? Rose?"

"Yes."

"Jesus, I wasn't sure whether I should pick up . . ."

"I know."

"But it rang so long, and I thought . . ."

"It's all right. All right." She paused. "Jack?"

"Yes."

Her hands were shaking. "I . . ." God, why was she having so much trouble saying it? "Oh, God, Jack—I do want to be with you again. I do."

"I know. I want you too."

"Write your phone number down before you go, please. I'll call you. Can I? Will it be all right? And you take my number down."

He hesitated. "All right."

"Good. If it's best for you—you call me. But I still want your number. Do you mind?"

"No. And Rose?"

"Yes."

"I'll call you soon. Really soon."

"All right," she said, hearing the eagerness in her own voice. "But if you can't reach me, keep trying—all right?"

"Okay."

"I'll see you," she said. Moments later, descending into the subway, she was smiling.

CHAPTER 14

HE WATCHED THE ORANGE JUICE GUSH AND BURP IN THE PLAS-
tic bubble, his nostrils filled with the aromas of pizza, hot dogs
and burnt coffee. A bank of flashing electric bulbs on the ceiling
and around the doorway glowed red, white and blue and shattered the blackness of night. Pimps and prostitutes proposi-
tioned the natives right outside the open glass doors.

The young black boy behind the counter handed him his
orange juice and change, waving to one of the hookers, smiling,
his broken front tooth acting as a whistle when he shouted,
"How's it movin', sugar?"

"Real good, nigger, real good." She tossed her long mop
of black hair to the other side of her face and kept walking.

He sipped his juice as his thoughts moved to the magic
called night. He let the word form itself within his mind, like
a spider forms a web. Night. He whispered the word and then
whispered it again. A time from dusk to dawn, he reflected,
when no light of the sun is visible. When the bright light of
the sun's accusing eye disappears, letting forth the darkness,
the concealment. Night, he whispered again, letting himself
get turned on. A period of affliction, of intellectual and moral
darkness. The period after life; death.

He watched the orange globules of air fight for firmness,
foam to the top and dissolve. Night watch. The juice tasted
good. Night owl, nighthawk, nightwalker, all crawling about
in the night. And they were all out there, the nightwalkers,
like a pack of slithering angleworms crawling about in the
gutter.

But he did not feel like that, like a worm. No. He preferred to think of himself as a night rider. One of the elite. One of the secret band of masked people who moved effortlessly through the blackness of night.

The words started to crowd his mind now, the lights blinking faster, the whores laughing and joking right in front of him. "Nightstick," he whispered, and his phallus grew hard and its throbbing red glans moistened. Nightshade, and he could smell the strong scent, experience its narcotic effect.

His hand gripped the plastic cup of juice tighter, and still the lights blinked faster, blurring his vision. Night blindness. He rubbed his eyes hard with the back of his hand. A whore stood just outside the door and beckoned him to come outside. Her breasts were pressed together, bulging from the top of her blouse. Nightmare. He was having one—the whore seeming to sit on his chest like some great succubus, forcing him to sink down, succumb to temptation. It's just a nervous disorder, the voice whispered inside his head. You're nervous, that's all. She's not really sitting on your chest. He couldn't breathe. Relax, the voice said, relax. The whore stuck her tongue out, licked her lips, her ruby red lips, as she moved closer. "You want some, baby? I mean, you look like you want some." The front of his pants was wet, his phallus bulging. "Man, you sure look like you want some." He had to move away, wanted to move away, but he couldn't. Nighttide, nighttime, nightwear . . . he couldn't stop the words from coming, couldn't stop her from teasing him, taunting him; his head was about to bust open like an egg smashed against the pavement.

Nightingale, and his thoughts shifted, hearing the sweet songs sung in the night during breeding season. Nightcap, nightclub, and he pushed past the whore and headed for the subway. He knew the feeling he now felt would be nightlong. And he would cherish it.

CHAPTER 15

THIS SAME SATURDAY, AT A LITTLE PAST NINE O'CLOCK IN THE evening, long-legged, smooth ivory-skinned Julie Lemon stood shooting the breeze with Rose as they waited for Mitzie to fill their drink orders. All at once her large dark eyes under rather severe brows glistened with profound insight.

"Christ, I'm a pushover," she said, snuffing her cigarette. "Say something sweet to me and I melt, dissolve all over the place. Show me a stiff dick and I get wet. No, really—my shrink kept wondering what made me tick. Last week he said he finally found out what it was."

"Oh, really—what?" Rose asked, counting her change.

"Nothing."

Rose stopped counting.

"That's what he said. Nothing. That there was nothing there but a soft heart, whatever that means."

Rose shook her head. She had just gotten started, having walked into the Cottontail Club only minutes ago, and still hadn't had time to adjust to the atmosphere.

No bar in the Village was more wildly lighted than the Cottontail Club when it was jumping. And tonight it was jumping. It glowed and glittered like a full blast of fireworks on a hot Fourth of July night. Under the beckoning neon sign (a cocktail waitress whose bunny's tail wagged), the jukebox flashed with psychedelic lights, the table lanterns snapped and sputtered, and the strip lights around the stage blinked on and off like eyes that had suddenly been hit with a foreign object.

Nina, a young, well-built N.Y.U. economics major with

symmetrical buttocks, more top-heavy than topless, bumped and ground stage center, her skin flashing red, then orange, then blue, the palms of her hands making erotic waves through the smoke-filled air. A trickle of sweat ran down the front of her chest, between her massive breasts. With one finger, she wiped the sweat away, then, with a smile, she licked the finger, still displaying her charms in rhythmic pulsations.

Rose shook her head again to clear it. Nina was the real thing, all right. No nonsense there. She watched Nina strut her stuff, watched the crystal globe suspended above her head spin slowly, sending a thousand little specks of light across the room—a room of all men, just a few couples at the tables and the booth in the corner.

"Here you go, girls." Mitzie placed two rum and Cokes on Rose's tray and three beers on Julie's tray.

"That's me, all right," Julie said. "I get all the cheap drinkers." She turned with her tray and almost ran into Danny Blue Eyes.

"How's the best-looking broad in town doing?" he asked.

"That depends on who I'm doing it with." Julie brushed past him, having no trouble moving through the crowd while making various parts of her body dance for Danny.

"Hey, Nick, what's been going on in this dump?" Danny dropped his arm over Nick's shoulder. "Christ, it smells like a six-day orgy in here."

Nick smiled wryly. "Talent scouts come in here all the time. They don't seem to mind the smell."

"Cute." Danny grinned cynically and pinched Nick's cheek. "Real cute." Then he ducked into the men's room.

Mitzie leaned over to Nick. "Why don't you tell that pissant to go screw himself."

"Because I don't want trouble," Nick said, his colorless eyes roaming the bar. He was capable of measuring and calculating to the drop just how much liquor Mitzie was pouring into a customer's drink. "Damn it, Mitzie. Can't you see all those empty glasses lined up on the bar? Come on, honey— fill them. Fill them, for Chrissakes."

Mitzie smiled and moved away. Nick always liked it when Mitzie smiled. An attractive thirty-two-year-old woman, she knew the ropes. She had had more experience than anyone in the room, yet she still looked fresh. Blond hair piled casually on her head, she always had a sparkle in her pale blue eyes, always a childish joy in her thin voice. With high pointed breasts, thin waist and well-rounded hips, she was everyone's favorite.

Nick stood up abruptly and reached behind the bar for a fresh cigar; then he glanced at Rose. Sure enough, she was staring at him, expressionless.

"How much are the tables doing?" he asked, though the total clearly showed on the service bar register.

"One twenty-nine." She shrugged wearily.

Nick pouted, thoughtful, shaking his head. "And people wonder why the IRS has taken a lien on the place." He rolled his eyes toward God. "You see," he said to God, "that's what I get for hiring an artist."

"I just got started," Rose protested. Like someone who has just confessed some terrible crime, she stood gravely still.

Nick held a match to his cigar and inhaled, then coughed. When he was able to talk, he said, "Ah, come on, Rose, get a move on. Move it."

"Okay," she whispered, and nervously picked up her tray and moved into the crowd.

Afterward, when she had delivered her drinks, hardly able to stop thinking about Jack, weak with anxiety—and with guilt, too—she stepped up to the bar and nearly collided with Julie.

"Please, Lord—protect me from sleepwalking women," Julie said. She tipped her head to one side and smiled. "Still not feeling so good, are you?"

Rose thought about it, sliding her tray onto the bar, then shook her head. "It isn't that."

Now Danny Blue Eyes moved by, his movements smooth and restrained, his trousers so tight that his crammed genitals were as clearly visible as his clenched fist. "See you later," he said to Julie. Without glancing back, he went to the far side of the bar and sat.

Julie turned, rolled her eyes toward him, and smiled. "Here I go again," she said, "getting all wet and gooey."

"You really shouldn't fool around with him," Rose said without deliberation; it simply came out.

"Oh, hell, he's all right. I had a date with him last night."

"You're kidding." Rose blinked in astonishment.

"No."

Mitzie stepped gingerly to the edge of the bar. "What'll it be this time?"

"Two scotch and waters," Rose said.

Julie scowled. "Four beers!"

"Coming right up." Mitzie winked at Rose, then chuckled, moving away down the bar.

Rose regarded Julie with curiosity for a moment. It would have been easy to say Julie was more an assortment of cheap items—watch, necklace, wig, clothing—than a person; in part it was true, but it didn't take into account two bad marriages and a broken homelife as a child.

"Julie?"

"Yeah?"

"You really shouldn't get involved with him. He's pretty rough."

Julie smiled cynically. "Rough. You don't have to tell me." She rubbed her hand across her breasts. "He nearly bit them off last night. I told him if he kept it up, I'd have to get him a bottle."

Rose tensed. "Why do you talk like that?"

"Why, you just come from church or something?"

"I just think you should have a little respect for yourself. You can do better than Danny."

"Oh, really? Who? Nick? And if not him, some other slob. At least Danny has the connections and the dough."

Mitzie slipped the drinks and the beers professionally onto the trays. "There you go."

"Don't worry, honey," Julie said, "I know what I'm doing." She quickly disappeared into the crowd.

"Hey, Rose." Mitzie took hold of Rose's arm. "There's a guy at the other end of the bar looking for you."

"Me?"

"Yeah."

Rose didn't recognize any of the men sitting there. "Which one?"

"Right there. The one in . . ." Mitzie broke off. "Well, I'll be damned. He was just sitting there."

Rose swallowed past the sick feeling rising in her throat. "What did he look like?"

Mitzie shrugged. "I don't know. I really wasn't paying attention."

"You must have seen him. His face?"

"No, I was talking to a customer. Hey, you all right? I mean, you're not in trouble, are you?"

"No. No trouble."

Rose delivered her drinks, glancing at the empty stool at the far end of the bar. Images flooded her mind now as a hand reached out for her waist. She brushed the hand away, suddenly feeling cheap and dirty.

The guys were cheering now; Nina had removed her shorts, and stood there totally naked gyrating to the music. Somebody was reaching out to fondle her. Nick pushed the guy back, shouting to Nina to stop the nonsense and leave the stage.

The hand again slid over the tabletop toward Rose, inviting her to take it.

"Lay off," Rose said with an edge to her voice.

The thin corpselike man jerked his head up, his cheeks gray as ashes. "At least the dancer up there is giving us something for our money," he said stiffly.

"Oh, really," Rose scowled. Usually she ignored the insults, the remarks. The men who came into the Cottontail Club were nothing more than a sea of blurred faces, one indistinguishable from the other. Just a collection of harmless voyeurs who got their kicks ogling naked women. But tonight she found it necessary to defend herself, defend her presence there. "I've a question for you. You think just because I work here, that gives you the right to treat me anyway you please, don't you?"

"Maybe," he said, making wet rings on the table with his glass.

"Tell me, how much did you pay for your drink?"

"Four dollars."

Rose pointed to Nina. "For that price, what you see is what you get. Enjoy it!"

Rose flounced away from the table, still angry. If she felt the least bit sorry for him, she also felt repelled.

For the next couple of hours, she moved slowly—too slowly—between the bar and the tables. As the night wore on, she could feel the weight of each step as though her feet were encased in cement. Nick had kept an eye on her. He had shaken his head, amused, annoyed, yet somehow Rose could see he had felt sorry for her. It was one of those nights. Nick had always said: Win some, lose some, and some get rained out.

Nick smiled. "How'd your dreams go last night? Dream of anything interesting?"

"As a matter of fact I did. I dreamt of you."

"No kidding? Bet you had one hell of a time."

"Not really. I was so bored, I woke up."

Some time after midnight Rose noticed that the table crowd had thinned out somewhat, all the couples had gone, leaving the majority of action focused around the bar.

Uncomfortable as she was feeling—the eye-aching wealth of neon, the noise, the oh-so-terribly-sad collection of men— she minded nonetheless that it would soon be time to go home; minded it more with each fresh glance at the still unoccupied stool at the far end of the bar. Time to hit the streets again. Time to— Damn it, who was the man who was asking for her? A sudden sharp image began to reawaken.

Faster and faster Cheryl had run . . . but not fast enough . . . because eventually he had taken hold of her . . . one of his huge hands wrapping itself around her throat. She had struggled to break free. A violent, useless struggle because he had been too powerful. Too hungry.

Now it was Rose who was running, in her mind, as fast as she could.

She turned, peering into the smoke-clogged atmosphere. A sea of grinning faces washed over her in waves. She tried desperately to understand what was happening to her. Where had this night person in her mind come from? What did he want? Rose clung to the edge of the bar waiting for some burst of illumination, some all-transforming light to give her an answer.

"Rose? Are you all right?"

Mitzie had spoken in a loud clear voice that had broken Rose's introspection.

"What's the matter, honey?" Mitzie toyed with the two gin and tonics she had placed on Rose's tray. "Tired?"

"A little."

"You'll be done soon."

Rose nodded and lifted her tray.

"Oh, by the way. Did your girlfriend ever get in touch with you?"

"Girlfriend?"

"Yeah. She came in here Thursday night looking for you.

Right after you left. You couldn't have missed her by more than a couple of minutes."

Rose felt her throat go dry. "But . . . I asked Nick. He said no one came in Thursday. . . ."

"What does Nick know when he's been drinking? She was here all right. A good-looking gal. Around thirty, maybe younger. Dressed like a schoolteacher. Kind of plain if you know what I mean."

"Cheryl."

"Yeah. Cheryl. She never reached you?"

"No." Rose leaned unsteadily against the bar.

"Jesus, that's funny. She said she was going to call you as soon as she got back to her hotel. Seemed pretty important that she reach you."

"Hotel? She said hotel?"

"I think so."

"Did she mention which hotel?"

"Let me see . . . oh, yeah. The Dixie on Tenth Avenue."

"Are you sure?"

"Oh, it was the Dixie all right. I remember thinking, what's a dame like this doing bedding down in the Dixie? Jesus, that's where I met that jerk I was married to. . . ."

. . . Mitzie had married a musician at age twenty. It had lasted two years—two years of sadness and emotional upheaval, even physical abuse. Three months after they married, he had started playing around with other women. Having been raised with the old-fashioned ideas about love, honor and obey until death do us part, Mitzie had endured his infidelity as long as was humanly possible until finally she divorced him. The experience had left deep and lasting scars.

"It was my fault, I guess," Mitzie went on. "I should have known he was a loser—" But Rose couldn't concentrate on what Mitzie was saying. She heard instead a loud crashing sound coming from the kitchen, then Julie screaming. It didn't register with Rose what was happening until she saw Mitzie rushing toward the kitchen door.

"Stay out of it, Mitzie." Nick had taken hold of her arm.

"Let go!"

"I said stay out of it." Nick held fast.

Julie's voice rang out from the kitchen. "You son-of-a-bitch. Leave me alone!"

Rose stood aside and, through the small oval window, watched Danny Blue Eyes do what he'd often bragged he did: "Rough up his lady." Only this was a bit more than roughing up; frozen with horror, she saw Danny's hand double into a fist, and this time instead of a slap, his fist landed across her jaw like a hammerblow, sending her flying into a pile of linen.

"Come on. Say that to me again. Come on!" he screamed, and with a swoop of his arm sent a crate of eggs crashing to the floor. "Get up," he said, dragging her up onto her feet.

She broke away, trying to duck under the sink. Danny looked down at her with his cold blue eyes. "What's the matter, cat's got your tongue?"

"You bastard!" she screamed.

"Still with the nasty mouth?" He took hold of a kitchen knife, at the same time pulling her to her feet.

"Jesus, Nick. He's going to kill her." Mitzie tried to break free of Nick's grasp. Everyone else in the club had by this time turned their attention toward the kitchen.

Rose panicked as she watched Danny slide the knife across Julie's throat, wrenching her head back by her thick blond hair. It was the subtlest move he'd made, graceful almost, and it had the effect of stopping the crowd cold. Even Mitzie drew back with a muffled cry.

"Well, now—did you say something?" He pressed the knife into Julie's ashen flesh. She started to give way, weeping with fear, her legs buckling under her.

Abruptly, he released his grip and she dropped to the floor. "Next time you see me," he said, "you talk with respect or I'll cut out your goddamn tongue. You understand?"

"Yes," Julie whimpered.

"Good. Now maybe we understand one another. . . ."

The crowd stirred slightly, hoping for more action, more excitement.

But it was all over.

Coming from the kitchen, Danny paused to straighten each of his lace cuffs, then hit the door with the palm of his hand. Everyone but Mitzie backed away. She stood her ground, every line of her body an illustration of contempt.

Danny saw it. "You got problems?" he asked.

Mitzie shrugged loose of Nick's grasp. "You're going to get it one of these days. And I'm going to be there to enjoy it."

He nodded. "And then again, you're liable to get it, and I'll be there to enjoy it."

"And who's going to give it to me? You?"

"Mitzie, please—" Nick tried moving her away.

"Let me alone." She pushed Nick aside. "You bastard, you just try fucking with me, and see what happens." She stood there staring Danny down.

He remained immobile, scarcely breathing, then turned away as though Mitzie was not worth any more of his attention. Effortlessly, he moved toward the door.

"And stay out of here," Nick hollered after him.

There was a smile, not his hard familiar smile, just a smile on Danny's lips as he left the club.

CHAPTER 16

As THE NIGHT DREW ON, THE CITY TOOK ITS SHADOWS FROM the sinking moon, and the night grew more and more solemn for Rose. For some time after leaving the club she could not think. To see Julie beaten like that, actually beaten and bloodied, lying there in pain, screaming for someone, anyone to help her, and yet no one had moved except Mitzie.

Rose sighed, shifted her position in the seat slightly. Outside the window lights were flashing again as the subway made its snakelike way uptown.

Moments later, she stepped nervously onto the Seventy-ninth Street platform. All at once she had an odd sense of the nocturnal in her, the darkness inside the light, the black around the moon.

Coming up from the subway, she hesitated. Around her the neighborhood loomed silent. Yet she could feel him again, in the air around her, almost visible. A solitary figure, small and weasel-like, moved past her and quickly disappeared into the subway. She moved in the opposite direction.

She hesitated once again at the corner of Amsterdam Avenue, then crossed the street and moved up the slight incline of pavement toward her apartment. Ahead of her were two shadows, both her own. The moon forming one, the streetlamp the other. Two separate entities, one thin and almost imperceptible, the other long and black; herself forming the trinity. The Father, the Son, and the Holy Ghost. Jack, his wife and she. She, and Jack and Lance. Cheryl and she and . . . the Holy Ghost.

She suddenly realized he had moved closer to her. Perhaps had even entered her body in some strange way, and she thought, abstractly, with no flicker of intention, of last night's dream session. Did something happen at the Institute last night that she wasn't aware of? Jack had said five direct hits. Yet she hadn't been able to remember the last one. Four direct hits with total recall and then a blank. Why? Why couldn't she remember the last dream she'd had?

Inside her apartment she removed her coat and lay down on the couch for a moment to think, maybe grant herself a few hours' sleep. Lying there, inert, folded into a ball of anxiety, she saw the last few days travel past her mind's eye like a movie. She probed through a maze of images, her eyes darting from one end of the room to the other, focusing, refocusing, what was she looking for? A clue. Something was going terribly wrong, she knew that. What that something was, she wasn't sure.

Night, blackness—something was hurling itself at her, a body—Jack's body hurling through space, and then the shattering of glass. Where was the image coming from? She had asked Dr. Cindrella what had happened to the window of the sleep subject room. He had told her there had been an accident, nothing serious. Why didn't she remember it? Jack's hand—bandaged. Blood. The blood was coming from Cheryl's body as she lay beneath his massive legs; he had beaten and raped her. Who had beaten and raped her? Danny? No, that was at the Cottontail Club. But Mitzie said someone had asked for her. A man. Then he wasn't there. Empty stool, empty space . . . Hysteria rising, building, Rose got to her feet and entered the bedroom.

She felt exhausted, but knew she couldn't lie down, couldn't close her eyes. And then she saw it. Just a little slip of paper propped up against the clock radio next to the bed. Scribbled, hurried, a phone number. Jack's phone number. Staring at the paper left her uneasy. No message . . . nothing but an awkwardly written phone number. He should have at least written something, anything, so she knew that they had done more than just fuck. She knew hardly anything about Jack's life. She knew he was married and that it was probably going to be difficult to see him. She knew he wrote music and that he was a good lover. Now she wondered if he still made love to his wife, and if so, was he that good with her as well. But then again, she had asked Jack to take her to bed, not vice versa. Did that turn him on? Did he like being the one led into sex?

She had said please. Please make love to me. She had been begging. Did he see it that way? Had it been just sympathy? Rose stopped suddenly, becoming self-conscious.

At that moment the phone rang. She picked it up on the first ring. "Hello?" She listened. There was a low raspy sound on the line; then the phone went dead. Slowly she placed the receiver back into its cradle.

Promptly, her mind was filled with a full-length image of Cheryl. Cheryl standing at her door, suitcase in hand. Cheryl laughing, Cheryl running, falling . . . Rose felt herself suffocating with the onrush of images until Cheryl lay dead, piled in a bloody heap at his feet.

She lifted the receiver. Dialed information. Information received, she dialed again.

"Hello, Dixie," the sleepy voice said on the other end of the line.

"Yes. I'd like to speak with Cheryl Arthur, please."

"Room number?"

"I . . . I don't know." Rose bit the inside of her lip.

"Hold on."

Rose shook her head, grimaced. She clamped her arm around herself, closed her eyes, and squeezed. She was beginning to become a bit unglued. Just a bit.

"Not here," the voice echoed in her ear.

She opened her eyes. "What?"

"I don't find a Cheryl Arthur registered."

"But . . . but you must. There's some mistake."

"You're probably right." There was a mocking tone to his voice.

"What?"

"They do it all the time here. But she isn't in the register. Still, that doesn't mean she's not here."

"That's ridiculous!"

"Listen, lady, don't scream at me. I'm only the night clerk. It isn't my job to keep track of who's here and who isn't." He was beginning to breathe heavily. "I'm only the night clerk. That's all."

Rose tried to calm herself. "How can I find out for sure if she's there?"

"Manager. He'd know. But he won't be here until Monday . . . sorry."

With a desperate thrust of her arm, without knowing what she was doing, Rose slammed the phone down hard. "Dammit!" she screamed, and then threw herself across the bed, the tears flooding her eyes.

. . . She was silent now. She ran her hands over the soft sheets, thinking of Jack. Thinking that she would like to embrace him, make love to him. Her heartbeat had slowed . . . she was at the edge of sleep when the telephone rang. As if in a dream she picked up the receiver slowly. She knew that there would be no voice there, only breathing, his breathing, but she picked the receiver up anyway. Was she dreaming? Was it really Jack? Was he really telling her that he wanted to be with her? Tomorrow, yes. In the morning. Yes, I'd like that, she said. No, you didn't wake me . . . I just got home. I've been thinking about you all night. Don't get mad for what I'm about to say, okay, but I missed you. Are you mad? Good, I'm glad. Yes, I can't wait to see you either. Yes, tomorrow then. Good night.

She hung up.

And then she passed into a deep sleep. She dreamt of bodies— Mitzie's body being put into an ambulance. It was Mitzie, wasn't it? There was a sheet over the girl's face, but Rose knew it was Mitzie. A police photographer was taking pictures of the back seat of Mitzie's green Buick. The car was Mitzie's pride and joy and the back seat was now splattered with blood. Rose could see the bloody finger marks on the window as if Mitzie had struggled to free herself from him. A dark shadowy figure stood in the crowd, watching the attendants slide Mitzie's body into the ambulance. Was it him? Rose couldn't see his face, but knew it must be him.

. . . Rose's muscles tensed beneath the covers. "Jack," she whispered, and the man in the shadows moved, as if someone had called his name. The man's body was floating away, dissolving . . . "Jack, please don't go—stay." The man's body was far away now, dissolving into gentle ocean waves that washed him out to sea, and Rose let herself go along with him.

Far out, very far out to sea.

And a voice whispered, Godlike, "Go seek your lover. Go . . . seek your death."

PART TWO

PART TWO

CHAPTER 1

Sunday, October 19
2:00 P.M.

WINDS SHIFTED.

Jack cocked his head, sniffed, taking in a deep breath of salt air. He stood looking out over a long foam-line where gulls dove, hitting the water with sudden sharp thrusts of their beaks, scavenging for food. The sea lay still and green, like the felt cloth of a billiard table, after a night of rolling and howling.

At the edge of the seawall the tide lay shallow, lapping in gentle rhythms. Jack sipped again from his styrofoam cup, took a deep drag on his cigarette, then glanced at Rose.

The breeze ruffled her gently. A calm autumn breeze that dropped away like the fluttering of bird wings.

"Are you cold?" he asked.

"Not really." She smiled.

Then for a while she seemed lost to him, simply sketching on her pad an image of a blond figure in faded khaki standing motionless at the end of the seawall.

When she next looked up she saw that Jack's mood had shifted. He appeared suddenly pensive and shy.

"I used to come here as a kid," he said.

"Right here? This spot?"

"Not exactly this spot. Coney Island. Every Sunday," Jack said, grinning.

Rose sat back and watched the sun glitter warmly, vanishing for a second behind rolling clouds; appearing, vanishing again. Reappearing.

The warm breeze continued to lull them while Jack filled in the time gaps with snatches of childhood recollections, until he had switched the conversation to his marriage.

Rose put her sketch pad aside. "What will you do now?"

Jack gulped down the last of his coffee, crushed the cup; there was nothing he could do. Then with a directness that even surprised him, he said, "I don't know. It's futile to talk about it now. I don't have any of the answers."

The silence that followed was tense and confusing. He had changed so quickly, so completely, from one minute to the next. His shy face had fallen into hard lines and he gave no indication that he was aware of her presence beside him.

Rose looked at him searchingly. She heard nothing but her own strong heartbeat. Jack was the first man she had been with since Lance. There could have been others had she given them a chance. But she had always placed an invisible barbed wire in the way of any relationship up to this point. Men made her nervous and uneasy. But for some unexplainable reason, Jack made the barriers seem a sort of optical illusion, something she'd imagined. Being close to him was inevitable, something she could no more deny herself than the air she breathed. In some subtle way she imagined their destinies were already mixed up together like colors blended on her palette. She wondered if already it would be difficult or impossible to stop what they had started. She wondered if he wanted to stop. He had moved closer now. She could feel the warmth of him.

"I like this," Jack said. He lifted the sketch pad and studied it closer. "Do you sketch much?" he asked.

"Usually when I'm not involved with my painting. I use sketching as a sort of investigation, trying to figure out what to paint next."

"Have you been painting long?"

"Oh, yes. Very long."

"What made you know . . . I mean really know this is what you wanted to do?"

"I don't know," Rose said, studying hard the seascape in front of her. "I guess it was my aunt that started it all. I can still remember her reaction to a drawing of Sleeping Beauty I did." She smiled. "The fact that I copied it right out of a book made no difference to her. I was eight, I think. I'm not sure now. But as far as she was concerned, I was an artist right there and then. Actually, I think my getting involved with art had a lot to do with my solitariness as a little girl." She shrugged. "I can remember spending a great deal of time watching things from the sidelines. I'm still that way, I guess. A watcher."

Rose turned then, leaned back on both hands, looked down upon the surf below the wall. Tenuous wisps of mist slipped by, in gently writhed mutation against the dark stone, dissipating slowly.

"And you?" she asked. "What made you choose music?"

Jack paused before saying, "My father was a musician. Just hand him an instrument and he'd play it. Sometimes he'd sit down at this grand piano we had and play and sing 'Pennies from Heaven,' and he always seemed happy to me at those times. I guess I just figured if I played the piano and wrote songs I'd be happy too. . . ." Jack's voice was suddenly monotone, running along the edge of sadness. "But it didn't quite work out that way, did it?" He laughed nervously. "'Pennies from Heaven.' Sleeping Beauty. Is that really the stuff we're made of?"

"What's wrong with 'Pennies from Heaven'?"

"I knew sooner or later somebody was going to ask me that question." He shook his head heavily, like a sleepy dog.

"Well?"

"It's too hard to dance to," he intoned, flinging his arms out. "Oh, mother!"

"You're crazy, you know that?"

Jack turned, glancing at her sharply. "I don't know. Maybe I am. Maybe we all are." He looked again at the sketch pad. "Tell me something. Why do you work in such a place?"

"What place?"

"The Cottontail Club. Why do you work there?"

Rose blushed. "I—I don't . . . How did you know I worked there?"

He smiled, a smile so casual and relaxed that again his whole face changed. "I don't know . . . Dr. Cindrella mentioned it, I think."

His abrupt change in manner caused Rose to stand. She groped for something to say.

Jack rose to stand beside her. "Anything wrong?"

"I . . . never told Dr. Cindrella the name of the club."

Jack shrugged. "You must have mentioned it then."

"But you said *such* a place. Like you knew it was dirty or something."

"The name. You know—it sounds . . ."

"Like what?"

"Like a strip joint." He paused. "Is it?"

She looked at him for a moment. He reached for her hand, but she turned away, feeling young, naive and most of all angry. She felt put down by his question. And for no good reason at all she also felt dreadfully guilty.

"Hey, why are you getting so upset?" he asked.

"I'm not upset . . . it's just that I don't think it's necessary for me to suddenly be forced to justify my life."

"I only meant—"

"What's a nice girl like you, etc.—I know." The air had a distinct bit of fall to it now. It caught sharp in Rose's lungs.

"I think my reaction is understandable," Jack said. "I don't want to see you . . ."

"What?"

"Forget it." He turned away, moving closer to the edge of the seawall.

"Jack?" She placed her hand on his shoulder. "You talked to Dr. Cindrella about me?"

"We didn't really talk about you."

She could see Jack hedge. "Friday night . . . while I was asleep. Did something happen that I should know about?"

He turned to face her. "Like what?"

"I don't know. You and Dr. Cindrella were talking in the laboratory. It took quite a while."

"He was just showing me around."

"And then the experiment was changed suddenly. Long-distance rather than at the Institute. Why?"

"He told me that he wanted to see how good we'd be long-distance."

"You said five hits. Five for five, you said. I only remembered four."

"That's only natural. We don't always remember our dreams." He glanced away sharply, shifted his feet.

"The window in the sleep room was broken . . ."

"We told you what had happened. Cindrella broke the window while moving a piece of equipment."

"Why didn't I hear it?"

Jack laughed. "Hey, why the sudden interrogation? What do you want me to tell you?"

"I'm not sure," Rose said.

She looked away now and saw Mitzie's body lying under the sheet, the stretcher being shoved into the ambulance. She tried to reassure herself that it had all been a dream, but her mind quickly embraced the experience and began assembling a jigsaw puzzle. All she had been able to see was a dark form, seemingly suspended in the shadows. Then the torso, silhouetted, seemed to her to have been erased, rubbed out, almost gone. She regretted not having looked closer at the figure lurking in the darkness, because there was someone there, watching Mitzie being placed into the ambulance. Yes, she remembered that now, but she hadn't been able to see the face. Just a dark haze. Trousers and jacket both dark. A man. She had clearly seen it was a man. She had called Jack's name, the figure had moved away, deeper into the shadows, until . . .

"Are you all right?" Jack asked, and moved closer.

"Cold, that's all." She tugged on the collar of her coat. The wind had subsided again to a faint whisper.

"Shall we go back to the room?"

Rose stood as if frozen, confused, her hands clasped in front of her.

"All right," she murmured, and no longer knew what to think. Nevertheless, she was still lucid enough to understand that Jack had his arm around her, that the silence was broken abruptly by a familiar sound, the crunching of pebbles as they made their way back to the motel.

When Rose turned away from drawing the drapes, Jack was waiting for her. With soft padded steps he moved closer, yes, unmistakably closer; he was drawing her to him. His first gentle kiss was followed by a sudden fierce embrace. Rose tightened, feeling his hand move over her breast, molding it, shaping it with delicate insistence; his hand seemed to grab hold of her thoughts next, sending them whirling off into another time and place where she could not catch them. She tried feebly to resist but his arms were around her and moving also, guiding her onto the bed.

Suddenly his breath came hot against her neck. His hands stirred her in a rush toward her center, engulfing her. She was steaming, all of her steaming, oozing heat which flowed in a rush of sound; it was impossible to catch up, make sense of it all as he entered her.

Hot air rushed through her, burning, stopped her breath. With tense legs she pushed her pelvis upward to meet his thrust. His mouth moved over hers, feverish and wet, while his hands lifted her.

"Now," he whispered, his voice low and thick in his throat.

"Yes," she breathed fiercely, then tensed, frantically groping about in the sweet liquidity, straining, until with one final lunge they climaxed. Mutually.

They lay still for a moment, Jack's head resting on Rose's breasts. Softly, she stroked his hair. She gazed down at him, nervously awaiting his response. He smiled faintly, shook his head once in bewilderment.

"I'll say one thing," he said. "That was sure unexpected." He started to move.

She clung to him. "No, don't move. Just let's stay like this for awhile."

Jack smiled, avoiding her close inspection of him. She cradled him, rocked him, as he went from one breast to the other kissing them. Rose drew back a little; she hadn't meant to excite him again.

"Hey, come up here and kiss me," she said, trying to slow him down. Awkwardly, he raised himself over her and pressed his lips to hers. He was breathing hard as he moved down and began to bite her neck. Hard bites, almost vicious bites that caused Rose to moan, not from pleasure, but pain. His phallus had stiffened again. He passed his hand across her cheek, sighing quietly and richly. It was happening, so unanticipated, the rush of waves over new seas. Rose could feel the rapid pounding of his heart as he entered her again, climaxing almost instantly.

Embarrassed, he moved away from her, dropping his legs over the side of the bed. Rose didn't know what to say. What had just happened? All she knew was that they had just made love again, the act itself having no more meaning than a second cup of coffee. For the first time Jack had made her feel like an anonymous object. She didn't like the feeling.

Jack lit a cigarette, stared at himself in the mirror. Pressing his finger into the corner of his eye, he turned to face her.

"Would you like a cigarette?" he asked.

"Yes, please."

He handed her his, lighted another. He was pacing now,

looking for something to say. "You, ah . . . you were pretty angry out there on the beach."

She smiled. "I guess so."

"Why?"

"I don't know. I just thought I'd been had."

"Had?"

"You know. Alone with two men. Asleep. Suddenly I find out you had been discussing me."

"Very little, actually."

"Was it locker room talk?"

"Oh, Christ, Rose." He snuffed his cigarette.

"Hey, come on—I was only joking."

"No, you weren't." He paused. "I'm going to take a shower. Then maybe we'll go out to eat." He disappeared into the bathroom.

Rose caught sight of herself in the chipped mirror over the dresser. She didn't like what she saw. Her body looked thin and debauched. She glanced around the room. The green vinyl chair in the corner was torn, the carpet frayed and dirty. Stirring from the bed, she felt the springs dig into her buttocks.

Rose could hardly tell what she felt as she paced the room— guilty, shoddy, angry at having placed herself in this degrading situation, at the same time miserably inadequate. She shuddered. She was actually playing the game. Panting with desire and orgiastic ecstasy. Motel rooms in the middle of the day. For God's sakes, Jack was a married man. The thought stopped her. She sank slowly onto the bed.

Confusion, she thought, more than anything else, was the problem. It had caused an undercurrent which had swept them toward each other, then away. She could feel both Jack and herself trembling, shifting. Sometimes seeing each other and sometimes seeing in each other the faces of other people. Sometimes laughing and sometimes . . .

Suddenly, despite all efforts to prevent it, her eyes welled with tears.

Jack stood before the bathroom mirror and studied his naked body. He had lost weight and liked the way his rib cage, clearly defined, seemed to lend a certain sense of power to the rest of his body. Through the misty steam of the room, his flesh seemed to have a glow to it; rosy red, smooth and fresh.

The gold bracelet that dangled from his wrist seemed to add a touch of dramatic accent. Like he had just finished performing an orgiastic ritual, the bracelet part of his otherwise naked costume.

He touched himself, feeling the pleasure mounting again. The act of sex was becoming more important to him than the physical gratification, and Rose brought a certain spiritual sense to her lovemaking. Heady and light.

He lifted Rose's perfume from off the sink, dabbed it on his finger, passed the bottle under his nose. The scent was lush and sent the blood rushing to his head, dizzying him. Cara had stopped perfuming herself. He missed that. The taste of perfumed skin.

Cara. Cara. He struggled to free himself, but the stake held in his heart; even breathing hurt him, even that. He reached for his trousers, dug into the side pocket, taking away a small bottle of uppers. He washed the pill down quickly, desperately trying to stay high, intoxicated. He could not ignore the fact that he felt bitterly toward Cara. He resented her for having sullied his dream of her. He had constructed a reality for them to live in, and now that reality was gone. His bitterness toward Cara grew, deeper, wider, until it now turned on him, his own weakness, his own lack of ability to believe in their love gnawing away at his innards.

He turned suddenly, surprised to find Rose standing at the bathroom door. "You're dressed?" he said, and tried to smile. "That was quick."

"Jack, what are we doing here?" she asked, her sadness having taken hold of the small features of her face.

"What?" He wrapped the towel around himself, shoving the pill bottle back into his trouser pocket.

"I mean, we could have stayed at my place."

"You said you had two days off. I thought you'd enjoy getting away from the city."

Rose spoke what was really on her mind. "Jack, we're moving too fast. I feel we're not thinking, just doing. I feel out of control. Like being here. A motel—at first it sounded exciting. But it's not exciting. It's degrading."

"Oh?" He glanced at Rose and then, out of the corner of his eye, at his trousers. He smiled nervously.

"I guess you don't understand how I feel," she said softly.

"I think I can imagine," he said. His gaze met Rose's challengingly, but he merely gave a good-natured shrug and said, "Would you like to go home?"

"Do you mind?"

He smiled. "Not really."

CHAPTER 2

THEY WERE SILENT IN THE CAB, HE WITH HIS HAND IN HERS, disappointed, frustrated; Rose, confused and saddened. She sat rigidly, as if straining every muscle to appear relaxed. Nothing moved but her slowly blinking eyelids. From time to time she was aware of the driver peering at her in the rearview mirror. He had a disconcerting way of staring straight through her, his thin lips slightly parted, his eyebrows black and full, like visors.

He said nothing, preferring to puff steadily on his cigarette rather than to engage in conversation. Most unusual for a New York cab driver, Rose thought, and settled deeper into her seat. She was painfully conscious of the silence which followed. She moved her head, just a little, and gazed absently out the window.

Once inside the city, the driver began to mutter and make childish gestures at the tight traffic pattern that had suddenly materialized around them. Not words, actually, but low guttural animal sounds that stopped midway in his throat.

It was just as he was pulling up in front of the apartment—his cigarette smoked down to the nub, the meter turned off—that he spoke for the first time. "It's a dollar apiece extra for each bag," he said.

Rose slid forward on the seat. "But we handled our own luggage. I thought—"

"A dollar apiece," he repeated heavily.

"But—"

"It's all right," Jack said, and handed him a twenty. "Keep the change."

"What change?" he challenged.

"Sorry," Jack said, no apology in his voice.

The driver raised his arm in a quick, impatient gesture, threw the cab into gear and sped off, his tires screeching against the pavement.

"What a character," Jack muttered, allowing himself an ironic half-smile. Almost as an afterthought, he picked up the two bags and began walking toward the entranceway.

Rose seemed to be drifting now, floating in the shadow of Jack's movement. The hallway was too dark. The elevator too small and airless. Then there was a sound; a lock on the door clicked, a dead bolt released. Then another. Jack pushed open the door, stepped in, and gestured for Rose to follow. Somehow he was always two steps ahead of her now.

Moving into the apartment, Rose paused to look around. The inside of the apartment seemed dull and unreal. Shadows fell over the living room, slanting from corner to corner—pale light that seemed to separate as one passed through it. She stood rigidly, breathing carefully in and out, waiting.

After Jack had put on a fresh pot of coffee, he fluffed a pillow under Rose's head, making her comfortable on the couch.

"You don't have to treat me like an invalid, you know."

"I just want you to relax." He kissed her hand.

Minutes later Jack was showering again. Rose couldn't help feeling that his obsessive cleanliness was somehow due in part to his feeling trapped in an unclean situation. She wanted desperately to cry, to wash the thought from her mind, to cleanse herself. But her eyes remained dry.

With great persistence she pressed her fingers to her temples, pushing hard, as if seeing if she were still capable of feeling. Around her the apartment became more rigid and brittle, more still. Long blue shadows reached from the window down across her face. Shadows that no longer bespoke day, but purple dusk edging into night.

She slid a cigarette from the pack, tamped it on the coffee table, and lit it.

The light in the room changed again. The shadows darkened, spilled out across the room, filling it like a cup. Rose sucked in smoke, then lay back and placed her hand on her chest.

She forgot what she'd been thinking.

The seeming forgetfulness seemed part of it. Part of her present confusion. Then a sudden thought welled up into her consciousness, after a lapse of perhaps minutes, and she felt a shock of surprise, which gave way to panic. The front door to the apartment had been left unlocked. She knew in a flash that *he* was close. Probably right outside her front door. And then the doorknob turned. Slowly at first, but the knob was turning; the door cracked open a few inches and quietly swung wide.

"Oh, dear God, I'm sorry, Miss Carpenter. I thought . . . I thought you were away for a few days." Harmon Thomas, the building's super, stood awkwardly in the doorway, his usual cheery face a mass of nervous twitches.

Rose blinked. "Harmon?"

"Yes, Miss Carpenter. I'm sorry. I came up to fix your windows."

"Windows?" Rose sat up, trying to focus on the little man who hovered in her doorway, his pressed work shirt with starched collar, and matching slacks falling in neat lines over his ageless body.

"You said the windows were rattling. I thought this would be a good time. I thought . . ." He broke off, peering with fierce attention at the living room windows.

"It's okay, Harmon. We decided not to stay."

"Well, I'm sorry."

"It's all right." Rose smiled, glancing at his face to see what response she ought to make to calm his fears. All she saw was a pair of large, glinting eyes staring back at her, fierce brown pupils in tan webbing.

"I'm sorry, really," he said. "We'll get them fixed during the week. Sorry."

Rose smiled harder, offering him help. Without another word, he turned, somehow moving forward in the same instant, found the space he needed, and fled. Rose stared at the closing door with her mouth open.

She was both amazed and amused at Harmon's awkwardness, his confusion, and found herself chuckling. Ironically, she saw in him her own awkwardness and confusion. What had been wrong with her? She wasn't the first woman to find herself in a motel room, and she wouldn't be the last. What was all the fuss about?

Jack was easier to talk to now. They sat side by side on the couch making notes about life. Checking them off mentally, covering everything from food to entertainment to Zen Buddhism. They found they had read some of the same books, that they hated going to dinners that were served too late or were skimpy on food, that she enjoyed the music he wrote.

"Whew!" Jack sighed, wiping imaginary sweat off his forehead. "We would never have gotten past that."

"I saw one of your plays."

"Broadway?"

"Off-Broadway."

"Ah."

"Angel Dust."

"We bombed on that one."

"I thought you got robbed on that one. Your music was great."

"Not that great." He shrugged.

"Well, not that great," she agreed solemnly.

"Listen, you."

"It was great!" she shrieked as he pummeled her playfully.

"Okay. Now let me tell you that by the greatest of coincidences I saw your paintings at La Galleria."

"Coincidence?"

"Well, it was a coincidence that the gallery was listed in the phone book. When Cindrella mentioned you were hanging there, I just—"

"When did you have the time?"

"Last night after I left your apartment."

"And Lottie was still open?"

"Open and doing a great business. I loved your stuff. I would have bought one of your paintings on the spot, but—" He ground to an uneasy halt.

"No place to hang it," she finished softly. "I understand."

They steered back into easier waters. They leaned against each other, as though too weak to sit up straight. Mostly they laughed, as though this were what they needed the most. One fact seemed irrefutable. They enjoyed each other's company.

Jack seemed content now, his hand closed around a glass of straight scotch. His hair lay in curls across his forehead. Somehow, she thought, it was a princely image. He let go of his glass and slipped his hand into hers.

"I give up," she said. "Why does an eggplant . . . wait a minute . . . I've got the two jokes mixed up."

"The eggplant was an hour ago."

"But why does it—"

"Never mind," he said, laughing again. Then in a quieter moment, he added, "I think you and I are very much alike."

Rose smiled and was unable to keep from saying, "So do I."

At nine o'clock they sent out for Chinese food. Jack got a little sexy during the meal. Rose was uneasy about it, wondering if he'd try to waltz her to bed again.

He didn't. She was somewhat disappointed that he hadn't.

They spent the next hour watching television, cuddled up on the couch in the living room. It was a pleasant time and Rose felt genuinely relaxed.

At eleven-thirty, Rose hesitantly answered the telephone. It was Nicklas Nuzzo. "Oh, Christ, Rose. Where have you been . . . ?" His voice cracked.

"Nick?"

"I've been trying to reach you all day. All day . . ."

"Nick, what is it?"

Nick began to answer, and then, as though a caution light had flashed, he slowed. Something was definitely artificial about his gruff, "Uh, you sound good. Everything all right? Rose, I was just . . . I was . . ." His voice broke around the edges of his words; he was a distracted man who was trying for a semblance of normality.

"Nick, in the name of God, what's happened?"

"It's . . . ah . . ."

She realized he was crying in the pauses. That was the brittle quality, the cracking of the words. Tears. "Just say it. Come on now," she said quietly, her panic nearing grief, almost a kind of mourning, though as yet she didn't know . . .

"Mitzie. She was a good girl, Rose. A really good girl."

"Mitzie," Rose repeated numbly.

"She was killed. The bastard raped her, Rose. He stabbed her twelve times. Once wasn't enough. Twelve times."

Rose's reaction was instantaneous. Stunning, even to herself. She had spun, as though facing an invisible man, someone who had waited to watch her reaction to the news, someone who was watching her all the time now in one form or the other, someone who was amused. Laughing.

"What is it?" Jack asked, moving closer.

"Close the drapes."

"Why?"

"Just—"

"Okay. No problem." Alertly, he followed her instructions, staring at her over his shoulder from the window.

Him again, Rose thought. And no way to ever shut him out. No closing of the curtains, no changing of locks. He was inside of her now. Staring through her eyes. Listening through her ears. Laughing.

She felt herself begin to laugh, a horrible choked, suffocating sound, even as Nick's voice went on giving mechanical details. And crying. Crying. The parking lot attendant had found Mitzie at nine-fifteen this morning. Blood. Drenched in blood. Clothes torn from her body.

Rose shut her eyes, trying to block out the image. Nick's voice boomed, rang in her ears. A loud sound of ultimate grief that refused to pause, that refused to stop its incessant wailing. I . . . I watched them take her away. . . . She desperately sought to blot his words from her mind. Oh, God—how could anyone . . .

All at once Rose let out a terrible quavering cry; across her mind came a flood of black waves; she thrashed to free herself, head spinning.

Then the world flew to pieces in waste and profusion, and for a long time did not reassemble.

CHAPTER 3

Monday, October 20
7:00 A.M.

IN THE MORNING ROSE AWAKENED CRUSHED BY HER OWN HEAVY awareness, paralyzed from head to toe, as if she'd been drugged into sleep and had never quite recovered. It took her a good while to remember what was wrong; Mitzie Karp was dead. Suddenly the power to move took hold of her.

She sat up, as tired as if she hadn't slept at all, dropped her feet to the floor, and set her hands in her lap, momentarily baffled by how cold it was. The day was dark and gray, with rain that pelted the windows like small stones. Wind whistled through the cracks beneath the windows.

She stirred suddenly. A moment of dizziness came and went. She put on her robe and went to the window where she looked out over the city. Her mind, independent of what she might desire, would not relent, would not let go of Mitzie's death. She was sure that Mitzie's killer was the same man who had been stalking her for more than a week now. Everywhere she went, he had been there. At home, on the subway, at the Cottontail Club, at the Institute. Yes, even there. Jack hadn't told her the truth. The fifth dream. Something had gone decidedly wrong during the fifth dream. But neither Jack nor Dr. Cindrella would speak of it.

Rose turned to glance at the bed. Sometime during the night, Jack had left the apartment. For a long time he had lain there beside her, holding her. She had dozed off several times, only to awake to find him there, eyes open, his arm resting beneath her neck. Whatever restlessness he had felt, he had controlled it for her sake. At one point, she had tried to explain what she had seen. How she'd dreamt Mitzi's death before she'd known it had actually happened. She was waiting to hear his reaction before telling him any more . . . Cheryl . . . the man who stalked her in her mind . . . To her amazement, Jack had barely reacted, merely cradled her closer.

"Jack?" she whispered, puzzled.

"Yes?"

"Did you hear what I said?"

"Don't take it too hard, Rose. It's not a frightening thing."

"But—"

"It just proves what an extraordinary girl you are."

"You mean you believe in psychic power?"

"Everyone has visions," he said. "All people are psychic in some way or the other. You're an artist. You possess a truly amazing amount of creative power. And creative power doesn't reason. It produces unexpected mental images, with strong feelings behind them."

"But it frightens me," Rose murmured.

He nodded reassuringly. "It's tough to lose a friend. You start feeling all kinds of things. Guilt, grief, fear. It all comes out and you try to put it together—try to make sense of it."

Uneasily, she lay back again, considering it. In the circle of his arm, she had managed to find peace, only to awaken again and find him staring into space.

"You need to go now," she said, and felt his amazement that she could understand him that well.

"I don't think I should leave you," he said hesitantly.

"I just need to rest," she murmured. "Let the time go by." She sat up in bed. "I'm afraid all this has been awful for you."

"Don't be silly." He brushed a few hairs from her forehead. "Are you sure you're going to be all right?"

She nodded. "Sure. You go on."

Moments later she watched him collect his belongings, his watch, wallet, loose change from the dresser. She didn't want to see him leave. She shut her eyes for an instant, remembering the sound of Nick's voice, hearing his words. Never before had she been so totally overwhelmed.

"Jack?"

"Yes?"

She held her hand out. "Take them."

Jack stared at the keys that dangled from her fingers. "Are you sure?"

"I work late. You may want to meet me here sometime."

Jack took the keys, kissed her. And then he was gone from the apartment.

Rose sighed now and dried her eyes. Below in the rain-soaked corridors of the city, the sound of traffic continued to hum, incessantly, without end, until the sound seemed to be right there in the room with her.

Coming almost to the end of her strength, she managed to make her way to the kitchen. Awkwardly, she fumbled around—shoved two pieces of bread into the toaster. Then she fixed a strong cup of instant coffee.

Forgetting the toast, she moved into the living room where she dropped heavily into the armchair. She stared down at her coffee, swirling the black liquid around and around until the center had become an abyss that looked deeper and more deadly than imaginable. She had actually seen the scene of Mitzie's death. The last gory details of a brutal act. She had had a similar dream involving Cheryl. Was Cheryl also dead?

Draining her coffee, she moved back into the kitchen where she placed the empty cup in the sink. She moved slowly, hardly able to breathe. Should she phone the police? But what could she tell them? What did she actually know? Thinking this way, brooding, she returned to the living room.

An hour passed, or maybe two, and Rose mused, bouncing thoughts off the walls of her skull, causing hard thuds like one might hear during a game of racket ball. What was he? This man who drifted like a shadow through her mind. What did he want from her? She sat motionless in a kind of stupor.

Was it possible that she'd imagined it, imagined that Mitzie's death, the man in her mind and Cheryl were all connected? "Ridiculous," she whispered, not quite sure that it was. Here she sat, shaping reality from intermingled dreams—incapable of knowing which was which, yet weighing the results as if she'd gotten them fresh and clean out of a textbook.

She shuddered and tried to push the whole mess from her mind. Her thoughts refused to budge. Why couldn't she identify him? She had an image of him in her mind. Only a shadowy thin vapor, but there was at least a vague outline of him there, lurking. He did exist, she was sure of it, and somehow it all fit together.

It was two in the afternoon when she finally dressed. The phone was ringing. She let it ring several times before it came to her that it might be Jack; then she moved swiftly, crossed the bedroom and took the phone from the hook. "Hello?" she said, guarded.

"Rose? It's Lottie." The softness of her voice confused Rose, as if she were calling from a great distance away.

Rose nodded but did not speak, trying to think. It crossed her mind that she had let Lottie down in some way. That in all the confusion she had forgotten her.

"Rose?" Lottie's voice was louder now, shriller.

"Hello, Lottie," she said. Her voice was tearful.

"Rose, are you all right?"

"Not so good, I guess," she said. She was hardly breathing.

"I can imagine. I just saw the newspaper. Ghastly. That poor woman. As soon as I realized she worked at the Cottontail Club, I . . ."

"I know—" Rose faltered.

"And when you didn't show up Saturday night—"

"Saturday?"

"We were supposed to meet, remember. The Guggenheim. I tried calling you yesterday, but you weren't home. Then when I saw the paper this morning—"

Rose's body ached from the cold. The damn heat. Why didn't they put on the damn heat? She was shivering all over.

After a long moment Lottie said, "Rose, is there anything I can do?"

Rose thought of telling her all that had happened since she'd last seen her—the man who followed after her, Cheryl, Jack, seeing Mitzie dead upon the stretcher—but knew it would be impossible to say anything at all. She just didn't have the strength for it. Nor the stomach. Nor had Lottie, probably. Rose received instead a mental image of Lottie all safe and snug, tucked away in the back room of the gallery, her feet snuggled into her favorite pair of soft green slippers. Lottie, at least, was still immune to all that had happened. It gave Rose, at least for a moment, a kind of peace, a serenity that she did not wish to disturb.

Lottie had asked her something and was waiting for her answer. Finally she remembered what it was. "No, I'll be all right. But . . . thanks."

"I can come over there if you like. Or we can go for a drink, take in a movie."

"I'll get together with you soon. I promise."

When the conversation finally ended, Rose knew that the next time the phone rang, she would not be there to answer it.

Moments later she stood in the kitchen, reasoning with herself. She was sure that as soon as she got going her thoughts would clear.

Numbly she made two phone calls and then left the apartment.

Dr. Cindrella propped himself on his elbows, his chin resting on his hands, which were locked into one huge fist. Rose sat across the desk from him. He tried to concentrate on what she was saying. No, he hadn't minded her calling him. Coming to see him. It was understandable. What? Fears, yes. Her fears were ordinary enough. He had listened to hundreds of such cases. Delusions, hallucinations—punishment. He eyed her surreptitiously. Depression? Yes. Anxieties? Certainly. He wrote the words "wishful thinking" in blue ink at the head of his note pad.

Then, restless, he leaned back in his swivel chair, dropping the pen casually on the desk. "The club you work at. Do you feel morally right working there?"

Rose shrugged. "I have no real problem with it."

"Do you feel sexually driven to work there?"

"Absolutely not."

"Do you find a need to punish yourself?" He watched her carefully.

Rose straightened in her chair. "I don't see—" She broke off and stared at him.

"Does my question surprise you?"

She said nothing.

"Rose, it should be remembered that you create your own dreams. You decide who will or will not be there. You are the one who invites this stranger into your dreams."

"But that's just it. I don't."

"He is, after all, not really there, but merely a focal point of unresolved tension. When your tension abates, he will diminish. When the tension increases, he will be with you more often."

Rose floundered. "But . . . I actually saw him on the train. And then he called me."

"You may have seen a man on the train once. As for the

other times, you admit yourself that he was never there. As for the phone calls, again—tension, anxiety."

"No, he's there," she whispered hoarsely, realizing she was nearly inaudible.

"I understand your fear. Fear is a common emotion in dreams. It's nothing unusual. Dreaming on the whole is not a very pleasant pastime."

Rose knew a response was expected of her, but she took time to think about what Dr. Cindrella had just said. *Dreaming on the whole was not a very pleasant pastime*. Rose had always been taught to believe in dreams. Happiness, real happiness, lies in our dreams, her father had said. It was illusion without end. It was hope.

Abruptly Cindrella moved. He walked over to the window looking out at the street and drew the drapes closed. Rose blinked; the sun had been shining in her eyes.

"There, is that better?" he asked.

Rose smiled. "Yes, thank you."

Cindrella returned her smile, so warmly that it came as a complete surprise to Rose. "Let's put it another way," he said, seated once again at his desk. "Let us say a woman is walking down the street and she is afraid that someone is going to attack her. She turns the corner and sees a refrigerator crate partially hidden by a telephone pole. She faints because she believes she saw a man. We call that distorting objective reality. These are illusions or delusions. The crate is an illusion because there was actually something there. It becomes nothing more than a mistaken perception caused by the woman's mental state. A delusion on the other hand is a mistake in judgment or belief. A person believes something is true when it is actually false. Delusions are often nothing more than wishful thinking. A person wants something to be true, so they convince themselves that it is true. They make the world conform to their wishes. If there is no man at all, but the woman sees him even though there is no object that could possibly be mistaken for a man— this is an hallucination."

Images flooded Rose's mind, forming, changing swiftly, reshaping themselves at will. She still hadn't told Cindrella about Mitzie's death. She dreaded putting it into words, as though the words would bring the nightmare to life, make it happen all over again . . .

. . . Rose's mind moved into darkness as Dr. Cindrella leaned forward and spoke softly.

"You said you dreamt that he was coming after you with a knife. Making love to the knife. This is a purely sexual dream. The knife representing the male organ."

Rose stirred uneasily. "But you said that I invited him into my dreams. Are you saying that I'm asking to be seduced?"

He looked evasive. "I'm not sure. If you view sex as dirty. As degrading or dangerous. Perhaps. I would have to monitor more of your dreams. After a time, a sort of jigsaw puzzle forms. We put the pieces together and sometimes we are able to discover the whole picture. Dreams are not mysterious. They're merely pictures of what the mind is thinking. The thing to understand is that dreams are the creation of the dreamer's mind."

Rose stared at him. What exactly was he trying to imply? She eyed him suspiciously; then slowly, very slowly, like day surrendering to twilight, to night, she spoke of Mitzi Karp. How she had dreamt of Mitzi's death, and then Nick's phone call confirming her dream. Without so much as a pause, she moved on to Cheryl Arthur. How Cheryl had come to be in New York, their argument, and then how she had dreamt of Cheryl's being raped and murdered. Biting her lip to stop herself from crying, she watched Cindrella's face as she finished her story, and noticed that his expression had not changed.

For a moment it seemed Dr. Cindrella could not think of anything to say. Then, bending forward, he removed a cigarette from its pack and lit it. He said very softly, "Would you like one?"

"No. Thank you."

He inhaled. Paused. "Let's talk about Mitzi Karp first. A vision of someone passing away is not unusual. You hear of it all the time. A deceased grandfather reappears, or the so-called mystery of the watch that stopped, a warning that arrived too late. All quite normal. But Cheryl Arthur . . . well, this is a more complex matter. And I believe closely related to your problem."

"Problem?"

He nodded. "Yes. You said that while this girl, Cheryl, was being beaten and raped in your dream, you suffered right along with her. That you had actually felt his hand over your mouth."

"Yes."

"Then you felt as if you were being beaten and raped, is that correct? That you were being punished."

"I guess so," she said wearily.

"So, Cheryl becomes your substitute and receives punishment meant for you. Our next question is: Why is the dreamer being punished? For rebelling against authority. For violating one of the commandments within the conscience. For gratifying a forbidden wish, for committing a misdeed. It makes no difference—the dream is always the price one has to pay for doing something wrong."

"But . . ." Tears were forming in Rose's eyes. ". . . I don't feel that I've done anything wrong."

"Shall I be frank with you, Miss Carpenter?"

"Please . . ."

"It is not easy to separate from one's husband. Have you been thinking of him lately?"

"Yes," she said, sniffling, the ugliness of her situation surrounding her. She could feel her bitterness, taste it.

"Are you still angry with him?"

"Yes . . ."

"So when you think of your husband, you immediately think of the intruder. The base intentions of the intruder are quite clear. What is not so clear is that you have summoned the intruder in order to do away with your husband. In other words, you harbor a hostile feeling against your husband. You remove him from your mind by having another person intrude upon your thoughts. Also the intruder is there to punish you. He stands for an alien part of your own personality which you are reluctant to acknowledge as belonging to you. . . ."

Rose's fingernails had begun to dig into the arms of the chair. . . . Please, God, make him stop talking.

"Your dreams of this man seem to always include sex and aggression. You needn't be alarmed by this. Sex and aggression are necessary for man's survival and reproduction. Aggression is frowned upon in society . . ."

. . . make him stop. Please.

". . . so we seek outlets privately. One such outlet is the dream. So it is not surprising to find aggression in most people's dreams. Again, I'm stating all this in its simplest terms. Usually the sexual elements of a dream frame a larger, more complex picture."

Nervously, Rose turned away. God help her, it was true.

She didn't want to hate Lance, but she did. She truly did.

Dr. Cindrella stirred from his chair. He stood for a moment, hunched, before venturing from behind the desk. "Rose, believe me—I know that you feel as if you've been invaded by an outside force or being. But what has invaded you is actually what you yourself have created. Everything comes from the invisible to the visible. The mind being the launching pad. The more intense the desire, the more apt it is to reproduce itself. The mind functions on many levels. The moment you let some life experience disturb you, the mind becomes affected, upsetting its delicate balance. Unless one can adjust to the situation, tension develops—images emerge and one loses control." Roses's lack of response forced him to add, "You see, while you were here Friday evening, you did not dream of him."

"But I did," she said, frowning.

"No, you hit each target picture accurately. Each dream was absolutely connected to the target picture. I still haven't determined whether Jack is a gifted sender or you are a gifted receiver, but one thing is certain. You only dreamt what was being transmitted to you."

"No, he was here," she murmured. "You're just not telling me what happened."

Reese looked at her strangely. "Why would I . . ." he began slowly, then stopped.

"The fifth dream," she said solemnly. "Tell me about the fifth dream." Rose shook visibly.

He considered a moment. "Rose, most dreams follow a standard, highly organized sequence. Yours were no different. Your first two dreams were the shortest, a kind of overture. Two more followed, each slightly longer than the other, each having a sense of greater detail. The fifth, and for most people the final dream of the night, builds on material from all the previous dreams, forming a grand finale. Your—"

"But why couldn't I remember it?" she interrupted.

"We couldn't wake you at the end of your REM period. It is most unusual for a person to remember a dream after waking from a deep sleep."

"We?" she challenged.

"What?"

"You said 'we' couldn't wake you."

He smiled. "Sorry. It's a bad habit of mine . . . speaking of myself collectively."

Then, with infinite caution, he said, "It may interest you to know that many years ago I also found myself haunted by demons." He paused briefly to nod in communion with himself, his body bent forward in thought. "I too believed my demons were real. Oh, yes. In fact, I was so convinced of their absolute substance that I considered taking my life. Not a very pleasant thought, eh? Luckily, very luckily, my mother sought immediate help. After many hours of analysis, I came to see that my demons were merely thoughts, my subconscious fear of losing my mother. She was sick at the time, and I feared that she would soon be leaving me. That I would be left alone in a world that I neither knew, nor trusted." Slowly his voice trailed off, his gaze coming to rest on the ornate picture frame on his desk.

Now he hesitated—then said, "Rose, I want to help you. But you must trust me."

Rose looked into his eyes, remembering that she too had experienced a long spell of illness that had interrupted her schooling. Was Dr. Cindrella right? Was all this a reoccurring sickness? Had her separation from Lance driven her back to the roots of her childhood?

Rose was silent for a moment. Her eyes narrowed; her mouth and chin grew rigid. She looked directly at Cindrella and said, "You talked to Jack Squadron about me. I would like to know what aspect of me was discussed."

Cindrella actually took a step backward as if he had been struck in the face. "Jack said that we talked about you?"

"Yes," she said sharply.

"Well, he must remember something that I don't," he said stonily, fiddling with his coffee cup.

"Dr. Cindrella," she said with an accusatory tone to her voice, "I know how Jack cut his hand. I also know how the window was broken. Jack smashed the window, didn't he? To get to me."

Cindrella hesitated before speaking. "Well," he said gruffly, "if Jack Squadron told you this . . . I'm surprised. Because none of it is true." His voice was recapturing the anonymity with which he cloaked himself. "If I seem a bit abrupt—I apologize. But your accusation was a shock, after all. These things have a way of taking one by surprise." Deftly, he closed the file on his desk.

"Do you think it advisable to continue with the experiment?" Rose asked heavily.

He merely shrugged in reply. The question obviously seemed to him irrelevant. It was like asking a doctor if it was advisable to breathe or a farmer if it was advisable to plow his land. People *should* dream, and those dreams *should* be explored.

Rose found herself once again faltering. Dr. Cindrella, on the other hand, sat behind his desk, a confident, self-assured man with one thing on his mind. Dreams.

After agreeing to continue with the experiment, Rose left the Institute and headed back to her apartment, unaware that Alex Mana had watched her leave the building. Huddled in a corner, Alex waited until Rose had turned the corner before stepping from his concealment and crossing the street. He smiled and entered the Institute.

CHAPTER 4

AT THE SAME MOMENT ALEX MANA WALKED INTO REESE CIN-drella's office, Jack Squadron sat at the edge of his piano bench, staring out the window. Even after a hot shower and a clean shave, he still felt scruffy and used.

He had spent most of the morning working on a new song, but nothing came. He kept looking at his watch, but he had nowhere to go. Cara was still refusing to see him.

Absently, he took a small bite of toast that seemed to harden as he chewed. Putting the toast aside, he continued to take small sips of his coffee. He never touched the single poached egg and two strips of bacon he had prepared for himself.

"Christ," he breathed.

The apartment loomed silent around him, his slightest movement echoing through the living room of his six-room duplex on West Fifteenth Street.

Slowly he let his fingers run the keyboard until he slipped into Debussy's "Clair de lune." His playing was not inspirational; he had lost his enthusiasm for music and played like an adult beginner.

His fingers moved awkwardly, weak places turning up where he least expected them. He practiced the fractures until he set them, and played the piece again. His mind moved to thoughts of Rose, toyed with the idea of calling her. He had just decided to spend the evening with her when Cara slipped her key into the lock. His playing covered the sound.

Cara quietly put down her overnight bag and closed the door. She stared at him for a moment, his thick hair shining brightly, the sun highlighting his strong profile. She remembered the younger, gutsier kid who had gone out of his way to court her with boxes of candy and flowers and, once, a diamond stickpin.

Their years together had not changed him much physically, but they had pressed in on him emotionally, changing him from a happy-go-lucky extrovert into a pensive, moody introvert. He had congealed, condensed his essence within himself—a lonely place where she was not allowed.

She still could not understand why she had lost him. With the sickening taste of despair, she wondered if he could go it alone. If he could survive without her. Her own overwhelming sense of doom demanded that she let the question go unanswered.

Jack finished the piece and paused.

"Momma's home," she said in a weak voice, and Jack turned suddenly to face her.

"Cara," he exclaimed tonelessly.

She laughed shortly.

"What . . . you're home!"

"I'm home," she said promptly.

A light flashed in his fuzzy eyes for an instant as he peered at her in astonishment.

"The hospital was making me sick," she said with a sour grin. "I kept throwing up a lot."

"How do you feel now?"

"Restless."

"You look fine."

She sniffed. "What's burning?"

"Bacon. Would you like some?"

She didn't answer, and when he glanced at her, she seemed to be laughing inwardly. At what, he wasn't sure.

She seemed to be making an inventory of the apartment, checking to see if he had changed anything while she was away. He sat awkwardly, silently, and waited. In seconds she had straightened magazines, fluffed pillows and emptied an ashtray. Then she poured herself a drink.

Jack watched her feeling her way. Emotionally, not physically, feeling her way to a new perception of reality. Bewildered, he rose to his feet. Now he had his arm around her shoulders. She allowed herself to lean on him.

"Are you tired?" he asked.

"Exhausted!" She finished her drink in one gulp.

He moved her to the couch, where they sat. He eyed her nervously. "So, what are you thinking? Don't fudge—tell me your deep dark thoughts," he soothed.

"Fuck," she said, fumbling in her handbag for a cigarette. She flicked her lighter, inhaled, then let out a deep swallow of smoke like a steam engine getting up its steam. "Life is a bitch. A real bitch," she sighed heavily.

"Yeah." He was feeling distinctly uneasy.

The apartment was suddenly full of noises and unnameable problems. A wind had come up, whipped the trees beyond the window, whispered and creaked, much like voices. Something alive and huge ran through the atmosphere, knocking down his thoughts, then fleeing. No, he was fleeing. He had begun to move away from her.

"Don't go," she said desperately. "Please."

Jack smiled. "I was going to mix you another drink. I'm not going anywhere. I promise." Jack stalked to the liquor cabinet. He couldn't believe the way Cara looked. Her face was milk-white and covered with a slick sheen. Her eyes darted back and forth in a short spasmodic rhythm; her tongue licked her lips every few seconds.

Nervously, he poured her a glass of vermouth, took scotch for himself. All at once he felt a hand on his arm and turned. Cara kissed him, hard and long. A desperate kiss. Then she said in a low voice, "It's nice to be home." Her eyes never left his face.

"Hey, you just ambushed me!"

She laughed wanly, knowing full well he was trying to keep things light. "Well, now that I have you cornered, I have a confession to make. I missed you terribly." Jack let a sad smile move across his lips. "Well," Cara said steadily, "do you want to take it from there?"

"No." Jack feigned playfulness. "You carry the ball. I'm speechless." He handed Cara her drink.

She looked at him. Overcome by the futility of anything she could possibly do, she said, "Where do we go from here, Jack?"

"Where do you want to go?"

"I don't know," she said, seeming to look for the right words. None came. She lifted her glass. "To your health."

"And yours."

"Thank you."

They both sipped their drinks.

"While I was in the hospital," she said after a moment, "I had time to run my fingers through the Yellow Pages and make a list of all the hobby shops in the metropolitan area. I can use a hobby, don't you think? I've considered everything from glassblowing to collecting zarfs."

"Collecting what?"

"Zarfs—drinking mugs. Dangerous hobby, really. Glass-blowing sounds interesting. What do you suggest?"

Jack tried; he struggled to put himself in her place, to feel and think as she might feel and think. He made up his mind and said what he thought Cara would want him to say. "I think yesterday was a bummer—so what? Today is today. I think we should start having people up for dinner right away. Some close friends."

Cara stared off into space, while Jack watched her expectantly. Finally, she grunted and heaved herself back onto the couch. "Good," she said, being careful to avoid false enthusiasm. "We'll get Frank Austin over here. I'll feed him the same crap they threw at me for the last five days. Christ, I sure didn't have any trouble sticking to my diet."

"Diet?" Jack looked at her strangely. She was already too thin. "Are you dieting?"

"Oh, you're so fucking smart," she said without rancor. "When have I ever not been dieting?"

"But you shouldn't be on one now."

"Do you think I'm too thin?"

"Not too—just."

"Oh, that's jim-dandy."

"What is?"

She glanced at the drink in her hand. "I forget—I'm not supposed to drink."

"Why?"

"Because of these little suckers." She waved a pill bottle in front of his face.

"What are they?" he inquired.

"Pain-killers, sleeping pills—sedatives, who knows. Time to take one. Would you get me a glass of water, please."

"Sure."

When he ventured from the kitchen, Cara was standing by the window. She popped the pill into her mouth, swallowing it down with a gulp of water. She smiled at him without speaking. He could see she was thinking things over.

"Kiss me," she said, dropping her arms around his shoulders. They kissed. His hand mechanically reached for her buttocks.

"Do you want it?" she asked unexpectedly.

Jack answered quickly, automatically. "Of course." This lie depressed him. It always depressed him when it was necessary to lie to her.

"Good," she cooed.

She entered the bedroom first, turned on the light, then slowly glanced around the room. Jack and she had devoured each other in this room a thousand times, but today it seemed important to her that it be something special.

He stared at her.

"What would you like?" she asked.

Jack hesitated. "Leave just your heels on. And your bra."

"My watch?" she asked, slipping off her blouse.

"Yes, leave it on."

"Don't you undress, all right? Just open your zipper."

"All right."

He watched her strip. Something was missing. Nothing stirred inside him.

She turned to face him as she removed her panties, one leg at a time, balancing well on her high-heel shoes. "Will you remove the bra later?"

"Yes, later."

Her breasts heaved as she kissed him.

"Shall I walk around for you?" she asked.

"No. Just sit at the edge of the bed."

She sat and let Jack look at her, tossing her hair back, parting her legs slightly, letting the heels of her shoes dig into the hard wooden floor. Then she lay back and opened her legs wider, letting her hands rest on the inner portion of her thighs. "Do you still like it, Jack? Do you?"

Jack moved away, embarrassed. Cara knew in an instant what his problem was. She sat up on the bed. "Jack?"

"I'm sorry, Cara."

"Come over here and sit down." She patted the bed beside

her. He slumped down next to her. She took his hand and raised it to her face, rubbing it softly on her cheek, kissing it. "It's all right," she said. "We'll get back into it. Believe me . . . I love you." She leaned over his body, unbuttoning his shirt, and put her lips to his right nipple; his eyes closed, and then she reached for his soft penis and put it into her mouth, not really sucking it, but just encompassing it: sort of protecting it from its nakedness. A swallow of pride, of love, a warm, conscious act of communion.

When Jack next peered into the bedroom, Cara was asleep, curled up into a comfortable ball on top of the bedspread. He sat on the window seat and waited quietly, glancing occasionally from the rain-stained windows. He sat there for an hour, hardly moving. He dozed off once, but mostly he watched Cara sleep.

The soft October dusk was calm. He held out his hands. They were trembling slightly. It had not gone well with Cara. But, he reassured himself, it hadn't gone that badly either.

His face became slightly distorted as an image of Rose slipped past his mind's eye. His thoughts raced with sudden erotic bewilderment—and fear. Would he be able to see Rose again now that Cara was back? Cara. He dared not move, fearing to wake her. Fearing that she would be able to see his innermost thoughts. The strange thing, Jack decided, was that he loved Cara. So sad. That he could love her, and yet feel so apart from her. Different. That was it. He was different now. Rose and he made up something new. This newness had changed him. Cara had wanted to isolate him, to hide him away. Little did she know, it was now too late.

Poor Cara. Did she know that eventually he would have to cast her adrift? Sink or swim, it would have to be done.

CHAPTER 5

Monday, October 20
5:30 P.M.

THE GIRL, REFLECTED DETECTIVE LOU JAFFY, HAD BEEN A real knockout. He bit dispassionately into ham and cheese on a hard roll and followed it with a cold swig of beer. He always ate after a particularly messy homicide, not because he had a need any longer to prove something to himself, but rather due to the habit of years.

Yep, the girl had been very attractive, he thought, glancing at his watch. He had just returned from the morgue where he'd viewed what was left of Mitzi Karp's body. She had been raped and then murdered. Someone had used her body as a dart board, having punctured it twelve times with an ice pick. Scanning her body as it lay on the porcelain table, he had asked himself the same old questions: What kind of person commits such a crime? And what kind of person ends up being the victim?

He shifted in his chair slightly and ran the coroner's report on Mitzie Karp over in his head. "Crushed trachea, fractured jaw and multiple stab wounds inflicted within the chest region and between the shoulder blades. Semen discovered on the victim's face, hands, and in her throat. Blood type discernible from semen: Type B."

Jaffy was a good cop. Smart and quick with paperwork, a feel for what was important and what was bullshit. He could keep his mouth shut when it needed to be shut; he could open it when it needed to be opened. He had a fair amount of vitality left for forty-seven and he was courageous and tough.

He had acquired the toughness over the years. It came of forcing himself to act in times of crisis. Of being shot in the chest and coming back. Of looking into the sea of waxen faces, of seeing gaping mortal wounds and cultivating the ability to tune it all out. To sift through human tragedy, searching for threads of truth, and to weave of that truth a net for the enemy. The enemy became his personal enemy, hated and relentlessly pursued. The hate for the enemy was his gift to the victim.

Jaffy was winding down now. The beer had hit him just right. The first few days on a case were hard because so much kept coming at you. The victim, the survivors, the scene of the crime, the kind of crime, suspects who had histories of similar crimes, searching the area for possible witnesses. Sifting the witnesses. Who hadn't wanted to see something and saw it anyway? Who wanted to see something and hadn't? Where had the victim come from, where was she going and who knew about it?

He would interview every possible witness personally, trusting no one to make impressions for him, listening over and over to tapes of likely witnesses. Finding the holes, the inconsistencies. Seeing the evasive look in the eyes. Finding out how many people thought they saw the same person. Getting the police artist to sketch out the person. Putting the sketch on the front pages of the newspaper, on television news. Making the rounds of all the local bars in the area. So much of this type of thing started in a bar.

Although Jaffy belonged to the Sex Crime Squad, due to the nature of the crime he had been temporarily reassigned to Homicide. Different aspects of the Mitzie Karp case were assigned to each detective, the rationale being that they would sneak up on the killer from all directions. Jaffy was to focus on the victim's relationships. The interdepartmental race was on. Fair enough.

Jaffy reached for his hat and left the office.

Rose Carpenter lived in 10E. Jaffy pressed the button and lifted the small intercom phone. He waited, but there was no response. He pressed the button again, twice this time.

"Yes?" Rose's voice sounded faint.

"Miss Carpenter?"

"Yes."

"My name is Lou Jaffy. Detective. New York Police Department. Can we talk for a few minutes?"

The girl on the other end hesitated for a moment, as if she hadn't heard right. "Detective?"

"Yes. Twentieth Precinct."

"Talk? About what?"

"It's about Mitzie Karp. I'm investigating her death."

"Oh."

The silence lasted so long that Jaffy was about to ring again when the buzzer snapped the front door free. He flung the phone down hastily and reached for the door.

Stepping from the elevator on the tenth floor, Jaffy removed his hat, scratched his partially balding head and moved down the hallway to 10E. He pressed the bell, then sneezed. He reached into his pocket, took away his handkerchief and blew his nose. He became suddenly aware that he had been waiting for the door to open for what he thought was an unusually long time. He pressed again, muttering something about when you press bells you expect people to open the goddamn door.

"Miss Carpenter?" he called.

Rose flung the door open so suddenly that she scared the hell right out of him.

"Yes," she cried.

"God."

"Sorry. I . . . I wasn't dressed."

"It's all right. I jog."

"What?"

"My heart can take it. Getting frightened half to death, I mean."

"Come in, please."

"Right." He sneezed. "Sorry."

"God bless you."

"I've always liked that." He grinned. "I hate to sneeze when I'm alone and miss the blessing."

Rose immediately found him odd-looking for a detective. A small man in his mid-forties, his body was slender and wiry; he shuffled his feet as he walked. Dressed in a plaid sports coat, white shirt and striped tie, he more resembled a door-to-door salesman than a detective.

"Miss Carpenter?" he was saying now with an air of officially beginning their conversation.

"Yes," she murmured, allowing herself to be prodded.

"How do you do. Detective Lou Jaffy. Sex Crime Squad. Twentieth Precinct."

"May I see your badge?"

"Oh, yeah. Sure." He held his identification in front of him.

Rose hardly looked at it. "You should take a closer look," he said, "it could be a phony."

Rose suddenly found his voice pleasingly deep, resonant, and kind.

"I wouldn't know whether it was false or not," she said.

"Then why ask to see it?" he said without rancor.

"Television."

"Right."

"I watch a lot of television."

"Right."

Rose watched him take in the apartment, his deep blue eyes darting from one corner of the room to the next.

"Nice place," he said, and then gave Rose an appraising look.

"Thank you."

"Big."

"Just the one bedroom." Rose smiled shortly.

"Compared to mine—it's big!" He placed his crumpled hat on the dining table.

"Please, sit down," Rose offered nervously.

"Thanks." He planted himself solidly in one of the dining chairs. She took a seat across the table from him. "Well, now— I just have a few questions," he said, taking a small note pad and pencil from his breast pocket.

"About Mitzie?"

"A shame. A real shame," he breathed.

"I know . . ."

"What was she? Thirty-two." He shrugged. "Who knows why these things happen. But they do and that's why I'm here."

"I understand."

"You know, I just said to my wife the other night—it seems crime is woven right into the fabric of our society. What's the answer? More laws? Fewer laws, stiffer penalties, lesser court sentences? Who knows. It's like the weather, we all talk about it but we can't seem to control it. We're smarter today, better educated. We have better equipment—still, the criminal mind is relentless. And sexual crimes, well . . ." He broke off, scratching the bald spot on the top of his head.

Rose reached for a cigarette. Jaffy lit it.

"So . . ." Jaffy paused, appearing to be at a loss for words.

"Would you like a cup of coffee?" Rose asked.

"No, thanks. It makes me nervous." He gave her a warm

smile. "So . . . tell me about Saturday night. At the Cottontail Club. There was a fight . . . let's see." He glanced at his note pad. "A Miss Julie Lemon was physically assaulted by Danny Romano. Is that right?"

"Yes."

"Mitzie Karp had a few words with Romano right after the fight. Ugly words."

"That's right."

"Nicklas Nuzzo, your boss, said that you and he were right in the thick of it."

"I was standing with Nick."

"Do you remember what Romano said to Mitzie before he left the club?"

Rose shook her head. "Not really."

He glanced down at his pad and read. "'You're going to get it one of these days and I'm going to be there to enjoy it.' Do you remember Mitzie saying that?" he asked patiently.

Rose hesitated. "Well, she said something like that. Yes."

He continued to read from the pad. "'And then again, you're liable to get it, and I'll be there to enjoy it.' Do you recall Romano saying that?"

"Yes. Something similar."

Jaffy sighed. "Then Romano did threaten her?"

"No. Not exactly. I mean, that's really not a threat, is it?"

Jaffy folded his arms and stared down at his note pad. He nodded briefly.

"Do you think Danny did it?" Rose asked.

"Not sure. We have an APB out on him now. I believe he could have."

Rose began to tap her fingers nervously against the tabletop. Jaffy went on then about Mitzie's background. In high school, she was virtually uncontrollable, especially by her parents. She'd had an abortion and was arrested once for prostitution—a fact Jaffy's voice underscored.

Rose stirred. "Prostitution? That can't be right."

"It's a matter of police record."

"If it happened, you can add to that record it was because of her husband."

Jaffy shrugged.

"He controlled her with his fists. A real hero type. Mitzi told me about him."

"Anyway," he went on, "what I'm most interested in knowing is what she was into now. Perhaps . . ."

Rose interrupted, purposeful, a little flame of impatience leaping in her. "What makes you think she was into anything?"

He hesitated, then said, "I'd better explain."

"Yes, why don't you."

"Motive. That's what I need to understand. Was her death a whim to satisfy a depraved appetite, or was it . . . let's say revenge."

"Revenge?"

"Yes. Sex has always been a prime ingredient in badger games, extortion rackets—blackmail. Sometimes it gets out of hand."

A stabbing annoyance rushed through Rose. "That's ridiculous. Mitzie wasn't that kind. Why are you trying to accuse her of these things? Because she worked at the Cottontail Club? I work at the club. Are you accusing me of the same thing?"

His lips curved, and his expression moved into a pleasant smile. "I'm not accusing her of anything. Part of my job is to find out why these things happen, that's all."

Rose was angry now. "Well, her death wasn't because she was involved in blackmail! That much I'm sure of."

"Fine."

There was a long silence.

In a cool and deliberate expression of what was really on his mind, he said, "I also wanted to ask you about your friend. The one who came into the Cottontail Club Saturday night."

"My friend?" Rose stirred uncomfortably.

"Yes. Julie Lemon said that he came in earlier. Then again right after you left the club. Around one-thirty. Mitzie Karp was talking to him most of the night after that."

"I . . . don't know who that could be," she said, her stomach knotting.

"Strange. Miss Lemon said that he seemed to know you pretty well. At least that's what Mitzie had told her."

"I have no idea who he was." Rose reached out and snuffed her cigarette.

Jaffy smiled reflectively. For what seemed like a minute he sat there. Finally, he said, "You see, the trouble is, no one really paid that much attention to him. We can't seem to get a description. I thought . . ."

"I really wasn't expecting anyone." His gaze became intense, but he didn't comment. Rose added nervously, "Guys do that all the time. Use one girl's name to get to know the other."

"Then you don't believe he was actually a friend of yours?"

"No," she said impatiently.

Jaffy eyed her skeptically but let the matter drop.

Rose watched as he wrote the information down in his note pad. The sight of him scribbling gave her pause to think. In her mind, she saw Mitzie's green Buick. Mitzie being slid into the ambulance with a carelessness that said DOA. Far back in the darkness, someone watched. Rose started as Jaffy thumped his pencil against his pad and seemed to hesitate. She had the sudden crazy instinct to tell him of the dream, every improbable detail.

She looked at him, sharp-eyed as a cat. What purpose would it serve? He would merely stare at her with amusement as Jack had done. Or shake his head pityingly as Dr. Cindrella had done, eager to believe her a witless child. No, she decided, this was not the time.

Lou Jaffy sighed, scratching his eyebrow. "Do you know if Mitzie had a falling-out with anyone. Nick? Any of the other waitresses?"

"She had no enemies that I know of."

"Did she ever mention anything that might help us? Personal things?" Jaffy looked at her quizzically, as if he hoped to be let in on some great secret.

"No," Rose said flatly. "She was a very happy girl. No problems that I know of."

"Okay," he said, tugging on his earlobe. Rose had the impression that he was disappointed. "Well, I guess that about covers it," he said. He stood up slowly and reached for his hat. "If I have any more questions, I'll be in touch."

He stepped toward the door. "By the way, were you aware that Mitzie Karp had worked for Romano at one time? As a model."

"No, I wasn't," she said quietly, not meeting his gaze.

"That's where Nicklas first met her. I hear Romano was pretty steamed when she went to work for Nick. Now, that doesn't surprise me. But what does surprise me is that Romano let her go. It makes me ask, was Romano indebted to her?

Were there favors owed? You see—sex and crime usually go hand and hand. It's hard to determine where one leaves off and the other begins."

"In what way?"

"Well, I really don't think I should . . ."

"No, please. I'm curious."

"Well now, it's only a pet theory of mine, you understand. But I believe there's a comparison to be made between both acts. For instance, a thief forces his way into a house. What do we have? The act of penetration. We call it breaking and entering. A fairly apt description for the sexual act. And the next thing a thief does after committing the crime is to withdraw, escape. After the sex act, the result is the same. Withdrawal, both physically and emotionally. No doubt most people would find this farfetched, but I believe the comparison is there. Sometimes a criminal gets carried away, and he commits both acts at the same time. He doesn't mean to. He merely wanted to break in. Steal. But suddenly he discovers there is a woman in the house—alone. He can't help himself. He goes one step further. This could very well be the case here. Someone waited for Mitzie in the back seat of her car. To steal. That's all, and then got carried away. Or someone wanted to punish her—not much, just a little. Who knows? One thing is certain. It happened. My job is to find out who did it and why."

He fell silent, then gazed directly at Rose. "Do you mind me asking you a personal question?"

"No."

"I'm sure you've been asked this a thousand times, but I'm curious. Why do you work at the Cottontail Club?"

Rose shrugged. "It's a job. It pays well. Why do you ask?"

"I don't know. Maybe because I have a daughter your age. I worry about her. A lot. You understand. It's tough today. It's like the whole world is having a nervous breakdown. I hate to see it happen to her. Thank God she's married now, expecting her first child."

Rose smiled weakly. "That's nice."

"Yeah." He looked at Rose narrowly. "You know, if this was the perverted act of a twisted mind, then I suggest that you be careful. These things have a way of repeating themselves."

Rose became aware of the tight, urgent tone in his voice. She nodded blankly.

"So . . . there's nothing else you can think of," Jaffy concluded. "Nothing you may have forgotten? Just some little thing . . . I don't know."

"Mitzie," she said unexpectedly. "You don't know Mitzie." With relief, she realized this was what had been bothering her. Mitzie's past, this was all he knew. The uncontrollable teenager. Prostitution. Nothing about Mitzi the survivor, who was a hell of a lot more than all those black marks on a piece of paper. "She was a wonderful human being," Rose said quietly, tears welling in her eyes. "Something really special. Maybe that's not important, but—"

Jaffy scribbled briskly. "I've made a note of it. But, Miss Carpenter, a life like that—keeping company with the wrong element . . . mixing drinks for the drunks and listening to their stories . . . all that takes a toll. It can't be helped, you know."

"It didn't ruin Mitzie," she said stoutly.

He simply shrugged. "It killed her," he said regretfully. "Well, I'll be in touch." He stood as if frozen in a slight bow, his hands clasped in front of him. After a moment he removed the cigarette from his mouth, then crossed silently to the door and let himself out.

Rose sighed, loathing the image before her, yet she was unable to stop her brush from moving. She stroked viciously at the canvas, stroked blacks, and greens, and brilliant reds; paused, studying, smudged with a dirty rag . . . Why couldn't she see him, capture his image? Her night person.

She frowned, stroked again, her forearm moving in a series of quick, fierce movements. The light from the window suddenly burst upon the canvas before her, heightening the image, which leapt forward, then just as quickly receded as the room dimmed. Holding the brush down at her side she paused, stared without seeing, breathless.

Before her the uncompleted painting still stood, devoid of light, of life—a woven composition of harsh lines, a flicker of an eye, a splash of red dripping over a black center.

The corners of her mouth tightened, drew down slightly. Meaning: what has meaning . . . Far off, in the twilight reaches of her mind, a great, dark image stood, growing, gaining in fury. . . . Why hadn't she told Jaffy about her dream? About *him?*

She thrust her hands against her eyes. Rubbed hard.

Paint with the thrill of agony—someone had once said.

I can't. I can't capture his image. It keeps jumping. I . . . I can't see. I CAN'T SEE!

She took her hands from her eyes, opened them. At the center of the canvas an image was forming, circular, delicate, sweeping to the far edges now. She stared at it. Inside the circle another image, moving, growing larger, spreading.

She pulled herself up and backward with a start. The painting seemed to be changing shape of its own accord. No, there must be order. An artist must create order.

Now all movement stopped.

Stood still.

Slowly she got to her feet.

No, you're dead. You can't get up—you're dead.

Straining, each step an effort, she moved to the window, where she looked out over the gray slab of a city, hugging her body for warmth. Her mind seemed to work independently of her will, so that she found herself thinking of the one thing she did not want to think about. Lance. Where had it all gone? she wondered. All those wonderful dreams, the promise of everlasting love and devotion. Lance had meant everything to her. He had been all things to her. Friend, lover, husband; so much so, that for a time she believed that she would disappear without him.

Suddenly the telephone was ringing. She turned with a start. Was it Jack? Oh, please dear God, let it be Jack. Hurriedly, she picked up the receiver. "Hello?"

Raspy and low, the breathing slithered into her ear. Then came the muffled voice, saying, ". . . Just be ready."

"What?"

". . . Just be ready," the voice whispered again.

Before Rose could respond, the phone went dead. Her eyes shifted to the receiver and saw that it was shaking in her hand. Almost at once she slammed the phone down. Breathless, she waited. Waited for the phone to ring again. If she could only talk to him. Really talk to him. Maybe that's what he needed. Someone to talk to. If only he would call back, stay on the line—talk to her; then everything would be all right.

Transfixed, she stared at the phone until she was certain that he wasn't going to call back. Not now at any rate. Still she remained rooted, unable to move, thinking twenty things at once—thinking, among other things, what Dr. Cindrella had said. That every time she thought of Lance, she subconsciously invited the intruder into her mind.

She blinked at the phone. Was that what had just happened? Had the phone rung at all? She wasn't sure now. Had she really heard a voice on the other end of the line?

On impulse she reached for her pocketbook, fished around until she found Jack's number, then dialed. She stood hunched over the kitchen counter, waiting.

"Hello?" Jack's voice sounded odd. Dazed.

Flustered, she laughed. "Jack?"

"Rose?" Jack spoke in a half-whisper.

"Yes."

There was a slight pause.

"I just called to see if you were real," she said, stroking her hair, still laughing.

"What?"

"Real. That I hadn't imagined you. But you're there, all right."

"Yes, I'm here," Jack said solemnly.

"Do you miss me? Lie if you have to, or . . ."

"Rose, Cara has come home," he said hastily.

"What?"

"She's asleep now."

Her expression darkened. "But . . . when?"

"A little while ago. Caught me by complete surprise."

"Oh." Rose paused for a moment, not knowing what to say. "I'll . . . I'll hang up then."

"No. Rose, I want to see you."

"But . . ."

"Tonight. You're off tonight, aren't you?"

"Yes."

"Can you meet me?"

Rose regarded the situation silently.

"Rose?"

"Yes—I'm here."

"Please. I need you. I can explain everything when I see you."

"You don't have to explain. I understand."

"Will you meet me? Say, eight o'clock?"

"Where?" she asked, gritting her teeth.

"There's a little bar on the corner of Thirteenth Street and Eleventh Avenue. The Seahorse. It's near my apartment. I can't really be gone that long. I'm sorry to ask you to come down here, but . . ."

"No, it's all right. I'll be in the area. It's fine." She gave a flat laugh. "Jack, I do understand. And I'm glad you feel the way you do."

"Are you?"

"Yes, I . . ." She broke off.

"I've got to hang up now."

"All right. I'll see you at eight."

Abruptly the line went dead. Rose let a few seconds pass, maybe more, before hanging up the phone. She reached for a cigarette, tapping it firmly on the counter top before lighting it. Suddenly she found herself resenting Jack. Resenting the fact that she had been forced again to lean on the shoulders of a man.

For a short while, after Lance and she had separated, she'd felt self-sufficient, strong. There was something exhilarating about being unattached. But now her independence was working against her. When had it all begun to change? When . . . dear God . . . had her life become a series of painful disasters?

She sat for a long time staring at the front door. She knew she was thinking, but when she tried to focus on her thoughts, her mind seemed to unravel. She floundered, then remembered. The Dixie Hotel. Was Cheryl still there?

She crushed out her cigarette.

Twelfth Street and Tenth Avenue. The Dixie Hotel.

Moments later, she had her coat on and was heading out the door.

CHAPTER 6

NOT QUITE AN HOUR LATER, ROSE WAS LED INTO THE HOTEL manager's office, located to the rear of the building. Outside, traffic moaned through the congested streets, the sound a harsh murmuring that rattled the windows of his small, airtight office.

The manager, studiously ignoring her presence, scrutinized an assortment of cigars in a humidor on his desk. Finally he selected one, closed the lid, and looked up at Rose with the cool, appraising eyes of an insurance adjuster about to knock down a claim.

"Her suitcase will be here in a minute," he wheezed, then smiled slightly.

Rose did not return the smile. Instead, she lit a cigarette and settled back, trying to loosen the knot in her stomach.

"You her sister?" he asked.

"No. Just a friend."

The manager stared at her, almost squinting, as if there were a message written across her face. "That isn't what you said before," he mumbled.

"What?" Rose flicked her ash.

"Before. You told the desk clerk you were a relative."

"That was to get his attention," Rose said sarcastically.

He affected a look of deep confoundment, and was about to speak, when the office door opened. A smallish man, with a rounded head attached to his plump body with no intervening neck, stepped briskly into the room.

"Put the suitcase on the desk, Marty."

The man did as he was instructed and left the room, glancing back at Rose as he closed the door.

"This her suitcase?" the manager asked, chewing on his cigar.

Rose stiffened. "Yes."

He lifted the identification tag and read. "Cheryl Arthur, Two-eight-one Ocean Drive, Miami, Florida."

For whatever reason, Rose could not remember ever feeling what she now felt as she watched him fumble with Cheryl's suitcase.

"May I look inside?" she said glumly.

"I don't see why not." He pressed the latch and lifted the lid of the suitcase.

Rose moved behind the desk, noticing that the manager was smiling, a morbid smile, his thin lips pressing the juice out of his cigar. Closer now, she noticed that he smelled of the kind of liquid soap found in a public washroom.

"Not much in there," he said.

"You checked her room Friday evening?" Rose asked, staring into the suitcase.

"Saturday evening. We were filling up fast. That's why we moved her out."

"What made you think she wasn't coming back?" Rose pushed aside Cheryl's pale green negligee and came face to face with a small picture of Lance in a gold frame. She picked it up.

"She said she was only staying a day or two. When we hadn't heard from her by Saturday afternoon, we checked the room. The bed hadn't been slept in. When I questioned the maid, she said the bed had never been slept in. That's when I knew she had skipped out."

"Skipped out?" Rose repeated, gazing at the picture. Lance was posed seductively, lounging on the arm of a couch wearing only a small terrycloth bathrobe. His tanned body was almost entirely exposed. Humiliated, ripped with jealousy, Rose dropped the picture back into the suitcase.

"Like I said, not much in there." A grin appeared on the manager's face.

"You said you thought she skipped out?"

"Oh, yes. It happens all the time. People take a room on speculation for a day or two. Then when something turns up for them, they decide to skip out without paying." He shrugged. "She must have found what she was looking for."

When Rose looked back at him, his eyes had a strange vacancy to them, yet he grinned tightly and added, "Like I said, it happens all the time."

"She never paid you for the room?"

"That's right."

"How much does she owe?"

"Let's see. Three nights at . . ."

"Two nights. Thursday and Friday."

"Three. It was well after checkout time when we moved her out."

"How much?"

"Ninety dollars plus tax."

"Will you take a personal check?"

"Sorry," he said, no apology in his voice.

"If I bring you the money in cash. May I have her suitcase?"

"If you show proper identification and sign for it."

"Fine," Rose said stonily.

"There's also a storage charge."

"A what?"

"We charge five dollars a day for storage. We'll figure that out the day you pick up the suitcase."

Rose shook her head in disdain.

He smiled slightly, almost coyly. "You don't like me much, do you?"

"Not really." Rose picked up her pocketbook.

"Well, at least you're honest." His smile had crossed over now, and was openly ironic. "Our policy here is clear enough. We supply rooms, no questions asked. Until people leave without paying. Then we get tough. We don't have much of a choice." He paused for a moment, then added, "I'd like to help you, really. But I've got this problem. I can't see cheating the hotel so your friend can go around cheating other people." He smiled.

You sanctimonious crumb, Rose thought, and stormed from the hotel.

The evening edition of the *Post* was still carrying Mitzie Karp's death on page two. Rose stared at the picture. It was all too familiar. Mitzie's body covered with a white sheet, being slid into the back of the ambulance. The picture was identical to the image in her dream.

Rose tucked the paper under her arm and headed for the Seahorse.

Jack met her at the door. Her resentment of him immediately vanished. She clung to him for a desperate moment.

"I'm glad you've come," he said softly.

"So am I."

Inside the bar, Jack glanced at the bigger of the two men, who was tending bar closest to the door. They sat at a corner table, Jack angling his body into the plush chair away from the bartender's view. He wondered if the man had recognized him on the way in. If he had realized Jack was in there four nights ago causing a disturbance. Apparently he hadn't.

After ordering two martinis, Jack turned to face Rose directly for the first time. She smiled awkwardly and reached for a cigarette. Jack did the same. Cigarettes lit, drinks on the table, they still hadn't uttered a word.

Through the pale swirl of smoke, their eyes met for an instant, then moved away.

"She was showering when I left," he said offhandedly.

"How is she?"

Jack found himself almost stammering. "Depressed. On edge."

"Do you think . . ." Rose broke off.

"What?"

"She's not . . . suicidal, is she?"

"No, I don't think so."

Rose felt a swift rush of relief.

Jack managed to smile in a lopsided way and wished he could have totally believed that. But he wasn't sure. Cara was ticking away inside like a time bomb. She was really capable of anything.

"Would you like to order something to eat?" Jack said, breaking the awkward silence.

"No. Thanks."

He glanced at his watch. His heart was beating oddly. It was as though he were experiencing the concentrated essence of the last week all at once.

"Have you ever felt like two people?" he asked. "Like someone has cut you in two, so that one part is constantly crawling around looking for the other?"

"Jack, it's not your fault."

"I know." He looked at his glass reflectively. "But still, it makes me feel strange. When I try to look at it from Cara's point of view, I have to admit, I don't feel much of anything. All I seem to feel is this anger that it's all happening to me, and not to someone else."

Rose stared at her glass for a moment. "Maybe you're discovering that you love her more than you realize."

"I don't know." He shrugged.

"You feel guilty, don't you? About us."

"I'm here, aren't I?"

"But you don't like the idea—I can tell."

Until this moment, he hadn't known what he was going to say, whether he would tell Rose it was all over between Cara and him, or stand his ground and tell Rose it had been nice while it lasted, but Cara came first. The problem was he felt no guilt at all. Neither for what he was doing, nor for what he had done in the past. He took a deep drag on his cigarette, taking time to understand his feelings. Finally he said, "I have to think about us. You and me."

Rose drew a breath, shifting her weight in the chair. "But we hardly know each other."

"Is that the way you feel?" He gave her a rueful look.

"Not really. But I don't want to be the one who gets in Cara's way. I know how she must feel."

"Do you know how I feel?"

"I'm trying to."

He regarded her silently. There was a look of sadness in her eyes, like a little girl lost. He felt suddenly unable to help her, unable to help himself really. He had been so confused the last few days that it was like trying to work himself through a maze of briars, with thorns turned at sharp angles; no matter which way he turned, his flesh was torn, which sent him scurrying in a new direction, only to become tangled again. More cuts, more confusion.

In desperation he blurted out, "I think I'm in love with you, Rose."

And Rose thought: This is where I say go home to your wife, Jack. Don't call me, don't think of me too often, don't even look at other girls and compare them to me. "I think I love you too." She had said it against her will, the words battling their way past her protesting lips.

"Are you sure? Absolutely sure?"

"Are you?"

He took a long uneasy moment, and said, "Yes."

"So am I," she answered with surprising speed, then moved forward, pressed her thigh against the leg of the table, bracing herself. The still air was heavy with the smell of burnt candle wax and alcohol. She could feel her passion stirring. A quiet exultancy had begun to work in her, moving lightly, then surging.

"Will we be able to find time together?" she asked. "Real time?"

Jack was suddenly distracted. He watched as the bartender moved to draw the drapes over the front window.

"What's the matter?" she asked.

"Oh . . . the bartender—he looks familiar."

She studied Jack's face for a moment. His lips were pursed slightly. He was drifting away from her, thinking hard about something. She continued studying his features against the pale backlight of the bar; such a sensitive face; it hadn't seemed to age much in thirty-three years. Only slightly. The small lines around his eyes, perhaps that was it. No, the eyes themselves. They bore his age.

She sighed, knowing that her longing for him ran deep.

"I want to go home," she said suddenly, her fingers spread out across the table, clawlike and tense. "With you."

"Soon," he said in a half-whisper. "I'll come to you soon."

"Not tonight?"

He shook his head halfheartedly. "I can't." Then, looking into the thin face that seemed so near and yet so far away, he added, "I promise. We'll be together soon." He said it like a blood oath.

Rose sighed deeply. "I'm glad."

Jack glanced nervously at his watch.

Rose asked, "Is it recess time already?"

"I'm afraid so. I told Cara I was going shopping. The store will be closed soon."

The last remains of smoke coiled loosely, drifted over the faint glow of the candle. Jack stared at Rose now as if he had never seen her before. The same but different. She stared back at him, her eyelids blinking beneath slim black brows.

"I'll be with you tonight," he whispered. "In your dreams."

"In my dreams," she said shortly, and reached for her coat.

* * *

She did not look back at him as the door closed behind her. In the street, traffic flowed steadily; the curb as usual was lined with cars parked bumper to bumper. She stood for a moment facing the river, and the sharp night wind whipped against her face.

She put her back to the wind and walked over to Tenth Avenue, then turned north, heading for the subway. The street was spotted with the usual stores: supermarket, hardware store, cleaners and the five-and-dime. All were protected by heavy metal gates.

At the corner she paused, and the image of Cheryl's bloody body flashed before her. *Please, Rose, we must talk . . .* She turned abruptly and crossed the street, as if her sudden movement would dislodge Cheryl's image and send it skittering into the night. She walked on, head bent, and found herself in a quieter part of town. Here the evening mist moved in a hazy way, seeping into crevices and settling on the windshields of parked cars; dried stiff limbs of a solitary tree creaked in the wind.

Suddenly the surrounding area had a feeling of déjà vu about it. The street loomed semilit, each light at either end of the street casting a soft steady glow, while at the center of the street a lamplight flickered on and off, sending brief shocks of light into recessed doorways, then rendering them dark as caves. First a strident raw light, then total blackness.

Rose jerked to a stop. She stood on watery legs inspecting the street. It all seemed so familiar. The long row of shabby buildings. The flashing streetlamp. And across the street, isolated, its face a crumbling mask of decay, a red-bricked building that had long since outlived its usefulness. It stood silent and alone, its guts torn out, its windows vacant and peering.

In that instant Rose knew that it was the building in her dream.

The same building in which she had seen Cheryl raped and murdered. Once again the dream flashed through her mind. The building's crumbling walls, the narrow windows, the crack that extended from the roof and ran scarlike in a zigzag direction, until it vanished just above the sealed entranceway. It was all the same.

Promptly, the lamplight flickered on, sending the sharp light of speculation skimming through Rose's mind. Cheryl must have first checked into the Dixie Hotel, then gone on to the Cottontail Club. Not finding Rose there, she would have headed back to the hotel, walking down Fourteenth Street to get back to the hotel.

At the corner of Tenth Avenue, Cheryl would have crossed the street, never noticing the flickering light, the momentary lapse of darkness. She would have walked past the building, and— Yes, it was possible.

Was Cheryl's body in that building?

Rose hesitated a moment longer, waited for some vision, some burst of illuminating, all-transforming light—a thunder-bolt, perhaps—something, anything to confirm the fact that she wasn't losing her mind, that, indeed, Cheryl's body was in that building.

The streetlight flickered.

All around her now, blackness.

She felt a brief jolt of fear, her eyes shifting from the dark-ened face of the building to the semilit street corner.

Should she go into the building? See for herself?

She blinked the thought away as she blinked away the sweat that ran in rivulets down her forehead. If she hesitated a moment longer, she believed, she would see her doom, solid as the blackness, all around her.

Slowly she turned and began walking away.

Moments later she was gone from the neighborhood.

CHAPTER 7

Monday, October 20
9:30 P.M.

DARKNESS.

Then a sudden burst of light.

From behind the window of the monitoring room, Reese Cindrella could see the diamond-bursts of light go on and off in the sleep room at ten-second intervals. Staring into the darkness, he felt something inside his brain tug, tug again; a vicious pulling. Vexed for an instant, he tried to review the day's findings.

Alex Mana had demonstrated extraordinary paranormal phenomena, including psychokinetic powers. Using only his mind, Mana had caused a door to open and close by itself, a book to levitate for a moment in the air, and had shattered a mirror. Reese had heard of such powers, but today was the first time he'd actually witnessed them. "A spark of electricity is God in motion," Mana had said, then let the book that had been levitating fall to the floor.

At that precise moment, Reese had felt a sudden draft. A cold stream of air that had erupted from Mana's body. He had known then, conclusively, that Alex Mana could completely control the world around him. A hundred times, this eye-opening day, he had seen with dizzying vividness what the human mind was capable of.

And now, as before, Reese Cindrella stared at the monitor in dumb amazement. Once again Mana was doing the impossible.

Seated alone in the sleep room, it was Mana's task to predict which of the three lights mounted on the panel in front of him would light next. Right, left, or center? Having made his selection, he was to press the corresponding button under the light. If the light lit above the button he had pressed, the monitor recorded a direct hit. Thus far Mana had 92 percent accuracy. Precognition. The ability to predict that which hasn't happened yet. Alex Mana had this ability 92 percent of the time.

Reese turned slowly and wiped a large bead of sweat from his brow. Who was Alex Mana? And from what source did he draw his power? More importantly, could Reese gain control of this power? Use it to serve his own ends?

A pinprick of light flashed in the darkness. Reese glanced at the monitor. Another direct hit.

The blackness was full of flies and bees, and he was one of them: mad drone and buzzing, legs scraping toward remote slits of light, too mindless to know what life was . . . a mob of acrid-smelling insects committing suicide against man's light, against man's clever God-like bubbles.

Alex Mana breathed fiercely through his wide nostrils, making an awkward gesture of exorcism with his hand to drive away the thought. Another thought quickly sprang up in its place.

"I had him put away," his mother is saying. "The Lucian Children's Home. For playing hooky. He always had problems. Always."

The judge nods.

"I don't believe he molested that girl like they say. But I believe he was there. And if he is guilty, he deserves what he gets." His mother wipes tears from her eyes.

"It's a terrible thing to raise children," she adds. "I've always told him, you've got to respect yourself and other people. And then something like this happens. I just can't believe it."

The judge looks at her sternly. "When you had him sent away, weren't you aware he would meet the worst kind of people?"

"He was playing hooky . . . messing around with drugs. So I took him to family court and had him declared a person who needed supervision." She pauses for a moment. "When he came home, he was real good at first. He stayed home nights. He even helped clean the house." She blinks back the tears in her reddened eyes. "But then he got sick; I don't know what happened to him. He spent eight months in a hospital.

He was mentally disturbed, that's what they said. When they released him, he started with the drugs again. So we moved here. It didn't do any good though, and now this. I can't believe he would do such a terrible thing . . ."

Alex was crying now as he watched the light flash on the panel before him. Left. Who do they think I am? I function. I function—well. There's nothing wrong with me. See, Mama, I don't need drugs anymore.

Right.

I'm educated now. Higher significant data can only be acquired by going into ourselves. We are the observers—the interpreters of the world.

Right.

All this chaos, Mama, is in man's bewildered imagination. In his fearful ignorance. I have this vision now, Mama.

Center.

That I am the unsuspected resources of all ages. Me. Inside me. The moon is no longer unreachable. They call me mad. But I'm not mad, Mama. I'm quite sane. Everything is going down smooth, all the time now, Mama. I'm on top of it. Really on top of it. Watch me.

Left. You see, a direct hit.

Right, right. Again. I'm fantastic.

Left, center, right—center. I'm on fire, Mama.

10:00 P.M.

Rose slowly turned back the quilt, her gaze fixed on the dormiphone beside her bed. Jack and she had agreed to reset their timers for twelve, three, and six o'clock. At each time interval a matching sound would play over each dormiphone. Upon hearing the sound, they would awaken and record their dreams. This done, they would return to sleep and continue dreaming.

Rose turned off the bedside lamp and stood for a time in the darkness. She tried to imagine Jack there.

Slowly she got into the bed. She thought about dreams, the possibility of Jack experiencing hers. She being able to experience his. They would send each other messages; was it possible to make love together in a dream? Not merely through the imagination, but actually, physically make contact. Brain activity was known to be electrical; like a flash of lightning they could create physical pleasure. They could actually make love.

Make love, she thought.

Make love . . .

Finally, with considerable effort, she forced her eyes shut. She imagined herself sliding her hand into Jack's. A strong hand, she thought, yet light to the touch; in the crevices of her mind she saw its shape, the smooth flat palm, the elegantly long fingers . . . so loving and still was the hand, and then, Rose sensed the hand was beginning to move; like a strange explosion of flesh, it grew, expanded, larger and larger and larger until it was immense and throbbing with life, until it had grasped all of reality into its huge sweating palm.

Rose tried to pull away, but it was too late. She *was* the hand as it moved slowly toward her throat. No, not her throat— someone else's. The hand was clutching someone else's throat, tighter, squeezing, squeezing, squeezing . . . NO, DEAR GOD—NO!!

Suddenly the vision was gone and Rose held tight the side of the bed, making crying sounds, sounds that dissolved quickly into the night, and just as quickly her dream fled and she gave up all awareness . . .

And slept.

11:35 P.M.

Cara listened as Jack's breathing became heavy. He must be dreaming, she thought. She could only see a small portion of his face. His lips were twitching as if attempting to smile. He sighed deeply and rolled over on his back. His hand brushed against her side and then lay still. For a moment, she imagined the entire weight of his body on hers. His thrusting motion as he penetrated her. But the memory seemed to have outlived itself, and vanished quickly.

She watched him sleep silently now. There was little or no movement in his body. His respiration seemed to have completely stopped. Beneath his eyelids, she imagined his eyes staring into themselves, rather than staring out into the room. They seemed to have no awareness of her. She was nonexistent to him at that moment.

She didn't want to be there. Not like that. Not alone next to a corpse. She longed to hear his hoarse breathing, to feel the jerking of his muscles, the heaving of his chest. Anything but that dead emptiness.

As if Jack sensed her discomfort, he rolled over on his side to face the wall. And then, from below in the living room, a swift throbbing rhythm mounted, tense piano chords that slammed furiously.

Cara turned to listen. Was she imagining it? No, she could clearly hear someone banging on the piano. Jack's muscles jerked suddenly beneath the sheets. Still the grotesque banging of the piano continued.

She stirred from the bed. Putting on her robe, she moved into the hallway. Was this another attack of anxiety?

She hesitated for a brief instant, then turned on the hall light. Heart thumping, she moved to the edge of the stairs. The banging on the piano grew louder. She stared into the darkened room below. There was no sign of movement. Only the discordant sound of the piano.

Quickly she moved to the bottom step. The sound ceased. She stood for a long time gazing at the piano. Then walked around the house aimlessly, trying to escape the fear that she was actually going insane. But it still wasn't real unless voiced. She must not let herself think, speak. Hold tight. That's all she had to do was to hold tight.

She sat quietly and waited. She was breathing evenly. Her eyes were closed. She had a random thought: Jack was asleep, dreaming. As in the old days, she wondered what images were shimmering through his mind. Her heart thumped in anxiety. "Damn you," she moaned. "Damn you!" she cried.

She wanted to lash out at Jack, turn her sorrow to anger—anger she could deal with—but she couldn't find her voice.

Then, as if guiltily, as if she had sinfully elevated her needs above Jack's, she prayed—prayed because she needed to pray—and now as she uttered her mournful plea, an immense holy gap opened up in her heart and began to swallow her alive.

The last sound she heard was the ringing of her own words, like the rusty gears of an old universe.

11:45 P.M.

. . . Madness.

Where does "normal" extrasensory experience end and "madness" begin?

Reese Cindrella peered through the thick lenses of his glasses, studying the movements of Alex Mana as he prepared himself for sleep. Was Mana gifted or was he mad? Were they one and the same thing? Reese's gaze intensified. Before him the tall, muscular young man moved with great care. His movement was slow and precise. His piercing blue eyes barely moved, yet Reese knew he was constantly looking, watching. Hollow-cheeked, pale-complected, he seemed undernourished, and Reese wondered if he ate regularly. Probably not. Yet his body seemed vital and strong.

Reese's curiosity mounted as he watched Mana carefully place an ornate silver box on the table beside his bed. A pack of cigarettes and lighter were placed just as carefully beside the box. This accomplished, he pulled the sheets and covers taut so that there wasn't the least crease showing. Then he removed a thinly laced handkerchief from his overnight bag and placed it on the pillow. All this was accomplished with absolute ritualistic precision.

Reese knew that Mana was preparing himself for entry into the sleep world. That this fastidious ritual helped him withdraw from the activities of the day world. All people, more or less, go through the same procedure. Brush their teeth, urinate, put on their favorite pair of pajamas, turn off the lights—all carried out in a general pattern unique to the individual.

But Mana's actions also served another purpose. The objects that he had surrounded himself with were more of a crutch than anything else. As if he needed proof that while he slept the day world would still be there. As if he needed proof positive of a continuous existence.

Reese took this as a sign of fear. That Mana was afraid to relinquish his day life and pass into a completely different state of being. He was sure Mana viewed sleep as a form of death, as an unknown cosmos, with its own special dimensions, where the body goes from the vertical perspective to the horizontal position, from maximum movement to complete inactivity. A state of being where control had to be given up.

Reese felt a slight chilling sensation travel through his body. Once Mana was asleep, his defensive maneuvers of the day world would disappear. Reese would then be able to discover the real man. Perhaps even be able to isolate the source of his power.

"I'm going to sleep in the nude," Mana said without looking up. "Do you mind?"

"Not at all," Reese said softly.

Mana smiled, not quite meeting Cindrella's eyes but clearly pleased with himself as he removed his trousers and placed them neatly over the chair.

There was a moment of stillness as Reese viewed Mana's naked body. His heart was beating like a wild bird. Was Mana deliberately exposing himself for his benefit?

Mana quickly and soundlessly slipped between the sheets, like a hand inserting itself into a well-fitted glove. "All right, Doc. Hook me up."

Reese moved professionally, attaching the electrodes to Mana's temple and neck. Mana smiled up at him, so bright and innocent a smile that Reese couldn't help but smile back.

"What's the matter, Doc? You look nervous."

"Nervous? Not at all." His smile faded.

There was a long stretch of awkward silence as Reese hooked up one last electrode to Mana's temple. But this electrode was not of the usual kind. Reese had decided to film Mana's brain activity on a closed-circuit, modified television scanner, especially built for in-depth probing. Reese wondered if Mana knew what he was up to.

At that instant the door to the sleep room slammed shut. Reese glanced quickly at Mana. "Did you just do that?"

"Nope." His lips formed a supercilious smile.

At the same time the room grew cold, and was gripped by an unexplainable turbulence. Relax, breathe, everything will be all right, Reese reassured himself.

"I don't seem to be well," Mana said. He grabbed Reese's hand and placed it on his forehead. "I think I have a fever."

"No . . . no, you're fine." Reese's eyes blurred as he tried to extricate his hand from Mana's grasp.

"You're shaking. Why?" Mana asked.

"It's been a long day."

"You don't like me touching you, do you?" He let Reese's hand slide free.

"It's not that . . ."

"I didn't mean to. It was just automatic."

"I understand."

"The greatest sense in our body is our touch sense. Did you know that?"

"What?"

"The skin. It's the most sensitive of our organs." He stared at Reese for a moment, his mouth slightly open. "We love, we feel, we hate through the touch corpuscles of our skin," he said in a toneless, metallic voice. "Our whole body is covered with this veil of sensitivity. Even the cornea of the eye—the orifices. The mind of the skin . . . incredible."

Reese stared at him, not quite sure what he was driving at.

"I'm afraid I've lost you," Mana observed stonily.

"I'm afraid you have," Reese replied.

"Touching. I like it. I like to touch. Body heat. The womb." He mouthed his words precisely. "Rocked in the cradle of the deep. Bathed in Mama's amniotic fluid. Enveloped by soft walls of skin. I guess it starts there." His eyes shifted to the door, held on it, piercing. "Sex isn't so bad either. Is it?"

Reese never answered, but Mana continued as though he had.

"It's a kind of pain really. An ache. Sex. But it's also a source of warmth and that part is nice." He turned again to stare directly into Reese's eyes. "The feel of things is important. To reach out, to touch, to stroke, rub . . . that's what I tried to tell them. The doctors said that I had to stop touching. That it was all in my mind. One doctor said that I was suffering from a severe case of melancholia. Another, schizophrenia. Two of the more seasoned doctors concluded that I was a hopeless hysteric. Perhaps narcissistic. But I knew better." He broke off suddenly, as if his recall had exposed him to severe mental exhaustion.

"Were you institutionalized during analysis?" Reese asked.

"Eight months. A hospital in upstate New York. They told me that I had two convulsions in one day. That my brain was damaged. Can you beat that." Seemingly embarrassed, he slid deeper beneath the covers and molded his pillow.

"I thought you were born and raised in Kansas?"

"I was born here in New York. My mother and I moved to Kansas when things didn't go right." He stretched his neck. "They didn't go right out there either." At this point he settled his head on the pillow and seemed to sink into a mood of sorrowful regret.

Cindrella turned, slowly, as if to stir no breeze, his attention having wandered down a new path. Alex Mana had been institutionalized. The report from the National Parapsychology Society had not stated this. Were the two doctors who had tested Mana in the Kansas City State Prison aware of this? Reese hovered for a moment, realizing he knew very little of Mana. The thought was at once annoying and frightening.

Annoying because he had been so anxious to test Mana that he had neglected to investigate the young man fully. He hadn't called the doctors listed in the article. He hadn't asked to interview Alex before testing him. He hadn't contacted the prison. And frightening because Mana had extraordinary paranormal power. Words like schizophrenia and hopeless hysteric had never entered Reese's mind. In order to control this power, Reese had to be sure of its source.

Dammit!

Dammit, dammit, dammit!

"Well," Reese said, and started to move toward the door. It was too late to think about all that. Too much had already been set into motion to stop now.

"Oh," Mana breathed, "do you get off here?"

"I do. But you don't."

"Right."

Reese moved closer to the door.

"Are you putting out the lights now, Doc?"

"Yes."

"Good. Good, I'm tired," Mana muttered nervously, and Reese knew that he was afraid of the dark. Afraid to leave the world of identifiable objects. Afraid to enter a world in which people saw with their thoughts rather than with their eyes.

Reese hesitated a moment longer, then turned out the lights.

12:03 A.M.

Rose found herself walking down a long, dark corridor. The nurse had told her to stay in her room. But the whimpering would not stop.

Rose remained asleep on her back, rigid, in a position of tense resistance, watching herself as a little girl open the door at the far end of the hallway.

They had come for her by car. It was understood that she was to enter a private hospital adjoining the asylum. By mistake, she had been taken, not to the private hospital, but to a small wing of the asylum itself.

The nurse had helped her undress, had slipped a small brown gown over her slender shoulders and had immediately put her to bed. Rose shook with fear as the sky darkened, then the room itself. But she did not cry.

She gazed steadily around her, trying to see any signs of life. There were none. Only the great bars on the windows seemed to move, to loom out at her. The scream of an old woman came first. An animal noise that paralyzed her with fear.

The low moaning and whimpering came later. Much later. It continued for almost an hour until Rose couldn't stand it any longer. She had tried to block it out of her mind, but the sound persisted.

Finally she had gotten out of bed, opened the door to her room and peered out. The corridor was empty. But the whimpering continued.

Moving slowly, she made her way down the hallway. At all cost she had to quiet the whimpering, hear it no more. She looked wildly around her; then, feeling that she was about to die in her struggle, she took hold of the doorknob and pushed open the door.

Instantly, rising out of the darkness, came a horrible sight. A young dark-haired man with greenish skin sat huddled in the corner, his knees drawn up against his chin. Totally naked, he sat like a mummy, moving nothing but his eyes and whimpering. Steam and moisture seemed to emanate from the pores of his sagging skin.

Rose gasped, trying with all her strength to close the door, to run as fast as she could back to the safety of her room. But the image of the young man struck out at her and her own fear entered into a horrible combination—images mixing with emotions. It was impossible for her to move. Something snapped, and for a brief instant, she felt as though she were him. That young man. That they were one and the same person.

Slowly he reached his hand out to her in a state of helpless infancy. Saliva ran from the corners of his mouth as he muttered, "Love . . . me."

Rising to his feet, his body jerking, the young man moved toward her, his outstretched fingers kneading the space in front of him as he reached out to take hold of her.

His face moved startlingly out of the shadows, a small shaft of light touching his eyes; his face had changed now, grown older—not a young face at all, but the face of an old man. He looked as though he had aged to the point of death. Rose's breath drew in sharply as he took hold of her throat.

Then came the scream. Her scream.

The light was on in the room now.

Rose stared at the dormiphone beside her bed. Sitting upright, sweating, she listened.

"Love me." The two words repeated on the dormiphone.

Rose's mind was reeling. Her body felt battered and drained. She quickly reached over and hit the switch on the dormiphone. She leaned back against the headboard and let her body fall limp.

"God," she breathed. It had all come back to her. The asylum. That night. The young man. After all these years, he was still with her.

Slowly, she pulled the covers over her naked body. She remained still. Shaking. Watching. Waiting.

12:05 A.M.

Jack hit the switch on the dormiphone and smiled. Still half-asleep, he jotted down several pleasant thoughts on a piece of paper.

Caught in the twilight zone between waking and sleeping, he heard the voice within him whisper:

". . . and I knocked on the large square door
That I found in my nocturnal wanderings.
All grown over with moss and roses,
It beckoned me to enter.
I turned the knob and came face to face
With a stranger I felt I knew.
For the door was the door to my secret heart
And the stranger, of course, was . . ."

Jack heard a laugh. His laugh. He went back to sleep, unaware that Cara was no longer lying in bed beside him.

CHAPTER 8

Tuesday, October 21
2:00 A.M.

It was a little after two when Reese Cindrella opened his eyes.

He lifted his head slowly. He had been dozing in the monitoring room, moving in a kind of dream in and out of reality. He had imagined himself on his knees, looking for something in the dust. His mind was crowded, swollen with images from his past. At last he had heard a babyish cry coming from the sleep room.

Now he hastened to glance at the monitor. Had Alex Mana entered his first REM period? No, the pen tracings indicated a slow brain wave. Mana had been hovering there for more than an hour now. He was at stage four of the sleep process, but hadn't moved into the dream state.

Reese got to his feet feeling as gray and vague as the shadows that danced ahead of him in the hallway.

He opened the door, stepped out, and softly closed the door behind him.

Inside the office, he poured his fifth cup of coffee, hesitated, then moved into the hallway where he drew back the curtain on the front door and peered out through the thick green glass.

His tension was almost unbearable as he glanced at the darkened streets of the city. He felt lost. He took a deep breath and forced his muscles to relax. It hadn't helped. Neither had his short snooze.

The night was black and still, yet he could feel the movement of the unseen beings who swirled and spun around in his mind like a wind gusting through trees.

For a minute or more he stood staring out, his eyes lifeless:

In his mind, the image of his mother seated in the living room, her frail body draped with lace, her eyes—when she turned her face to him—dark blue and cold. Then, though the image of her was still vivid in his mind, he began to receive a sense of her leaving him. Subtly, she had begun to slip away, and no matter how hard he tried, he knew she would soon be gone.

He wondered whether he would be the same man he was today if she had loved him as much as she had loved his brother Michael. Would he have the same obsessions and desires? So many desires all adding up to one obsession. He felt a strange moment of joy. His eyes flashed. "I have begun something important," he whispered inwardly. "A labor of love that makes me feel alive again. With all its strains and necessities and humiliations—I am alive. And I will not let anyone stop me. Not you, Mother. Not anyone."

He sighed heavily and let the curtain fall away. Again, and overwhelmingly, he felt images from his past crowding his mind.

By the time he had reached the monitoring room, he was weeping silently. In the sleep room Mana was lying perfectly still, having finally entered the dream state of sleep. Reese stared at the monitor. The pen tracings of the EEG were going wild.

Almost at once Mana shifted onto his side. His eyes were beginning to make rapid movements back and forth as his breathing and pulse rates jumped into activity, fluctuated wildly, creating "autonomic storms." He turned again, kicking the sheets from his body.

There was no turning back now.

Reese moved forward to study the special closed-circuit television he'd wired to Mana's brain. Rigid patterns were beginning to form. It was working. Mana's brain was actually putting images into existence. Impossible, he thought, yet there they were, vague shadowy images that leapt forward, then blended together—faster, more images, clearer, steadier. Reese was actually doing it. He was actually recording Mana's center of thought; his consciousness, memory, emotions and imagination. Three pounds of gray matter protected by the cranium and he was about to enter it.

Without warning, Reese felt himself drop away into a void, dissolve into a yellow mist that raised him upward, outward, until all was cool in color and all-embracing. An image flew by, another and another, until his imagination promptly exploded.

Strangely, he imagined himself traveling through Mana's body, traveling quickly up his spinal cord and entering his brain: first the medulla, where he stopped for a moment to regulate Mana's respiration and heart action; then he moved above to the cerebellum, pushed past its fine grooves, and crossed over a bridge of nerve fibers connecting the higher and lower brain.

Gushing full blast into the midbrain, he stopped to look at the world through Mana's eyes. A thousand images flew by. He couldn't make sense of any of them. All at once, time stretched out in front of him like the dark drifts and crosscuts of a mining tunnel. Swiftly there came a rush of wind, a half-glimpsed image of eyes.

Reese's whole body had begun to quiver.

He stumbled forward to the thalamus, where Mana's present emotion was running rampant; tornado-like, it sucked up everything in its path, twisting it, destroying it, leaving a flat desolate landscape in its wake. With a violent thrust, Reese was sucked into its explosive force and thrown forward.

Breathlessly, he arrived in the cerebrum, where he stared into two hemispheres divided by a deep fissure. White matter everywhere, consciousness, imagination, then he saw it—the tumor. Abscessed, inflamed, it had begun to produce pus. Ugly thick pus that started to flood the area like a river of lava.

Time, and blood, and pain, they were all rushing at Reese now. And images. Hundreds of images that seared his vision. Huge blood-soaked hands, the slashing blade of a knife, the partially naked body of a girl who lay dying on the dust covered floor of an abandoned building. More images, faster, faster, faster, the girl again. And blood, blood everywhere. With a scream for help, he tried to take his eyes from her body.

The darkness rushed and jabbed around him, closed in. He could feel the muscles in his face jerk violently as he stared at the television screen. He watched as a twisted figure of a man knelt over the girl's body, darkness and blood covering him. Suddenly the current of time stopped and the image changed.

The screen darkened; then with a burst of light, Rose Carpenter's face came into focus. Eyes bulging, Rose appeared in pain. She was calling out, reaching out. "Help me," she cried. "Help me." Her voice was quickly drowned out by another voice, which grew and grew until it was a howl.

"You lied!" Mana's voice came screaming over the intercom. "You've recorded the session."

Reese spun around. Mana held him fast in his gaze. He stood growling, his swollen eyes burning like fiery comets. Half-wild, Mana burst into laughter, the sound coming into the monitoring room like the grinding of metal on metal. Then came the sudden shattering of glass.

Reese ducked, but not fast enough.

The plate glass window of the monitoring room burst open and flew forward, a huge piece of the glass slicing Reese's cheek with the neat proficiency of a razor blade. Catching him just below the eye, the glass cleanly sliced his skin before smashing off the back wall.

Reese dropped quickly to the floor, writhing in the shadows, the blood pumping outward in gushes, as though the brain were still telling the heart to keep operating, to keep functioning.

"LIAR!!" Mana screamed, his voice mixing with a sudden roaring. All at once flames leapt up in the hallway. Reese pressed his hand over the gash on his cheek and staggered backward. The flames jumped higher, a living red weed sprung by a silent command.

Now, the hallway was darkened over with smoke and grime. It was almost impossible to see anything. Reese lurched to the door and peered out. In the sleep room he could see Mana's face plastered with a fixed, grinning satisfaction.

Then the fixed grin on Mana's lips broke; his face seemed to be replaced by another face. Then another and another. Each face hideous and grinning. More and more and more until the hallway was completely black. Reese could see nothing, but could feel Mana hurtling toward him.

"Goddamn you!" Mana screamed through smoke and flames. "Goddamn you!"

Reese felt a sharp pain in his chest. It was the last thing he felt as he too screamed. With hands like claws in front of him, he lunged.

Both men lunged.

Now all that remained was the hissing and crackling of the fire, burning and consuming ravenously.

3:00 A.M.

He lay still for a while merely breathing.

Where was he?

The bed was cold and clammy, the air chilled and oppressive, and that was all there was. Except for a blinding headache. Lying flat on his back, Jack groaned, then called out, "Cara?"

He reached over and discovered the bed was empty next to him. He sat up, not quite awake yet, and turned on the light. The room was suddenly staring bright.

"Cara?"

He leaned forward, straining. His vision blurred, focused, blurred again. Someone had called out for help. "Help me," the voice had cried. Had he imagined it? He blinked, trying to drive the heaviness from his eyelids. It flitted through his mind that perhaps he *had* imagined it. But, no—he became conscious of his own thought process now—no, he had distinctly heard someone calling out for help.

Awake and on his feet now, he stared at the dormiphone. Quickly he rewound the tape. Pressing the button, he listened. After a moment: "Help me." But that was not the voice he had heard. Or was it? He hit the button, rewound the tape and listened again. He was confused now. Where was Cara?

Hurriedly he moved into the hallway. The hall light was on but the rest of the apartment was dark. "Cara?"

At the top of the stairs he paused and, leaning forward a little, looked into the darkness below. He held his breath, listening for sounds. Nothing. Yet, he felt a strange uneasiness gaining on him.

He stood rigid, trying to think; then abruptly it came to him. Rose . . . he had seen her face. Twisted, crying. "Help me," she had cried. "Help me." And then glass breaking. Flames.

Suddenly he was frightened.

"Cara!" he screamed, running from one room to the other, slamming on lights. In the kitchen, he paused. He heard the wind rattle the outside shutters. Then, silence laced with a general calm.

Perversely, the consolation didn't last. Whatever comfort he drew from the specific lull, there was also an immense sense of misgiving. It occurred to him that it was suddenly too quiet. As all sounds withdrew, sucked, as it were, into uncharged spaces, he straightened, listening intently. His gaze traveled the walls and, beyond, to the streets. All was still. He listened, gazing silently. There was no sound.

His glance came to rest finally on a tiny piece of notepaper propped on the kitchen table. With haste, he lifted the paper.

The note was short and to the point. Cara wanted out. She knew that he had gone to see "that girl" tonight. She had listened in on their conversation. She wanted a divorce as soon as possible. In the meantime, she would stay in at a hotel.

Eyes riveted to the paper, he read the note again, then slowly lowered his hand, letting the note fall to the floor.

"Christ," he breathed, and realized, perhaps for the first time, that it was final. That he had actually lost Cara. That their marriage was over. He waited for a fresh thought, but none came. Yet some inner whispering caused him to stir.

As soon as he had dressed, he left the apartment and started walking. He wasn't going anywhere and there wasn't any hurry. He cut over to Ninth Avenue and headed south. There were a few prostitutes walking the streets, an old derelict crouched in a doorway. With trembling hands, the man reached out to Jack.

"I need help. Can you help me?" he asked with the sour smell of drunkenness.

They stood there, looking at each other.

"Please, buddy," he whispered. "Help me . . ."

Jack quickly dug into his pocket and handed him a dollar.

"Hey, man, I'll never forget you for this. Never." Quickly, he disappeared into the darkness.

A bad dream.

To a person in the city, blank and stopped as a cadaver, the world itself was a bad dream. A blend of the shabby and the exotic: oriental rugs, vases, fine lace set out in display windows, while in doorways lingered the destitute and the crazy.

A cool wind rushed by and Jack was momentarily transported, moving with considerable speed through the streets of the city. Beneath him, rising and falling to the beat of steel wheels, the subway rumbled. All at once he made an abortive movement as though to go back to his apartment; then he was off, moving into the night, his brown patent leather shoes flashing in the moonlight.

3:30 A.M.

The soprano screech of brakes punished her ears. Rose raised her face to the cold dark sky, feeling the burning of nausea in the pit of her stomach, the upsurge of anger and confusion, the stinging of sweat in the corners of her eyes.

She moved down Fourteenth Street, heading toward the river. She had paid little attention to the traffic as she'd crossed to the other side of the street. There were few people out. Those who were moved past her with complete indifference.

Cheryl Arthur is dead.

Horrible, but true.

Cheryl Arthur is dead. And her body has been left to rot in the abandoned building in my dreams.

As the last strains of the thought drifted away, Rose came to an abrupt halt. She stood on a deserted street corner virtually concealed by heavy shadows, while ahead of her the street loomed quiet and still.

Almost immediately, she saw a small shaft of light pulsating in the darkness. Quick and tentative, it moved toward her. She couldn't tell what it was, whether it was real or unreal, or in what combination; only that it was moving toward her; except, there was an image forming now, swift, quivering. Then, terminated.

The image of Cheryl was gone.

Rose stood still. It had happened so fleetingly, she wasn't altogether sure she had seen her; perhaps the image had not been real. Yet, it was easy to believe that she had just seen the other side of hell, that she had gone someplace far away, knowing that she had left someone behind: a girl shivering on the street corner, her skin as dry as parchment, her breath coming in short, strange gulps of air.

Now the pavement turned soft, the air heavy, as she moved further down the street. Ahead of her the streetlamp flashed on, and for a long time she studied the details of the building to which she was heading. The building in her dream.

She approached slowly, cautious not to invade the area too roughly. She looked up, her torso straining as she attempted to see beyond its battered walls.

Abruptly, the streetlamp went off. Overhead, the glow of a full moon, the silver and ebony of the clouds that drifted quickly across the sky. It was that kind of night. Swift, dangerous, unfettered.

Her eyes wandered trancelike over the face of the building. How frosty beautiful it looked, she thought, its naked frame motionless against the night. Only her eyes moved now, looking for a way in.

She stopped walking.

Then she started to walk again, hearing her own footsteps, listening for others. She circled wide, wider, and then she saw it. An opening in front of the building, barely discernible. A few boards had been pried loose, leaving a small sliver of space. Still, it was wide enough for her to squeeze through.

She moved closer, listening to her own sound, her own footsteps. Yet, why did she have the sense something else was moving with her? Not wind. Someone. She turned to stare at the twisted black street behind her. Nothing more than a deserted avenue.

She waited a moment longer, waited until the streetlight flashed on, then quickly slid into the building.

Once inside, she stopped.

How odd that this moment struck her as the most important link in a whole chain of events. This brief, quivering hesitation. The macabre dreams behind a curtain of gauze—those should have been far more important: Or the rapid beating of her heart, or the stripped-nakedness of the building she now stood in, or the ever-present footsteps wherever she had gone. The phone calls. His breathing—him. But, no—those aspects had only led her to this moment.

Leave the building, she told herself. Leave the building before it's too late.

This, she realized, might be the last sensible thought she would ever have.

Drawing a deep breath, she began to make her way up the narrow wooden staircase. Each step was an effort. The stairs seemed built for the legs of a more nimble species, their rise almost as steep as a ladder's. She forced her eyes upward; the dim, long walls wavered.

On the first-floor landing she stopped to listen. She thought she had heard something behind her. Satisfied with the absolute silence, she began to climb to the second floor.

The faint outline of a door at the top of the stairs drew her on. Her sudden weariness was agonizing. Each wave of fatigue forced her gaze to tighten on the door where, through the gapes of holes that were once windows, light from the streetlamp entered, brushing the space ahead of her in faded watercolors.

Now she placed her hand on the doorknob. She gripped the brass knob tighter and, her mouth thin with determination, pushed the door open. She felt the last of her strength vanish with the effort.

Cautiously, she took the first step, then stopped to allow her eyes to readjust. A small shaft of moonlight forced its way through the broken roof above her head. Faintly, at first, the room began to take shape.

Archways, two of them, massive and jagged as bat wings. A dead stretch of green wall and an alcove as black as a grave. Packing crates ripped open; chunks of packing insulation scattered over the floor. A wooden chair, which apparently had been smashed off the wall, was now a pile of kindling. More debris, tons of it. It seemed all of New York had dumped its garbage into this one room. And then she saw what she had been looking for. Ahead of her and to her left stood two fifty-gallon oil drums.

Sweat broke out on Rose's brow.

Was Cheryl's body in one of them?

She stood dazed for an instant, but then weariness gave way to anger. "Son of a bitch," she said between tight lips. Without further thought, she entered the room.

Her anger gave way to weariness again as she hesitated beside the drums. She stood rooted to the exact spot where she had seen Cheryl raped and murdered. She peered at the floor. Because the wooden planks were so grimy and dark and roughly textured, she had some difficulty telling if there was any blood soaked into them. Quite clearly, there was not the enormous puddle she had expected to find. Nor was there any sign that a struggle had taken place. The dust was as thick and undisturbed here as in the rest of the room.

She took a step, stared blindly at the two drums, her eyes blazing with a force that sucked all remaining logic from her body. One drum was filled with rags and newspapers, the other with a greenish, slimy water. She remembered him stuffing newspapers into the drum. Yes, newspapers.

Her hands were moving rapidly now, throwing the papers

to the floor. Then she yanked rags out. Her movement became frantic as she removed an assortment of debris. Faster, she dug in, throwing garbage to the side. Faster . . . Faster.

The stink was unbearable.

Oh, God, she thought wildly. I must be going crazy. She looked blankly down at the half-empty container. Cheryl was not there. Tears had begun to shimmer at the corners of her eyes.

Numb, disbelieving, she slumped on a packing crate, her arms limp beside her, her head hung. The only thing she could feel was the sick pounding of the blood rushing through her temples. It was one of those times when she needed desperately to talk to herself, to share with herself her deepest feelings, to work out her confusion and get her mind back on the right track. But the rushing of blood within her head seemed to prevent all that.

Rose began to shake. She wept.

She was alone and scared and very mixed-up.

She stared at the dark floor and told herself that it had only been a dream after all. That it hadn't been a prophecy, an omen. It had merely been a dream. Just a bad dream. A disturbing nightmare.

In the distance, traffic hummed. It was a cold, lonely, mournful buzzing that brought her to her feet. Wiping tears from her eyes, she moved to leave the room. But something kept after her. Desperately, she tried to rid herself of the thought, but the idea refused to relinquish its hold on her.

Check the other drum. Check the other . . .

In a sudden frenzy of haste, she moved to the second container. For a moment she was breathless, and dark shadows closed around the edges of her vision. Then, with a quick gesture, she brushed aside a soggy wad of Kleenex that floated atop the water.

A mild emotional explosion now as she thrust her hand into grimy liquid. Her hand disappeared and then her elbow. She touched something. Something was caught between her fingers. Alarmed, she withdrew her hand; Cheryl's head came with it. Eyes open and bulging from her water-soaked flesh, jaw locked in an expression of terror, her head bobbed like an apple on top of the water; a withered green-eyed mask of death that now began to sink back into the slime from which it came.

Rose turned and as she turned she screamed. A wild, despairing scream that caught in her throat. Almost at once the sound dropped into her stomach, knotting it.

Then, between two gasps of desperate air, she heard it. The sound of someone breathing. At first, she thought it was only her own mounting hysteria, and that she had imagined a deeper sound. She held her breath, but the breathing kept on.

An icy shiver raced up her spine. She whirled, looked into the darkness. The alcove, which had been pitch-black when she came into the room, was shimmering with a thin veil of light. She stared at it expectantly, realizing it was the perfect place to hide. But if anyone had been hiding there, waiting for her, he would have come out by now.

A sudden noise broke the silence behind her. She turned and threw her arms up to fend off her attacker. But there was no one there. She was still alone in the room.

Nevertheless, she was convinced that what she had heard was breathing, and not her own. It had been too deep, too heavy to be her own. No, quite clearly she sensed another presence.

Noise again.

In the alcove.

With a soft cry of alarm, she spun around. And there in the shadows, she saw piercing eyes that darted and burned.

She started to back up, cautiously retreating toward the door which seemed miles away.

He moved now out into the open, but his face was lost in the shadows.

The instant she saw him, Rose froze. She stopped backing toward the door even though he had begun to move toward her. His face, she wanted to see his face. What she saw instead was the knife he held in his gloved hand. The glint of the blade drew her attention.

"No," she whimpered. "Please . . ."

He moved slowly across the space that separated him from her, stepping carefully through the debris. As he moved, sharp slivers of light glinted on the cutting edge of the blade.

"NO!" Rose screamed and broke for the door. She knew that she had gained only seconds, no more than that, because she had barely started down the first flight of stairs when she heard clattering footsteps behind her. Amplified by the narrow staircase, the sound echoed with a kind of menace. He was gaining on her.

She could hear his heavy breathing as he drew closer.

She darted across the first-floor landing and ran down the remaining stairs, two at a time.

"Help me," she screamed, and then, catching her heel on the ragged edge of the steps, she began to fall. Her head whipped back as she toppled forward. She fell, screaming, until her body came to lie in a crumpled heap at the foot of the stairs.

Then she felt the paroxysm, the ache, the throe of pain. She let go and her circle of vision began to close . . . but not before she saw the immense figure of a man come to stand over her. His massive shoulders and swollen head seemed to fill the whole of her world, and she thought of the vast organs that gave him life—the black thumping of his heart, his huge lungs breathing, inhaling and exhaling, the countless cells revitalizing themselves with the sucking in of air that streamed hot vapor from his nostrils, that sent blood flowing to his great gray cabbage of a brain.

"Please," Rose whispered, "don't kill me."

She closed her eyes then. And with God's mercy, lost consciousness.

PART THREE

PART THREE

CHAPTER 1

DETECTIVE LOU JAFFY PARKED HIS BUTTOCKS ON THE EDGE of his desk, which was bare save a tattered green blotter with black-tipped corners. Once or twice, in an unconscious gesture, he nodded his head as though confirming his latest speculation. He was thinking about the last seventy-two hours. He drew a deep breath and closed his eyes. His mind immediately shifted to a small burnt-out room: the monitoring room at the Institute of Parapsychology.

He still couldn't understand why Reese Cindrella's death had been so easily dismissed as an accident. He paused, recalling his conversation with Detective Lieutenant Burke.

"Look, Lou, there's no tits and ass involved here. No rape—nobody has been sexually assaulted. Just a simple death by fire. So why are you here?"

"So you think this was an accident?"

"What else?"

"How do you explain the glass shattering like that?"

"A sudden pressure. Look around you. The room's loaded with highly charged equipment."

"But the window was blown inward—from the hallway."

"Blown in? It could have just fallen in."

"There's glass clear on the other side of the room. Clear into the bathroom."

Burke grimaced; at the same time ash fell from his cigarette, and he rubbed it into his jacket. The suit he wore, a brilliant blue poorly chosen for his red hair and sallow color, was frayed at the cuffs, raveled at the collar.

"Lou, do me a favor," he said. "Go home."

"No."

"What in the hell is your problem?" he asked gruffly.

Jaffy looked at him in some surprise. "Rose Carpenter. I read you her statement. She said—"

"And I told you what Cindrella had in his files on her. She is suffering from delusions. Repressed sexual fantasies."

"Can I see the file?"

"Jesus, Lou—you're a real pain in the ass. No, I mean it. I'd like to close this case, okay? If I let you start poking around, I won't see my wife and kids for a week!"

"Just a little peek."

Burke, a frown cemented to his jaw, murmured, "Okay, Lou. But I want the file on my desk first thing in the morning."

"You got it." With a sudden motion, Jaffy donned his hat and headed for the door. "By the way," he said, and turned back to face Burke. "Has the mother identified the body yet?"

"Nothing much left to identify. She verified that the ring and watch were his. We're running down his dental records now."

Tipping his hat back, Jaffy scanned the dark shadows of the room. It appeared as a deep well of blackness surrounded by charred walls. The dusty air struck him with the smell of ash. He studied the minute specks of broken glass scattered like a multitude of stars in the rubble. "Strange, isn't it?" he said.

"What is?"

"Only three rooms burned. The office, the other rooms weren't at all—"

Burke wearily shook his head. "What's to burn, Lou? The building is all glass and brick. The ceiling soundproofed—fire retardant."

"Yet he wasn't able to get away from the fire."

"He probably panicked. Passed out. Fell and hit his head."

Jaffy studied the room a moment longer, debating what Burke had said. "Perhaps. Perhaps," he muttered. Then with a last smoothing touch to the brim of his hat, he turned and quit the room.

Jaffy sighed now and opened his eyes. Reaching into his desk, he removed a small tape recorder which he had used to record Rose Carpenter's statement. He had questioned her shortly after she had been admitted to Roosevelt Hospital yesterday morning. He had also questioned Patrolman Machette, the officer who had found her. He hit the button and listened to Patrolman Machette's words.

"It was 3:30 a.m. and I watched her enter the building. I didn't know what was going down, so I decided to check things out. I entered the building through the back. By the time I reached the first-floor hallway, I heard a scream. When I got to her, she was lying at the bottom of the stairs near the front of the building. She looked up at me and . . . I don't know why . . . she said, 'Please don't kill me.' Then she passed out. No one else was in the building that I know of. I immediately called for an ambulance."

Jaffy pondered Patrolman Machette's statement for a moment as the tape continued to run. Then came Rose Carpenter's voice.

". . . it all started with a dream. No, a vision. I saw Cheryl's body exploding before my eyes. She was sitting in my apartment, just sitting there, you know, and then I watched her disintegrate right before my eyes. Anyhow, we talked and I left for work. That night, when I got back to the apartment, she was gone. She left me a note saying she'd be in touch. But she never did. I was worried. I went to bed. That's when I had the dream. That's when I saw her raped and murdered. In that building. That's why I went there. I . . . suddenly . . . I found myself standing over her. She was in the barrel. Just where I saw him put her. No, in the other barrel, the one with the rags in it. But she wasn't in that one, she was in the one with the water. And then I felt someone else there too. He was there. He's been following me, calling me. I'm sure he killed Mitzie too. I had the same dream after she was killed, and he was there too. He killed Mitzie. I'm sure. When I woke up I was here in the hospital . . . I was . . . I tell you, Cheryl was in that barrel. She's dead. And he was there. He's always there—everywhere I go. He's going to kill me too. Oh, God, what's happening to me? Cheryl was murdered, I tell you. And he's after me now . . ."

Jaffy shut the recorder off. "What a world," he breathed. "What a world." Reaching into his breast pocket, he removed his note pad and flipped to page 6. On the page was listed:

Dixie Hotel—Cheryl Arthur.
    Institute of Parapsychology.
    Jack Squadron.
    Stoneridge. Rose Carpenter.

He had underlined each entry with green ink.

He reached for Cheryl Arthur's suitcase and dumped it on his desk. Opening the lid, he reexamined its contents. A picture of Lance Frazier (Rose's husband).

What was his picture doing in her suitcase?

A bottle of Quaaludes.

Were drugs involved?

Maybe prostitution. Something. Cheryl Arthur was apparently missing. Where was she? Not in the barrel as Rose had stated. Jaffy had gone to the building. It had been searched from top to bottom. Nothing was found.

Jaffy knew the street well. He had checked with shopkeepers, doormen, neighbors; for two years previously, he had conducted three sex-slaying investigations in that same vicinity. Yes, Jaffy knew the area well.

Idly, he eyed the contents of the suitcase. He had a nagging feeling of having missed something. What? Now the thing to do was to take it from the beginning. Go over it all again. Opening the desk drawer, he took away the Jack Squadron/ Rose Carpenter file he had taken from the Institute.

Placing it on the desk, he unwrapped the second half of his corned beef sandwich and sat, wishing he had a beer. There were a lot of loose ends: Was Rose really suffering from delusions? Was Cheryl Arthur really dead? Was there one man doing the killing? Where did Reese Cindrella fit in?

He looked at his watch. Almost two. It would be a long afternoon. He sighed, put his foot up on his desk and took a bite from his sandwich.

4:00 P.M.

Rose lay staring at the pinholes in the acoustical tiles above her head. She wasn't sure for how long. She closed her eyes and maybe she slept and maybe she didn't. When she opened her eyes again, she saw the continuing nightmare unfolding before her.

Dr. Cindrella was dead. Jaffy had told her, his alert eyes watching for her smallest change of emotion. What she felt instead of grief was almost panic. It was all rushing at her, blending into a blur of death that threatened to engulf her.

Jaffy had sat there, waiting.

"Dr. Cindrella," she had said in a clear flat voice, "was a very nice man. I'm sorry he's dead."

"Are you?" mused Jaffy softly.

"I'm sorry they're all dead," Rose said, crying. "Dr. Cindrella . . . Mitzie . . . Cheryl. What's happening?"

Jaffy's watchful expression relaxed. "Sleep now," he said. "Rest."

Now the pinholes in the tiles above Rose's head seemed to move, coming together, then fanning out. She couldn't lie in that uncomfortable position any longer. She had to get moving. She rose slowly and glanced at her watch. Where was Jack? He had promised to pick her up today by four o'clock. She worried now that the doctor had changed his mind and refused to let her leave the hospital. "A concussion is nothing to take lightly, young lady," he had said after he had examined her yesterday. "You must take it easy. I'll make my decision tomorrow."

As soon as she had been able, she had called Jack. Upon her request, he had gone to her apartment, thrown some of her clothing into her overnight bag and come straight to the hospital. The first thing she had done was to tell him what had happened. She could still see the changing expression on his face as he listened to the details. First puzzlement, next sorrow, and then complete understanding. If nothing else, Rose felt that at last Jack had finally believed her.

Rose hesitated now and became aware of how badly she ached. She ran her fingers over the bruise on her forehead

where the skin had been broken. Parts of her body were swollen
and sore. Still, she had to get going. It didn't matter where.
All she wanted was out of this room, this hospital. She felt
hemmed in. She picked up the phone and dialed Jack's apartment. There was no answer.

She sat staring from the gauze-curtained window. She
watched people amble along the walkway that ran alongside
the building, along the garden path to the end of the courtyard.
Normal. Everything looked so normal. She blinked her eyes,
tears filled them, blurring her vision—but somehow providing
a measure of relief.

She tried dialing Jack again at four-thirty. Again no answer.
Again a sudden loss of faith. Of courage. She waited a few
minutes, and tried once more. Still no answer. She checked
with the switchboard operator. There was nothing wrong with
the phone. They were just not answering.

Rose tried to sit quietly. It was too hot and she was too sore
and just couldn't get comfortable. She moved onto the bed.
She felt worse.

She was up again and moving. The only way she could
keep halfway calm was to keep walking. Whenever she stopped
she began to panic, to sweat, and had to move again.

She was moving now, and kept moving.

3:30 P.M.

Jack Squadron ducked into the phone booth and dialed.
Except for a cup of coffee, he hadn't eaten all day. His head
was spinning as he waited for Frank Austin's secretary to put
him through. He realized that Cara wasn't actually Frank's
patient, but hoped like hell she had contacted him. Once or
twice, over the years, Cara had called on Frank to solve smaller
problems. None that called for a psychiatrist, but just the advice
of a close friend.

Jack was sweating profusely when Frank came on the line.
"Hello? Jack?"

"Yeah, Frank." It took a few seconds for him to ask, "Have
you heard from Cara yet?"

A heavy sigh followed by, "I'm afraid I haven't."

Jack shook his head wearily. "Dammit. Goddamn it!"

"Jack, take it easy."

"Oh, God . . . Frank, how can I take it easy? Cara's roaming around somewhere—she hasn't much money—she's sick. Who knows what's going to happen to her?"

"I'm sure she's all right."

"Bullshit!"

"Have you been at the apartment all day?"

"Yes. I even stood in the lobby for awhile. I hung around the entrance hoping . . . Frank, we have to find her."

"I can understand your concern."

Jack glanced at his watch. "Frank, I've got to go. I'll keep in touch. If she does call you, Christ, Frank—talk some sense into her head. We can work things out."

"Where can I reach you?"

"I don't know, I . . ."

"Jack, this is no time to be wandering around."

"Goddamn it, Frank. Don't preach to me. I know she's not your patient, but you were supposed to keep an eye on her. You didn't even know she left the hospital. If she needed professional help—you should have gotten it for her."

"I did my best . . ."

"Please, Frank . . ." Jack shrugged. "I'm sorry. I know it's not your fault. I'm sorry. Look, I really have to go. I'll check with you later. See you." Jack hung up. The question now was: What would Cara do next? This morning, yes, it was this morning that he had taken a letter away from the mailbox. No postage stamp, no name written on the envelope, not even sealed; it contained a letter from Cara. Jack took the letter from his pocket now and began to reread it slowly.

Jack: Because I have left the apartment, it does not mean I have left you. I may be watching you right now as you read this letter. When you are with her—I will know. My eyes will always be there—watching. Forever yours, Cara.

A siren's scream broke Jack's concentration. All at once the street was a mass of converging patrol cars. Jack looked out over Columbus Avenue. The sun had started to fade. Stuffing the letter into his pocket, he moved slowly, then faster, walking uptown, heading for the Twentieth Precinct. Detective Jaffy had called him first thing this morning. Would Jack mind stopping by? Jack wished now that he had gone earlier. But somehow the day had gotten away from him.

He glanced at his watch. He'd never be able to pick Rose up at the hospital in time. He had tried calling her several times, but the line had always been busy. The story of his life.

Minutes later he entered the Twentieth Precinct. The desk sergeant motioned him upstairs. As Jack climbed the steps, he could still hear the loud screeching of sirens outside the building. Someone dashed past him and flung open a door to his right.

"Lieutenant?" he shouted into the room.

"Yeah?"

"There's been a shooting on Eighty-seventh. Between Columbus and Amsterdam. The victim's not dead. They have the suspect trapped on the roof of the Garland Building."

"Get the car. We'll go over together."

"Right." The officer turned and headed for Jack.

"Can you tell me where I'd find Detective Jaffy?" Jack asked.

"Down the hall to the left," the officer said without stopping.

Jack moved on, pushed open the door to the waiting room. Outside of a policeman seated behind his desk, the room was empty. "I'm here to see Detective Jaffy."

"Name?"

"Squadron. Jack."

"Have a seat." After a short exchange over the intercom, Jaffy appeared. He was smaller than Jack by several inches, probably five-seven or -eight, but very thin. In his mid-forties, he was still in good physical shape. He must work out, thought Jack.

"Mr. Squadron?"

"Yes."

"Glad to meet you." Jaffy extended his hand. His grip was firm. "Come on in." He turned to the officer. "Hold all calls." Jaffy walked ahead of Jack into his office. Furnished in gray metal, the office seemed part motel and part institution. A few bad watercolor prints that hung on the walls, a throw rug and a fake plant scored on the motel side. The metal desk, chairs and chalkboard helped proclaim it as an institution. The two windows behind the desk faced south and were bare of drapes or blinds. The crudeness of tenement living was the only view.

Jaffy closed the door. Without speaking, he indicated that

Jack should be seated. In order to maintain his sense of rightness and authority, Jaffy seated himself properly behind his desk, lit a cigarette and opened the folder in front of him.

"I just have a few questions. I hope you don't mind."

"No," Jack mumbled.

"It's about Rose Carpenter." Jaffy exhaled; he had not finished. "Tell me, Jack—how well do you know her?"

Jack shrugged. "Not very. We met last week."

"During a dream telepathy session, right?"

"Yes."

"You see, what I really need to know is how well you know her emotionally."

"I don't understand."

"I had a brief chat with Rose yesterday morning. Right after they brought her in. About her accident. Did she tell you what happened?"

"About finding her girlfriend. Yes."

"And the man who is supposed to be after her. Did she tell you that too?"

"Yes."

"Do you believe her?"

Jack hesitated. "I'm not sure."

Jaffy's mind was already racing, analyzing the way in which Jack had hesitated before answering the question. Jaffy had a thing about people's hesitations. He felt that he could judge the emotion behind the answer by the length and breadth of the hesitation: Love, hate, anger, fear, truth or lie.

In this case, making a quick assessment, Jack's hesitation indicated (a) fear, and (b) lie. Jaffy was beginning to feel a slight twinge of suspicion.

Flicking the ash from his cigarette, he said, "Rose was institutionalized at age nine. Stoneridge in upstate New York. Did you know that?"

Jack shook his head. "No."

"She had a schizophrenic episode. Do you know what that is, Jack?"

"Not really."

"She lost her perception of reality. Suffered from delirium and hallucinations. I checked. I called Stoneridge this morning. That's what they told me. In other words, she was living in a world of fantasy."

Jack started to speak and then abruptly stopped. He seemed

to catch his breath. For a moment both men silently, unwillingly, acknowledged the uncomfortable gap in the conversation.

"I'm sorry . . . these things are never pleasant." Jaffy smiled compassionately across the desk.

"Did Rose tell you about Stoneridge?" Jack asked.

"No."

"Then how did . . ."

Jaffy tapped the folder in front of him. "I found the entry in her folder. The one Dr. Cindrella compiled prior to the experiment."

"You haven't wasted any time."

Jaffy gave him a long, searching look, then said slowly, "Jack, I'll be honest with you. The whole thing is really a puzzle to me. Mitzie Karp was raped and murdered. Rose tells me now that she saw the death scene—in her dream. She also saw Cheryl Arthur raped and murdered—in her dream. Then what happens, Cheryl Arthur turns up missing. All this happens while Rose is involved with a dream telepathy experiment. Next thing we know, Dr. Cindrella turns up dead. So I take it one step at a time and what do I come up with? Is Rose telling the truth, is she suffering from delusions, or is she lying?"

"Why would she be lying?"

Jaffy shrugged. "To protect someone maybe. Or to protect herself. Maybe there are other things involved here that we can't see. Extortion, prostitution . . ."

"Prostitution? Why? Because Rose works at the Cottontail Club?"

"That's right. The place is loaded with them."

"That doesn't mean Rose is involved with any of it."

"I didn't say she was. On the other hand, I have to check all the angles."

"Anyway, what's all this got to do with me?" Jack frowned.

"I've got to find out more about Rose Carpenter. Who she is. What she is. You've spent time with her. Fill me in . . ."

"I don't know anything about her," Jack said with a certain edge of contempt to his voice.

"Goddamn it," Jaffy exploded, "we may be in the middle of mass murder here, and you're playing games! You think about it, Jack. You take just one slightly insane person who has lost touch with himself; and what do you have? An animal. He's liable to be out there right now. Have you ever seen people behave in a climate of fear? Watch what extremes they are driven to? Rose is going through it right now. If she is telling the truth, she might be next. You want that? Would that make you feel any better?"

Jaffy glanced at Jack's face. It was firm and expressionless, save for a certain granitelike belligerence set into the jawline. His cheeks were sunken, but a day's growth of beard filled his face out. His eyes remained steady. Jaffy sensed a touch of ruthlessness, a downright no-nonsense thrust.

Jaffy turned away. "All right, Jack," he said. "Have it your own way. I have just a few more questions—then you can go." He rummaged through the folder in front of him. "It states here that you're married."

"Yes," Jack answered mechanically.

"That you're a composer."

"Yes."

"Did Dr. Cindrella tell you why he picked you for the experiment?"

"No."

Jaffy paused, sensing that Jack was lying. Why, he wasn't sure. He pushed on. "I notice here that Rose had five dreams during the night. All marked as direct hits. I did some checking. That's quite a feat, wouldn't you say?"

"Yes."

"The interesting thing is that Dr. Cindrella did not record the fifth dream. The other four he recorded in detail. Under the fifth dream his only comment is . . ." Jaffy read from the sheet. "'Extraordinary. Subject had crossed over. Experienced a new dimension.'"

Visibly irritated, Jack glanced at his watch.

Jaffy leaned forward. "Do you know what the doctor meant by that note?"

"No," he mumbled.

"Okay, Jack, you can go."

He wasted no time in moving toward the door.

Jaffy slammed the folder shut. "Just in case you're interested, I've asked Rose to come here tomorrow morning. I want her to look through our files. See if she can't identify the man she claims is after her."

Jack turned suddenly. "I didn't know she had actually seen him."

"She hadn't. At least, not clearly. I thought that perhaps

one of the pictures would strike home. It's a shot." Jaffy looked at him for a moment longer, then asked, "By the way, you wouldn't happen to know what blood type you are, would you?"

"No, I . . . I really couldn't tell you."

"Right."

Jack, puzzled by the look in Jaffy's eyes, turned and left the office.

Moments later he was on his way to pick up Rose.

CHAPTER 2

"Yeah! It's all happening right here on FM 99.
WXLO. Look outside, man—we got frost. Thirty-
four degrees midtown with the sun nowhere, I say
nowhere to be found. Brrrrr. That's all right—do
the morning with us and we'll warm you into the
morn. Time 7:01 and moving. Speaking of moving . . ."

Rose reached out and switched off the clock radio. Slowly,
she commanded her body to move. After a small muscular
struggle, she managed to sit up. Her body felt numb and im-
personal; a computer, moving by rote, no longer by any force
or will of her own. Early morning was clearly not her best time
of day.

She cast a sour glance around the room . . . it looked like
a setting for a disaster movie. Her life had become that way.
Cluttered. Everything thrown in all the wrong places. Under-
garments dangled everywhere. The bedside table had been turned
into an eating nook. Cups and plates and silverware. Everything
everywhere.

Throwing the covers aside, Rose stood.

She hesitated, undecided which way to turn.

The room was colder now, colder than it had been last night.
Jack and she had made love before he left. In her quest to rid
herself of all anxiety, she had reached out for him, asking for
no commitment, no giving, no sharing, only his embrace, his
touch; the sex of the thing.

In the bathroom now, Rose stared at her body—her small

waist, flat stomach, the nipples of her breasts stiff from the cold; the huge tuft of silky black hair; and in this moment, she noticed for the first time the red slashes on her shoulder, neck and forehead.

Her eyes widened, and in horror she suddenly remembered the dream she'd had last night. She had screamed out in pain. The knife's sharp blade had slashed across her shoulder. Then grazed the side of her neck. She'd gasped as the blade slashed across her forehead. She had been slashed again, and again, while her arms and legs kept thrashing out, swinging and clawing to stay off her attacker.

Dimly, she had heard him whisper, "Come to me . . ."

"Oh, God," she had wept. "Help me."

"Give up. Rest. Be mine for all eternity," he had whispered, bringing the blade down again.

Then he had vanished.

Rose blinked into the mirror, unable to take her eyes off the slash marks on her body. She stood waiting, anticipating. Seconds. Minutes. Her waiting became so intense, so suffocating that she knew she was not waiting of her own volition. The waiting was being demanded of her by someone outside herself.

"No," she whispered, "it has to be a dream. A dream." But the slash marks were there. If she had only been dreaming, why were they there?

An hour later Rose stepped onto the pavement and ran into instant bedlam: garbage trucks grinding up yesterday's garbage; shopkeepers sweeping the walkways in front of their shops; children shoving and yelling as they made their way to school. It all seemed too loud.

She paused to glance at the card in her hand. It was a color postcard of the Eiffel Tower. It had arrived in the morning mail. "How I wish you were here," her mother had written. Then added: "No, on second thought, darling, I'm glad you're not. This is better than our first honeymoon."

Rose laid the postcard against her cheek. "Oh, how I wish *you* were here," she whispered, picturing her still-youthful mother, her exuberant father. But they were not there. She glanced at the card one last time before slipping it into her bag.

Then, looking thin and disoriented, she stepped quickly into the throng, strode down to Columbus Avenue and turned north. The Twentieth Precinct was only a few blocks away. She slowed a bit, sidestepped a woman walking her dog, and almost collided with a jogger going in the opposite direction. She began again to hasten her pace, the sidewalk changing from a dull gray to a gleaming granite as she passed from shadow to sunlight.

A slow smile of recognition appeared around her eyes and at the corners of her mouth as she glanced at the sudden brilliance of sky where swiftly changing clouds rode. The sun had risen higher, bright-faced, a warm, mellow hue to its light. Its very presence was golden and gentle and reassuring.

She was able to see color in the world now—the bright orange and yellow russet of leaves on trees lining the park, the rows of gleaming cars, reflections in glass, undisturbed images intertwined with the greens and browns of vegetation. Wherever the sun shone, things that were invisible became evident: color, people . . . herself.

It was a perfectly still mirror world in which the only movement came from the fleeting clusters of vaporous clouds galloping across the sky. There seemed no sound whatever from the great things around her. Space vanished. Time stood still.

For a brief instant, Rose yearned to wander the narrow streets of Greenwich Village where old, ornate houses huddled in unifying comfort. Where she could sit in an outdoor cafe and sip wine and talk art with Lottie. Where she could browse the bookstalls and eat oysters with their succulent texture and their strong taste of the sea. Where everything, oh, yes— everything was sharper and clearer and more peaceful.

Shadows now as the sun dipped behind the clouds.

Footsteps in the shadows.

Him again.

Abruptly, Rose stopped, teetering on the ragged edge of her consciousness. She was suddenly—and against her will—driven to her lowest potential.

"A quantity less than zero," a voice whispered. "If people learn they are destined to die, they tend to oblige. Just be ready."

The words sounded in her mind as clearly as though they had been spoken aloud. They were his words. His voice. Rose turned, startled, glancing around. Up to this point he had always been outside of herself. But now he was speaking to her from within.

"My tongue is your truth," he whispered. "Your womb— my death. Black fuzz that fills the mouth, shadows the brain . . ."

"Stop it," Rose said aloud.

Images pressed in, shot by—exploded.

"STOP IT!" she screamed, and people turned to stare.

Rose looked around, felt a rush of vertigo, not so much of her body as of her soul. She saw life now without reason, without purpose. Everything was crumbling. She glanced at her watch and saw that the sweep of the second hand had stopped. Time had stopped. It really didn't matter.

Nothing mattered.

Brushing tears away, Rose now felt her indifference deepen. In a mental blindness, she pulled her coat collar up tighter around her neck and moved away down the street.

CHAPTER 3

THE LADIES' ROOM ON THE FIRST FLOOR OF THE TWENTIETH Precinct was small and poorly lighted. Rose remained motionless just inside the door and waited for the policewoman to finish inspecting herself in the full-length mirror. Snapping her bra into place under her uniform, she smiled at Rose, then left the room.

Softly yet clearly in the silence that followed, the words came again, spoken in a whisper, spoken directly into the core of her being.

". . . Just be ready."

Rose lifted her hand to her face, stared evenly into the mirror and, as if drawn against her will, went about changing her appearance. Her hand was unsteady as she plucked out the first hair from her eyebrow. Then another. And another.

". . . We change and we have secret worlds. Don't be afraid. It won't hurt."

Eyebrows entirely removed, she applied a heavy rouge to her cheeks. For an instant, she wondered if she were not applying her own blood to her cheeks. Such a pretty color, she thought, and her world suddenly exploded in an avalanche of heat. Wet heat. With a sense of great wonder and joy, she applied a second coat of lipstick, deep and glowing red, and a second coat of powder, light powder, ghostly, all the time listening to the soft tapping in her brain.

"The hair. Change the hair."

Closing her eyes, she felt a darkness wash over her, and in the darkness she felt his eyes smiling at her.

"Disturbed . . . what do they know?"

Sweeping her hair away from her face, she opened her eyes. She quickly pinned it back into a severe bun, leaving the features of her face sharp and cutting.

". . . That's right. Let the machinery take over. Tell your story as though I never existed. They won't believe you anyway. Remember, I don't exist."

Unbuttoning the first two buttons on her blouse, she pulled the sheer material apart, allowing as much cleavage to show as possible. She lingered a moment longer, gazing into the mirror, running her tongue over her lips to moisten them. She enjoyed the taste, enjoyed watching her tongue lick the red fleshy folds of her mouth.

"And this is the girl I was telling you about," the voice whispered.

Another voice, ancient and wizened, said: "She's like all the others. Nothing more than a tramp. Get her away from me. Kill her if you must, I don't care, just make her go away."

Rose remained still.

Then in the faint light of a new day, she smiled and shut her thoughts—not off, but away—and left the room.

"Ah, Miss Carpenter," Lou Jaffy said, somewhat startled by Rose's appearance. His first thought: Drugs. She's on drugs. She was certainly a very different-looking girl from the girl he had interviewed at the hospital two days ago. Only drugs could do that to a person. He gestured to a chair beside his desk. "Please, sit down."

Rose circled past the desk to the window and stared out. She made a quick movement to her throat, then let her hand drop away.

Jaffy held her fast in his gaze. Two red gashes cut across her forehead and neck. Her eyes were larger than normal, and frightened. From the moment she had entered his office, he had noticed a change in the atmosphere. It was charged with a kind of negative energy.

"Please," he offered, "won't you be seated."

Rose turned and stared at him an instant; then her eyes averted his gaze, darting hectically around the room. A police station. How had she gotten there? She looked at the world through a fog now. She couldn't remember coming there, entering the building—climbing the stairs. She blinked, blinked again—the only light in the room was a dim overhead circular fluorescent which made her eyes ache—and she gave up her effort, her struggle to understand, and sat in a hard wooden chair to the right of the desk. She heard—or perhaps only saw, peripherally—the man behind the desk, who seemed to be shuffling papers in front of him. Otherwise, silence.

"What happened?" Jaffy asked offhandedly. "Accident?"

"What?" she muttered.

"The cuts. On your face . . ."

"Scratches. A neighbor's cat."

"Ah," Jaffy nodded. "May I get you a cup of coffee?"

"No, thank you."

All at once there was a disturbance in the hallway. A plainclothesman hollered into an adjoining office. "We've spotted him. Green E-type Jaguar. That fuck!"

"Where?"

"Heading north on the FDR. It's that son-of-a-bitch. I know it."

The two men rushed through the hallway and down the stairs as Jaffy got up and closed the door. He smiled apologetically at Rose. "Never a dull moment."

As though waking from a restless sleep, Rose stared with a dazed incomprehension at the man who was now pouring himself a cup of coffee.

"Are you sure you . . ."

"No," Rose said shortly.

"Just a few questions before we take a look at the files. All right?"

"Did you catch him yet?" Rose asked, not quite knowing why.

"What?"

"Danny. Danny Romano. He killed Mitzie."

Jaffy remained perfectly still, his face masking his surprise at her unexpected declaration. "What makes you so sure Romano killed Mitzie Karp?"

"Who else could it have been?" She was still unable to look at him.

"Interesting," he muttered.

"What is?"

"When we spoke in your apartment, you seemed reluctant to accept Romano as Mitzie's assailant. In fact, despite overwhelming evidence at the time, you seemed to totally discount the possibility."

In the rather odd silence which followed, Rose glanced down at her lap, her head falling forward slightly. She began to speak, to open her lips, but something stopped her. Why had she said it was Romano? What was wrong with her? She couldn't think. She . . . just couldn't think straight. It was as if a window fan had broken loose inside her head and was whipping itself into a frenzy, causing her to say things she didn't want to say, to do things she didn't want to do.

"I . . . I just thought maybe . . ." She broke off, unable to go on.

Jaffy drew himself up in his chair, sighed heavily. "No— no, I'm afraid Romano had nothing to do with her death. First he is the wrong blood type. Second, we know exactly where he was the night she was murdered. All the witnesses check out."

Rose nodded. When she looked Jaffy in the eyes, he smiled.

"Well, now . . ." he said, swallowing coffee and cigarette smoke at the same time, "I've had a chance to examine Dr. Cindrella's files at the Institute since we last talked. I thought perhaps if I went through his files . . . something would turn up." Jaffy paused, deliberating whether or not he should bring up Cindrella's death. He quickly ran past the notion. "I'll say one thing. I sure found it interesting. Dr. Cindrella seems to have tested everyone. In one session he tested the difference between sailors who had been tattooed once, sailors who had been tattooed more than once, and sailors who had never been tattooed at all. Then he tested sailors who wished they had been tattooed and sailors who hadn't and didn't want to be. After all that, do you know what his conclusion was?"

Rose shook her head.

"He found that most sailors were dull. Tattooed or otherwise. Imagine that. Prior to that, he tested survivors of the Holocaust. And before that, schoolteachers from grades one through nine. I'll tell you one thing. After reading some of their dreams, it's no wonder we're having problems with our children."

Rose suddenly found herself gazing at the window. Something had drawn her attention to it. A sound. A scraping sound. Her body tensed as the sound grew louder.

"Is something wrong?" Jaffy asked.

"Oh, no—nothing. May I have a cigarette, please?"

"Oh, sure." He tapped a cigarette from his pack and handed it to her. Her hand was shaking as he lit it.

"Thank you." She inhaled deep, letting the smoke fill her lungs. She glanced at the window again. "Can I look at the pictures now? I've . . . I haven't been sleeping well, and . . ."

"Of course. I'm sorry." He paused. "The point I was making is that I really only found one little scrap of interesting material at the Institute." Without any further preamble, he slid a piece of yellow paper across the desk. "Would you take a look at this, please."

Rose studied the piece of paper. On the top line was written: MANA. Beneath the word was a series of lines that connected other words. TELEPATHY—PRECOGNITION—PSY-CHOKINESIS. Another line connected the three words with the word STOCHASTIC. The last line connected all of the above to ROSE CARPENTER.

"Do you know what it means, Rose?" Jaffy swiveled in his chair and leaned forward on the desk.

Rose's face clouded. "No," she said softly.

"I've had several parapsychologists take a look at it. They can identify all the entries except one. MANA. None seemed to know what the word represented. I thought perhaps you might know . . . that perhaps Dr. Cindrella had discussed it with you."

"No, he hadn't."

Jaffy stroked his chin. "Do you know what the word 'sto-chastic' means?"

"Not really."

"Interesting word. It's from the Greek, originally meaning 'target' or 'point of aim.' There's a new movement in para-psychology that swears by it. Swears that someday we'll be able to attain absolute knowledge of what is to come. That we'll be all-seeing. Nothing will be random. In other words, we will be able to take the guesswork out of our lives. Some people are already supposed to have this gift. Apparently, Dr. Cindrella thought that you were one of them. You dream that people die, and sure enough—they die. At least, Mitzie Karp did. It appears you are able to receive important data on events before they occur. For whatever reason, you have become a target, a point of aim. Now I . . ."

"I don't understand any of it," Rose mumbled.

"Let's talk about the man in your dream."

"I've already told you—he always appears to me in shadows."

"But you said you first ran into him on the subway."

"I was mistaken." Rose stirred uncomfortably.

"Mistaken?"

"Yes."

Jaffy sighed, exhaling a cloud of smoke, then stood and removed his jacket. He knew that Rose had suddenly shifted gears. That she was on the run now, panicked, and that she was capable of saying almost anything to throw him off the track.

"Rose, you're running away from me. Why?"

Rose fell strangely silent. She looked again to the window. She felt a tapping inside her brain. A physical strangeness. And wrapped around that strangeness lay the deep velvet of a night she had once lived through. A night long ago. "I don't think you understand the danger," she muttered.

"Danger?"

"To me. My life. He's going to kill me."

"Who is going to kill you?"

"Him."

"The man on the subway? The one in your dream? Who?" Jaffy showed the first signs of impatience.

"You don't believe me, do you?"

"Give me proof."

"How can I give you something I don't understand myself?"

"Then perhaps it's all a delusion. There really is no man after all. Is that possible?"

"Then who killed Mitzie? Cheryl?"

"We don't know Cheryl Arthur is dead. Only missing."

Rose shook her head sadly. "No, she's dead. I know it."

Jaffy was beginning to feel twinges. A gut feeling? A hunch? No, that was all bullshit. No, what he felt was more like a vague uneasiness.

1. Cheryl Arthur turns up missing. Rose Carpenter turns up in the hospital the next morning claiming to have seen her body. Cheryl Arthur's suitcase contains a picture of Rose' husband. Is there a connection?

2. Mitzie Karp is raped and murdered. Rose Carpenter saw her death scene in her dream. So she said. They both work a

the Cottontail Club. Does the Club fit into the picture?

3. Rose Carpenter and Jack Squadron go through dream testing together. A few days later Dr. Reese Cindrella turns up dead. Accident, my ass! Maybe he found out something he shouldn't have. Dreams can sometimes be very revealing.

4. What is MANA?

5. Where does Jack Squadron fit in? He's married, yet he appears to be playing footsie with Rose. How many others was he playing footsie with? Mitzie Karp, perhaps?

6. Could Jack Squadron be the one I'm looking for?

7. Is that what Rose is covering up?

Jaffy paused a moment longer, the question-and-answer game nagging at him. There was something about the whole business that reeked of the madness that one goes through in trying to pick a winning lottery number. Pick the right one and you hit the jackpot. Pick the wrong one and you end up empty-handed. The real question to be answered was: Is Rose Carpenter telling the truth, or is she lying? Is she gifted, or is she suffering from delusions?

Jaffy led Rose to a small, musty room at the far end of the hallway. To the center of the room sat a huge oak slab of a table and several metal foldout chairs. A cork bulletin board hung from the south wall, haphazardly covered with newspaper clippings, wanted posters and memos. Venetian blinds hung crooked from the two narrow windows, and the black-tiled floor looked like it hadn't been cleaned in months.

"You look uncomfortable," Jaffy said as he extracted three large portfolios from one of the filing cabinets.

Rose mechanically shook her head. "I'm just a little tired, that's all."

There was a sticky silence.

"If you'd rather not look at these right now . . ."

"Now you think it's useless, is that it? What made you change your mind?"

"Like you said, his face is always in shadows."

"That means you don't trust me, doesn't it?"

Jaffy considered for a moment. Intuition said go ahead, tell her the truth. Caution said there was at least an outside chance she might turn something up, say something later that would be useful.

"Take as long as you want looking at these. If any picture seems even vaguely familiar, let me know. All the men you'll be looking at are repeaters." He laid the portfolios on the table. "If you need anything, I'll be in my office."

Rose watched him amble slowly from the room. Awkwardly, she sat at the table, her head whirling, her thoughts disorganized. Filtering through her mind was a succession of disturbing images: the sharp edge of a knife's blade slashing across her neck; Jack making love to her; Mitzi's face smiling as she served up the drinks at the Cottontail Club. Then, without warning, pain blocked her memory and dulled all thought. Hesitantly, she turned the first page.

Her eyes dismissed the opening pictures with a cursory glance, until finally her gaze came to rest on a young boy, sixteen, no more, with soft eyes and a full head of curly hair.

In a way, the boy looked like a younger version of Lance. No, she cautioned herself, she wasn't imagining it. He did look like Lance. Rose felt herself getting drawn in deeper. Oddly, she didn't mind. Lance was a reality; so was this boy. And reality was what she was hoping for. Encouraged, she moved on to the next picture, and the next, and then the next. Oh, please, God, let him be here. Let his face appear full-blown before my eyes, so that I can say, Yes! That's him. That's the man who wants to kill me!

She could feel a slight tremble in her hand as she frantically considered each face, stared into each new set of eyes. Calm eyes, peaceful eyes—eyes that stared back at her . . . a man doesn't choose his life. His life chooses him. Evil eyes, vacant eyes. An eye for an eye, the power of seeing, the power to judge, cold eyes, eyes that smiled—he wasn't there. HE WASN'T THERE!

Jaffy came back into the room as Rose was scanning the last of the photos.

"Find anything?"

Rose shook her head. "No," she whispered, her teeth biting down hard on her lower lip to stop herself from crying. It was no use. Like a sudden rush of a river, it all came pouring out of her. She tried to bury her face in her hands.

"Hey, come on. It'll be all right." Jaffy quickly moved to her side. Rose remained crumpled in the chair, sobbing helplessly. Jaffy had not been prepared for this. He tried to speak, but really didn't know what to say. As such, he was caught off guard. He just stood there watching her, thinking about his own daughter, thinking about all the daughters who were out there, somewhere, and that maybe, just maybe, they might end up like Mitzie Karp before the day was over.

Rose had felt very strange when she had entered the police station that morning. She felt even stranger now that she was about to leave it. Hesitantly, she hit the bar on the front door and passed into sunlight.

Then everything seemed to stop, to wait, to hold its breath in a state of extreme tension. Something was about to occur, some horrible catastrophe. The anxiety was overwhelming, choking the very life out of her. The senselessness of it all. People, things . . .

Rose looked around frantically.

The street was still. Nothing moved. There was no sound of footsteps. No cars. There was nothing. She was a nonperson in a city that didn't exist. Someone who was imprisoned in the fleeting figments of her imagination, while every fiber and sinew of her life was permeated with an alien tyrant, a brute authority who tumbled in and out of her consciousness at will.

Now hardly a moment passed when dark thoughts didn't pass through her mind, soft whisperings in a language she couldn't understand. The words were, of course, recognizable. But the meaning—what was their meaning?

With a conscious effort, Rose began to make her way to Columbus Avenue. She wanted only one thing: to go back into her apartment, to hide, to crawl into a deep dark hole and pull it in after her.

She took another awkward step. The neighborhood was quiet. Its silence a density, almost tangible. She sighed. As she did so, she again became aware of someone. Someone close by, watching her.

She glanced behind her.

Only rows of dilapidated brownstones and the gaping mouth of an alleyway. Except for a solitary woman reading an Apartment for Rent sign on the opposite side of the street, the block was empty.

At the corner Rose stopped again to look over her shoulder. Had she imagined it? The slow, shuffling footsteps behind her.

Where was the woman? The street was totally deserted now. When Rose turned back, she was startled to find the woman standing in front of her.

"Which way is Central Park?" asked the woman, her voice almost a whisper.

Rose stared into her ageless eyes. Finally she managed to raise her hand and point east. "That way," she said.

"Thank you." The woman whirled away and hurriedly crossed Columbus Avenue.

Rose drew a breath and headed south on Columbus Avenue toward home. There were more people now. More sound. At the corner of Eighty-first Street she paused to glance around.

The woman had changed back to Rose's side of the street and now stood swaying in a doorway. Nervously, she tugged at her coat collar. Although the street was busied with people, Rose had no trouble seeing the woman's movements.

Rose turned, quickly crossed the street, yearning to rid herself of the woman's presence. She kept moving, passed the museum, until at last she came to the end of yet another block where she turned left, knowing she only had a few more steps to go.

Her legs ached as she pushed open the outer door to her building. She glanced to the corner and saw the woman watching after her.

Rose plunged up the stairs, fumbled for her keys and let herself into the lobby. Instinctively, she moved to the elevator—punched ten. The door slid open.

Everything was a blur as the elevator cranked its way upward. The cheap scent of perfume and whiskey assailed her nostrils. She felt her head. Hot. Her clothes beneath her raincoat were drenched in sweat.

As the elevator door opened, she paused for a moment, then carefully stepped into the hallway. In one of the apartments, she couldn't tell which, loud rock music was blaring. Her legs were starting to give way as she moved toward her apartment. Leaning on the wall several times for support, she finally managed to reach her front door. She slipped the key into the lock and turned. Turned it again. And again and again. Nothing.

She glanced at her keys. She had been using the top key for the bottom lock and vice versa. And something else. She had been distracted by a piece of blue stationery peering at her from beneath her door.

Once inside, she dropped onto the couch and waited for the hammering in her chest to subside; waited until her breathing returned to normal. Only then did she read the letter.

Dear Lovebirds:

Do you sit with your heads touching like other lovebirds do? With your green and creamy gray skins melting into one? Sit still. Don't move. Don't blink. Yes. Perfect. Is there a cure for your sickness? But do you want to be cured? Can you be cured? No matter, someday you're going to pay for it.

I wish I could see your faces right now.

I'll bet you are both thinking of me all the time. Wondering. Is she dangerous? Will she try to destroy us? Destroy herself? You both should feel very proud. Do you?

Where am I? Is that what you are wondering? Perhaps across the street. Or perhaps right in the next apartment, or in the next building, watching you as you walk around your apartment naked. You really should get drapes to put over your windows. Plants won't do.

You should not worry about me though. It's the system that you should be worrying about. It knows. It will punish you. It always does. The system always does. It taught me a valuable lesson. Love destroys all things.

Fondest regards,
Ex-Mrs. Squadron

CHAPTER 4

Thursday, October 23
5:30 P.M.

ROSE SAT ROOTED, LISTENING TO TRAFFIC HUM THROUGH THE streets below. So many thoughts ran through her mind that her sitting may have lasted an hour; it may have lasted only a moment. It was the voices that frightened her the most. Thin vaporous voices that spoke in fractured sentences, pulverized double-talk and abrupt changes. This is a dream, she told herself, a dream, a dream, a very bad dream, but even the worst dream eventually ends, and she sat, waited, trying to hold herself together until it was over.

She had begun again to think about her own marriage. How else could one think of marriage? Words like "commitment" crossed her mind. She had believed in such things once. She had been brought up to believe that marriage should be forever. Her white knight, her rose garden, where had they all gone? Replaced by half-empty closets, busted bank accounts, and the fear of spending the rest of her life alone. New rules, new priorities—what were they anyway? Why the hell didn't she know?

Rose sat back, trembling and sweating profusely. She lit a cigarette and stared with an idiot's gaze at Cara's letter spread before her on the coffee table. From the moment she had read the first cruel words, she had run the gambit of emotions and the effort to remain calm had been a great strain.

Shattering . . . overwhelming . . . in just one short letter, Rose had collided with another person's suffering.

Ironically, she was doing to Cara what Cheryl had done to her. She was taking a love that belonged to someone else. A love between two people. A sacred trust. But it was different with Jack and her, wasn't it? Wasn't it?

Face up, she lay back on the couch; stared with open eyes at the ceiling. Oh, Cara, I'm so sorry. So damn sorry. Forgive me. Please.

Abruptly the rock music in the adjoining apartment blared into life again, causing her to rise with a start.

She tried glancing again at Cara's words, but nothing could have persuaded her to reread the letter just now.

Instead she prowled restlessly about the apartment in deep and disturbing thought. Oblivion lapped at consciousness and she struggled desperately to convince herself that none of this was her fault. Guilt tried to transform itself while the jangling bell ripped across her nerve ends.

She reached out and lifted the receiver.

"Hello?" Her head ached and the sound of her own voice echoed back into her brain like an explosion.

"Rose?"

"Yes? Who—"

"For Chrissakes, Rose—where the hell have you been?" Nick's voice was harsh and raspy, like a piece of sandpaper. She could tell it was business as usual.

"Nick, I—"

"I've been calling you . . ."

"Please . . ."

"Is everything all right?"

"Yes, fine."

"Then what the hell's going on? You were supposed to work the first shift Tuesday and Wednesday night. Dammit, Rose, I'm dying here. Dying!"

Rose tried to ignore Nick's harsh tone.

"I've been in the hospital, Nick."

"Hospital?"

"Yes. I had an accident . . ."

"You just said you were all right . . ."

"It was nothing serious."

"What happened?"

Rose moved quickly through her story, leaving out Cheryl's body and her dream.

Nick was not satisfied. He asked more questions, most of them personal, as if he wanted to squeeze the last ounce of

drama from the event—a striving after shock value, like all
those dozens of people you see gathered around a man on the
street who has just suffered a massive heart attack.

"What were you doing in the building?"

It was a good question. Rose was sure that her silence told
its own story. It suddenly occurred to her that there were tears
in her eyes; she hastily reached for a dish towel and wiped
them away.

"Rose?"

"Yes, Nick . . ."

"Look, I'm in big trouble here. Julie Lemon quit last night.
I'm up to my ass in customers with no way to handle them.
You coming in tonight?"

"Nick, I can't."

"Rose, for Chrissakes . . ."

"Please, I . . ."

"Tomorrow night's Friday. You gotta come in tomorrow
night. Work the weekend. Goddamn it, Rose, I need help!"

Rose hesitated, drawing in a deep lungful of smoke.

"Come on, Rose. What do you want me to do, beg?"

"I'll be in better shape after I get a little sleep."

"That's what I said. Forget tonight. But I need you for the
weekend. Okay?"

Rose agreed. At which point, an unreasoning anger took
hold and she wished she could smash her fist into Nick's pudgy
face.

"Thanks, Rose. I owe you one."

"Yeah. You owe me one."

Rose hung up without saying goodbye. From that point on
her every movement was an exercise in slow motion. She had
to eat. Something. Without thought, she crushed out her cigarette and started to prepare a small salad. Dropping a tomato
onto the cutting board, she reached for the knife. Slowly, methodically, she began to slice the tomato.

Reality. She had taken the word seriously once—long
ago . . . two weeks ago. Her reality now was what? It crossed
her mind that she had missed both of her art classes this week.
Something she hadn't done in years. Her thoughts were coming
quicker now, one piled on top of the other.

—You really should go into analysis, Rose, really. Artists
should get to know themselves.

—Oh, yes, nothing is more yours than your own dreams.

—To see at all, you must isolate and select . . .

—You really should go into analysis, Rose.

—By the way, most women who are depressed see themselves as losers and victims in their dreams.

—You really should go into analysis, Rose.

—Art is a thing of the mind . . . of the mind . . .

Rose watched as the blade sliced neatly through the ripened redness of the tomato, its juicy pulp spilling onto the cutting board.

—You really should go into analysis, Rose. Dig deeper into yourself. For your art. Having a dream is like having a conversation with yourself. Dig deeper, Rose. Deeper. This is your creation. You made it. It's your very own. Your baby.

Rose froze suddenly. Someone—yes, someone—was moving outside her door.

No, she scolded herself, and quickly pushed the thought aside. No, it was only her imagination. She knew all too well the extraordinary facility people had for imagining things. For creating mental images to their own liking. A foolish notion, she told herself. A fantasy. There was no one really out there.

She was just about to put down the knife when she had a flash of panic, knowing that she *did* hear someone moving outside her door. She stood still and listened. Dammit! There was someone out there. Perhaps her neighbor fishing around in her purse for her key. Or one of the building's maintenance men. Or the super. Almost anyone. No reason to panic. But still, she hesitated a moment longer. Whoever it was had on soft-soled shoes, and was walking very lightly. Suddenly the movement outside the door stopped, and Rose had the impression that whoever it was had also stopped to listen. Abruptly the sound of padded footsteps moved away from her door.

Rose quickly stepped forward and pressed her eye to the peephole. The hallway directly in front of her door was empty. With the knife still in her hand, she opened the door slightly, only a few inches, allowing herself to see further down the corridor. Still she saw nothing, but she was certain someone was there. She sensed it. She opened the door wider, giving herself a better angle from which to see.

Then she heard it, the quiet, hushed sound of someone breathing. If she pulled the door open just a little further, she would be able to see the entire corridor: she pulled. Someone moved. Rose darted into the hallway just in time to see a woman duck into the fire stairwell.

"Oh, my God," Rose gasped. It was her. The same woman who had followed her home. Cara? Was it Cara? Of course it was!

7:00 P.M.

Rose's state of mind was such that when she heard the doorbell ring she reached for the kitchen knife. She stood staring vacantly at the front door without breathing. The doorbell rang again. Suddenly she heard the tumbler of the upper lock turn with a noisy click. The lower tumbler clicked next.

She took a step back and waited.

The door was pushed open, then stopped with a jerk against the safety chain.

"Rose?"

Jack's voice.

"Jesus," she breathed, putting down the knife. She moved swiftly to the door. "God, I'm glad it's you," she said, releasing the chain.

Jack stepped quickly over the threshold. "What is it? What's wrong?" he asked stonily.

"I didn't know you were coming back tonight."

"I said I would." He stared at her for a moment. She looked tired. Like she hadn't slept in days. And something else. Her face. Twilight illumined her features and steeped her face in a light so diffused that her flesh appeared gray. Lifeless. It wasn't until Jack stepped closer that he realized it was the makeup she was wearing. And her eyebrows . . .

Rose groaned. "Jack, Cara was here. She left this letter. Under the door." Rose handed him the piece of stationery.

Mechanically, he took the letter and read it. He could feel Rose watching him, waiting for some kind of reaction to the words Cara had written. He was slightly concerned now, not because of the letter but because of the way Rose was reacting to it. He could feel the anger flooding through him. Just who he was angry with, he wasn't sure. He remained still for a moment, waiting for the slight trembling of his hands to subside.

"Jack, she sounds . . ."

"Dangerous, I know." He paused, then shifted his position, dropping the letter to the table, partially to give emphasis to what he was about to say, and partially with the hope that Rose would not see that his hands were still trembling.

"It's all right," he said, "I know where she is. She's staying at the Dixie Hotel. She called Frank Austin about an hour ago."

"The Dixie Hotel? That's where Cheryl—"

"I know. It's right around the corner from our apartment." He shook his head wearily. "Leave it to Cara."

"What are we going to do?"

"Nothing tonight. I'll go over there in the morning and try to straighten things out." He put his arms around her. "Don't worry, everything is going to be fine. Just fine."

Rose willingly let her body collapse against him.

Jack did most of the talking over the meal. It was another world he described, a world of sympathy for Cara, of friendship more than love, a cynical, hardhearted, backward look at the truth.

"Actually," he concluded, "we really never should have gotten married."

Rose felt that he really didn't believe that. That in some magical way, he was still very much in love with her, and probably always would be.

A momentary silence was agreed upon as they worked at forgetting an unpalatable subject. Jack sprawled on the sofa, his face partially in shadow, as Rose slipped the dishes into the dishwasher. He looked at her almost without recognition. His eyes pulled together to form a wrinkled brow, and with a sigh, he reached into his pocket and withdrew a pack of cigarettes.

Minutes passed and Jack mused, drawing in deep gulps of smoke, sucking the smoke up through his head, blowing it from his nostrils like a locomotive letting off steam. One thought followed another, causing ripples, then waves, until at last he quit thinking, in fear he was listening to the echo of mindlessness.

It was nearly nine o'clock when Rose mixed them both a drink. They sat beside each other on the sofa.

"God," Rose groaned, tossing hair off the back of her neck.

"Tired?"

"Exhausted."

"Don't you have to work tonight?"

"I told Nick I'd work the weekend."

"Oh."

"How are you feeling?"

"All right." Jack took out another cigarette, lit it. "What happened to your face?" he asked, reaching for an ashtray.

"What?"

"Those marks. What happened?"

Rose found it hard to know how or where to begin. She began awkwardly. Really, she was like a nervous animal who stirred at every sound, glanced here and there at a door slamming in the hallway, people shouting below in the courtyard, and never gave herself up totally to what she was talking about. She touched the slash on her forehead with distaste as she spoke of the knife's sharp blade. She went on talking, describing the event detail upon detail; she omitted no detail relevant to making herself completely understood.

She swirled the last of her gin and tonic in her glass and couldn't help but notice Jack's downright incredulity. It seemed preposterous; she knew that. She sighed.

"Maybe you scratched yourself while you were dreaming," Jack suggested, his arm raised, his hand at the back of her neck.

Rose found herself reluctant to look at him. "No. He . . . he was actually cutting me with the knife."

"How is that possible?"

"I don't know." She caressed his hand abstractedly. "One night, a person has a dream. They dream they are going to die. How they're going to die. The details of the dream are so clear, so truthful, that they know eventually it will come true. That it must come true, or—"

Rose caught her breath and stared at the foamy liquid in her glass as though it held the absolute certainty that she was right. Rubbish, but, dear God, the possibility was real, the ice-cold possibility that she and this man were locked together in a similar destiny, and that this destiny had been agreed upon years ago.

Rose felt her heart pounding like a sledgehammer as the next thought hit her.

"Jack, I've met this man before."

"I know. On the subway, wasn't it?"

"No, before that. Long before that . . ." Her eyes grew dangerously large. "We've met before. Years ago!"

"I don't understand." Jack stared at her. Suddenly she seemed transformed into someone else entirely. Her eyes had become vacant crystals in a blood-drained face. They seemed to bore straight through the walls of the apartment and beyond. She sat absolutely still; not a muscle moved.

"I'm back there now," she muttered. "I know it's happening, but I can't stop it. No one can."

Suddenly Jack began to feel a subtle vibration. He turned to look around the room. Everything seemed to be in order. Yet he could feel the vibration.

"He is close to me now," Rose said. "Closer to me than he's ever been."

Jack turned, confused. It seemed to him that Rose had stopped breathing. He slid around to face her. He could see she had fallen into some sort of trance.

"Rose?" he cried, taking her face into his hands. "Are you all right?"

"What?"

"You were just . . . are you all right?"

In the next instant a look of confusion mounted upon her face, deepened into terror. Abruptly, her lips squeezed together, her eyes rolled back, and she began to weep, uncontrollably.

CHAPTER 5

HALF AN HOUR LATER, ROSE REVEALED NO SIGNS OF HER emotional breakdown. In fact, she seemed almost in a good humor. Speaking in a relaxed tone, she offered, "I'll make some more coffee. How about it?"

"No, thanks. I've had enough."

"Are you sure?"

"Yes." Jack paused for a moment. "Are you going to be all right?"

Rose nodded, put her hand over his and squeezed it. A tight smile pinched her lips.

For an instant Jack looked at her in perplexity. This was not the same girl who had been in the room with him an hour ago. Not at all. It was like being with two women now. Even as she had been talking, her hair had come undone and the jet-black curls fell loosely over her forehead, giving her a look of promiscuity. A sensuousness radiated from the pores of her skin like steam on a bathroom mirror.

He watched as she drew back slightly, resting on one elbow, allowed her leg to extend out beyond the slit of her dressing gown, allowed her slipper to dangle from her tiny foot. Her long fingers, spread out like a claw, drifted slowly up her arm, giving a sexual implication to the movement. Her breasts were partially exposed, the cut of her dressing gown dropping low, suggestive.

He reached over and kissed her hard. She closed her eyes idly and moved her mouth against his as if she were tasting wine. When they paused, Rose's breath was coming in quick, short spurts.

"Come on," she whispered, taking his hands and pulling him to his feet.

Jack stood immobilized, frozen, in the center of the living room, his mind not being able to give him directions. People were moving now in the corridors of his mind; quickly, slowly, hurriedly, like ants under attack, they scurried from one end of his thoughts to the other, arms around shoulders, waists, voices urgent. Jack gasped at the unexpected hand on his shoulder.

Startled, he regarded the girl before him without recognition. "No, I don't . . ."

"Right here?" she asked.

He felt the shifting of weight, the careful movement toward him. He didn't want to face her. No, not now. Pretend, smile— in a few minutes he would be able to ease himself from the apartment, go away, somewhere, another town maybe, another country . . .

"Jack!"

He hesitated. Smiled. "Give me a few minutes. Okay? I'll be right in."

"Promise?"

"Yes."

"Don't be long." Slowly, she backed into the bedroom.

Jack crossed to the window and looked out over a city cloaked in darkness. Lights shimmered in the distance, like stars, and the silence about him became doubly oppressive.

A plaything, he mused, and his vision blurred. That's all he was, a plaything. Cara was using him. Rose was using him. He had been used all his life, and that was the cruelest abuse of all. A sudden, uncontrollable anger leapt within him, and his thoughts burned with it for a moment. Then lust collided with anger and set off a sharp spark in his brain, destroying all thought, all feeling, but one. The exercise of his sexuality— his desire and its consummation.

She stood up and slipped off her gown, as he watched. She felt him wanting her. Sitting down on the bed beside him, she opened the front of his trousers. She watched his face; he let his head roll back a little and let his eyelids droop. She took his phallus in her hand and began to stroke it.

"Wait," he said, and stood up. Rose lay back on the bed

and watched him remove his trousers and shirt. When he turned to face her, she moved forward and took down his briefs.

He ran his hands lightly over the back of her head, her neck, letting her establish her own movement. Then he slid both hands down her back and pulled her closer.

She kissed his phallus, then pulled back. He held the tension on her back, still hopeful that she would go on. Instead, she moved away, saying, "I want you in me."

She slid further back onto the bed and waited. For a brief moment Jack stood there in seeming indecision, then knelt on the bed next to her. He ran his fingers down her body, slowly, playfully, outlining her breasts, her belly button, stopping when he got to her pubic hair. Hesitantly, he looked into her eyes and smiled.

"You're a very beautiful girl," he said softly.

He half sat, then let his body drop next to hers.

Now, alone and naked with Jack, the emotions she least understood but needed most to feel came quickly, easily, and her confusion was overtaken by her hunger. A hunger that seemed to come from some outside source, yet so deep within her that she could no longer deny it. She suddenly wanted him to open her up, wanted him to experience every facet of her, wanted to be loved in all ways.

Slowly, he reached for her breasts. She moaned beneath his touch and could see his phallus had grown to full erection.

As he entered her, she closed her eyes. Slowly, he began to move. She continued playing with the hairs on the back of his neck as she quickened his pace.

She moaned, feeling an odd pleasure ripple through her body. Rolling her head to one side, her face slipped down between the pillows. All at once Jack dropped the full weight of his body on top of her and shoved violently forward. With each repeated thrust, she moaned, her body sinking deeper into the mattress.

She was climaxing now. At least she thought she was. Actually, she was gasping for air. The pillow was completely covering her face. She couldn't breathe. Jack's body pressed down harder.

She panicked, trying to wrench the pillow away from her face. Her nails ripped across the material, but the pillow remained covering her face. She heard Jack moan, whimper like a child in pain.

"Now," he screamed.

Oh, my God—I can't breathe!

Rose gasped, feeling Jack pressing down, harder and harder, his body rigid. Everything started to fall away. Suddenly Jack's body rolled away from her, his hand taking the pillow with him.

Rose gasped, her lungs taking in a sudden flood of oxygen.

With her second deep intake of breath came the sight of Jack moving away from her, flowing effortlessly across the room, drifting through the darkness in a wild silence like the wake of bells.

There was total silence then and no movement.

Ambition should be made of sterner stuff, Jack reminded himself as he left the building. The ease with which Rose had accepted the incident dumbfounded him. She had regarded him thoughtfully, saying nothing, displaying neither surprise nor hostility nor despair. How calm she had been.

Her calmness baffled him.

He glanced at his watch. Ten-thirty. Rose had been asleep when he had decided to leave the apartment. Or was she? A sudden little wind scooted paper across the sidewalk. His gaze sharpened. The night caught in his heart. All the shadow and glow of a full moon called out to him. It was that kind of night—taut, swift, deep in abortive emotions and longing. He smiled, his eyes flashing in the moonlight.

He moved softly away from the building.

The temperature seemed to plummet ten degrees by the time he had reached the mouth of the subway. He glanced around the vacant night, quivering, sore, and pressed his hand into his pocket, fishing around for loose change.

A pitiful-looking creature lurched from a darkened doorway, mumbling and coughing, his outstretched hand begging for a small token of money. Before Jack had a chance to respond, the man doubled over and began to vomit, spewing forth a mixture of liquor and pain, and stood huddled afterward next to a parked car, weak, shaking, unable to straighten up.

Jack moved quickly away and disappeared into the subway.

11:15 P.M.

Cara Squadron dropped the keys to her hotel room on the dresser and kicked off her heels. She wasted no time in removing her clothes.

Shakily, she stood naked before the mirror, looking at herself. She hated what she saw. She was nearly fifty, but in the harsh overhead light of the room, she thought she looked much older. She stared at her milky-white complexion, the dark circles under her eyes. Her lips were chapped and almost devoid of color.

Licking her lips, she glanced critically at her body. Her breasts appeared to sag more than usual. She cupped each breast firmly and lifted them higher, squeezing the nipples slightly, trying to tease life back into them. She remembered how much Jack had enjoyed watching her do this while they were making love. Having mounted him, she would hold her breasts and fondle them, making sure to point them in his direction. He would become instantly aroused and pull her hips down harder, shoving it in deeper.

Of course, she had been younger then, prettier, and willing to do anything for him sexually. *Younger and prettier*. The words swirled in her head as images flashed before her eyes, cavorting within the mirror's frame. Mirrors are not for admiring oneself, she mused, but for wondering at, and wondering into. A piece of glass by which we try and catch a moment in time and hold it there. Wonder upon it. There is so little to really wonder about when you get right down to it, and yet so fucking much to wonder about when you get right down to it. Fifty years. A lifetime. Seen, heard, felt—not felt, worse—not understood, standing here, rattling on like pennies in a child's piggy bank.

Fuck it!

She lit a cigarette and switched on the TV set. Most times it helped her forget her troubles, no matter what the program, but tonight the controlled images on the screen only helped to agitate her more. She punched out the main light—it was causing a glare—and crossed to the bed where she spread her long naked body out like a polar bear basking in the sun.

Her edginess persisted. Perfectly understandable. She lay there dormant, in a state of suspended animation, but the restlessness continued within her mind. A divorce would be acceptable. Stop. A new thought; like turning a new page in one's life. Never. Never, never! She glanced desperately at the TV screen. Christ. She would have to do something to take her mind off who the hell knew what.

A short rap on the door; then: "Telegram."

"What?" she muttered to herself.

The silence seemed to last forever.

"Mrs. Squadron? Telegram."

There it was again, she thought. That voice—a musical lilt she could listen to forever. "Telegram," she whispered as she got up and turned the sound down on the TV set. She knew it could only be from one person. Frank Austin. He was the only one who knew she was there. Probably a clever little pick-me-up message:

> You've got bats in your belfrey,
> Don't you see,
> Let me come over
> And we'll have some tea.

Cara smiled. "Just a minute."

She threw on her robe and moved to the door. "Telegram? For me?"

"Mrs. Squadron?"

"Yes."

"It's for you."

"Can you put it under the door?"

"Sorry. You have to sign for it."

"Oh, all right. Hold on." She removed the safety chain and hit the safety lock on the door handle. One minute Cara was opening the door of the room. The next a great hand, fisted, came out of the darkness and slammed into the center of her chest, plummeting her backward onto the bed. She tried to scream, but his hand slapped itself across her mouth. His free hand darted quickly between her legs. Grinding his body against hers, he laughed and moaned simultaneously. She was blinded with fear. It wasn't happening, couldn't be happening.

Groping for the fly of his trousers, he removed his penis, huge and wet, and quickly shoved it between her legs.

Cara's eyes held on his face. Light flickered from the TV screen, but he had dropped his body forward, blocking out all light. As he pushed in harder, she strained away from him and kicked with both legs.

"Cunt," he whispered. "Open up."

Completely panicked, determined to resist, she lifted her knees and jammed them against his chest, biting down on the flesh of his hand at the same time.

Three brutal blows across her face with his fist stunned her; the light started to fade; her legs were being spread again. He flung his body across her, pressing down with his full weight.

She opened her mouth to scream. He hit her again in the face. Again, this time sending her to the floor. She rose on all fours, whimpering, groping her way across the room. He mounted her from behind, driving her to the floor.

"Scream," he whispered, "and I'll kill you." He flashed the knife in front of her eyes.

She tried to turn on her side.

He forced her to the floor to stop her body from squirming and twisting. He grabbed hold of her breasts and squeezed hard, causing the veins around her brown nipples to bulge.

She kicked again with both legs, trying to topple him. Hunching her back, she tried to rise. He yanked her down to the floor, trapping her flat. And then she felt it. An ache. A sharp stabbing pain as the knife punched its way into her back.

She took the last ounce of strength and breath left in her body and screamed. The knife came down again, puncturing her skin just below the shoulder.

The light started to fade. "Oh, yes—" she whispered. "Just let me die."

She made one last effort to turn and face her assailant. The light from the TV flickered and she gasped as the knife struck for the third time. She screamed: "Jack! No!"

And then there was blackness.

CHAPTER 6

Friday, October 24
9:30 A.M.

ROOM 300 WAS THE INTERROGATION ROOM OF THE TWENTIETH Precinct. Jaffy crushed a paper water cup and tossed it casually into the basket. The stenographer sat ready in the corner, apparently uninvolved but alert to all that went on. Leaning against the filing cabinet to Jack Squadron's right was Kenny Clark, the assistant district attorney. Seated on the corner of the table to Jack's left, Captain Derek Jones, Homicide Squad, Manhattan West.

Jaffy stepped forward.

"Now Jack," he said, "we're going to ask you questions, loads of questions. Those questions and your answers will be taken down by the stenographer. Any answers you make may be used against you in future proceedings. Do you understand?"

"Yes."

"Now you know you don't have to answer any of the questions if you don't want to. You have the right, by law, to remain silent. Is that clear?"

"Yeah," he muttered, examining his surroundings through narrowed eyes.

"You can still call a lawyer if you like."

"Just get Frank Austin over here," Jack said, showing little outward interest.

"He knows you're here," Jaffy said, pacing slowly back and forth, the first of the continual cigarettes he would smoke drooping from his mouth. "We've already questioned him.

He'll be here right after lunch." Jaffy stared at Jack, then at the stenographer, then at Jack again.

"For the record, Jack—state your name."

"Jack. Squadron . . ."

"Speak up so the stenographer can hear you."

"Jack Squadron!"

"Address?"

"Four-sixteen West Fifteenth Street."

"What do you do for a living?"

"Composer. Music."

"How old are you?"

Jack sighed. "Thirty-three."

Jaffy paused for a moment, stood erect, crushed his cigarette into the ashtray. "Did you rape your wife, Jack?"

"No," Jack replied, his fingers gripping the arms of his chair.

"Do you know who did?"

"Christ!"

Jaffy blinked his eyes slowly, pleased by Jack's anger. "Does the question bother you?"

"Yes."

"Why?"

"I'm scared, that's why. You arrest me because my wife claims I tried to kill her. You won't let me talk with her—see her . . ."

"Why would your wife lie to us?"

"I don't know. Maybe she thought it was me. Wanted it to be me. She's been sick . . . I told you that. Confused. Ask Frank Austin. He'll tell you."

"How long have you known Rose Carpenter?"

"A week."

"Have you ever gone to bed with her?"

"That's none of your goddamn business!"

Captain Jones slid from the table. "Watch your mouth, smart guy." The captain's deep voice hardly ever rose into the middle register; it was like the bass string of a musical instrument. "We can treat you two ways here. Like a man or like a criminal. Now which is it?"

Grimacing, he sat back on the table and folded his arms to indicate that he was finished.

"Did your wife know you were going out with Rose?" Jaffy asked.

Jack hesitated. "I don't know. Maybe."

"Is that why she was staying at the Dixie Hotel?"

"I don't know why she went there."

Jaffy caught Kenny Clark's eye and gave him a sign. Clark groped in his briefcase as Jaffy moved to the window. The blinds were partially open. The double windows gave a view of brick tenements behind the station. Jaffy stood with his back to the window, watching, waiting, making mental notes.

Clark stepped forward, adjusted his glasses, and in a ponderous, nasal tone began to read aloud from a slip of paper. "Jack: Because I have left the apartment, it does not mean I have left you. I may be watching you right now as you read this letter. When you are with her—I will know. My eyes will always be there—watching."

Jack's eyebrows rose in surprise. "You searched my apartment. What right—"

Clark removed his glasses. "All legal, Mr. Squadron. Let me explain that I'm a lawyer, not a policeman. We are not here to trap you. Only to get at the truth. You will not be deprived of your rights under the law. Detective Jaffy explained that you don't have to answer our questions. It was stated before. Let me state it again. Your answers are voluntary."

Jaffy stepped forward as Clark stepped back.

"Jack, did your wife know you were having an affair with Rose Carpenter?"

Jack hesitated. "Yes."

"You recognize the letter just read to you?"

"Yes."

"Did you and your wife argue over it?"

"No."

"Did you feel trapped when you read the letter?"

"I don't know what I felt."

Captain Jones stood. "Okay, Jack, tell me about your wife's body again."

Jack blinked, confused. "You mean the way I found her lying there?" Jack glanced at Jaffy.

"No, no, Jack," the captain said. "Over here. Tell *me*."

Jack looked at the intense, muscular man who stood to his left. "Well, I . . . I entered the hotel . . ."

"What then?"

"I went up to Cara's room."

"How?"

"Elevator."

"And?"

"I don't know. The next thing I remember—I heard a bunch of screams . . ."

"I like that. Screams in bunches."

"That's right."

"And you immediately ran to her?"

"That's right. But . . . but I was too late. I found the door open . . ."

"Of course," the captain remarked. "Kind of like an immaculate conception. You running into yourself at the open door."

"I don't have to take that from you."

"Listen, you," the captain cried, pointing his finger into his face, "with the evidence we've got here, you're as good as convicted."

"I tell you, she was just lying there on the floor. There . . . there was blood all over the place. All the lights in the room were off . . ."

"Then how did you see the blood?"

"The . . . TV was on—no sound, there was no sound. But the TV was on."

"When the manager found you standing over her, he said the sound from the television was blaring."

"No. No, it wasn't. It couldn't have been."

"Maybe you turned it up to drown out her screams."

"No, I heard footsteps. Someone running down the back stairs."

"With your wife screaming—the television blaring?"

"No! There was no sound."

"You wanted to punish your wife, isn't that right?"

"Yes."

"She was ruining your life."

"Yes."

"And she laughed at you. Probably called you names . . ."

"No, we—"

"So you tried to kill her. You cut her with the knife then tried to rape her. Or did you rape her first, then stab her? That's really what you did, isn't it? You beat her, raped her, and then tried to stab her to death."

"Nooo! I love her. I LOVE HER!"

"Remarkable! After raping and stabbing her six times he is more in love with his wife than ever. I'm sure she'll be glad to hear that." He paused. "That is, if she lives."

Jack began to sob softly.

Jaffy stepped forward and indicated to the captain that Jack needed a breather. It was the sort of thing Jaffy felt embarrassed watching. Crucifying a suspect—watching him break down. Not that he wasn't a strong cop. He was. He was just weary of it all. There had been times when there was nothing more important to him than solving a case. Those were the good old days. Exciting, challenging, when he was filled with conviction and purpose. Each case was more extraordinary than the next, and he jumped in with penetrating interest. Even a sense of perverse joy.

But somehow, after years of seeing the misery, the suffering, he found himself becoming more compassionate. He looked at it all now as a sickness. A sorrowful sickness that needed understanding rather than brutality.

Punching a cigarette from his pack, he offered it to Jack. Jack surfaced from his slumped position, grateful for a moment of peace.

"Thanks," he said, and Jaffy said, "Sure," and lit his cigarette. Kenny Clark spoke in a low whisper to the captain as he scribbled on a yellow pad. Jack couldn't make out what they were saying, but he was sure they were talking about him.

"I'm sorry, Jack," Jaffy said. "I mean I'm really very sorry, but we have to get at the truth."

"Yeah. The truth," Jack muttered.

Jaffy shrugged. "These things are never pleasant."

"They're not supposed to be!" cried the captain. "Now let's get on with it."

Jaffy gazed at him, marveling. Everything that the big man was thinking, feeling, it seemed to Jaffy, lay as open on his face as his gun did on his hip. Momentarily embarrassed, Jaffy tugged on his earlobe. With a sigh, he said, "You see, Jack, by your own admission your relationship with your wife was on shaky ground. Her letter states that she intended to make your life miserable. I know that you're fond of her and she has genuine love for you, but maybe—"

"Will she live?" Jack asked shakily.

Jaffy gazed at him blankly and could see that Jack was a long way off, trying to work out a problem. "They have her in intensive care. She lost a lot of blood. One of her lungs was punctured—"

"Jesus," Jack breathed.

"I've asked the hospital to keep us informed."

"Thanks."

Jaffy paused. "Jack, I'm going to level with you. I'm not even supposed to be dealing with you at this point. I mean, murder may now be involved. Next you'll have to deal with Homicide. They're not going to be that easy on you."

Jack slowly removed the cigarette from between his lips. "Murder? I don't understand. I thought—"

"Jack, murder's murder. It's clear-cut, if you know what I mean. With me, it's all semen, corruption, rape. I mean, if that's all it turns out to be, and you cooperate, things will go a lot easier for you. Let's say that you went to the hotel to talk it out with her. But the closer you got to the hotel, the more angry you became. You wanted to punish her. Rape is a form of punishment. But she put up a fight..You lost your head . . ."

Jack laughed. "You're grasping at straws," he cried. "Aren't you? You know damn well I didn't do it! Christ, you're all crazy."

Jaffy's face hardened. "Jack, the knife had your fingerprints all over it."

"So what? He could have been wearing gloves."

"What made you pick up the knife?"

"A natural reaction."

"You had an awful lot of her blood on your clothing."

"I told you. I picked her up. Held her in my arms."

"The manager said you were standing over her when he walked in."

"I must have put her down. Stood up. I was just going to call the police when he walked in." Jack laughed again. "Give yourself a rest. You haven't got a case. I don't care what she said, you don't have a case."

Jaffy slowly shook his head. "Suit yourself," he murmured wearily.

That concluded the interdepartmental section of the interrogation. Jaffy turned to matters of immediate concern to Homicide. "Jack, do you know a Mitzie Karp?"

"Never heard of her," Jack said smugly.

"Rose never mentioned her to you?"

Jack looked at the tip of his cigarette. "Oh, yeah. You mean—"

"October twentieth. Four P.M. Raped and then stabbed twelve times. Yeah, that Mitzie Karp."

"Rose mentioned her. What's that got to do with me?"

"Ever been to the Cottontail Club?"

"I've never been there in my life."

Jaffy clicked his tongue. "I hate to contradict you, but we both know that's an outright lie. You were there the night she was murdered. Twice. You talked with her half the night. You were one of the last customers to leave the club."

Jack's face froze. "Who said so?"

"Julie Lemon. One of the barmaids. And the owner, Nick Nuzzo; they have both made a positive identification."

"That's bullshit. I've never been to any Cottontail Club."

"Saturday evening. Sunday morning, October nineteenth. Where were you?"

"I . . . I don't remember."

"That's because you don't want to!"

"No, I wasn't there."

"Were you with Rose Carpenter?"

Jack paused. "That was five, six days ago. I can't remember . . ." Jack broke into nervous laughter, choked on it, the sweat beading on his brow. "This is ridiculous. You're not accusing—"

"Were you having an affair with Mitzie Karp too?"

"That's preposterous." He sat rigidly in the chair, as if to hold the structure of the argument within his control.

Jaffy took up a position behind the table where he reached for a brown folder. "Jack, your blood has been checked out by a hematologist. You're type B. Semen, whether you know it or not, can be a substitute for blood. The semen ejaculated by Mitzie Karp's killer was type B. Do you know what the odds of that are? Blood type A, forty percent. Type O, another forty percent. Blood type AB, five percent. That leaves B, your type. Fifteen percent."

Jack's face slowly disintegrated under the laser scrutiny of Jaffy's eyes.

Outside, it had begun to rain. Buckets of it, mixing together with sudden cataclysmic crashes of thunder, flashes of lightning. Heavy layers of air mass were violently pushed apart. Then it quieted and time moved forward, the room darker in the constant downpouring of rain.

"I've also done a little checking on you before last night," Jaffy continued. "From what Rose said, I figure that Cheryl Arthur turned up missing Thursday evening, the sixteenth of October. That she never returned to the Dixie Hotel that night. So I did a little nosing around. And what do I find? That night you were in a bar on Thirteenth Street and Eleventh Avenue. The Seahorse. The bartender remembered you well. It seems you got into a fight with a young lady after she refused to let you put the make on her. That you threatened her. Grabbed her. Ripped her blouse. They literally had to escort you from the bar." Jaffy moved around to the other side of the table. "Suddenly, I get curious. I draw a map of the area and bam! It hits me right between the eyes. The Dixie Hotel, the Seahorse, the building Rose claims she saw Cheryl Arthur's body in, all within a four-block radius, walking distance from your apartment. Even the Cottontail Club is in walking distance. Easy enough for you to be at each scene of the crime, yet barely out of your own neighborhood. Now don't sit there and tell me that all this is coincidence."

Jack's heart leaped in his chest and he felt himself reddening. "This is nonsense. All nonsense! Okay, maybe I was in the Cottontail Club, maybe I was in the Seahorse, but I didn't rape and kill those girls!"

Kenny Clark stepped forward. "Girls? He didn't say Cheryl Arthur was dead. He said she was missing." Clark moved closer to Jack. "Is Cheryl Arthur dead, Jack? Is she?"

All eyes turned on him.

"Come on, Jack," Jaffy soothed, "talk to the man. He's the only one who can help you."

Jack tightened his lips and refused to answer.

The captain joined the other two. They now had Jack squeezed in from all sides. "I'm tired of listening to you lie. You've been lying to us all morning. Now you got one last chance to tell the truth, or—"

Jack swung his body around to face the stenographer. "You. You there. Take this down. No, look at me," he demanded. "I am being forced to answer questions. I have a right to a lawyer. I want one now. I have a right to make one phone call. I want to make a phone call."

"All of a sudden the prick wants a lawyer," the captain bellowed.

Jaffy said, "For Christ's sake, Jack—you raped your wife; why not admit it?"

"Because it's a lie!"

"Her blood and flesh were found under your fingernails."

"I want a lawyer!"

"You'll get one, but in the meantime, let's keep talking."

The next two hours passed with the same badgering tactics. Jaffy went on to establish the fact that Frank Austin admitted Jack never got along with young women. That in point of fact, he seemed to hate them. The captain worked the pauses, directing a myriad of barbs at Jack, but if they took effect it was not apparent. Kenny Clark kept up an assault of quietly posed questions. From his earlier days in criminal law, he still had a vivid imagination that could make this sort of technique work. Soft-spoken, almost smiling, his questions were intensely physical as he reconstructed each act of violence. The object was to strip Jack down, make him feel naked. It was a favorite ploy used by the Nazis in concentration camps. Stripped naked, people were easier to handle. But it didn't work. Jack remained calm. Too calm.

Recess was finally called.

Jack was escorted to room 305, a holding room with four bare walls, one table and one chair. He stood hunched at the window, his finger massaging his upper lip. A gray slab of a courtyard with a single tree lay below and to his right. He had an impulse to jump. It would be taking a chance, but if he hit the tree just right, careened across the sidewalk, was able to hurl himself up over the wall—yes, it could be done.

He was sweating heavily under his jacket in the stuffy, close air. Outside, heavy drops of rain pelted the window. His upper arms moved like oil against his body as he reached into his pocket for a cigarette. There was none. He opened his mouth and tried to breathe more freely as he leaned against the cool windowpane. How many floors up was he? he wondered. It looked to be three.

All the same. If it had to be done, it had to be done. The

door opened behind him and the voice asked: "What do you want for lunch?"

"Nothing. Just a pack of cigarettes."

"Are you sure?"

"Yeah."

There was the briefest of hesitations, then the door closed with a dull thud. Jack's eyes never left the courtyard. He nodded. If that's the way Cara wants it . . . Suddenly he straightened, alert, staring. "Possible," he said in a half whisper, wryly smirking. "Very possible . . ."

Jaffy lit another cigarette, drew the smoke in thoughtfully, plucked a piece of loose tobacco from his upper lip, and said, "I'll say one thing for him, his intestinal fortitude is incredible. Up to his eyeballs in trouble, yet he won't give an inch."

"We don't have any witnesses, that's why," Clark said, shrugging on his raincoat. "He knows that. Even if his wife goes ahead with her testimony, a good lawyer would have him waltzing the hell out of court with a slap on the wrist."

Jaffy rose and began to prowl the office. "Can we stall?"

"Stall, hell. We've got to lay our hands on something. Even then it's not going to be easy. Without witnesses—"

Jaffy nodded almost imperceptibly.

They discussed briefly the legal aspects of the evidence. Jaffy was forced to agree with Clark—they didn't really have much.

"He's one clever son-of-a-bitch," Clark moaned, then added, "What about the Carpenter girl? Maybe she knows something."

Jaffy took a deep breath. "I don't know . . ."

"Get her over here."

"It's useless for me to question her again. I tried. She doesn't trust me."

"Throw her onto someone else. Have her questioned again."

Jaffy walked Clark to the door, where he watched him disappear down the steps. Jaffy remained alone in the corridor for a moment, then reentered his office. He brewed a fresh pot of coffee on his hot plate. His eyes cocked in space. What could he do or say to Jack that would stop him dead—really jar him loose? There Jack is, Jaffy thought. Here you are. Don't let him get away from you.

Abruptly, he reached for the telephone.

CHAPTER 7

Friday, October 24
11:15 A.M.

OFF IN THE DISTANCE THE TELEPHONE CONTINUED TO RING.

Rose remained lying on her stomach, her face pressed into the pillow, her arms crushed beneath her body. For a split second she wondered where she was. Licking her lips, she extracted her left arm from beneath her body, next her right. Then something within her body seemed to release itself and she groped for the phone.

"Hello?" she said, her eyes barely open.

Detective Jaffy's words were no more than a murmur. Like a tightrope walker, he meandered around the implications of everything that had happened—was happening. His voice came to Rose as a disconnected jumble. Then as a stake through the heart. "Impossible," she breathed, trying hard to keep the on-rush of emotions from invading her thoughts. Jaffy moved swiftly into details: Raped and stabbed . . . Cara . . . Dixie Hotel last night.

Rose listened disbelievingly as images flew by. Jack and her, lying in bed last night, making love. She had fallen asleep, yet had sensed Jack putting on his clothes. She had awakened suddenly. She was alone. Very alone. It had been several hours later when she realized Jack wasn't coming back, and slipped again into a deep sleep.

Rose now glanced at the empty space in the bed next to her. He had been lying there last night. Touching her. Kissing her. How helpless he was, how like a little boy. Lying in her arms, clumsy and warm, his embrace awkward, his breath hot upon her, he had begged her to caress him. He had appeared so helpless. So . . . childlike.

Rose could not free herself of the paralysis of the moment, the frightening knowledge that it might have been she brutalized instead of Cara.

Jaffy's voice began to wind down as he spoke of Mitzie Karp and Cheryl Arthur. In one short sentence he accused Jack of being involved with both girls. "Most likely," Jaffy concluded, "Cheryl Arthur is dead."

Rose felt a kind of faltering inside her, a kind of stumbling; the whole of her world gave a lurch and there was nothing to hold on to, no certainty anywhere. For an instant she couldn't remember what day it was. Friday? Yes, she was sure it was Friday. She brushed hair out of her eyes.

Jaffy was talking again. Could she come to the police station later today? She fought to clear her thoughts. Then her gaze—veiled by eyelashes as thick as tree trunks—wandered to the painting by the window. A red blotch of paint was running freely down the canvas, dripping steadily on the floor.

Rose sat up. The room was cool and dim.

Something seemed to hum in the walls.

"Say around seven o'clock?" Jaffy asked. "I can send a car for you if you like."

"No, I'll . . . no, all right—seven o'clock. I'll be there." Her voice was nervous and shrill.

"Are you going to be all right?"

"Yes. I . . . please, I can't talk now . . . please."

She placed the receiver in its cradle.

In the next moment Rose broke down and wept uncontrollably, but made no sound, the pain caught in her chest, unable to make its way to the outside world.

The telephone began ringing again. Rose made a gesture as if to answer it—no, let it ring—and sank back. She was not going to answer it this time. She waited, tensely, her eyes riveted to the painting.

Images began to parade through her mind. They spread out like a veil of soft fiber, overlaying all other of earth's images, large and small.

Overhead, the creaking of floorboards, the sudden sound of water rushing through pipes. Rose's head split, and she closed her eyes and saw the blood in her own head. The water slowed.

Are you afraid?

Not of death.

Of what?

Him.

You're going to die.

Cold. She was so cold, so cramped, so tired, so weak that she could not go any further. All at once Cheryl's face rushed forward in the blackness of her vision. Stripped of life, it descended the mad river of her sight in wild turnings, striking her vision dead center.

Rose could not open her eyes to fight back. She could not lift her head. She moaned. And moaned. There was nothing else she could do.

Dr. Frank Austin had wet feet.

The rain had stopped some twenty minutes ago, but he'd been sloshing around in it for the better part of an hour, trying to catch a cab. A point he emphasized with considerable disgust.

He was a tall man, Jaffy noted, escorting him slowly up the stairs. He looked even taller in his black raincoat that billowed from his broad shoulders like a cape. He held a black attaché case in his right hand, his gloves in the other, and he walked up the granite steps as if he were attending a funeral.

"You see," Jaffy said, glancing at the hall clock. It was a few minutes past three. "Criminal investigation has its own rules. The problem is, no case resembles the other. Especially where homicide is concerned. So each investigation runs its own course. Creates its own precedent. This means we're always starting from scratch. Criminals follow no set patterns, display no recognizable signs. I mention this because of Jack. Now if he did murder these girls . . ."

"What is it you want?" Austin asked, having become conscious of his squeaking shoes.

"What I'd really like," Jaffy said swiftly, "is for you to probe the possibility that he *did* murder those girls. Talk with him. I know he is a friend . . ."

Austin stopped at the top of the stairs, having gone white. "That's right. A personal friend. I find it hard to believe that he would—"

"Dr. Austin. He tried to kill his wife. Surely you believe that?"

"Not necessarily," Austin protested earnestly.

"You did speak with her?"

"Yes."

"And?"

He hesitated. "Cara's been very sick. Bent on destroying herself. Perhaps Jack as well."

"But she did tell you that it was Jack who attempted to kill her?"

"Yes," he said gravely.

"You indicated to me over the phone that Jack was suffering from emotional problems. Did you know that he was placed in an orphanage at the age of six?"

"Yes."

"So he probably has some very strong feelings toward his mother. He was living with her at the time, I believe."

"You're being a bit Freudian, aren't you?"

"Hatred of a mother can do strange things to a person. I don't believe I have to tell you that."

Frank Austin looked vaguely perplexed. They began to walk again down the third-floor corridor.

"Human beings never change," Jaffy said sadly. "Neither do their motives. Being in my profession, I'm reminded constantly that as long as people exist, they'll go on killing each other for the same reasons. No matter how simple those reasons may be. And with the same unwavering commitment. What I'm saying is, if Jack did kill those women—he'll kill again. I think it's important that we get at the truth."

Jaffy turned and opened the door to room 305.

Frank Austin entered the room first and walked directly to Jack, who stood up. Jack looked intensely at him, then put out his hand.

"What do you say, Frank. Remember me?" He laughed, a nervous laugh, as Frank shook his hand. "Cross my heart, Frank—these bastards are crazy. I had nothing to do with it."

"Sit down, Jack. Let's talk." Austin moved away to the window. Jaffy closed the door and turned to face the room. He could see that Jack had shifted gears again. He was playing the clown. Casually trying to make light of his situation.

"I'd offer you a chair, Frank—but as you can see . . ."

Jack was like an unpredictable child now, Jaffy mused. A good sign. He might do anything, say anything. Jack smiled at Jaffy. Yet his body, independent of what he might desire, would not relax. Cockily, he extracted a cigarette from its pack, lit it, then flourished it in Jaffy's direction.

"Well, I guess this has been a long day for some people," Jack commented, casually releasing smoke from his nostrils.

Jaffy nodded. "It isn't over yet."

Austin cleared his throat. "Jack? Did you try to kill Cara?"

Jack lurched toward him. "Is that why you're here? To ask me the same dumb fucking questions they've been asking me all morning?"

"I came here to help, if you'll let me." Austin turned to face him.

"Help? If you really want to help me, you'll tell them that Cara is sick. Tell them, Frank. That I've spent the last ten years of my life, for Christ's sake, trying to make her happy. Tell them what she did. How she stuck her hand into the fire. You aren't going to take her word, are you, Frank? Are you?"

"No," Austin said softly. "Still, I'd like you to listen to me for a moment."

He shrugged. "Sure, Frank. I trust you. Go ahead."

Austin took a pipe from his pocket and began stuffing it with tobacco. He did this slowly and thoroughly, Jack's eyes upon him, and when he was finished he gathered the remaining loose tobacco in the palm of his hand and dumped it into the wastebasket.

Jaffy knew the doctor was stalling, trying to determine the right place to begin. Beginnings were important. Start in the wrong place and you've had it.

Pipe lighted, Austin said, "Are you frightened, Jack?"

"Yeah, of course." His words were almost inaudible. "I was scared to death last night. Today I feel empty. Degraded. All I want is out—cut loose and start again."

"With Cara?"

Jack glanced at Jaffy. A look of confusion crossed his face. He glanced back to Frank. "What do you mean? She hasn't—"

"No. I just came from the hospital. I think she's going to be all right."

"Good, good," Jack breathed.

Austin stared thoughtfully at him. "Jack, do you know what 'dissociation' means?"

"What?"

"Dissociation. It's like when a person dreams they are falling. They see themselves falling; they know that they are about to die. But then a strange thing happens. At the moment of impact—they wake up. Their mind will not let itself live through that moment. It's too intolerable. That's what happens in our awakened life as well. Some things are just too horrible to imagine, so our mind dissociates—it shuts out the act from our conscious mind."

Jack began to squirm. The muscles at the side of his mouth tensed. He inhaled nervously and expelled the smoke with characteristic force.

"What Dr. Austin is suggesting," Jaffy snorted, "is that maybe you did try to kill Cara, only you don't remember."

"I thought I could trust you, Frank," Jack said softly. "That you wanted to help me. But—"

"Jack, it's possible," Austin interjected quickly. "Your subconscious mind wanted desperately to free yourself from her. To punish her for ruining your life. But after you attack her—you dissociated yourself from your actions, because you love her."

Jack shook his head sadly. "You don't know what you're saying. . . ."

Jaffy watched Jack's face closely. Though his eyes were glazed, somehow he appeared more relaxed, as though he had vented the last of his anger. "No, Frank, you don't know what you're saying."

Jaffy inched forward. "Jack, would you be willing to submit to a polygraph?"

Jack laughed nervously. "Why should I put myself through that?"

"Because it's the best way for you to clear yourself."

Jack turned to face Austin, studying him with an odd expression on his face. Finally, he said, "No, no—I'm not going to take a lie detector test."

"Why?" Jaffy asked shortly.

"Because lies can become truth. Suppose I did want to hurt Cara. I'd have to tell the truth about my desire. Really making believe so strong that I did do it because I felt that maybe I should have, could have—and it registered in my mind as the truth. Suppose my whole life was like that. Wanting to do things and missing out on them and then always punishing myself. I mean, if I am like that, then why take the chance?"

Austin shook his head. "Jack, I don't think you realize what's at stake here. They're accusing you of murdering two other women."

"Do you believe them?"

"You're not giving me much choice."

Jack smiled. "You know, Frank, my biggest ambition in life is to beat you in just one set of tennis. That's all—just one. We'll have to get together real soon and play. Okay?"

"You're talking nonsense." Austin frowned.

"A profound observation," Jack said with a grimace. As if reaching for the climax, his hands went up in the air. "Enough, Frank. Enough."

Austin said, "Just what is it you're trying to prove?"

Jack shrugged indifferently. "Perhaps I'm conducting my own funeral. Accept that, Frank—that's all you'll get."

"That's no answer. Give me an answer."

"I don't have to give you anything. I am what I am. That's all any friend has a right to."

"There's Cara. You're going to have to face her. Sooner or later, you're—"

Jack slammed the ball of his hand against the back of the chair. "What the hell do you think this is, a game of darts? Wipe the board clean and start again. She ran out on me!"

"That's not true . . ."

"It is true."

"Don't you feel anything for her?"

"I feel nothing." He caught himself, put his hand to his forehead, and glanced away. "Frank, try and understand. It is impossible for me to relate to a single incident in my life. What is it you want me to do? To arbitrarily feel something for her that I have never been able to feel?" Confused, he made a vague, wild gesture with his hand. "I'm tired of rummaging through my head to understand the situation, to understand her. For ten years I've been walking around with my mind in a sling because of her. Isn't that enough? Isn't it, Frank? I've been living in a hell. I don't see people, I see one-dimensional figures—optical illusions, that's my reality. Well, it's going to stop. Stop, dammit. I will not feel guilty for that woman any longer."

Jack stood shaking, twisting his gold wedding ring around on his finger, rhythmically. He stopped suddenly, seeing the flat and hostile look in Austin's eyes. Despite this, Jack grinned.

"Forgive me, Frank," he said in a slow easy tone, "but right now I feel like an abscess that has just been drained. Besides which, the art of conversation takes patience and practice, the likes of which I have neither."

Austin glanced at his pipe. "Jack, there's something that happened between you and Cara—something important. If we could return—go back to a certain starting place—go over it all again, slowly, we might be able to find out what that something was."

"And what do we do then—make penance? Bury ourselves alive—kill ourselves? What?"

Austin appraised him for a moment.

"You are morally obligated—for Cara's sake," he said sharply.

"I owe her nothing." His eyes flashed at him, held in a momentary flicker of contempt. "She ran out on me."

"And so she has failed you. Well, if she failed you, Jack, then it's just barely possible that you have failed her. That you have both failed each other."

Jack nodded, smiling faintly behind the frozen glint in his eyes. "You know, Frank, no matter how right I think I am, words from you and suddenly I'm wrong. Ridiculously wrong. You make me feel as if I have betrayed the whole world, apologizing for myself." He stared vacantly at Jaffy, then let his gaze return to Austin. "And you enjoy it, don't you? Wallowing in the muck. Wandering through the perversity of people's minds. Well, go on, Frank. Search the basements, throw open the trunks, clean out the attic—GO ON!" In a seeming rush of anguish, he whispered, "Go home, Frank. You've completed today's assignment. I'm sure you've been nicely paid for it."

Those were Jack's last words. Austin tried to engage him in further conversation, but Jack only stared out the window, refusing to speak. He sat transfixed. As his mind receded, he sat limp, his arms dangling at his sides, his face ashen, sweat upon his upper lip. Once he was heard to mutter, "I should have cut her fucking heart out."

It was almost five-thirty when the call came through the switchboard at the Twentieth Precinct. It was routed through to Lou Jaffy's office, and when Jaffy answered his phone, he was surprised to hear again from his caller.

"Oh, yes, Dr. Clairmont. What can I do for you?"

Clairmont said, "About that paper. The diagram that you showed me . . ."

Jaffy's mind was still reeling from Jack Squadron's conversation with Dr. Austin, and really wasn't paying much attention. "Yes?"

"Well, I got to thinking about it. You know—MANA. It dawned on me after you left that perhaps MANA was a person's name. That got me thinking."

"Go on."

"Well, there is a very gifted paranormal subject by the name of Mana. Alex Mana."

"Do you know him?"

"No. But I've studied reports on him. He was tested extensively while incarcerated at the Kansas City State Prison."

"Are you sure?" Jaffy started in his chair, his arm extended in pursuit of pad and pencil.

"Yes. Quite sure. I have the report right here in front of me. Alex Mana. I knew that I had heard that name, but I—"

"Kansas City State Prison. Is he still there?"

"No, I believe he was released about six months ago."

"Do you know why he was in prison?"

"That I couldn't tell you."

"Thanks, Doctor, you've been a big help."

Hanging up, Jaffy tore the sheet of paper from the pad and hurried downstairs. He handed it to the officer. "Tony, put this information on the wire right away. I need an answer in a hurry."

"Right."

"A real hurry."

"You've got it."

Jaffy took a deep breath, turned, and slowly started back up the stairs. The walls seemed to be closing in on him. *What did it all mean?* Probably nothing. He would most likely come to find that this latest bit of information meant nothing. The trouble was he didn't believe that for a second. He had no idea what he actually *did* believe. What he felt was a vague uneasiness. Who was Alex Mana? Everything he had thought thus far told him Jack Squadron. Had he been mistaken? No, he was sure he hadn't. Yet—

Closing the door to his office, he moved to the window where he peered out. He could hear the barges hooting on the river. The fog was thick, heavy, blending with the gray sky. The tenements—a uniform bleached red—seemed to lean against each other for support.

If Alex Mana was connected, if it was more than a coincidence that his name turned up in Dr. Cindrella's elaborate equation, then he could be out there right now.

Alex Mana suddenly tumbled lazily, head over heels, through Jaffy's mind.

He had no face.

But he was tumbling, nonetheless, and it took all of Jaffy's strength not to duck.

CHAPTER 8

Friday, October 24
6:35 P.M.

ROSE OPENED HER EYES, PRAYING THAT HER NIGHTMARE WOULD end. She drew her hand back and gasped. Cheryl's face was still there, floating just above the water, her hair adrift like seaweed. From her throat trickled a thin stream of blood. Her lips and chin were also heavily caked with blood. Blood seeped from an open wound on her cheek, flamed from the slashes on her forehead.

Rose turned quickly, feeling herself in the grip of something hard, metallic, like a hook cutting into her flesh. Fear-sweat gushed from every pore of her skin as she watched Cheryl's eyes roll back into her head. Around her the water bubbled and swirled, turned a deep red, sucking Cheryl into its murky depths. Within seconds, her face bled away. The water was neither swirling nor sucking now; it had changed to gentle stillness, but it was still glistening—blood red.

Below, a large metal door seemed to beckon. The world turned slightly on its endless journey, and a corpse of a girl lay submerged beneath the water. The image of Cheryl reappeared, burst across her vision like a sunspot. The intense image seared her eyes, yet she couldn't look away. Why not? Why not—one might as well as not.

Not what? She had forgotten. Well, then . . . She watched her bare feet move across the floor, weak and frail. Something new began to stir in her, deeply and heavily. She moved in absolute silence, moving as if in a trance or a dream, making her eyes tear again. Cheryl . . . is very near, Rose thought. Very close. She could feel her presence.

With a series of aborted thoughts, half-gestures, she began

to dress. After stepping awkwardly into her jeans, slipping on her sweater, she moved into the living room. The floor creaked. Gusts of wind leapt at the window and rattled the pane.

Her eyes darted swiftly about, focusing, refocusing, probing the nightmare world that had descended upon her. And then she felt it. A vague, fluttering vibration emanating from within. She felt herself being entered and she knew it was him. Her eyes narrowed to tiny pinpricks of intensity. They were together now, in the silence, flowing in the same direction, time itself a tangible element that carried them forward, yet back to the past as well. Rose felt him thinking within her. He felt nothing. He allowed himself no closeness, no intimacy with others. He was terrified of people. It was only Rose that he wanted.

"Come to me . . ." he whispered.

Her arms shot out to steady herself. Clinging to the kitchen counter, she realized that the voice rising in her brain was a voice that belonged to her. But she could not control it. Something began to swell up inside of her, a sensation of terror. She thought: Don't speak again. Not one more word.

"The two of us are alike, you and I . . ."

"Leave me alone!" Rose screamed. For a moment there had been a silence in which she caught her breath, and now the silence was broken by a thin whining voice inside her head.

"Love me," the voice pleaded. "Come to me . . ."

Rose stared out the window. Night. Black. The city had grown cold, an inhuman place; black and gray and fuzzy.

And she knew, absolutely knew, that the time had come.

PART FOUR

CHAPTER 1

Friday, October 24
8:00 P.M.

DETECTIVE LOU JAFFY SAT PATIENTLY WAITING. FROM TIME to time he took a sip of coffee from his cup. Feet propped on his desk, he stared idly out of the window. Faint light shone behind a drawn shade on the third floor of a squat, five-story tenement directly behind the station. Another light flashed on on the second floor. The shrill sounds of kids playing came wafting through the partially opened window. Also a cool breeze that felt refreshing against his sweating brow.

Jaffy's gaze left the tenement and sought the lighted top of his desk, where a transcript of Jack Squadron's testimony, a thick, confusing document, was lying. What had Jack said that had made Jaffy suspicious as hell? He lingered over the transcript until his mind became a blur.

Turning suddenly, Jaffy glanced at his watch. Rose was already an hour late. He reached for the phone. Dialed. After several rings, he hung up. "Probably on her way," he muttered.

A light rap on his door.

"Yeah?" he barked.

His door snapped open. A tall, husky officer moved forward and dropped the report on his desk.

"Right off the wire." He smiled.

"It's about time," Jaffy said, scooping up the paper. "Help yourself to coffee."

"No, thanks. I'm off the stuff."

"No shit? What gets you moving in the morning?"

"Sex." The tall, husky officer smiled and left the room.

"Leave the door open, will you."

"Right," he said, and disappeared down the stairs.

Unhurriedly, Jaffy read the report. "Alex Mana. Sex offender. Arrested March 12, 1973. Apprehended for offering a female decoy cop twenty dollars to commit a sex act. He was charged with misdemeanor commercial sex and pleaded guilty to disorderly conduct. He was fined fifty dollars and given a conditional discharge.

"Arrested January 17, 1974, on a sexual abuse charge involving 'public lewdness' and 'subjecting another person to sexual contact without the person's consent.' He pleaded guilty to the lesser charge of disorderly conduct, and was given a conditional discharge.

"Arrested February 3, 1977. Charged with molestation, rape, and attempted murder of a sixteen-year-old girl. Convicted and sentenced to six to ten years in the Kansas City State Prison.

"Released from Kansas City State Prison February 16, 1983."

Jaffy pivoted in his chair slowly. "Christ," he breathed. He continued to study the report. The strange thing, Jaffy mused, was that the world, his world, was expanding—it was now one person larger, while at the same time he could feel himself getting smaller. He was sure that Jack Squadron was his man, yet . . .

He hit the button on the intercom. "Tony?"

"Yeah?"

"Is the captain still in his office?"

"Yeah."

"Good. Good. I need to see him. Tell him I'm coming down."

The captain stared at the report. Jaffy took up a position beside his desk. There was the sound of the captain's lighter as he clicked forth the flame to his cigarette. He stood up suddenly and without a word closed the door to his office. He remained silent for a moment longer, his cigarette drooping from his mouth as he paced back and forth, laying a trail of cigarette ash across the office floor.

"Well, what do you think?" the captain asked gruffly.

Jaffy shrugged. "I'm not sure."

"If you ask me—it all fits."

"I'm not convinced," Jaffy muttered in response.

"No?" He shook his large head angrily. "Well, I'll tell you one thing, Lou—when a guy rapes, or tries to kill once, you can bet your ass the son-of-a-bitch will rape and kill again. He's got the right profile, you have to admit that."

"We don't even know if he's in the city."

"Then what the hell was his name doing on Cindrella's chart? Tell me that."

"I checked Cindrella's office. If he was working with Mana, there would have been records."

"Maybe Cindrella's death was no accident. Maybe Mana killed Cindrella. To get rid of the records. Cindrella may have uncovered something during one of the sessions."

"Possible."

"Shit! Lou, we have to start from the beginning. Go over it all again."

"What about Squadron?"

"Forget him for the moment."

"That's hard to do," Jaffy said sullenly.

"Lou, what the hell is wrong with you? Mana has a record of violence, sexual violence. He also happens to be a parapsychologist's banquet. Cindrella turns up dead. And whose name do we find at the top of his list? Mana! Cindrella even had Mana linked with Rose Carpenter. What the hell do you want, Lou—a brick to fall on your fucking head?"

"I don't know. Call it a hunch." The captain opened his mouth to speak. Jaffy held up his hand. "I know. Percentages. But Squadron also has all the earmarks. No record—granted. But as sure as I'm standing here, he killed Mitzie Karp. Probably Cheryl Arthur as well."

"We've been working on him since this morning. Not an inch. He hasn't given an inch."

"What about his wife's testimony?"

"You heard what Austin said. The woman is not reliable." The captain sighed heavily. "Even if he did try to kill his wife, the man is a lightweight. Probably got emotionally involved in something he couldn't handle. Now Mana—that's a heavyweight. Whoever killed Mitzie Karp is a heavyweight!" The captain paused to draw in a lungful of smoke. Exhaled. "Get on it, Lou. I'll notify the others. Let's get Mana's picture on the wire."

"What about Squadron?"

"Let him rest."

"But—"

The captain sighed impatiently, signifying that the conversation was concluded.

Wearily, Jaffy left the captain's office for his own, and in the hallway, his ear at the stairwell, thought he heard the faint sound of crashing glass. He ascended a half flight, and heard voices shouting. A rush of footsteps came next. Moving quicker, Jaffy lurched up the stairs and almost collided with a police officer. The blood had drained from his face.

"He jumped," the officer bellowed.

"What?" Jaffy stepped forward.

"The bastard jumped from the window!"

"Who?"

"Squadron."

"Jesus Christ!"

Jaffy lurched forward, taking the stairs two at a time. When he hit the third-floor landing, Frank Austin was standing there shaking.

"What happened?" Jaffy cried.

Austin tried to clear his throat, to speak. Instead, he collapsed into a furious spasm of coughing.

"Are you all right?"

He nodded.

Jaffy moved away down the hall. The door to room 305 was wide open. Entering the room, Jaffy saw immediately that the window had been smashed with a chair. Stepping through broken glass, Jaffy leaned out the window, strained his eyes to see down into the darkness. Searchlights flashed below in the courtyard.

"Any sign of life?" Jaffy shouted.

"None. He probably made it over the wall."

Jaffy hollered, "You stupid sonofabitch. Stop acting like an idiot and do your job. Get after him!"

Jaffy watched two cops leap the wall and disappear over the other side. One cop was still prowling the grounds.

"Any blood?" Jaffy asked.

"Yeah. Plenty of it! He ain't getting very far. From the looks of it, he's fucking dead already."

"Don't bet your pension on it!" Jaffy turned from the window and glared at the officer in charge. "What the hell happened?"

He shrugged. "He was with Austin. Austin was here. I figured—"

"You figured? Well, you figured wrong. Goddamn it! Get the car out front. Now!"

8:05 P.M.

Dead pale, dressed in sweater and jeans, Rose pressed the basement button. The elevator door slid closed. The bottom dropped from beneath her as the elevator descended to the lowest depths of the building. Something—an elusive glimpse, a fragment of a lost image she had seen a long time ago—flew past her. The image tried to take shape in her mind, as though it were trying to adhere to her brain. But it slipped away, and what she had almost remembered remained nothing more than a shadow.

The elevator stopped suddenly. The door slid open.

Rose stepped from the elevator and found herself in a dark musty corridor running the length of the basement. The main lights were out. Only a bare hundred-watt bulb glowed directly in front of her. Toward the far end of the corridor the light thinned out, revealing a seemingly endless expanse of crevices and shadow.

Rose paused, forcing herself to separate the night sounds around her, what belonged and what didn't. The elevator clicked and moved upward behind her. She turned. The panel light indicated that the elevator had stopped on the first floor. Then the light moved again up to the twelfth floor. She turned back to face the corridor.

She could feel Cheryl's presence again. She tried wrenching the picture of Cheryl's face out of her mind. She could see her so clearly. Too clearly.

She hesitated, then moved until she stopped in front of the maintenance room. The smell of sawdust and varnish rushed toward her. Stepping inside, she realized that it was not one room at all, but a series of rooms. Three in all. The first room appeared to be almost livable, with a small unmade bed, a threadbare chair and a night table. Beyond this room, a second room, which was empty except for a mop and bucket.

Reaching the doorway to the third room, she paused. Lining the wall was a long aluminum tub that glistened in the darkness. Her only light source was behind her now, making it impossible to see much of anything else. She reached into the room, groping for the light switch. She clicked it. Clicked it again. The room remained dark.

Momentarily immobilized, she stood there, listening. But there was no sound. She was listening only to a silent darkness. She wondered if she dared enter the room. The stillness held. Slowly, she took a few steps, waited. Silence.

Then, in her vague semiconscious state, she became aware of being enveloped by a warming sensation. Something soft was near her, around her, touching her. Yet there was a firmness in the touch. The sensation stopped as she stepped further into the room, then began again, stronger—drawing her more purposefully toward the aluminum tub.

Closer, she stepped closer, until she had reached the tub, where she slid a huge metal lid away to one side. Scratch. A metal scratch. She did not move. She had heard that sound once before at nighttime, metal against metal. And the lid, she realized now, was not a lid at all, but a metal door. The same door she had seen moments ago. The door that had beckoned to her.

Her impulse was: run from the room. But she knew it would serve no purpose. Wherever she ran, her night person would be there. Waiting. Fear . . . always fear, she thought.

She took courage now. It had been a number of moments since she had slid the metal door to the side. Slowly, she bent down and peered into the tub.

Abruptly, Cheryl's face leapt up at her. A shrieking scream of flesh with bulging eyes and blood-soaked lips. Her body surfaced just as quickly—leaving Rose no time to think, to react—bobbed atop the water like a cork for an instant, then began to sink.

Rose stood paralyzed. Not a vision this time. She was actually looking at the body of Cheryl Arthur.

Snap.

Something cracked behind Rose.

She turned. She peered into blackness and sensed rather than saw—someone. And in the next instant, his face loomed out at her from the darkened corner. His upper lip curled back, showing his teeth like a wild dog. Steam seemed to pour from his body, his skin glistening yellow in the shadows.

"Rose . . ." he whispered, and then began to chuckle.

His voice, she thought. His!

His chuckle grew into a raspy laughter and he roared till saliva started to drip from the corner of his mouth. He drew himself up.

"Love me . . .." His eyeballs rolled behind the rough skin of his closed lids. He raised his arms, thrashed them about slowly, groping like a blind man. In that instant, childhood terror and adult terror merged. Rose saw flashes of the young man at Stoneridge, it had been so many years ago, but here he was, exactly as she had seen him then, reaching out for her, begging for love.

His eyes suddenly shot open.

Rose shuddered, her breathing quickened—her eyes fastened themselves upon his. She felt as if a gauze had been ripped away from her face and from his, that they were back in time, in space, confronting each other as they had done so many years ago.

Dr. Cindrella, she thought. "Dr. Cindrella," she cried. It was impossible. He was dead. Dead, she thought over and over again.

Yet there he stood, his body hunched, his face twisted into a hideous mask. His flesh was burnt and charred; there was a large open gash on his cheek. With arms wide, hands imploring, wet gray hair hanging limply about a pale blood-drained face, he began to move toward her, beseeching her to love him. "Love me," he pleaded.

"NO!" he screamed in another voice. "Get her out of my house. She's like all the others. A little tramp!"

"Mother," he wailed.

"Kill her!" screamed a higher pitched voice.

He stopped then, stared at her through another's eyes. Eyes that gazed in disgust. Eyes that leapt with anger and fierce hatred as he started toward her again.

Rose felt her knees go weak. Suddenly she was totally defenseless against his gaze. He moved. The knife flashed before her eyes.

The glint of the blade sent her arms flying through the air. The metal door fell to the ground between them with a loud crash. And then she was running. Running faster than she had ever run before.

She stumbled in the hallway, recovered without actually falling, and started for the elevator. It was still on the twelfth floor! Glancing around quickly, she ducked into the laundry room.

Dimly, she heard Cindrella cry out.

"Rose, don't run away from me. Please, I love you. Don't run away!" His words skimmed through the still air, seeming to reach out for her.

She slammed the door shut. Snapped the lock. Why hadn't she tried for the stairs? Screamed? She should have screamed. It was too late now. The laundry room was set back in the deepest part of the building. Who would hear her? She stared at the locked door, breathless, disbelieving.

"Rose," he whispered. "Open the door. Please, Rose. I won't hurt you. Really, I won't."

Rooted in fear, she spent precious seconds surveying the room she was now trapped in. Two washers to the right, one to the left. Next to that, two dryers. Against the far wall, a low vinyl couch. Almost at once she pictured herself helpless upon the couch, his body pressed hard on top of her. The sharp pungent smell of soap powder, sweat, and Clorox suddenly assailed her nostrils, and she started to gag.

"Rose!" he screamed, the sound of his huge fist banging on the door. "Please," he whimpered. "Let me in."

Silence now as she turned to stare at the door. She could sense he was still there, waiting. She turned again, and then saw it. What she had been looking for. A small narrow window high in the south wall just above one of the dryers. Another way out. She could squeeze through the window into the court-yard. There was a small wooden fence to climb, but—now she realized there was a water pipe partially blocking her way. She moved closer, glancing up. She would have to squeeze around it.

Almost in a whisper: "Still, it can be done."

Quickly, she opened the dryer door, stepped on the ledge and raised her hand toward the pipe.

As she began to climb on top of the dryer, crying out within herself, begging for time to do what had to be done, she heard his body smash against the door with a violent thud. Her eyes shifted. She slipped, reached out for the pipe, missed, and fell crashing to the floor. There was a bone-jarring wrench as her hip collided with cement, then her face. She expelled her breath in pain, and then sat quite still. Blood flowed from her nose.

She held her head back to stop the bleeding. Almost at once, she became aware of the sudden stillness. She leaned forward. Listened.

Pressing her finger to her nostril, she stared hard at the door. The silence had a quality of menace about it. After waiting another moment, she began to get curious. Where was he? What was he doing out there?

She rose to her feet and, steadying herself against the wall, began to slide toward the door. A soft glow of light filtered in from beneath the door. If he were there, the light would be broken. She was starting to believe that he had given up and gone when something moved outside the window.

The glass burst inward, shattered, as Cindrella's foot jammed itself between the frame. Rose screamed and lurched for the door. Cindrella jumped down through the window, covering his face with his hands.

Rose was outside the room and running.

The door smashed off the wall behind her. Gasping, she reached for the fire exit door. With her lungs about to burst in her chest, she started to climb the stairs. Everything inside of her started to pull apart . . . the bands of tension snapping as she climbed higher.

She had barely entered her apartment and locked the door when she turned and saw the door handle move, first to the right and then to the left. In panic, she fled to the kitchen phone, forgetting to fasten the safety chain. She dialed 0 and waited.

The top tumbler rolled over in its lock.

Rose stared at the door in disbelief. How was that possible? She had changed the locks!

"You know, miss, if someone wanted to get in here, these locks wouldn't stop them. You need bigger locks."

"And if someone really wanted to break in, would bigger locks stop them?"

"Well, you're right there. If people want something badly enough—they always seem to find a way to get it."

"Hello, Operator!" Rose cried. "Please, give me the Twentieth Precinct. Hurry. Someone is—"

"Name?"

"What . . . what?"

"Name. I need the name . . ."

Rose dropped the phone when the bottom tumbler rolled over. Picking up a kitchen knife, she dashed into the bedroom, heading for the bathroom. Once inside the bathroom, she locked the door. For a moment there was silence. She moved backward toward the window, never taking her eyes from the door. Turning now, she tried to open the window and call for help. She pushed. The window was sealed shut by old paint that had hardened within its seams. She pushed harder. The window refused to budge. She stopped suddenly when she heard it. She turned and saw the doorknob moving. Oh, God. The doorknob moved again, slowly. This was done in silence at first, but after several attempts, it began to rattle violently, and then, a moment later, a foot began to kick furiously against the base of the door.

"Rose! Rose, open the door . . ." the voice pleaded.

And then with a violent blow to the door, Cindrella smashed his way into the bathroom.

CHAPTER 2

EVERYTHING FELL AWAY; THE SIGHT OF THE DOORFRAME SPLINtering open, the knife Cindrella held in his hand, the whole world—everything slid away like a violent landslide, leaving Rose helpless with Cindrella's cold eyes staring at her and the sound of someone calling her name.

"Rose? Rose, where are you?"

An intent listening expression flashed in Cindrella's eyes as he glanced over his shoulder. He had turned too late. Jack lunged at him, locked his fingers around his throat and began to squeeze. Cindrella raised his arm, snapped it back, jamming his elbow into Jack's rib cage, sending him stumbling into the bedroom.

Jack buckled but did not fall. Instead, he crouched, trying to prepare himself for the next attack. It came quickly. Cindrella drew the knife back and began slashing violently. Jack spun, the razorlike edge of the blade crisscrossing in slashing diagonals before his face. The knife flashed again. Jack threw his arm out in a reflex gesture of self-defense. The blade cut him cleanly. The pain instantly felt.

Jack cried out, once, then smelled a blood stench in his nostrils. Despite his sudden fear, he hurled himself at Cindrella, bringing his knee up into his groin. In agony, Cindrella doubled over onto the floor. Jack moved toward him, but slipped in his own blood. Cindrella raised dizzily to his knees, then rose completely. Jack seized him and, nearly pulling his arm half out of its socket, flung him across the room. Cindrella fell headlong into the lamp, knocking it over.

Jack heard the knife skitter across the floor. He lurched toward the sound. But Cindrella had gotten there first.

They were not inches from each other now. Staring. Dark eyes in thin shafts of light. Images welled up in front of Jack's eyes; a jarring sound assaulting his ears. He was inside a dark room—Rose's bedroom—staring at a man who meant to kill him.

Somewhere beyond sirens reached a crescendo, and then stopped.

Jack turned. Both men turned.

In the next instant, Cindrella dashed from the room.

Jack started after him.

"NO! STAY HERE!" Rose stood shaking in the bathroom doorway.

Confused, bent partially over, Jack hesitated. He was losing strength. With a sudden expulsion of breath, he said, "I'll kill the son-of-a-bitch!" Then started to move again. "No!" Rose screamed, a prolonged, muffled scream that followed after him as he crossed the living room. Within seconds, he had rushed into the hallway, moved forward to the elevator, hugging the wall for support. He felt a stabbing jolt of pain in his arm, then a fresh eruption of blood that drenched his jacket and ran down his arm.

He paused to let the pain subside. His face, puffed out like a hornet's nest from the fall he'd taken while jumping from the window, instantly took up the pain. He raised his hand to his face, touched lightly. Then he heard it, the footsteps in the stairwell. He pulled open the exit door and stepped into the narrow corridor. The footsteps grew louder, then faded as they raced for the rooftop.

Jack felt a hollowness in the pit of his stomach as he raced after them.

He hit the top landing where he flung open the outside door. There was darkness. He surveyed the rooftop stretching to his right. That portion of the roof was empty. He let go of the door and started to move. He was still unable to see past the water tower or the other half of the roof.

A sudden sound to his left caused him to stop. He had no idea whether it was Cindrella or not. The wind was whistling through the legs of the tower, which loomed like a forgotten giant in the darkness. He quickly veered in the opposite direction. Pressing his body between the tower and the ledge of the building, he accelerated his speed.

Without warning, the lip of the roof narrowed. His one leg dropped over the edge and he could feel himself falling. Quickly he lunged for the railing. As he regained his balance, he saw something move to his right. He moved too, but not fast enough. The blow caught him in the back of the neck. He fell forward, hitting the roof with a sickening thud. Almost at once mist filled his eyes, sounds and shapes became abstract, blurred. He rolled over on his side, wondering how long it would take Cindrella to finish him off.

There was confusion then, commands shouted, the hurried sound of footsteps. And then a figure came into focus.

"Over here!" Jaffy shouted, and knelt beside him. In the next instant he was sitting Jack up like an invalid. Jack flinched, winced at the pain lodged at the base of his neck.

"Are you all right?" Jaffy asked.

"Yeah. He's still on the roof. It's Cindrella."

Jaffy stared at him in dumb amazement. "Cindrella?"

Jack nodded.

A few seconds passed before Jaffy was breathing again, before he could grasp what Jack had said.

"Does he have a gun?"

"I don't think so. Just a knife." Jack extracted a handkerchief from his pocket and wrapped it around his arm. He pulled it into a knot, then pressed his arm against his side—anything to stem the bleeding.

"You stay here," Jaffy said in a low voice, motioning for the other officers to fan out along both sides of the roof. Jaffy took center, moving forward toward the water tower.

Someone dashed from the darkness toward the edge of the roof.

Jaffy stepped quickly past the tower and came face to face with Cindrella. Not more than ten feet away, he stood crouched at the edge of the roof, his arm extended, the knife held firmly in his hand. His eyes grew wider, his lips stretched into a grotesque grimace as he stared evenly in Jaffy's direction.

"Look, we don't want to hurt you," Jaffy said placatingly. "Give it up."

"Stay away!" Cindrella cried, flicking the knife in the air.

Officers appeared on either side of him.

"I said, stay away!"

They moved closer. Cindrella instantly backed up and stepped over the railing. "Come any closer, I'll jump."

The officers continued to move toward him.

"I'm not bluffing!" He turned slightly and looked down. Moisture trickled across his face.

"All right!" Jaffy cried. "All right. Let's talk it over."

Without warning, another officer emerged from the darkness and lunged.

"No!" Jaffy cried.

Cindrella flung his body away from the building, trying to reach the neighboring roof. With a violent thud, his body slammed against the opposite building and started to fall.

Reaching out, his hand caught hold of a metal rod which extended from the side of the building. The weight of his body swung down and around, twisting the rod, causing it to bend slightly. He hung with his legs swinging against the building, looking frantically for a foothold. People were shouting now, voices hollered to each other . . . he tried to reach for the rod with his other hand, failed. The rod bent further. Blood was starting to run down his wrist, the rough edge of the metal rod having cut the palm of his hand.

Glancing over his shoulder, he could see into the opposite apartments. A young girl talking on the telephone. In another window the vivid color of a television set glowing in a darkened room. No more than ten feet away people were living their lives, unaware that he was fighting for his.

His arm began to tremble from the steady strain of clinging to the metal rod, and he understood fully, perhaps for the first time, that he was probably going to die. There was a sudden gripping in his gut, a sharp pain that caused him to gasp. He had to do something.

Glancing down, he saw that his feet were kicking the top edge of a window. If he swung back, then dropped and pushed forward at the same time, there was a slight chance he would be able to thrust his body into the apartment below. But if the glass didn't break, or he missed the window, he would . . . He closed his eyes, listening to the distant cries.

"Hold on," Jaffy shouted. "We're sending someone over."

Cindrella wasn't waiting. He quickly tested his plan. He drew back and then swung forward. Yes, he was sure he would be able to kick through the top part of the window. But he needed more leverage for his swing. If he pushed away from the building with his feet, his body would push out further—come into the window at a better angle. He could imagine it happening. If you imagine it—then it is true.

The rod bent further. The veins and nerves in his arm were beginning to explode. He stared down between his legs at the gray slab of cement twelve stories below. Impossible as it seemed, isolated, suspended in that blackened vertical abyss, he could still make out every detail of the cement that lay below him. He studied it intently for a moment, as if to read his entire life written there, sensing instantly that the end might be written there as well.

"Most births and deaths occur at night," a voice whispered, and he could feel a small chill of fear working its way up his spine. Ironically, he was present to witness his own deathwatch. He was both observer and participant.

The gray slab below receded suddenly; the drop now appeared endless. Huge globs of sweat sprang out and moistened the palms of his hands. Everything began to shatter within him. He waited a second longer, drew a deep breath, rolled himself up into a ball, placed his two feet against the building and pushed. He swung out and dropped, driving his legs against the top of the window.

He heard the glass shatter, felt himself falling forward, but only one leg had punched through the window. His other leg hit the windowpane, and his body stopped, hooked for a second and then dropped. He went down quickly, very quickly, turning over once or twice, his body falling as limp as a rag doll, until he landed with a splash on the cement slab below.

He had one last instant of consciousness before it was over. Then the night closed over him, leaving his mangled body lying still in a deep puddle of his own blood.

CHAPTER 3

Saturday, October 25
12:00 Noon

LETTING THE SMOKE SIMMER THROUGH HIS NOSTRILS, DETECtive Lou Jaffy turned deliberately away from Kenny Clark and gazed out the steamy window at the bleak, dull tenements that loomed out of the dirt and grime of the city.

What troubled him and nearly shook his faith was that Kenny Clark wanted to close the case. Almost everyone who discussed the case with him suggested that Clark was right.

Unlike many of the men around him, Jaffy was not so easily convinced. "You see," Jaffy said tentatively, "I'm still not sure Jack Squadron isn't our man."

For the first time, Clark's angular face hardened. "Lou, we want you to drop it."

Jaffy looked at him gravely. His sad jaw had the hint of a smile. "Just like that?"

Jaffy knew that he hadn't proven it was Cindrella who had killed those two women, nor that he had attempted to kill Cara Squadron. All Jaffy was certain of was that Cindrella had attempted to reach Rose Carpenter. For what purpose, even that wasn't clear. Cindrella may have killed only one girl. He may have murdered both girls, and more. But then again, he may have murdered no one.

If Cindrella was the murderer, why had he waited so long to do away with Rose? The question was: Who could prove that Cindrella had committed those crimes? His victims could not testify against him. There were no eyewitnesses to the crimes. How could Jaffy be sure that, after all was said and done, there hadn't been two murderers?

In Jaffy's head the questions continued, rumbling, bubbling, stewing until the pot began to boil over, and from the force, his lips began to move again and he was speaking aloud.

"Kenny—Cara Squadron has suddenly changed her story. No, she says now, it was not Jack at all. When I showed her the picture of Cindrella, along with six or seven others, she couldn't identify him."

"Lou, face facts. It was dark in her room that night. She was in complete shock." He watched as Jaffy shook his head disbelievingly. "Okay, Lou—let's try all over again." They were both silent for a moment, considering what trying-all-over-again meant. "Let's start with Rose Carpenter. The first thing we found in Cindrella's hotel room was a torn-to-shreds picture of a nude model who looked very much like Rose Carpenter. We're only lucky that he didn't have time to do to her what he did to the picture. We also found Rose's *Goldilocks* painting hanging there. The woman at the gallery clearly identified him as A. Adam. He was registered at the hotel under the same name. A. Adam. Next we discover that he was with Rose at Stoneridge. Something snapped back there. When he saw that picture—it snapped again. Frank Austin explained all that to you. There is no doubt he killed Mana. Mana's records were also found in his hotel room, along with Mana's belongings. It's obvious that Mana knew about his involvement with Rose. That's why he had to do away with him. He even placed his jewelry on Mana's body to make it look like he died in the fire. What more proof do you need?"

"We can't link him with the two girls! He's never been to the Cottontail Club. He couldn't possibly have known Cheryl Arthur. No, it's still wide open as far as I'm concerned."

"Jesus, Lou!" Clark shook his head violently. "It's all over. Over and done with. The thing to do is stop thinking about it. Christ, I've got troubles enough. I don't need this."

Clark's stomach was burning. On top of everything else, he was sure he was getting an ulcer. "Look, Lou—you said it yourself. We have no witnesses. Squadron's wife denies flatly now that it was Jack."

"Why? Why did she do that? Because it suddenly occurred to her that with Cindrella on the scene—her husband was off the hook."

"Lou, he *is* off the hook. What do I tell the press? Oh, yeah, we caught the guy red-handed, trying to kill Rose Carpenter. After he stuffed the other girl into a washtub in the basement. When we chased him, he jumped to his death. Not because he was guilty. Hell, no—the other guy did it! Come on, Lou."

"You really have no doubts?"

"None whatsoever."

"That isn't what you thought when we were questioning Squadron."

"We didn't know Reese Cindrella was still alive then. Lou, it's an open-and-shut case. Let's leave it that way." Clark let that sink in. "The DA feels the same way. So does the chief."

"But—"

"No buts about it. The Homicide boys are satisfied—your end is rape. That's all—rape. I was against assigning you to Homicide in the first place. But no, they tell me—let everyone in on the action. A team. Well, the team has called it quits, Lou. Take a rest."

Jaffy smiled menacingly. "One big happy family—right, Kenny?"

"That's right."

Clark picked up his briefcase. "Don't let it get to you, Lou. In the next few days there will be a nice juicy rape case and you'll be in the saddle again. You won't even remember this case existed."

They eyed each other wearily. Jaffy's smile persisted even when he finally realized that his wings had been clipped. Clark was smiling too. But Jaffy had outgrown the Kenny Clarks just as he had outgrown so many other notions. Faith in democracy, justice, let right be done, truth will out. Truth depended on circumstances, on people's willingness to fight for it, as to whether it prevailed or not. Truth was the silent minority—very rarely heard from. And it was possible, just possible, that the madness had only just begun.

CHAPTER 4

Saturday, October 25
12:15 P.M.

JACK NEEDED SOMEONE TO ACT AS A BUFFER.

Frank Austin sat behind the desk in his office and crushed out his cigarette. He noted that Rose was still in a state of confusion. Jack sat off to the left and gazed out the window.

Austin leaned forward. "In other words, in all aspects of human activity, Cindrella had reached an adult normal level. However, he had remained a child in one area." He stared evenly at Rose. "To him, you were both always back there. Together at Stoneridge. Whenever he thought of you, he reverted back to being a young man. In a common boy-meets-girl situation, apparently he was instantly attracted to you. Love at first sight. A chemical attraction and it lasted all these years. Naturally, over the years, his feelings became confused. Dangerously so. You were loved, yes. But you were also a threat to the unwavering love and devotion he felt for his mother. That's where Jack came in. Emotionally incapable of dealing with you directly, he used Jack to transmit his feelings to you. Jack was sort of a go-between. Nothing more."

He abruptly stopped speaking—Rose was surprised by that—and after a brief glance at Jack, he took up where he'd left off. Apparently Jack had nothing to say.

"He used Alex Mana as well. As a source of energy. It seems the man had extraordinary powers which Cindrella used to get to you. Harnessing this energy, he directed it through Jack. You, I'm afraid, were the target." He shrugged. "Jack, well . . . he was merely used as a conductor for someone else's desires. I suppose Mana discovered what Cindrella was up to, so . . ."

Jack rose suddenly and edged his way toward the large mirror on the far wall.

What was confusing to Rose was the peculiar look of subdued pleasure Jack had written across his face; she had never seen it in his expression before. He looked tired, exhausted, and yet . . .

She sat quietly on the couch and watched as he considered his image in the mirror. She could not speak. Fatigue and shock had prevented her from sorting things out clearly or sensibly during the past twelve hours.

For a while Jack was silent. Then he began to speak, in a soft, slow voice. Offhandedly, he allowed the tips of his fingers to rub the stubble of his face, as if trying to make sense out of what he was about to say. ". . . Cara admits now that it wasn't me."

"We know that now," Austin said with a sigh.

Everything was moving too fast. Rose glanced at Austin and then to Jack. For a moment both men silently, unwillingly, acknowledged the tension that hung in the room. And then it passed.

"Cara's been sick," Jack muttered. "I suppose all along she knew it wasn't me. Why would I do such a thing?" Jack glanced in the mirror again, saw Rose watching, and looked away guiltily. "Hey, what the hell—no harm done." When she met his gaze evenly, he flushed and looked away.

Now, sitting silently between the two men, Rose wondered why Jack could not face her alone. What was he afraid of? What did he hope to accomplish by meeting her like this?

"Rose, perhaps it's best to say what has to be said." Austin paused for a moment, adjusting himself in his chair. "As I've already explained to Jack, the emotions you both experienced this past week, well . . . I'm afraid they were—how should I put it? Borrowed. What passed between you and Jack was really meant to pass between you and Cindrella. In a way, you and Jack were acting out his fantasy, his delusion. It's important that you both understand that."

Perhaps it was the way in which Austin had said this, or perhaps it was the silence that followed. But now the stillness was impossible to bear. Apparently Jack did not trust himself to speak. Rose watched as he gave her a covert glance, afraid perhaps to look at her openly, completely. Still, after a moment, he did manage to say, "Things will be better now. For us. Cara and me. I know it." He shrugged. "All my life I loved the idea of being in love. So naturally the idea of loving Cara was easy. I think it will be again. I'm not sure whether Cara still loves me, but she gets apoplectic with jealousy. I'm her possession." He smiled. "Cara has some curious ideas. She wants to live in California now. Get a small place where we can live out the illusion together. A tiny place. A doll's house, I guess. She's tenacious, I'll say that for her. Next thing you know we'll be going out and buying a rubber baby." He paused for a moment, his face falling into hard lines. "To tell you the truth, I always preferred miles of brick to rows of trees. There's nothing like being safely walled in, is there? But I'll go, I guess. It's what she wants." He smirked. "Can you picture me sitting on a patio eating pineapple? What the hell, I guess we'll retire together in matching wheelchairs."

His outpour halted momentarily. It wasn't until this moment that Rose realized Jack had been drinking. He turned to face Austin, and in the motion, his body blundered against the coatrack and set it rocking. His arm shot out to steady it.

"Frank, you better nail this thing down before it kills someone."

"We all have our problems," Austin said sadly.

"Yeah, well . . ." Jack looked at his watch. "Cara's waiting for me. I've got to go." He glanced at Rose. "You do understand, don't you? About us? About Cara?"

Rose nodded, but she did not speak.

"I'll see you," Jack said.

Rose watched him walk to the door. In an instant, he opened the door, stepped into the hallway, and then he was gone.

He did not look back.

She felt her body trembling. She had hoped he would look back one last time. That perhaps he would acknowledge that he had cared just a little.

Rose turned to meet Austin's gaze. There was momentary silence. Then, with a deliberate tone of condolence, he said, "I'm sorry. Truly sorry."

Back at her apartment, Rose stopped crying, went into the bathroom and daubed her face with cold water. She tried to make her face up but decided her eyes were too swollen; she could do little to produce any glamour, so she gave up and returned to the bedroom.

The next few hours passed quickly, and surprisingly enough—things eased up. Rose did the same things she usually did, but instead of there being a strange unreality to the scene, everything seemed brighter and clearer, as if someone had removed a yellow filter that had been placed over her life. And gradually, without realizing it, she found herself smiling as Lottie entered the apartment.

She stood speechless, feeling a mixture of confusion and awkwardness. She also felt the peace and joy that the sight of Lottie had always aroused in her. Apparently, Lottie was also confused, not knowing what to say. Rose could see she was trying to behave as though the past two weeks had never occurred. Rose certainly didn't want to rake up the past . . . there was only pain in going back. What the hell, she told herself, things never really go smoothly in this life. Despite her sense of foreboding, she would make an effort. A real effort this time to make things turn out differently.

"So," Lottie said finally, "how have you been?"

Rose looked straight into her blue eyes. She would not allow the past to touch her, she told herself; and in thinking, the inevitable idea spread its possibilities through her mind. Her next thought pleased her. That she had nothing more to fear.

EPILOGUE

In the two years after Reese Cindrella's death, the following occurred:

Rose Carpenter was married and eleven months later gave birth to a baby girl. She now lives in Boston with her husband and daughter. Her paintings can be seen hanging in the Museum of Modern Art in New York City.

Jack and Cara Squadron moved to Hollywood, California. Jack continues to write music, while Cara teaches tennis at the Hollywood Country Club.

Detective Lou Jaffy was made chief of the Sex Crimes Unit of Manhattan.

Julie Lemon was arrested and indicted on four counts of blackmail, extortion and involvement in the badger game.

Danny Romano was deported back to Italy.

The Cottontail Club burnt to the ground. The whereabouts of Nicklas Nuzzo—unknown.

The Institute of Parapsychology was converted into a day-care center for preschool children.

And a local Hollywood newspaper carried this article on page 2 of its morning edition:

Three Women Victims of
Sex-Related Murders

Hollywood — Police said the latest discovery, the body of Cindy Wilson, raped and stabbed nine times, leads them to believe there is an apparent connection with the area's other sex killings since September 10.

Police say Wilson's body was found Monday night in her van, two blocks from her apartment at Franklin and La Brea.

Wilson had been stabbed to death, and her body, which had been bound and gagged, was left propped up in a seated position.

The three woman victims reportedly were all murdered in the same fashion, police said.

One of them, Georgi Harper, 19, identified by police as a prostitute, was the first to be slain, on September 10. Her body was found in the back seat of her car in a Studio City parking lot.

The body of Darlene White, 23, was found eight days later in an abandoned nightclub on Sunset Strip.

Los Angeles Police Commander Timothy Black said he would not speculate on the motives for the murders.

We . . . have dreamt the world. We have dreamt it as firm, mysterious, visible, ubiquitous in space and durable in time; but in its architecture we have allowed tenuous and eternal crevices of unreason which tell us it is false.

—Borges, *Labyrinths*